THE
YELLOW
WALL-PAPER

AND OTHER STORIES

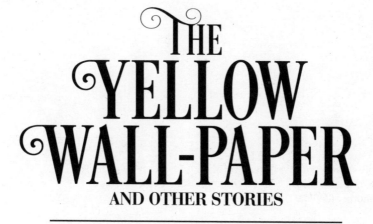

THE YELLOW WALL-PAPER

AND OTHER STORIES

CHARLOTTE PERKINS GILMAN

This edition published in 2021 by Arcturus Publishing Limited
26/27 Bickels Yard, 151–153 Bermondsey Street,
London SE1 3HA

Typesetting by Palimpsest Book Production Limited

Cover design: Peter Ridley
Cover illustration: Peter Gray
Design: Dani Leigh

AD006400US

Printed in the UK

Contents

Introduction

CHARLOTTE PERKINS GILMAN was an eminent American feminist author best known for her semi-autobiographical short story "The Yellow Wall-paper" (1892).

She was born in Hartford, Connecticut on July 3, 1860, the only daughter of librarian, editor and writer Frederic Beecher Perkins. From him she inherited a talent for writing and a strong commitment to social reform. But he was a distant father and eventually abandoned his young family, and they were forced to rely on Charlotte's paternal aunts for support, one of whom was the author Harriet Beecher Stowe (author of *Uncle Tom's Cabin*).

Despite her mother's obsessive distrust of men, Charlotte developed friendships with boys during an otherwise isolated and lonely childhood. She later described herself as a "tomboy" in her autobiography.

At the age of 18, she attended the Rhode Island School of Design, and after graduating, she supported herself as a painter and art teacher. But writing remained her abiding passion in tandem with her support for women's suffrage and social reform.

In 1884, she married the allegorical "colorist" artist Charles Walter Stetson against her own instincts and after the birth of their first and only child, a daughter, the following year, Charlotte succumbed to severe post-partum depression. The illness and the treatment advocated by a sceptical medical profession, which dismissed such disorders as mere female hysteria, soured her marriage and the couple eventually divorced. But the experience provided the inspiration and raw material for the short story which brought its author to prominence.

The first-person narrative of "The Yellow Wall-paper" takes the form of a series of journal entries by a woman who has been confined in an isolated mansion by her husband, a physician, who has prescribed a "rest cure" for what he believes is a nervous disorder. With nothing to occupy her mind, she gradually descends into psychosis, losing contact with reality and suffering hallucinations during which she sees a woman trapped behind the pattern of the wallpaper in her room. The story was seen as a powerful allegory for the oppression of women in American society.

Charlotte, however, was not embittered by the experience and after their divorce in 1894 she sent her daughter to live with Stetson and his second wife, whom she felt would be a better mother than she could have been. Following the separation, Charlotte moved to Pasadena, California where she became an active campaigner for women's suffrage and social reform and contributed articles, poems, short stories, and novellas to various journals that she also edited.

In 1900, she married her first cousin, attorney Houghton Gilman, and they lived happily until his death 34 years later. On August 17 the following year, after having been diagnosed with terminal cancer, Charlotte took her own life by inhaling an overdose of chloroform.

The Yellow
Wall-paper

IT IS VERY seldom that mere ordinary people like John and myself secure ancestral halls for the summer.

A colonial mansion, a hereditary estate, I would say a haunted house, and reach the height of romantic felicity—but that would be asking too much of fate!

Still I will proudly declare that there is something queer about it.

Else, why should it be let so cheaply? And why have stood so long untenanted?

John laughs at me, of course, but one expects that in marriage.

John is practical in the extreme. He has no patience with faith, an intense horror of superstition, and he scoffs openly at any talk of things not to be felt and seen and put down in figures.

John is a physician, and *perhaps*—(I would not say it to a living soul, of course, but this is dead paper and a great relief to my mind)—*perhaps* that is one reason I do not get well faster.

You see, he does not believe I am sick!

And what can one do?

If a physician of high standing, and one's own husband,

assures friends and relatives that there is really nothing the matter with one but temporary nervous depression—a slight hysterical tendency—what is one to do?

My brother is also a physician, and also of high standing, and he says the same thing.

So I take phosphates or phosphites—whichever it is, and tonics, and journeys, and air, and exercise, and am absolutely forbidden to "work" until I am well again.

Personally, I disagree with their ideas.

Personally, I believe that congenial work, with excitement and change, would do me good.

But what is one to do?

I did write for a while in spite of them; but it *does* exhaust me a good deal—having to be so sly about it, or else meet with heavy opposition.

I sometimes fancy that in my condition if I had less opposition and more society and stimulus—but John says the very worst thing I can do is to think about my condition, and I confess it always makes me feel bad.

So I will let it alone and talk about the house.

The most beautiful place! It is quite alone, standing well back from the road, quite three miles from the village. It makes me think of English places that you read about, for there are hedges and walls and gates that lock, and lots of separate little houses for the gardeners and people.

There is a *delicious* garden! I never saw such a garden—large and shady, full of box bordered paths, and lined with long grape-covered arbors with seats under them.

There were greenhouses, too, but they are all broken now.

There was some legal trouble, I believe, something about the heirs and co-heirs; anyhow, the place has been empty for years.

That spoils my ghostliness, I am afraid, but I don't care—

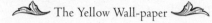

there is something strange about the house—I can feel it.

I even said so to John one moonlight evening, but he said what I felt was a *draught*, and shut the window.

I get unreasonably angry with John sometimes. I'm sure I never used to be so sensitive. I think it is due to this nervous condition.

But John says if I feel so, I shall neglect proper self-control; so I take pains to control myself—before him, at least, and that makes me very tired.

I don't like our room a bit. I wanted one downstairs that opened on the piazza and had roses all over the window, and such pretty, old-fashioned chintz hangings! but John would not hear of it.

He said there was only one window and not room for two beds, and no near room for him if he took another.

He is very careful and loving, and hardly lets me stir without special direction.

I have a schedule prescription for each hour in the day; he takes all care from me, and so I feel basely ungrateful not to value it more.

He said we came here solely on my account, that I was to have perfect rest and all the air I could get. "Your exercise depends on your strength, my dear," said he, "and your food somewhat on your appetite; but air you can absorb all the time." So we took the nursery, at the top of the house.

It is a big, airy room, the whole floor nearly, with windows that look all ways, and air and sunshine galore. It was nursery first and then playground and gymnasium, I should judge; for the windows are barred for little children, and there are rings and things in the walls.

The paint and paper look as if a boys' school had used it. It is stripped off—the paper—in great patches all around the head of my bed, about as far as I can reach, and in a great place on the other side of the room low down. I never saw a worse paper in my life.

One of those sprawling flamboyant patterns committing every artistic sin.

It is dull enough to confuse the eye in following, pronounced enough to constantly irritate and provoke study, and when you follow the lame uncertain curves for a little distance they suddenly commit suicide—plunge off at outrageous angles, destroy themselves in unheard-of contradictions.

The color is repellant, almost revolting; a smoldering, unclean yellow, strangely faded by the slow-turning sunlight.

It is a dull yet lurid orange in some places, a sickly sulphur tint in others.

No wonder the children hated it! I should hate it myself if I had to live in this room long.

There comes John, and I must put this away,—he hates to have me write a word.

We have been here two weeks, and I haven't felt like writing before, since that first day.

I am sitting by the window now, up in this atrocious nursery, and there is nothing to hinder my writing as much as I please, save lack of strength.

John is away all day, and even some nights when his cases are serious.

I am glad my case is not serious!

But these nervous troubles are dreadfully depressing.

John does not know how much I really suffer. He knows there is no *reason* to suffer, and that satisfies him.

Of course it is only nervousness. It does weigh on me so not to do my duty in any way!

I meant to be such a help to John, such a real rest and comfort, and here I am a comparative burden already!

Nobody would believe what an effort it is to do what little I am able,—to dress and entertain, and order things.

It is fortunate Mary is so good with the baby. Such a dear baby!

And yet I *cannot* be with him, it makes me so nervous.

I suppose John never was nervous in his life. He laughs at me so about this wall-paper!

At first he meant to repaper the room, but afterwards he said that I was letting it get the better of me, and that nothing was worse for a nervous patient than to give way to such fancies.

He said that after the wall-paper was changed it would be the heavy bedstead, and then the barred windows, and then that gate at the head of the stairs, and so on.

"You know the place is doing you good," he said, "and really, dear, I don't care to renovate the house just for a three months' rental."

"Then do let us go downstairs," I said, "there are such pretty rooms there."

Then he took me in his arms and called me a blessed little goose, and said he would go down to the cellar, if I wished, and have it whitewashed into the bargain.

But he is right enough about the beds and windows and things.

It is an airy and comfortable room as any one need wish, and, of course, I would not be so silly as to make him uncomfortable just for a whim.

I'm really getting quite fond of the big room, all but that horrid paper.

Out of one window I can see the garden, those mysterious deep-shaded arbors, the riotous old-fashioned flowers, and bushes and gnarly trees.

Out of another I get a lovely view of the bay and a little

private wharf belonging to the estate. There is a beautiful shaded lane that runs down there from the house. I always fancy I see people walking in these numerous paths and arbors, but John has cautioned me not to give way to fancy in the least. He says that with my imaginative power and habit of story-making, a nervous weakness like mine is sure to lead to all manner of excited fancies, and that I ought to use my will and good sense to check the tendency. So I try.

I think sometimes that if I were only well enough to write a little it would relieve the press of ideas and rest me.

But I find I get pretty tired when I try.

It is so discouraging not to have any advice and companionship about my work. When I get really well, John says we will ask Cousin Henry and Julia down for a long visit; but he says he would as soon put fireworks in my pillow-case as to let me have those stimulating people about now.

I wish I could get well faster.

But I must not think about that. This paper looks to me as if it *knew* what a vicious influence it had!

There is a recurrent spot where the pattern lolls like a broken neck and two bulbous eyes stare at you upside down.

I got positively angry with the impertinence of it and the everlastingness. Up and down and sideways they crawl, and those absurd, unblinking eyes are everywhere. There is one place where two breadths didn't match, and the eyes go all up and down the line, one a little higher than the other.

I never saw so much expression in an inanimate thing before, and we all know how much expression they have! I used to lie awake as a child and get more entertainment and terror out of blank walls and plain furniture than most children could find in a toy-store.

I remember what a kindly wink the knobs of our big old

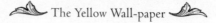

bureau used to have, and there was one chair that always seemed like a strong friend.

I used to feel that if any of the other things looked too fierce I could always hop into that chair and be safe.

The furniture in this room is no worse than inharmonious, however, for we had to bring it all from downstairs. I suppose when this was used as a playroom they had to take the nursery things out, and no wonder! I never saw such ravages as the children have made here.

The wall-paper, as I said before, is torn off in spots, and it sticketh closer than a brother—they must have had persever-ance as well as hatred.

Then the floor is scratched and gouged and splintered, the plaster itself is dug out here and there, and this great heavy bed which is all we found in the room, looks as if it had been through the wars.

But I don't mind it a bit—only the paper.

There comes John's sister. Such a dear girl as she is, and so careful of me! I must not let her find me writing.

She is a perfect and enthusiastic housekeeper, and hopes for no better profession. I verily believe she thinks it is the writing which made me sick!

But I can write when she is out, and see her a long way off from these windows.

There is one that commands the road, a lovely shaded winding road, and one that just looks off over the country. A lovely country, too, full of great elms and velvet meadows.

This wallpaper has a kind of sub-pattern in a different shade, a particularly irritating one, for you can only see it in certain lights, and not clearly then.

But in the places where it isn't faded, and where the sun is just so—I can see a strange, provoking, formless sort of figure, that seems to sulk about behind that silly and conspicuous front design.

There's sister on the stairs!

Well, the Fourth of July is over! The people are all gone and I am tired out. John thought it might do me good to see a little company, so we just had mother and Nellie and the children down for a week.

Of course I didn't do a thing. Jennie sees to everything now.

But it tired me all the same.

John says if I don't pick up faster he shall send me to Weir Mitchell in the fall.

But I don't want to go there at all. I had a friend who was in his hands once, and she says he is just like John and my brother, only more so!

Besides, it is such an undertaking to go so far.

I don't feel as if it was worthwhile to turn my hand over for anything, and I'm getting dreadfully fretful and querulous.

I cry at nothing, and cry most of the time.

Of course I don't when John is here, or anybody else, but when I am alone.

And I am alone a good deal just now. John is kept in town very often by serious cases, and Jennie is good and lets me alone when I want her to.

So I walk a little in the garden or down that lovely lane, sit on the porch under the roses, and lie down up here a good deal.

I'm getting really fond of the room in spite of the wallpaper. Perhaps *because* of the wallpaper.

It dwells in my mind so!

I lie here on this great immovable bed—it is nailed down, I believe—and follow that pattern about by the hour. It is as good as gymnastics, I assure you. I start, we'll say, at the bottom, down in the corner over there where it has not been touched, and I determine for the thousandth time that I *will* follow that pointless pattern to some sort of a conclusion.

I know a little of the principles of design, and I know this thing was not arranged on any laws of radiation, or alternation, or repetition, or symmetry, or anything else that I ever heard of.

It is repeated, of course, by the breadths, but not otherwise.

Looked at in one way each breadth stands alone, the bloated curves and flourishes—a kind of "debased Romanesque" with *delirium tremens*—go waddling up and down in isolated columns of fatuity.

But, on the other hand, they connect diagonally, and the sprawling outlines run off in great slanting waves of optic horror, like a lot of wallowing seaweeds in full chase.

The whole thing goes horizontally, too, at least it seems so, and I exhaust myself in trying to distinguish the order of its going in that direction.

They have used a horizontal breadth for a frieze, and that adds wonderfully to the confusion.

There is one end of the room where it is almost intact, and there, when the crosslights fade and the low sun shines directly upon it, I can almost fancy radiation after all,—the interminable grotesque seem to form around a common center and rush off in headlong plunges of equal distraction.

It makes me tired to follow it. I will take a nap, I guess.

I don't know why I should write this.

I don't want to.

I don't feel able.

And I know John would think it absurd. But I *must* say what I feel and think in some way—it is such a relief!

But the effort is getting to be greater than the relief.

Half the time now I am awfully lazy, and lie down ever so much.

John says I mustn't lose my strength, and has me take cod liver oil and lots of tonics and things, to say nothing of ale and wine and rare meat.

Dear John! He loves me very dearly, and hates to have me sick. I tried to have a real earnest reasonable talk with him the other day, and tell him how I wished he would let me go and make a visit to Cousin Henry and Julia.

But he said I wasn't able to go, nor able to stand it after I got there; and I did not make out a very good case for myself, for I was crying before I had finished.

It is getting to be a great effort for me to think straight. Just this nervous weakness, I suppose.

And dear John gathered me up in his arms, and just carried me upstairs and laid me on the bed, and sat by me and read to me till it tired my head.

He said I was his darling and his comfort and all he had, and that I must take care of myself for his sake, and keep well.

He says no one but myself can help me out of it, that I must use my will and self-control and not let any silly fancies run away with me.

There's one comfort, the baby is well and happy, and does not have to occupy this nursery with the horrid wallpaper.

If we had not used it, that blessed child would have! What a fortunate escape! Why, I wouldn't have a child of mine, an impressionable little thing, live in such a room for worlds.

I never thought of it before, but it is lucky that John kept me here, after all, I can stand it so much easier than a baby, you see.

Of course I never mention it to them any more—I am too wise,—but I keep watch of it all the same.

There are things in that paper that nobody knows but me, or ever will.

Behind that outside pattern the dim shapes get clearer every day.

It is always the same shape, only very numerous.

And it is like a woman stooping down and creeping about behind that pattern. I don't like it a bit. I wonder—I begin to think—I wish John would take me away from here!

It is so hard to talk with John about my case, because he is so wise, and because he loves me so.

But I tried it last night.

It was moonlight. The moon shines in all around just as the sun does.

I hate to see it sometimes, it creeps so slowly, and always comes in by one window or another.

John was asleep and I hated to waken him, so I kept still and watched the moonlight on that undulating wallpaper till I felt creepy.

The faint figure behind seemed to shake the pattern, just as if she wanted to get out.

I got up softly and went to feel and see if the paper *did* move, and when I came back John was awake.

"What is it, little girl?" he said. "Don't go walking about like that—you'll get cold."

I thought it was a good time to talk, so I told him that I really was not gaining here, and that I wished he would take me away.

"Why, darling!" said he, "our lease will be up in three weeks, and I can't see how to leave before.

"The repairs are not done at home, and I cannot possibly

leave town just now. Of course if you were in any danger, I could and would, but you really are better, dear, whether you can see it or not. I am a doctor, dear, and I know. You are gaining flesh and color, your appetite is better, I feel really much easier about you."

"I don't weigh a bit more," said I, "nor as much; and my appetite may be better in the evening when you are here, but it is worse in the morning when you are away!"

"Bless her little heart!" said he with a big hug, "she shall be as sick as she pleases! But now let's improve the shining hours by going to sleep, and talk about it in the morning!"

"And you won't go away?" I asked gloomily.

"Why, how can I, dear? It is only three weeks more and then we will take a nice little trip of a few days while Jennie is getting the house ready. Really dear you are better!"

"Better in body perhaps—" I began, and stopped short, for he sat up straight and looked at me with such a stern, reproachful look that I could not say another word.

"My darling," said he, "I beg of you, for my sake and for our child's sake, as well as for your own, that you will never for one instant let that idea enter your mind! There is nothing so dangerous, so fascinating, to a temperament like yours. It is a false and foolish fancy. Can you not trust me as a physician when I tell you so?"

So of course I said no more on that score, and we went to sleep before long. He thought I was asleep first, but I wasn't, and lay there for hours trying to decide whether that front pattern and the back pattern really did move together or separately.

On a pattern like this, by daylight, there is a lack of sequence, a defiance of law, that is a constant irritant to a normal mind.

The color is hideous enough, and unreliable enough, and infuriating enough, but the pattern is torturing.

You think you have mastered it, but just as you get well underway in following, it turns a back-somersault and there you are. It slaps you in the face, knocks you down, and tramples upon you. It is like a bad dream.

The outside pattern is a florid arabesque, reminding one of a fungus. If you can imagine a toadstool in joints, an interminable string of toadstools, budding and sprouting in endless convolutions—why, that is something like it.

That is, sometimes!

There is one marked peculiarity about this paper, a thing nobody seems to notice but myself, and that is that it changes as the light changes.

When the sun shoots in through the east window—I always watch for that first long, straight ray—it changes so quickly that I never can quite believe it.

That is why I watch it always.

By moonlight—the moon shines in all night when there is a moon—I wouldn't know it was the same paper.

At night in any kind of light, in twilight, candlelight, lamplight, and worst of all by moonlight, it becomes bars! The outside pattern I mean, and the woman behind it is as plain as can be.

I didn't realize for a long time what the thing was that showed behind, that dim sub-pattern, but now I am quite sure it is a woman.

By daylight she is subdued, quiet. I fancy it is the pattern that keeps her so still. It is so puzzling. It keeps me quiet by the hour.

I lie down ever so much now. John says it is good for me, and to sleep all I can.

Indeed, he started the habit by making me lie down for an hour after each meal.

It is a very bad habit, I am convinced, for, you see, I don't sleep.

And that cultivates deceit, for I don't tell them I'm awake—O no!

The fact is I am getting a little afraid of John.

He seems very queer sometimes, and even Jennie has an inexplicable look.

It strikes me occasionally, just as a scientific hypothesis,— that perhaps it is the paper!

I have watched John when he did not know I was looking, and come into the room suddenly on the most innocent excuses, and I've caught him several times *looking at the paper!* And Jennie too. I caught Jennie with her hand on it once.

She didn't know I was in the room, and when I asked her in a quiet, a very quiet voice, with the most restrained manner possible, what she was doing with the paper—she turned around as if she had been caught stealing, and looked quite angry—asked me why I should frighten her so!

Then she said that the paper stained everything it touched, that she had found yellow smooches on all my clothes and John's, and she wished we would be more careful!

Did not that sound innocent? But I know she was studying that pattern, and I am determined that nobody shall find it out but myself!

Life is very much more exciting now than it used to be. You see I have something more to expect, to look forward to, to watch. I really do eat better, and am more quiet than I was.

John is so pleased to see me improve! He laughed a little the other day, and said I seemed to be flourishing in spite of my wall-paper.

I turned it off with a laugh. I had no intention of telling him it was *because* of the wall-paper—he would make fun of me. He might even want to take me away.

I don't want to leave now until I have found it out. There is a week more, and I think that will be enough.

I'm feeling ever so much better! I don't sleep much at night, for it is so interesting to watch developments; but I sleep a good deal in the daytime.

In the daytime it is tiresome and perplexing.

There are always new shoots on the fungus, and new shades of yellow all over it. I cannot keep count of them, though I have tried conscientiously.

It is the strangest yellow, that wall-paper! It makes me think of all the yellow things I ever saw—not beautiful ones like buttercups, but old foul, bad yellow things.

But there is something else about that paper—the smell! I noticed it the moment we came into the room, but with so much air and sun it was not bad. Now we have had a week of fog and rain, and whether the windows are open or not, the smell is here.

It creeps all over the house.

I find it hovering in the dining-room, skulking in the parlor, hiding in the hall, lying in wait for me on the stairs.

It gets into my hair.

Even when I go to ride, if I turn my head suddenly and surprise it—there is that smell!

Such a peculiar odor, too! I have spent hours in trying to analyze it, to find what it smelled like.

It is not bad—at first, and very gentle, but quite the subtlest, most enduring odor I ever met.

In this damp weather it is awful, I wake up in the night and find it hanging over me.

It used to disturb me at first. I thought seriously of burning the house—to reach the smell.

But now I am used to it. The only thing I can think of that it is like is the *color* of the paper! A yellow smell.

There is a very funny mark on this wall, low down, near the mopboard. A streak that runs round the room. It goes behind every piece of furniture, except the bed, a long, straight, even *smooch*, as if it had been rubbed over and over.

I wonder how it was done and who did it, and what they did it for. Round and round and round—round and round and round—it makes me dizzy!

I really have discovered something at last.

Through watching so much at night, when it changes so, I have finally found out.

The front pattern *does* move—and no wonder! The woman behind shakes it!

Sometimes I think there are a great many women behind, and sometimes only one, and she crawls around fast, and her crawling shakes it all over.

Then in the very bright spots she keeps still, and in the very shady spots she just takes hold of the bars and shakes them hard.

And she is all the time trying to climb through. But nobody could climb through that pattern—it strangles so; I think that is why it has so many heads.

They get through, and then the pattern strangles them off and turns them upside down, and makes their eyes white!

If those heads were covered or taken off it would not be half so bad.

I think that woman gets out in the daytime!

And I'll tell you why—privately—I've seen her!

I can see her out of every one of my windows!

It is the same woman, I know, for she is always creeping, and most women do not creep by daylight.

I see her in that long shaded lane, creeping up and down. I see her in those dark grape arbors, creeping all around the garden.

I see her on that long road under the trees, creeping along, and when a carriage comes she hides under the blackberry vines.

I don't blame her a bit. It must be very humiliating to be caught creeping by daylight!

I always lock the door when I creep by daylight. I can't do it at night, for I know John would suspect something at once.

And John is so queer, now, that I don't want to irritate him. I wish he would take another room! Besides, I don't want anybody to get that woman out at night but myself.

I often wonder if I could see her out of all the windows at once.

But, turn as fast as I can, I can only see out of one at one time.

And though I always see her she *may* be able to creep faster than I can turn!

I have watched her sometimes away off in the open country, creeping as fast as a cloud shadow in a high wind.

If only that top pattern could be gotten off from the under one! I mean to try it, little by little.

I have found out another funny thing, but I shan't tell it this time! It does not do to trust people too much.

There are only two more days to get this paper off, and I believe John is beginning to notice. I don't like the look in his eyes.

And I heard him ask Jennie a lot of professional questions about me. She had a very good report to give.

She said I slept a good deal in the daytime.

John knows I don't sleep very well at night, for all I'm so quiet!

He asked me all sorts of questions, too, and pretended to be very loving and kind.

As if I couldn't see through him!

Still, I don't wonder he acts so, sleeping under this paper for three months.

It only interests me, but I feel sure John and Jennie are secretly affected by it.

Hurrah! This is the last day, but it is enough. John is to stay in town overnight, and won't be out until this evening.

Jennie wanted to sleep with me—the sly thing! But I told her I should undoubtedly rest better for a night all alone.

That was clever, for really I wasn't alone a bit! As soon as it was moonlight, and that poor thing began to crawl and shake the pattern, I got up and ran to help her.

I pulled and she shook, I shook and she pulled, and before morning we had peeled off yards of that paper.

A strip about as high as my head and half around the room.

And then when the sun came and that awful pattern began to laugh at me I declared I would finish it today!

We go away tomorrow, and they are moving all my furniture down again to leave things as they were before.

Jennie looked at the wall in amazement, but I told her merrily that I did it out of pure spite at the vicious thing.

She laughed and said she wouldn't mind doing it herself, but I must not get tired.

How she betrayed herself that time!

But I am here, and no person touches this paper but me,—not *alive!*

She tried to get me out of the room—it was too patent! But

I said it was so quiet and empty and clean now that I believed I would lie down again and sleep all I could; and not to wake me even for dinner—I would call when I woke.

So now she is gone, and the servants are gone, and the things are gone, and there is nothing left but that great bedstead nailed down, with the canvas mattress we found on it.

We shall sleep downstairs tonight, and take the boat home tomorrow.

I quite enjoy the room, now it is bare again.

How those children did tear about here!

This bedstead is fairly gnawed!

But I must get to work.

I have locked the door and thrown the key down into the front path.

I don't want to go out, and I don't want to have anybody come in, till John comes.

I want to astonish him.

I've got a rope up here that even Jennie did not find. If that woman does get out, and tries to get away, I can tie her!

But I forgot I could not reach far without anything to stand on!

This bed will *not* move!

I tried to lift and push it until I was lame, and then I got so angry I bit off a little piece at one corner—but it hurt my teeth.

Then I peeled off all the paper I could reach standing on the floor. It sticks horribly and the pattern just enjoys it! All those strangled heads and bulbous eyes and waddling fungus growths just shriek with derision!

I am getting angry enough to do something desperate. To jump out of the window would be admirable exercise, but the bars are too strong even to try.

Besides, I wouldn't do it. Of course not. I know well enough that a step like that is improper and might be misconstrued.

I don't like to *look* out of the windows even—there are so many of those creeping women, and they creep so fast.

I wonder if they all come out of that wall-paper, as I did?

But I am securely fastened now by my well-hidden rope—you don't get *me* out in the road there!

I suppose I shall have to get back behind the pattern when it comes night, and that is hard!

It is so pleasant to be out in this great room and creep around as I please!

I don't want to go outside. I won't, even if Jennie asks me to.

For outside you have to creep on the ground, and everything is green instead of yellow.

But here I can creep smoothly on the floor, and my shoulder just fits in that long smooch around the wall, so I cannot lose my way.

Why, there's John at the door!

It is no use, young man, you can't open it!

How he does call and pound!

Now he's crying for an axe.

It would be a shame to break down that beautiful door!

"John, dear!" said I in the gentlest voice, "the key is down by the front steps, under a plantain leaf!"

That silenced him for a few moments.

Then he said—very quietly indeed, "Open the door, my darling!"

"I can't," said I. "The key is down by the front door, under a plantain leaf!"

And then I said it again, several times, very gently and slowly, and said it so often that he had to go and see, and he got it, of course, and came in. He stopped short by the door.

"What is the matter?" he cried. "For God's sake, what are you doing?"

I kept on creeping just the same, but I looked at him over my shoulder.

"I've got out at last," said I, "in spite of you and Jane! And I've pulled off most of the paper, so you can't put me back!"

Now why should that man have fainted? But he did, and right across my path by the wall, so that I had to creep over him every time!

An Extinct Angel

THERE WAS ONCE a species of angel inhabiting this planet, acting as "a universal solvent" to all the jarring, irreconcilable elements of human life.

It was quite numerous; almost every family had one; and, although differing in degree of seraphic virtue, all were, by common consent, angels.

The advantages of possessing such a creature were untold. In the first place, the chances of the mere human being in the way of getting to heaven were greatly increased by these semi-heavenly belongings; they gave one a sort of lien on the next world, a practical claim most comforting to the owner.

For the angels of course possessed virtues above mere humanity; and because the angles were so well-behaved, therefore the owners were given credit.

Beside this direct advantage complimentary tickets up above were innumerable indirect advantages below. The possession of one of these angels smoothed every feature of life, and gave peace and joy to an otherwise hard lot.

It was the business of the angel to assuage, to soothe, to comfort, to delight. No matter how unruly were the passions of the owner, sometimes even to the extent of legally beating his angel with "a stick no thicker than his thumb," the angel was to have no passion whatsoever—unless self-sacrifice may be called a passion, and indeed it often amounted to one with her.

The human creature went out to his daily toil and comforted himself as he saw fit. He was apt to come home tired and cross, and in this exigency it was the business of the angel to wear a smile for his benefit—a soft, perennial, heavenly smile.

By an unfortunate limitation of humanity the angel was required, in addition to such celestial duties as smiling and soothing, to do kitchen service, cleaning, sewing, nursing, and other mundane tasks. But these things must be accomplished without the slightest diminution of the angelic virtues.

The angelic virtues, by the way, were of a curiously paradoxical nature.

They were inherent. A human being did not pretend to name them, could not be expected to have them, acknowledged them as far beyond his gross earthly nature; and yet, for all this, he kept constant watch over the virtues of the angel, wrote whole books of advice for angels on how they should behave, and openly held that angels would lose their virtues altogether should they once cease to obey the will and defer to the judgement of human kind.

This looks strange to us today as we consider these past conditions, but then it seemed fair enough; and the angels—bless their submissive, patient hearts!—never thought of questioning it.

It was perhaps only to be expected that when an angel fell the human creature should punish the celestial creature with unrelenting fury. It was so much easier to be an angel than to be human, that there was no excuse for an angel's falling, even by means of her own angelic pity and tender affection.

It seems perhaps hard that the very human creature the

angel fell on, or fell with, or fell to—however you choose to put it—was as harsh as anyone in condemnation of the fall. He never assisted the angel to rise, but got out from under and resumed his way, leaving her in the mud. She was a great convenience to walk on, and, as was stoutly maintained by the human creature, helped keep the other angels clean.

This is exceedingly mysterious, and had better not be inquired into too closely.

The amount of physical labor of a severe and degrading sort required of one of these bright spirits, was amazing. Certain kinds of work—always and essentially dirty—were relegated wholly to her. Yet one of her first and most rigid duties was the keeping of her angelic robes spotlessly clean.

The human creature took great delight in contemplating the flowing robes of the angels. Their changeful motion suggested to him all manner of sweet and lovely thoughts and memories; also, the angelic virtues above mentioned were supposed largely to inhere in the flowing robes. Therefore flow they must, and the ample garments waved unchecked over the weary limbs of the wearer, the contiguous furniture and the stairs. For the angels unfortunately had no wings, and their work was such as required a good deal of going up and down stairs.

It is quite a peculiar thing, in contemplating this work, to see how largely it consisted in dealing with dirt. Yes, it does seem strange to this enlightened age; but the fact was that the angels waited on the human creatures in every form of menial service, doing things as their natural duty which the human creature loathed or scorned.

It does seem irreconcilable, but they reconciled it. The angel was an angel and the work was the angel's work, and what more do you want?

There is one thing about the subject which looks a little

suspicious: The angels—I say it under breath—were not very bright!

The human creatures did not like intelligent angels—intelligence seemed to dim their shine, somehow, and pale their virtues. It was harder to reconcile things where the angels had any sense. Therefore every possible care was taken to prevent the angels from learning anything of our gross human wisdom.

But little by little, owing to the unthought-of consequences of repeated intermarriage between the angel and the human being, the angel longed for, found and ate the fruit of the forbidden tree of knowledge.

And in that day she surely died.

The species is now extinct. It is rumored that here and there in remote regions you can still find a solitary specimen—in places where no access is to be had to the deadly fruit; but the race as a race is extinct.

Poor dodo!

A Day's Berryin'

THE SUN WAS very hot on the round humpy little hills above "the smut." It was hot enough down there, on the black cracked surface of the peat bog; or where the still blacker pools reflected the cloudless sky in filmy luster.

But up here it was hotter, and the lovely white moss crumbled under foot as you walked on it.

"That moss makes first-rate kindlin' if you keep it dry," said Dothea Hopkins, crushing through the brittle masses. "That is, I've always heard say it did—I ain't never tried it."

"Goodness! how hot 'tis up here!" ejaculated her sister in reply. She was a little thin woman, and apparently nimbler than Dothea, whose square back was now bent low over the huckleberry bushes, while a brisk, hopping sound in the six-quart pail she wore at her waist told of the day's work being already begun. "Yes, it takes just such sun to sweeten the berries," Dothea replied. "They're real good this year. It's rained some, so they ain't little, and now it's hot enough so s't they'll be sweet." She rolled a few about in the palm of her large hand, blew off the bits of leaf and twig and put them in her mouth.

"I like these better'n the blueb'rys, don't you?" she said.

"Well, I do' know's I do," responded her sister, still panting a little from her climb up the hill, and looking gingerly about her for the very thickest place to pick in.

Dothea's big pail had ceased to thump and rattle, and only gave forth a dull soft sound, long before Almira had found a spot to her liking. Once settled, however, she picked steadily and with care. You did not have to pick over Almira's berries—they could go on the table at once.

"The swamp blues is the best, I think," pursued Almira. "Them big bushes you can bend down and sit on—I used to when I was little. But after all I do' know's they're any better'n the low blues—the real little ones that knock against your shoes so heavy."

"The black ones is the best," said Dothea firmly. "Blueb'rys is good for a change, I admit, but for steady wear, 'n above all for cookin', give me good black huckleberries!"

"O, for cookin', of course, I thought you meant jest a matter of taste," said Almira, and they relapsed into silence, moving farther away from each other and picking steadily.

It was hot. The big stones crusted with lichen, that lay in the midst of the huckleberry patches, were too hot to sit on comfortably, and the stiff little juniper trees filled the dry air with aromatic breath. In the shade, a few large speckled mosquitoes lurked hungrily.

"It's an awful bad year for mosquitoes," suddenly burst out Almira. "Down stairs where I live in the city they've got screen doors and screen windows and nettin's over the beds, and then they complain."

"Is that Hines girl married yet?" inquired Dothea, brightening up at the mention of her sister's tenants.

"No, she ain't," said Almira.

Almira Hopkins had married a "city feller" in her youth; and while she never said much of her life with him and mourned him decorously in whole, half and quarter mourning when he died; still it was observed that she did not marry again.

"Marriage," she would say sagely, "is a lott'ry. I've got a house and lot, and I'm independent—why should I marry again?" Yet Almira had plenty of chances, for her "city house" was a solid attraction, and her domestic skill was added to year by year with marvelous new recipes. Still she serenely declined any further experiment, making no explanation, and lived up stairs in her small city home, in two or three slant-roofed rooms, renting the lower part.

"She ain't, and I don't think it's likely she will," continued Almira, "with that mother of her'n. How much did I tell you about her, anyway?"

"Only that she was strong-minded and queer, and hadn't a beau for all her good looks. But Bijah Sterns sells 'em potatoes; he knew her mother when they lived over in Pendleton, and he says she's got a beau now. Has she?"

"Well, it's hard tellin'," answered Almira slowly, "but I'll tell you what I know about it. That girl works like a horse anyway. Her mother frets to have her work so hard; but she will do it, and I suppose there's reason good. Did you bring anythin' to drink, Dothea, or shall I hev to go down to the spring?"

"There's cold tea, lots of it," replied Dothea. "We didn't git started till near noon time, anyhow; and we might as well eat now as ever, if you're ready. I've filled this pail, anyhow, and we want the one with the things in it."

So they sat down together in a shady spot, kept off the mosquitoes as best they might with waving of sweet-fern bushes, and continued to discuss the Hines girl's marriage.

"She's a good girl for all she's so queer," pursued Almira, "and her mother has kept her awful strict. Then when she come of age she kind of asserted herself, and done as she

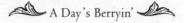

pleased. She don't do no manner of harm; only she won't be put upon as if she was a child any more. Her room is on the top floor with me and she pays reg'lar board to her mother. Pays some of the bills beside I guess, and does consid'able of the housework; but she's real independent and her mother can't abide it. She is a domineerin' sort of woman, I think, for all her religion.

"Well, when this young feller began to come—he was a photographer and good at his business, they said; but he had no faculty, and his folks were not up to what Mis' Hines wanted for her daughter.

"Anyhow, when he first come Mis' Hines never thought her Car'line would take up with him; and she was awful polite—kind of patronizin', I think. Car'line didn't like it, for she wasn't encouragin' him much, but her mother would ask him to tea, and set and talk with him Sunday evenin's while Car'line went to church. She would go to church regular and he wouldn't, not even for her company, it appears. So she'd go just the same to all the services, and her mother'd keep him to tea, as I say, and to spend the evenin'.

"Car'line never altered what she was doin' fer any man, or woman either. I never saw a young person so sot.

"Well, it run along, and bye 'n bye it begun to look as if she would have him after all. Then Mis' Hines turned right around. She'd been doin' all she could to encourage him, it looked to be, before that; more'n Car'line did by a long chalk. But now she thought the girl was goin' to have him, she began to behave—well, it was most peculiar, I think. Why, she told Car'line that he couldn't stay to tea no more, and that she'd got to tell him so! And here he'd been comin' right along every Sunday, and she keepin' him to tea as a reg'lar thing!"

"Well, of all things!" said Dothea. Dothea was unimaginative—unromantic. She had lived with her mother until that good woman, after five years in her chair and two in her bed, had died and left her the little house and a tiny bit in the bank. She was a nurse by profession, not from choice, particularly, but because she had been a nurse for seven years. This story of Almira's seemed to stir some faint memory in her broad breast, for she sat up straighter, shook the flakes of pie crust off her brown gingham apron, and asked, with some eagerness:

"What did she do?"

"Do? Why she had to tell him, of course. It come tea time, and we was thinkin', of course, he was goin' to stay, and there was no plate set, and Car'line's mother just rung the bell and said nothin'. So she had to tell him."

"What'd he do?" asked Dothea, eagerly.

"Oh, of course he said he wouldn't come any more. But Car'line held her head right up straight. I heard 'em, 'cause they was in the front hall, and I was up stairs lookin' out the window. 'I pay my board here,' says Car'line, 'and if I can't receive my friends here where I board, I will board somewhere else!'

"So he's comin' yet, but her mother don't speak to him, and I think he feels kinder stiff there now."

Dothea sighed a long, slow sigh.

"When'd Bijah Sterns get back from Idaho," asked Almira, suddenly.

Dothea colored a little.

"Last June," said she.

"And is he waitin' on you agin?" eagerly inquired Almira.

"He has called once or twice," slowly assented Dothea, looking far over the sun-burned meadows to where the white, dusty road lay like a piece of faded tape between its yellow-green border.

An old horse jogged slowly along in the sun, and a man sat dozing over the reins, his elbows on his knees.

"Come, let's go home," said she suddenly. "There's berries enough, and it looks as if 't was goin' to shower."

It was black in the north, and the air was hotter than ever. So they gathered up the pails, and reached the road by the shortest cut, the sweet fern breathing fragrant remonstrance, as they crushed it under foot.

"Why, Dothea! and here's Almira, too!" said Bijah Sterns from his wagon, overtaking them, as they walked single file in the narrow footpath by the fence, the dust rising in clouds from the laden grass.

"Get right in, and lem'me take you home. It's goin' to shower!"

"How lucky 't you should come along!" said Almira. "It's a special providence, *I* think."

Almira was rather nearsighted.

An Unnatural Mother

"DON'T TELL ME!" said old Mis' Briggs, with a forbidding shake of the head; "no mother that was a mother would desert her own child for anything on earth!"

"And leaving it a care on the town, too!" put in Susannah Jacobs, "as if we hadn't enough to do to take care of our own!"

Miss Jacobs was a well-to-do old maid, owning a comfortable farm and homestead, and living alone with an impoverished cousin acting as general servant, companion and protégé. Mis' Briggs, on the contrary, had had thirteen children, five of whom remained to bless her, so that what maternal feeling Miss Jacobs might lack, Mis' Briggs could certainly supply.

"I should think," piped little Martha Ann Simmons, the village dressmaker, "that she might a saved her young one first and then tried what she could do for the town."

Martha had been married, had lost her husband, and had one sickly boy to care for.

The youngest Briggs girl, still unmarried at thirty-six, and in her mother's eyes a most tender infant, now ventured to make a remark.

"You don't any of you seem to think what she did for all of us—if she hadn't left hers we should all have lost ours, sure."

"You ain't no call to judge, Maria Melia," her mother hastened to reply; "you've no children of your own, and you can't judge of a mother's duty. No mother ought to leave her child, whatever happens. The Lord gave it to her to take care of—he never gave her other people's. You nedn't tell me!"

"She was an unnatural mother!" repeated Miss Jacobs harshly, "as I said to begin with."

"What is the story?" asked the City Boarder. The City Boarder was interested in stories from a business point of view, but they did not know that. "What did this woman do?" she asked.

There was no difficulty in eliciting particulars. The difficulty was rather in discriminating amidst their profusion and contradictoriness. But when the City Boarder got it clear in her mind it was somewhat as follows:

The name of the much condemned heroine was Esther Greenwood, and she lived and died here in Toddsville.

Toddsville was a mill village. The Todds lived on a beautiful eminence overlooking the little town, as the castles of robber barons on the Rhine used to overlook their little towns. The mills and the mill hands' houses were built close along the bed of the river. They had to be pretty close, because the valley was a narrow one, and the bordering hills were too steep for travel, but the water power was fine. Above the village was the reservoir, filling the entire valley save for a narrow road beside it, a fair blue smiling lake, edged with lilies and blue flag, rich in pickerel and perch. This lake gave them fish, it gave them ice, it gave the power that ran the mills that gave the town its bread. Blue Lake was both useful and ornamental.

In this pretty and industrious village Esther had grown up, the somewhat neglected child of a heart-broken widower. He had lost a young wife, and three fair babies before her—this one was left him, and he said he meant that she should have all the chance there was.

"That was what ailed her in the first place!" they all eagerly explained to the City Boarder. "She never knew what 'twas to have a mother, and she grew up a regular tomboy! Why she used to roam the country for miles around, in all weather like an Injun! And her father wouldn't take no advice!"

This topic lent itself to eager discussion. The recreant father, it appeared, was a doctor, not their accepted standby, the resident physician of the neighborhood, but an alien doctor, possessed of "views."

"You never heard such things as he advocated," Miss Jacobs explained. "He wouldn't give no medicines, hardly; said 'nature' did the curing—he couldn't."

"And he couldn't either—that was clear," Mrs. Briggs agreed. "Look at his wife and children dying on his hands, as it were! 'Physician heal thyself,' I say."

"But, mother," Maria Amelia put in, "she was an invalid when he married her, they say; and those children died of polly—polly—what's that thing that nobody can help?"

"That may all be so," Miss Jacobs admitted, "but all the same it's a doctor's business to give medicine. If 'nature' was all that was wanted, we needn't have any doctor at all!"

"I believe in medicine and plenty of it. I always gave my children a good clearance, spring and fall, whether anything ailed 'em or not, just to be on the safe side. And if there was anything the matter with 'em they had plenty more. I never had anything to reproach myself with on that score," stated Mrs. Briggs firmly. Then as a sort of concession to the family graveyard, she added piously, "The Lord giveth and the Lord taketh away."

"You should have seen the way he dressed that child!"

pursued Miss Jacobs. "It was a reproach to the town. Why, you couldn't tell at a distance whether it was a boy or a girl. And barefoot! He let that child go barefoot till she was so big we was actually mortified to see her."

It appeared that a wild, healthy childhood had made Esther very different in her early womanhood from the meek, well-behaved damsels of the little place. She was well enough liked by those who knew her at all, and the children of the place adored her, but the worthy matrons shook their heads and prophesied no good of a girl who was "queer."

She was described with rich detail in reminiscence, how she wore her hair short till she was fifteen—"just shingled like a boy's—it did seem a shame that girl had no mother to look after her—and her clo'se was almost a scandal, even when she did put on shoes and stockings."

"Just gingham—brown gingham—and *short*!"

"I think she was a real nice girl," said Maria Amelia. "I can remember her just as well! She was so nice to us children. She was five or six years older than I was, and most girls that age won't have anything to do with little ones. But she was as kind and pleasant. She'd take us berrying and on all sorts of walks, and teach us new games and tell us things. I don't remember any one that ever did us the good she did!"

Maria Amelia's thin chest heaved with emotion; and there were tears in her eyes; but her mother took her up somewhat sharply.

"That sounds well I must say—right before your own mother that's toiled and slaved for you! It's all very well for a young thing that's got nothing on earth to do to make herself agreeable to young ones. That poor blinded father of hers never taught her to do the work a girl should—naturally, he couldn't."

"At least he might have married again and given her

another mother," said Susannah Jacobs, with decision, with so much decision in fact that the City Boarder studied her expression for a moment and concluded that if this recreant father had not married again it was not for lack of opportunity.

Mrs. Simmons cast an understanding glance upon Miss Jacobs, and nodded wisely.

"Yes, he ought to have done that, of course. A man's not fit to bring up children, anyhow—How can they? Mothers have the instinct—that is, all natural mothers have. But, dear me! There's some as don't seem to be mothers—even when they have a child!"

"You're quite right, Mis' Simmons," agreed the mother of thirteen. "It's a divine instinct, I say. I'm sorry for the child that lacks it. Now this Esther. We always knew she wan't like other girls—she never seemed to care for dress and company and things girls naturally do, but was always philandering over the hills with a parcel of young ones. There wan't a child in town but would run after her. She made more trouble 'n a little in families, the young ones quoting what Aunt Esther said, and tellin' what Aunt Esther did to their own mothers, and she only a young girl. Why she actually seemed to care more for them children than she did for beaux or anything— it wasn't natural!"

"But she did marry?" pursued the City Boarder.

"Marry! Yes, she married finally. We all thought she never would, but she did. After the things her father taught her it did seem as if he'd ruined all her chances. It's simply terrible the way that girl was trained."

"Him being a doctor," put in Mrs. Simmons, "made it different, I suppose."

"Doctor or no doctor," Miss Jacobs rigidly interposed, "it was a crying shame to have a young girl so instructed."

"Maria Melia," said her mother, "I want you should get me my smelling salts. They're up in the spare chamber, I believe—When your Aunt Marcia was here she had one of her spells—don't you remember?—and she asked for salts. Look in the top bureau drawer—they must be there."

Maria Amelia, thirty-six, but unmarried, withdrew dutifully, and the other ladies drew closer to the City Boarder.

"It's the most shocking thing I ever heard of," murmured Mrs. Briggs. "Do you know he—a father—actually taught his daughter how babies come!"

There was a breathless hush.

"He did," eagerly chimed in the little dressmaker, "all the particulars. It was perfectly awful!"

"He said," continued Mrs. Briggs, "that he expected her to be a mother and that she ought to understand what was before her!"

"He was waited on by a committee of ladies from the church, married ladies, all older than he was," explained Miss Jacobs severely. "They told him it was creating a scandal in the town—and what do you think he said?"

There was another breathless silence.

Above, the steps of Maria Amelia were heard, approaching the stairs.

"It ain't there, Ma!"

"Well, you look in the high boy and in the top drawer, they're somewhere up there," her mother replied.

Then, in a sepulchral whisper:

"He told us—yes, ma'am, I was on that committee—he told us that until young women knew what was before them as mothers they would not do their duty in choosing a father for their children! That was his expression—'choosing a father!' A nice thing for a young girl to be thinking of—a father for her children!"

"Yes, and more than that," inserted Miss Jacobs, who, though not on the committee, seemed familiar with its workings. "He told them——" But Mrs. Briggs waved her aside and continued swiftly——

"He taught that innocent girl about—the Bad Disease! Actually!"

"He did!" said the dressmaker. "It got out, too, all over town. There wasn't a man here would have married her after that."

Miss Jacobs insisted on taking up the tale. "I understand that he said it was 'to protect her!' Protect her, indeed! Against matrimony! As if any man alive would want to marry a young girl who knew all the evil of life! I was brought up differently, I assure you!"

"Young girls should be kept innocent!" Mrs. Briggs solemnly proclaimed. "Why, when I was married I knew no more what was before me than a babe unborn and my girls were all brought up so, too!"

Then, as Maria Amelia returned with the salts, she continued more loudly, "but she did marry after all. And a mighty queer husband she got, too. He was an artist or something, made pictures for the magazines and such as that, and they do say she met him first out in the hills. That's the first 'twas known of it here, anyhow—them two trapesing about all over; him with his painting things! They married and just settled down to live with her father, for she vowed she wouldn't leave him, and he said it didn't make no difference where he lived, he took his business with him."

"They seemed very happy together," said Maria Amelia.

"Happy! Well, they might have been, I suppose. It was a pretty queer family, I think." And her mother shook her head in retrospection. "They got on all right for a while; but the old man died, and those two—well, I don't call it housekeeping—the way they lived!"

"No," said Miss Jacobs. "They spent more time out of doors than they did in the house. She followed him around everywhere. And for open love making——"

They all showed deep disapproval at this memory. All but the City Boarder and Maria Amelia.

"She had one child, a girl," continued Mrs. Briggs, "and it was just shocking to see how she neglected that child from the beginnin'. She never seemed to have no maternal feelin' at all!"

"But I thought you said she was very fond of children," remonstrated the City Boarder.

"Oh, *children*, yes. She'd take up with any dirty faced brat in town, even to them Kanucks. I've seen her again and again with a whole swarm of the mill hands' young ones round her, goin' on some picnic or other—'open air school,' she used to call it—*Such* notions as she had. But when it come to her own child! Why——" Here the speaker's voice sank to a horrified hush. "She never had no baby clo'se for it! Not a single sock!"

The City Boarder was interested. "Why, what did she do with the little thing?"

"The Lord knows!" answered old Mis' Briggs. "She never would let us hardly see it when 'twas little, 'Shamed too, I don't doubt. But that's strange feelin's for a mother. Why, I was so proud of my babies! And I kept 'em lookin' so pretty! I'd a-sat up all night and sewed and washed, but I'd a had my children look well!" And the poor old eyes filled with tears as she thought of the eight little graves in the churchyard, which she never failed to keep looking pretty, even now. "She just let that young one roll round in the grass like a puppy with hardly nothin' on! Why, a squaw does better. She does keep 'em done up for a spell! That child was treated worse'n an Injun! We all done what we could, of course. We felt it no more'n right. But she was real hateful about it, and we had to let her be."

"The child died?" asked the City Boarder.

"Died! Dear no! That's it you saw going by; a great strappin' girl she is, too, and promisin' to grow up well, thanks to Mrs Stone's taking her. Mrs Stone always thought a heap of Esther. It's a mercy to the child that she lost her mother, I do believe! How she ever survived that kind of treatment beats all! Why that woman never seemed to have the first spark of maternal feeling to the end! She seemed just as fond of the other young ones after she had her own as she was before, and that's against nature. The way it happened was this. You see they lived up the valley nearer to the lake than the village. He was away, and was coming home that night, it seems, driving from Drayton along the lake road. And she set out to meet him. She must a walked up to the dam to look for him; and we think maybe she saw the team clear across the lake. Maybe she thought he could get to the house and save little Esther in time—that's the only explanation we ever could put on it. But this is what she did; and you can judge for yourselves if any mother in her senses *could* ha' done such a thing! You see 'twas the time of that awful disaster, you've read of it, likely, that destroyed three villages. Well, she got to the dam and see that 'twas givin' way—she was always great for knowin' all such things. And she just turned and ran. Jake Elder was up on the hill after a stray cow, and he seen her go. He was too far off to imagine what ailed her, but he said he never saw a woman run so in his life.

"And, if you'll believe it, she run right by her own house—never stopped—never looked at it. Just run for the village. Of course, she may have lost her head with the fright, but that wasn't like her. No, I think she made up her mind to leave that innocent baby to die! She just ran down here and give warnin', and, of course, we sent word down valley on horseback, and there was no lives lost in all three villages.

She started to run back as soon as we was 'roused, but 'twas too late then.

"Jake saw it all, thought he was too far off to do a thing. He said he couldn't stir a foot, it was so awful. He seen the wagon drivin' along as nice as you please till it got close to the dam, and then Greenwood seemed to see the danger and whipped up like mad. He was the father, you know. But he wasn't quite in time—the dam give way and the water went over him like a tidal wave. She was almost to the gate when it struck the house and her,—and we never found her body nor his for days and days. They was washed clear down river.

"Their house was strong and it stood a little high, and had some big trees between it and the lake too. It was moved off the place and brought up against the side of the stone church down yonder, 'twant wholly in pieces. And that child was found swimmin' round in its bed, most drowned, but not quite. The wonder is, it didn't die of a cold, but it's here yet—must have a strong constitution. Their folks never did nothing for it—so we had to keep it here."

"Well, now, mother," said Maria Amelia Briggs. "It does seem to me that she did her duty. You know yourself that if she hadn't give warnin' all three of the villages would a' been cleaned out—a matter of fifteen hundred people. And if she'd stopped to lug that child, she couldn't have got here in time. Don't you believe she was thinkin' of those mill-hands' children?"

"Maria 'Melia, I'm ashamed of you!" said old Mis' Briggs. "But you ain't married and ain't a mother. A mother's duty is to her own child! She neglected her own to look after other folks—the Lord never gave her them other children to care for!"

"Yes," said Miss Jacobs, "and here's her child, a burden on the town! She was an unnatural mother!"

According to Solomon

"'HE THAT REBUKETH a man afterwards shall find more favor than he that flattereth with his tongue,'" said Mr. Solomon Bankside to his wife Mary.

"It's the other way with a woman, I think;" she answered him, "you might put that in."

"Tut, tut, Molly," said he; "'Add not unto his words,'—do not speak lightly of the wisdom of the great king."

"I don't mean to, dear, but—when you hear it all the time"—

"'He that turneth away his ear from the law, even his prayer shall be an abomination,'" answered Mr. Bankside.

"I believe you know every one of those old Proverbs by heart," said his wife with some heat. "Now that's not disrespectful!—they *are* old!—and I do wish you'd forget some of them!"

He smiled at her quizzically, tossing back his heavy silver-gray hair with the gesture she had always loved. His eyes were deep blue and bright under their bushy brows; and the mouth was kind—in its iron way. "I can think of at least three to squelch you with, Molly," said he, "but I won't."

"O I know the one you want! 'A continual dropping in a very rainy day and a contentions woman are alike!' I'm *not* contentious, Solomon!"

"No, you are not," he frankly admitted. "What I really had in mind was this—'A prudent wife is from the Lord,' and 'He that findeth a wife findeth a good thing; and obtaineth favor of the Lord.'"

She ran around the table in the impulsive way years did not alter, and kissed him warmly.

"I'm not scolding you, my dear," he continued: "but if you had all the money you'd like to give away—there wouldn't be much left!"

"But look at what you spend on me!" she urged.

"That's a wise investment—as well as a deserved reward," her husband answered calmly. "'There is that scattereth and yet increaseth,' you know, my dear; 'And there is that withholdeth more than is meet—and it tendeth to poverty!' Take all you get my dear—it's none too good for you."

He gave her his goodbye kiss with special fondness, put on his heavy satin-lined overcoat and went to the office.

Mr. Solomon Bankside was not a Jew; though his last name suggested and his first seemed to prove it; also his proficiency in the Old Testament gave color to the idea. No, he came from Vermont; of generations of unbroken New England and old English Puritan ancestry, where the Solomons and Isaacs and Zedekiahs were only mitigated by the Standfasts and Praise-the-Lords. Pious, persistent pig-headed folk were they, down all the line.

His wife had no such simple pedigree. A streak of Huguenot blood she had (some of the best in France, though neither of them knew that), a grandmother from Albany with a Van to her name; a great grandmother with a Mac; and another with an O'; even a German cross came in somewhere. Mr. Bankside was devoted to genealogy, and had been at some pains to dig up these facts—the more he found the worse he felt, and the lower ran his opinion of Mrs. Bankside's ancestry.

She had been a fascinating girl; pretty, with the dash and piquancy of an oriole in a May apple-tree; clever and efficient in everything her swift hands touched; quite a spectacular housekeeper; and the sober, long-faced young down easterner had married her with a sudden decision that he often wondered about in later years. So did she.

What he had not sufficiently weighed at the time, was her spirit of incorrigible independence, and a lightmindedness which, on maturer judgment, he could almost term irreligious. His conduct was based on principle, all of it; built firmly into habit and buttressed by scriptural quotations. Hers seemed to him as inconsequent as the flight of a moth. Studying it, in his solemn conscientious way, in the light of his genealogical researches, he felt that all her uncertainties were accounted for, and that the error was his—in having married too many kinds of people at once.

They had been, and were, very happy together none the less: though sometimes their happiness was a little tottery. This was one of the times. It was the day after Christmas, and Mrs. Bankside entered the big drawing room, redolent of popcorn and evergreen, and walked slowly to the corner where the fruits of yesterday were lovingly arranged; so few that she had been able to give—so many that she had received.

There were the numerous pretty interchangeable things given her by her many friends; "presents," suitable to any lady. There were the few perfectly selected ones given by the few who knew her best. There was the rather perplexing gift of Mrs. MacAvelly. There was her brother's stiff white envelope enclosing a check. There were the loving gifts of children and grandchildren.

Finally there was Solomon's.

It was his custom to bestow upon her one solemn and expensive object, a boon as it were, carefully selected, after much thought and balancing of merits; but the consideration was spent on the nature of the gift—not on the desires of the recipient. There was the piano she could not play, the statue she did not admire, the set of Dante she never read, the heavy gold bracelet, the stiff diamond brooch—and all the others. This time it was a set of sables, costing even more than she imagined.

Christmas after Christmas had these things come to her; and she stood there now, thinking of that procession of unvalued valuables, with an expression so mixed and changeful it resembled a kaleidoscope. Love for Solomon, pride in Solomon, respect for Solomon's judgment and power to pay, gratitude for his unfailing kindness and generosity, impatience with his always giving her this one big valuable permanent thing, when he knew so well that she much preferred small renewable cheap ones; her personal dislike of furs, the painful conviction that brown was not becoming to her—all these and more filled the little woman with what used to be called "conflicting emotions."

She smoothed out her brother's check, wishing as she always did that it had come before Christmas, so that she might buy more presents for her beloved people. Solomon liked to spend money on her—in his own way; but he did not like to have her spend money on him—or on anyone for that matter. She had asked her brother once, if he would mind sending her his Christmas present beforehand.

"Not on your life, Polly!" he said. "You'd never see a cent of it! You can't buy 'em many things right on top of Christmas, and it'll be gone long before the next one."

She put the check away and turned to examine her queerest gift. Upon which scrutiny presently entered the donor.

"I'm ever so much obliged, Benigna," said Mrs. Bankside. "You know how I love to do things. It's a loom, isn't it? Can you show me how it works?"

"Of course I can, my dear; that's just what I ran in for—I was afraid you wouldn't know. But you are so clever with your hands that I'm sure you'll enjoy it. I do."

Whereat Mrs. MacAvelly taught Mrs. Bankside the time-honored art of weaving. And Mrs. Bankside enjoyed it more than any previous handicraft she had essayed.

She did it well, beginning with rather coarse and simple weaves; and gradually learning the finer grades of work. Despising as she did the more modern woolens, she bought real wool yarn of a lovely red—and made some light warm flannelly stuff in which she proceeded to rapturously enclose her little grandchildren.

Mr. Bankside warmly approved, murmuring affectionately, "'She seeketh wool and flax—she worketh willingly with her hands.'"

He watched little Bob and Polly strenuously "helping" the furnace man to clear the sidewalk, hopping about like red-birds in their new caps and coats; and his face beamed with the appositeness of his quotation, as he remarked, "She is not afraid of the snow for her household, for all her household are clothed with scarlet!" and he proffered an extra, wholly spontaneous kiss, which pleased her mightily.

"You dear man!" she said with a hug; "I believe you'd rather find a proverb to fit than a gold mine!"

To which he triumphantly responded: "'Wisdom is better than rubies; and all the things that may be desired are not to be compared to it.'"

She laughed sweetly at him. "And do you think wisdom stopped with that string of proverbs?"

"You can't get much beyond it," he answered calmly. "If we lived up to all there is in that list we shouldn't be far out, my dear!"

Whereat she laughed again smoothed his gray mane, and

kissed him in the back of his neck. "You *dear* thing!" said Mrs. Bankside.

She kept herself busy with the new plaything as he called it. Hands that had been rather empty were now smoothly full. Her health was better, and any hint of occasional quer-ulousness disappeared entirely; so that her husband was moved to fresh admiration of her sunny temper, and quoted for the hundredth time, "'She openeth her mouth with wisdom, and in her tongue is the law of kindness.'"

Mrs. MacAvelly taught her to make towels. But Mrs. Bankside's skill outstripped hers; she showed inventive genius and designed patterns of her own. The fineness and quality of the work increased; and she joyfully replenished her linen chest with her own handiwork.

"I tell you, my dear," said Mrs. MacAvelly, "if you'd be willing to sell them you could get almost any price for those towels. With the initials woven in. I know I could get you orders—through the Woman's Exchange, you know!"

Mrs. Bankside was delighted. "What fun!" she said. "And I needn't appear at all?"

"No, you needn't appear at all—do let me try."

So Mrs. Bankside made towels of price, soft, fine, and splendid, till she was weary of them; and in the opulence of constructive genius fell to devising woven belts of elaborate design.

These were admired excessively. All her women friends wanted one, or more; the Exchange got hold of it, there was a distinct demand; and finally Mrs. MacAvelly came in one day with a very important air and a special order.

"I don't know what you'll think, my dear," she said, "but I happen to know the Percy's very well—the big store people, you know; and Mr. Percy was talking about those belts of yours to me;—of course he didn't know they are yours; but he said (the Exchange people told him I knew, you see) he said, 'If you can place an order with that woman, I can take all she'll make and pay her full price for them. Is she poor?' he asked. 'Is she dependent on her work?' And I told him, 'Not altogether.' And I think he thinks it an interesting case! Anyhow, there's the order. Will you do it?"

Mrs. Bankside was much excited. She wanted to very much, but dreaded offending her husband. So far she had not told him of her quiet trade in towels; but hid and saved this precious money—the first she had ever earned.

The two friends discussed the pros and cons at considerable length; and finally with some perturbation, she decided to accept the order.

"You'll never tell, Benigna!" she urged. "Solomon would never forgive me, I'm afraid."

"Why of course I won't—you needn't have a moment's fear of it. You give them to me—I'll stop with the carriage you see; and I take them to the Exchange—and he gets them from there."

"It seems like smuggling!" said Mrs. Bankside delightedly. "I always did love to smuggle!"

"They say women have no conscience about laws, don't they?" Mrs. MacAvelly suggested.

"Why should we?" answered her friend. "We don't make 'em—nor God—nor nature. Why on earth should we respect a set of silly rules made by some men one day and changed by some more the next?"

"Bless us, Polly! Do you talk to Mr. Bankside like that?"

"Indeed I don't!" answered her hostess, holding out a particularly beautiful star-patterned belt to show to advantage. "There are lots of things I don't say to Mr. Bankside—'A man of understanding holdeth his peace' you know—or a woman."

She was a pretty creature, her hair like that of a powdered marchioness, her rosy cheeks and firm slight figure suggesting a charmer in Dresden china.

Mrs. MacAvelly regarded her admiringly. "'Where there is no wood the fire goeth out; so where there is no tale bearer the strife ceaseth,'" she proudly offered, "I can quote that much myself."

But Mrs. Bankside had many misgivings as she pursued her audacious way; the busy hours flying away from her, and the always astonishing checks flying toward her in gratifying accumulation. She came down to her well-planned dinners gracious and sweet; always effectively dressed; spent the cozy quiet evenings with her husband, or went out with him, with a manner of such increased tenderness and charm that his heart warmed anew to the wife of his youth; and he even relented a little toward her miscellaneous ancestors.

As the days shortened and darkened she sparkled more and more; with little snatches of song now and then; gay ineffectual strumming on the big piano; sudden affectionate darts at him, with quaintly distributed caresses.

"Molly!" said he, "I don't believe you're a day over twenty! What makes you act so?"

"Don't you like it, So?" she asked him. That was the nearest she ever would approximate to his name.

He did like it, naturally, and even gave her an extra ten dollars to buy Christmas presents with; while he meditated giving her an electric runabout;—to her!—who was afraid of a wheelbarrow!

When the day arrived and the family were gathered together, Mrs. Bankside, wearing the diamond brooch, the gold bracelet, the point lace handkerchief—everything she could carry of his accumulated generosity—and such an air of triumphant mystery that the tree itself was dim beside her;

handed out to her astonished relatives such an assortment of desirable articles that they found no words to express their gratitude.

"Why, *Mother!*" said Jessie, whose husband was a minister and salaried as such, "Why, *Mother*—how did you know we wanted just that kind of a rug!—and a sewing-machine *too!* And this lovely suit—and—and—why *Mother!*"

But her son-in-law took her aside and kissed her solemnly. He had wanted that particular set of sociological books for years—and never hoped to get them; or that bunch of magazines either.

Nellie had "married rich;" she was less ostentatiously favored; but she had shown her thankfulness a week ago—when her mother had handed her a check.

"Sh, sh! my dear!" her mother had said, "Not one word. I know! What pleasant weather we're having."

This son-in-law was agreeably surprised, too; and the other relatives, married and single; while the children rioted among their tools and toys, taking this Christmas like any other, as a season of unmitigated joy.

Mr. Solomon Bankside looked on with growing amazement, making computations in his practiced mind; saying nothing whatever. Should he criticize his wife before others?

But when his turn came—when gifts upon gifts were offered to him—sets of silken handkerchiefs (he couldn't bear the touch of a silk handkerchief!), a cabinet of cards and chips and counters of all sorts (he never played cards), an inlaid chess-table and ivory men (the game was unknown to him), a gorgeous scarfpin (he abominated jewelry), a five pound box of candy (he never ate it), his feelings so mounted within him, that since he would not express, and could not repress them, he summarily went up stairs to his room.

She found him there later, coming in blushing, smiling, crying a little too—like a naughty but charming child.

He swallowed hard as he looked at her; and his voice was a little strained.

"I can take a joke as well as any man, Molly. I guess we're square on that. But—my dear!—where did you get it?"

"Earned it," said she, looking down, and fingering her lace handkerchief.

"Earned it! My wife, earning money! How—if I may ask?"

"By my weaving, dear—the towels and the belts—I sold 'em. Don't be angry—nobody knows—my name didn't appear at all! Please don't be angry!—It isn't wicked, and it was such fun!"

"No—it's not wicked, I suppose," said he rather grimly. "But it is certainly a most mortifying and painful thing to me—most unprecedented."

"Not so unprecedented, Dear," she urged, "Even the woman you think most of did it! Don't you remember 'She maketh fine linen and selleth it—and delivereth girdles unto the merchants!'"

Mr. Bankside came down handsomely.

He got used to it after a while, and then he became proud of it. If a friend ventured to suggest a criticism, or to sympathize, he would calmly respond, "'The heart of her husband doth safely trust in her, so that he shall have no need of spoil. Give her of the fruit of her hands, and let her own works praise her in the gates.'"

Her Housekeeper

ON THE TOP floor of a New York boardinghouse lived a particularly attractive woman who was an actress.

She was also a widow, not divorcee, but just plain widow; and she persisted in acting under her real name, which was Mrs. Leland.

The manager objected, but her reputation was good enough to carry the point.

"It will cost you a great deal of money, Mrs. Leland," said the manager.

"I make money enough," she answered.

"You will not attract so many—admirers," said the manager.

"I have admirers enough," she answered; which was visibly true.

She was well under thirty, even by daylight—and about eighteen on the stage; and as for admirers—they apparently thought Mrs. Leland was a carefully selected stage name.

Besides being a widow, she was a mother, having a small boy of about five years; and this small boy did not look in the least like a "stage child," but was a brown-skinned, healthy little rascal of the ordinary sort.

With this boy, an excellent nursery governess, and a maid,

Mrs. Leland occupied the top floor above mentioned, and enjoyed it.

She had a big room in front, to receive in; and a small room with a skylight, to sleep in.

The boy's room and the governess' rooms were at the back, with sunny south windows, and the maid slept on a couch in the parlor.

She was a colored lady, named Alice, and did not seem to care where she slept, or if she slept at all.

"I never was so comfortable in my life," said Mrs. Leland to her friends. "I've been here three years and mean to stay. It is not like any boardinghouse I ever saw, and it is not like any home I ever had. I have the privacy, the detachment, the carelessness of a boardinghouse, and 'all the comforts of a home.' Up I go to my little top flat as private as you like. My Alice takes care of it—the housemaids only come in when I'm out. I can eat with the others downstairs if I please; but mostly I don't please; and up come my little meals on the dumbwaiter—hot and good."

"But—having to flock with a lot of promiscuous boarders!" said her friends.

"I don't flock, you see; that's just it. And besides, they are not promiscuous—there isn't a person in the house now who isn't some sort of a friend of mine. As fast as a room was vacated I'd suggest somebody—and here we all are. It's great."

"But do you *like* a skylight room?" Mrs. Leland's friends further inquired of her.

"By no means!" she promptly replied.

"I hate it. I feel like a mouse in a pitcher!"

"Then why in the name of reason?"

"Because I can sleep there! *Sleep*! It's the only way to be quiet in New York, and I have to sleep late if I sleep at all. I've fixed the skylight so that I'm drenched with air—and not drenched with rain—and there I am. Johnny is gagged and muffled as it were, and carried downstairs as early as possible. He gets his breakfast, and the unfortunate Miss Merton has to go out and play with him—in all weathers—except kindergarten time. Then Alice sits on the stairs and keeps everybody away till I ring."

Possibly it was owing to the stillness and the air and the sleep till near lunchtime that Mrs. Leland kept her engaging youth, her vivid uncertain beauty.

At times you said of her, "She has a keen intelligent face, but she's not pretty."

Which was true.

She was not pretty.

But at times again she overcame you with her sudden loveliness.

All of which was observed by her friend from the second floor who wanted to marry her. In this he was not alone; either as a friend, of whom she had many, or as a lover, of whom she had more.

His distinction lay first in his opportunities, as a co-resident, for which he was heartily hated by all the more and some of the many; and second in that he remained a friend in spite of being a lover, and remained a lover in spite of being flatly refused.

His name in the telephone book was given as "Arthur Olmstead, real estate;" office this and residence that—she looked him up therein after their first meeting.

He was rather a short man, heavily built, with a quiet kind face, and a somewhat quizzical smile.

He seemed to make all the money he needed, occupied the two rooms and plentiful closet space of his floor in great contentment, and manifested most improper domesticity of taste by inviting friends to tea.

"Just like a woman!" Mrs. Leland told him.

"And why not? Women have so many attractive ways— why not imitate them?" he asked her.

"A man doesn't want to be feminine, I'm sure," struck in a pallid, overdressed youth, with openwork socks on his slim feet, and perfumed handkerchief.

Mr. Olmstead smiled a broad friendly smile.

He was standing near the young man, a little behind him, and at this point he put his hands just beneath the youth's arms, lifted and set him aside as if he were an umbrella stand.

"Excuse me, Mr. Masters," he said gravely, but you were standing on Mrs. Leland's gown."

Mr. Masters was too much absorbed in apologizing to the lady to take umbrage at the method of his removal; but she was not so oblivious.

She tried doing it to her little boy afterwards, and found him very heavy.

When she came home from her walk or drive in the early winter dusk, this large quietly furnished room, the glowing fire, the excellent tea and delicate thin bread and butter were most restful.

"It is two more stories up before I can get my own;" she would say—"I must stop a minute."

When he began to propose to her the first time she tried to stop him.

"O please don't!" she cried. "*Please* don't! There are no end of reasons why I will not marry anybody again. Why can't some of you men be nice to me and not—that! Now I can't come in to tea any more!"

"I'd like to know why not," said he calmly. "You don't have to marry me if you don't want to; but that's no reason for cutting my acquaintance, is it?"

She gazed at him in amazement.

"I'm not threatening to kill myself, am I? I don't intend going to the devil. I'd like to be your husband, but if I can't— mayn't I be a brother to you?"

She was inclined to think he was making fun of her, but no—his proposal had had the real ring in it.

"And you're not—you're not going to?" it seemed the baldest assumption to think that he was going to, he looked so strong and calm and friendly.

"Not going to annoy you? Not going to force an undesired affection on you and rob myself of a most agreeable friendship? Of course not. Your tea is cold, Mrs. Leland—let me give you another cup. And do you think Miss Rose is going to do well as 'Angelina'?"

So presently Mrs. Leland was quite relieved in her mind, and free to enjoy the exceeding comfortableness of this relation.

Little Johnny was extremely fond of Mr. Olmstead; who always treated him with respect, and who could listen to his tales of strife and glory more intelligently than either mother or governess.

Mr. Olmstead kept on hand a changing supply of interesting things; not toys—never, but real things not intended for little boys to play with.

No little boy would want to play with dolls for instance; but what little boy would not be fascinated by a small wooden lay figure, capable of unheard of contortions.

Tin soldiers were common, but the flags of all nations—real flags, and true stories about them, were interesting.

Noah's arks were cheap and unreliable scientifically; but Barye lions, ivory elephants, and Japanese monkeys in didactic groups of three, had unfailing attraction.

And the books this man had—great solid books that could be opened wide on the floor, and a little boy lie down to in peace and comfort!

Mrs. Leland stirred her tea and watched them until Johnny was taken upstairs.

"Why don't you smoke?" she asked suddenly. "Doctor's orders?"

"No—mine," he answered. "I never consulted a doctor in my life."

"Nor a dentist, I judge," said she.

"Nor a dentist."

"You'd better knock on wood!" she told him.

"And cry 'Uncle Reuben?'" he asked smilingly.

"You haven't told me why you don't smoke!" said she suddenly.

"Haven't I?" he said. "That was very rude of me. But look here. There's a thing I wanted to ask you. Now I'm not pressing any sort of inquiry as to myself; but as a brother, would you mind telling me some of those numerous reasons why you will not marry anybody?"

She eyed him suspiciously, but he was as solid and calm as usual, regarding her pleasantly and with no hint of ulterior purpose.

"Why—I don't mind," she began slowly. "First—I have been married—and was very happy. That's reason enough."

He did not contradict her; but merely said, "That's one," and set it down in his notebook.

"Dear me, Mr. Olmstead! You're not a reporter, are you!"

"O no—but I wanted to have them clear and think about them," he explained. "Do you mind?" And he made as if to shut his little book again.

"I don't know as I mind," she said slowly.

"But it looks so—businesslike."

"This is a very serious business, Mrs. Leland, as you must know. Quite aside from any personal desire of my own, I am truly 'your sincere friend and well-wisher,' as the *Complete Letter Writer* has it, and there are so many men wanting to marry you."

This she knew full well, and gazed pensively at the toe of her small flexible slipper, poised on a stool before the fire.

Mr. Olmstead also gazed at the slipper toe with appreciation. "What's the next one?" he said cheerfully.

"Do you know you are a real comfort," she told him suddenly. "I never knew a man before who could—well leave off being a man for a moment and just be a human creature."

"Thank you, Mrs. Leland," he said in tones of pleasant sincerity.

"I want to be a comfort to you if I can. Incidentally wouldn't you be more comfortable on this side of the fire—the light falls better—don't move."

And before she realized what he was doing he picked her up, chair and all, and put her down softly on the other side, setting the footstool as before, and even daring to place her little feet upon it—but with so businesslike an air that she saw no opening for rebuke.

It is a difficult matter to object to a man's doing things like that when he doesn't look as if he was doing them.

"That's better," said he cheerfully, taking the place where she had been. "Now, what's the next one?"

"The next one is my boy."

"Second—Boy," he said, putting it down. "But I should think he'd be a reason the other way. Excuse me—I wasn't going to criticize—yet! And the third?"

"Why should you criticize at all, Mr. Olmstead?"

"I shouldn't—on my own account. But there may come a man you love." He had a fine baritone voice. When she heard him sing Mrs. Leland always wished he were taller, handsomer, more distinguished looking; his voice sounded as if he were.

"And I should hate to see these reasons standing in the way of your happiness," he continued.

"Perhaps they wouldn't," said she in a reverie.

"Perhaps they wouldn't—and in that case it is no possible harm that you tell me the rest of them. I won't cast it up at you. Third?"

"Third, I won't give up my profession for any man alive."

"Any man alive would be a fool to want you to," said he setting down, "Third—Profession."

"Fourth—I like *Freedom!*" she said with sudden intensity.

"You don't know! they kept me so tight! so *tight* when I was a girl! Then—I was left alone, with a very little money, and I began to study for the stage—that was like heaven! And then—O what *idiots* women are!"

She said the word not tragically, but with such hard-pointed intensity that it sounded like a gimlet. "Then I married, you see—I gave up all my new won freedom to *marry!* and he kept me tighter than ever." She shut her expressive mouth in level lines—stood up suddenly and stretched her arms wide and high.

"I'm free again, free—I can do exactly as I please!" The words were individually relished. "I have the work I love. I can earn all I need—am saving something for the boy. I'm perfectly independent!"

"And perfectly happy!" he cordially endorsed her. "I don't blame you for not wanting to give it up."

"O well—happy!" she hesitated. "There are times, of course, when one isn't happy. But then—the other way I was unhappy all the time."

"He's dead—unfortunately," mused Mr. Olmstead.

"Unfortunately? Why?"

He looked at her with his straightforward, pleasant smile. "I'd have liked the pleasure of killing him," he said regretfully.

She was startled, and watched him with dawning alarm.

But he was quite quiet—even cheerful.

"Fourth—Freedom," he wrote. "Is that all?"

"No—there are two more. Neither of them will please you.

You won't think so much of me any more. The worst one is this. I like—lovers! I'm very much ashamed of it, but I do! I try not to be unfair to them—some I really try to keep away from me—but honestly I like admiration and lots of it."

"What's the harm of that?" he asked easily, setting down, "Fifth—Lovers."

"No harm, so long as I'm my own mistress," said she defiantly. "I take care of my boy, I take care of myself—let them take care of themselves! Don't blame me too much!"

"You're not a very good psychologist, I'm afraid," said he.

"What do you mean?" she asked rather nervously.

"You surely don't expect a man to blame you for being a woman, do you?"

"All women are not like that," she hastily asserted. "They are too conscientious. Lots of my friends blame me severely."

"Women friends," he ventured.

"Men, too. Some men have said very hard things of me."

"Because you turned 'em down. That's natural."

"You don't!"

"No, I don't. I'm different.".

"How different?" she asked.

He looked at her steadily.

His eyes were hazel, flecked with changing bits of color, deep, steady, with a sort of inner light that grew as she watched till presently she thought it well to consider her slipper again; and continued, "The sixth is as bad as the other almost. I hate—I'd like to write a dozen tragic plays to show how much I hate—Housekeeping! There! That's all!"

"Sixth—Housekeeping," he wrote down, quite unmoved. "But why should anyone blame you for that—it's not your business."

"No—thank goodness, it's not! And never will be! I'm *free*, I tell you and I stay free! But look at the clock!" And she whisked away to dress for dinner.

He was not at table that night—not at home that night—not at home for some days—the landlady said he had gone out of town; and Mrs. Leland missed her afternoon tea. She had it upstairs, of course, and people came in—both friends and lovers; but she missed the quiet and coziness of the green and brown room downstairs.

Johnny missed his big friend still more. "Mama, where's Mr. Olmstead? Mama, why don't Mr. Olmstead come back? Mama! When is Mr. Olmstead coming back? Mama! Why don't you write to Mr. Olmstead and tell him to come back? Mama! can't we go in there and play with his things?"

As if in answer to this last wish she got a little note from him saying simply, "Don't let Johnny miss the lions and monkeys—he and Miss Merton and you, of course, are quite welcome to the whole floor. Go in at any time."

Just to keep the child quiet she took advantage of this offer, and Johnny introduced her to all the ins and outs of the place. In a corner of the bedroom was a zinc-lined tray with clay in it, where Johnny played rapturously at "making country." While he played his mother noted the quiet good taste and individuality of the place.

"It smells so clean!" she said to herself.

"There! he hasn't told me yet why he doesn't smoke. I never told him I didn't like it."

Johnny tugged at a bureau drawer.

"He keeps the water in here!" he said, and before she could stop him he had out a little box with bits of look-ing-glass in it, which soon became lakes and rivers in his clay continent.

Mrs. Leland put them back afterward, admiring the fine quality and goodly number of garments in that drawer, and their perfect order. Her husband had been a man who made a chowder of his bureau drawers, and who expected her to find all his studs and put them in for him. "A man like this would be no trouble at all," she thought for a moment—but then she remembered other things and set her mouth hard. "Not for mine!" she said determinedly.

By and by he came back, serene as ever, friendly and unpresuming.

"Aren't you going to tell me why you don't smoke?" she suddenly demanded of him on another quiet dusky afternoon when tea was before them.

He seemed so impersonal, almost remote, though nicer than ever to Johnny; and Mrs. Leland rather preferred the personal note in conservation.

"Why of course I am," he replied cordially. "That's easy," and he fumbled in his inner pocket.

"Is that where you keep your reasons?" she mischievously inquired.

"It's where I keep yours," he promptly answered, producing the little notebook.

"Now look here—I've got these all answered—you won't be able to hold to one of 'em after this. May I sit by you and explain?"

She made room for him on the sofa amiably enough, but defied him to convince her.

"Go ahead," she said cheerfully.

"First," he read off, "Previous Marriage. This is not a sufficient objection. Because you have been married you now know what to choose and what to avoid. A girl is comparatively helpless in this matter; you are armed. That your first marriage was unhappy is a reason for trying it again. It is not only that you are better able to choose, but that by the law of chances you stand to win next time. Do you admit the justice of this reasoning?"

"I don't admit anything," she said. "I'm waiting to ask you a question."

"Ask it now."

"No—I'll wait till you are all through. Do go on."

"'Second—The Boy,'" he continued. "Now Mrs. Leland, solely on the boy's account I should advise you to marry again. While he is a baby a mother is enough, but the older he grows the more he will need a father. Of course you should select a man the child could love—a man who could love the child."

"I begin to suspect you of deep double-dyed surreptitious designs, Mr. Olmstead. You know Johnny loves you dearly. And you know I won't marry you," she hastily added.

"I'm not asking you to—now, Mrs. Leland. I did, in good faith, and I would again if I thought I had the shadow of a chance—but I'm not at present. Still, I'm quite willing to stand at an instance. Now, we might resume, on that basis. Objection one does not really hold against me—now does it?"

He looked at her cheerily, warmly, openly; and in his clean, solid strength and tactful kindness he was so unspeakably different from the dark, fascinating slender man who had become a nightmare to her youth, that she felt in her heart he was right—so far.

"I won't admit a thing," she said sweetly. "But, pray go on."

He went on, unabashed.

"'Second—Boy.' Now if you married me I should consider the boy as an added attraction. Indeed—if you do marry again—someone who doesn't want the boy—I wish you'd give him to me. I mean it. I think he loves me, and I think I could be of real service to the child."

He seemed almost to have forgotten her, and she watched him curiously.

"Now, to go on," he continued. "'Third Profession.' As to your profession," said he slowly, clasping his hands over one knee and gazing at the dark soft-colored rug, "if you married me, and gave up your profession I should find it a distinct loss, I should lose my favorite actress."

She gave a little start of surprise.

"Didn't you know how much I admire your work?" he said.

"I don't hang around the stage entrance—there are plenty of chappies to do that; and I don't always occupy a box and throw bouquets—I don't like a box anyhow. But I haven't missed seeing you in any part you've played yet—some of 'em I've seen a dozen times. And you're growing—you'll do better work still. It is sometimes a little weak in the love parts—seems as if you couldn't quite take it seriously— couldn't let yourself go—but you'll grow. You'll do better—I really think—after you're married—"

She was rather impressed by this, but found it rather diffi-cult to say anything; for he was not looking at her at all.

He took up his notebook again with a smile. "So—if you married me, you would be more than welcome to go on with your profession. I wouldn't stand in your way any more than I do now. 'Fourth—Freedom,'" he read slowly. "That is easy in one way—hard in another. If you married me,"—She stirred resentfully at this constant reference to their marriage; but he seemed purely hypothetical in tone; "*I* wouldn't interfere with your freedom any. Not of my own will. But if you ever grew to love me—or if there were children—it would make *some* differ-ence. Not much. There mightn't be any children, and it isn't likely you'd ever love me enough to have that stand in your way. Otherwise than that you'd have freedom—as much as now. A little more; because if you wanted to make a foreign tour, or anything like that, I'd take care of Johnny. 'Fifth—Lovers.'"

Here he paused leaning forward with his chin in his hands, his eyes bent down.

She could see the broad heavy shoulders, the smooth fit of the well-made, coat, the spotless collar, and the fine, strong, clean-cut neck.

As it happened she particularly disliked the neck of the average man—either the cordy, the beefy or the adipose, and particularly liked this kind, firm and round like a Roman's, with the hair coming to a clean-cut edge and stopping there.

"As to lovers," he went on—"I hesitate a little as to what to say about that. I'm afraid I shall shock you. Perhaps I'd better leave out that one."

"As insuperable?" she mischievously asked.

"No, as too easy," he answered.

"You'd better explain," she said.

"Well then—it's simply this: as a man—I myself admire you more because so many other men admire you. I don't sympathize with them, any! Not for a minute. Of course, if you loved any one of them you wouldn't be my wife. But if you were my wife—"

"Well?" said she, a little breathlessly. "You're very irritating! What would you do? Kill 'em all? Come—If I were your wife?"

"If you were my wife—" he turned and faced her squarely, his deep eyes blazing steadily into hers, "In the first place the more lovers you had that you didn't love the better I'd be pleased."

"And if I did?" she dared him.

"If you were my wife," he pursued with perfect quietness, "you would never love anyone else."

There was a throbbing silence.

"'Sixth—Housekeeping,'" he read.

At this she rose to her feet as if released.

"Sixth and last and all sufficient!" she burst out, giving herself a little shake as if to waken.

"Final and conclusive and admitting no reply!"—I will not keep house for any man. Never! Never!! Never!!!"

"Why should you?" he said, as he had said it before; "Why not board?"

"I wouldn't board on any account!"

"But you are boarding now. Aren't you comfortable here?"

"O yes, perfectly comfortable. But this is the only board-inghouse I ever saw that was comfortable."

"Why not go on as we are—if you married me?"

She laughed shrilly.

"With the other boarders round them and a whole floor laid between," she parodied gaily. "No, sir! *If* I ever married again—and I won't—I'd want a home of my own—a whole house—and have it run as smoothly and perfectly as this does. With no more care than I have now!"

"If I could give you a whole house, like this, and run it for you as smoothly and perfectly as this one—then would you marry me?" he asked.

"O, I dare say I would," she said mockingly.

"My dear," said he, "I have kept this house—for you—for three years."

"What do you mean?" she demanded, flushingly.

"I mean that it is my business," he answered serenely. "Some men run hotels and some restaurants: I keep a number of boarding houses and make a handsome income from them. All the people are comfortable—I see to that. I planned to have you use these rooms, had the dumbwaiter run to the top so you could have meals comfortably there. You didn't much like the first housekeeper. I got one you liked better; cooks to please you, maids to please you. I have most seriously tried to make you comfortable. When you didn't like a boarder I got rid of him—or her—they are mostly all your friends now. Of course if we were married, we'd fire 'em all."

His tone was perfectly calm and business like. "You should keep your special apartments on top; you should also have the floor above this, a larger bedroom, drawing-room, and bath and private parlor for you; I'd stay right here as I am now—and when you wanted me—I'd be here."

She stiffened a little at this rather tame ending. She was stirred, uneasy, dissatisfied. She felt as if something had been offered and withdrawn; something was lacking. "It seems such a funny business—for a man," she said.

"Any funnier than Delmonico's?" he asked. "It's a business that takes some ability—witness the many failures. It is certainly useful. And it pays—amazingly."

"I thought it was real estate," she insisted.

"It is. I'm in a real estate office. I buy and sell houses—that's how I came to take this up!" He rose up, calmly and methodically, walked over to the fire, and laid his notebook on it. "There wasn't any strength in any of those objections, my dear," said he. "Especially the first one. Previous marriage, indeed! You have never been married before. You are going to be—now."

It was some weeks after that marriage that she suddenly turned upon him—as suddenly as one can turn upon a person whose arms are about one—demanding.

"And why don't you smoke? You never told me!"

"I shouldn't like to kiss you so well if you smoked!"—said he.

"I never had any idea," she ventured after a while, "that it could be—like this."

Three Thanksgivings

ANDREW'S LETTER AND Jean's letter were in Mrs. Morrison's lap. She had read them both, and sat looking at them with a varying sort of smile, now motherly and now unmotherly.

"You belong with me," Andrew wrote. "It is not right that Jean's husband should support my mother. I can do it easily now. You shall have a good room and every comfort. The old house will let for enough to give you quite a little income of your own, or it can be sold and I will invest the money where you'll get a deal more out of it. It is not right that you should live alone there. Sally is old and liable to accident. I am anxious about you. Come on for Thanksgiving—and come to stay. Here is the money to come with. You know I want you. Annie joins me in sending love. ANDREW."

Mrs. Morrison read it all through again, and laid it down with her quiet, twinkling smile. Then she read Jean's.

"Now, mother, you've got to come to us for Thanksgiving this year. Just think! You haven't seen baby since he was three months old! And have never seen the twins. You won't know him—he's such a splendid big boy now. Joe says for you to come, of course. And, mother, why won't you come and live with us? Joe wants you, too. There's the little room upstairs;

it's not very big, but we can put in a Franklin stove for you and make you pretty comfortable. Joe says he should think you ought to sell that white elephant of a place. He says he could put the money into his store and pay you good interest. I wish you would, mother. We'd just love to have you here. You'd be such a comfort to me, and such a help with the babies. And Joe just loves you. Do come now, and stay with us. Here is the money for the trip.—Your affectionate daughter, JEANNIE."

Mrs. Morrison laid this beside the other, folded both, and placed them in their respective envelopes, then in their several well-filled pigeon-holes in her big, old-fashioned desk. She turned and paced slowly up and down the long parlor, a tall woman, commanding of aspect, yet of a winningly attractive manner, erect and light-footed, still imposingly handsome.

It was now November, the last lingering boarder was long since gone, and a quiet winter lay before her. She was alone, but for Sally; and she smiled at Andrew's cautious expression, "liable to accident." He could not say "feeble" or "ailing," Sally being a colored lady of changeless aspect and incessant activity.

Mrs. Morrison was alone, and while living in the Welcome House she was never unhappy. Her father had built it, she was born there, she grew up playing on the broad green lawns in front, and in the acre of garden behind. It was the finest house in the village, and she then thought it the finest in the world.

Even after living with her father at Washington and abroad, after visiting hall, castle and palace, she still found the Welcome House beautiful and impressive.

If she kept on taking boarders she could live the year through, and pay interest, but not principal, on her little mortgage. This had been the one possible and necessary thing while the children were there, though it was a business she hated.

But her youthful experience in diplomatic circles, and the years of practical management in church affairs, enabled her to bear it with patience and success. The boarders often confided to one another, as they chatted and tatted on the long piazza, that Mrs. Morrison was "certainly very refined."

Now Sally whisked in cheerfully, announcing supper, and Mrs. Morrison went out to her great silver tea-tray at the lit end of the long, dark mahogany table, with as much dignity as if twenty titled guests were before her.

Afterward Mr. Butts called. He came early in the evening, with his usual air of determination and a somewhat unusual spruceness. Mr. Peter Butts was a florid, blonde person, a little stout, a little pompous, sturdy and immovable in the attitude of a self-made man. He had been a poor boy when she was a rich girl; and it gratified him much to realize—and to call upon her to realize—that their positions had changed. He meant no unkindness, his pride was honest and unveiled. Tact he had none.

She had refused Mr. Butts, almost with laughter, when he proposed to her in her gay girlhood. She had refused him, more gently, when he proposed to her in her early widowhood. He had always been her friend, and her husband's friend, a solid member of the church, and had taken the small mortgage of the house. She refused to allow him at first, but he was convincingly frank about it.

"This has nothing to do with my wanting you, Delia Morrison," he said. "I've always wanted you—and I've always wanted this house, too. You won't sell, but you've got to mortgage. By and by you can't pay up, and I'll get it—see? Then maybe you'll take me—to keep the house. Don't be a fool, Delia. It's a perfectly good investment."

She had taken the loan. She had paid the interest. She would pay the interest if she had to take boarders all her life. And she would not, at any price, marry Peter Butts.

He broached the subject again that evening, cheerful and undismayed. "You might as well come to it, Delia," he said. "Then we could live right here just the same. You aren't so young as you were, to be sure; I'm not, either. But you are as good a housekeeper as ever—better—you've had more experience."

"You are extremely kind, Mr. Butts," said the lady, "but I do not wish to marry you."

"I know you don't," he said. "You've made that clear. You don't, but I do. You've had your way and married the minister. He was a good man, but he's dead. Now you might as well marry me."

"I do not wish to marry again, Mr. Butts; neither you nor anyone."

"Very proper, very proper, Delia," he replied. "It wouldn't look well if you did—at any rate, if you showed it. But why shouldn't you? The children are gone now—you can't hold them up against me any more."

"Yes, the children are both settled now, and doing nicely," she admitted.

"You don't want to go and live with them—either one of them—do you?" he asked.

"I should prefer to stay here," she answered.

"Exactly! And you can't! You'd rather live here and be a grandee—but you can't do it. Keepin' house for boarders isn't any better than keepin' house for me, as I see. You'd much better marry me."

"I should prefer to keep the house without you, Mr. Butts."

"I know you would. But you can't, I tell you. I'd like to know what a woman of your age can do with a house like this—and no money? You can't live eternally on hens' eggs and garden truck. That won't pay the mortgage."

Mrs. Morrison looked at him with her cordial smile, calm and noncommittal. "Perhaps I can manage it," she said.

"That mortgage falls due two years from Thanksgiving, you know."

"Yes—I have not forgotten."

"Well, then, you might just as well marry me now, and save two years of interest. It'll be my house, either way—but you'll be keepin' it just the same."

"It is very kind of you, Mr. Butts. I must decline the offer none the less. I can pay the interest, I am sure. And perhaps—in two years' time—I can pay the principal. It's not a large sum."

"That depends on how you look at it," said he. "Two thousand dollars is considerable money for a single woman to raise in two years *and* interest."

He went away, as cheerful and determined as ever; and Mrs. Morrison saw him go with a keen, light in her fine eyes, a more definite line to that steady, pleasant smile.

Then she went to spend Thanksgiving with Andrew. He was glad to see her. Annie was glad to see her. They proudly installed her in "her room," and said she must call it "home" now.

This affectionately offered home was twelve by fifteen, and eight feet high. It had two windows, one looking at some pale gray clapboards within reach of a broom, the other giving a view of several small fenced yards occupied by cats, clothes and children. There was an ailanthus tree under the window, a lady ailanthus tree. Annie told her how profusely it bloomed. Mrs. Morrison particularly disliked the smell of ailanthus flowers. "It doesn't bloom in November," said she to herself. "I can be thankful for that!"

Andrew's church was very like the church of his father, and Mrs. Andrew was doing her best to fill the position of minister's wife—doing it well, too—there was no vacancy for a minister's mother.

Besides, the work she had done so cheerfully to help her husband was not what she most cared for, after all. She liked the people, she liked to manage, but she was not strong on doctrine. Even her husband had never known how far her views differed from his. Mrs. Morrison had never mentioned what they were.

Andrew's people were very polite to her. She was invited out with them, waited upon and watched over and set down among the old ladies and gentlemen—she had never realized so keenly that she was no longer young. Here nothing recalled her youth, every careful provision anticipated age. Annie brought her a hot-water bag at night, tucking it in at the foot of the bed with affectionate care. Mrs. Morrison thanked her, and subsequently took it out—airing the bed a little before she got into it. The house seemed very hot to her, after the big, windy halls at home.

The little dining-room, the little round table with the little round fern-dish in the middle, the little turkey and the little carving-set—game-set she would have called it— all made her feel as if she was looking through the wrong end of an opera-glass.

In Annie's precise efficiency she saw no room for her assistance; no room in the church, no room in the small, busy town, prosperous and progressive, and no room in the house. "Not enough to turn round in!" she said to herself. Annie, who had grown up in a city flat, thought their little parsonage palatial. Mrs. Morrison grew up in the Welcome House.

She stayed a week, pleasant and polite, conversational, interested in all that went on.

"I think your mother is just lovely," said Annie to Andrew.

"Charming woman, your mother," said the leading church member.

"What a delightful old lady your mother is!" said the pretty soprano.

And Andrew was deeply hurt and disappointed when she announced her determination to stay on for the present in her old home. "Dear boy," she said, "you mustn't take it to heart. I love to be with you, of course, but I love my home, and want to keep it is long as I can. It is a great pleasure to see you and Annie so well settled, and so happy together. I am most truly thankful for you."

"My home is open to you whenever you wish to come, mother," said Andrew.

But he was a little angry.

Mrs. Morrison came home as eager as a girl, and opened her own door with her own key, in spite of Sally's haste.

Two years were before her in which she must find some way to keep herself and Sally, and to pay two thousand dollars and the interest to Peter Butts. She considered her assets. There was the house—the white elephant. It *was* big—very big. It was profusely furnished. Her father had entertained lavishly like the Southern-born, hospitable gentleman he was; and the bedrooms ran in suites—somewhat deteriorated by the use of boarders, but still numerous and habitable. Boarders—she abhorred them. They were people from afar, strangers and interlopers. She went over the place from garret to cellar, from front gate to backyard fence.

The garden had great possibilities. She was fond of gardening, and understood it well. She measured and estimated.

"This garden," she finally decided, "with the hens, will feed us two women and sell enough to pay Sally. If we make

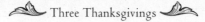

plenty of jelly, it may cover the coal bill, too. As to clothes—I don't need any. They last admirably. I can manage. I can *live*—but two thousand dollars—*and* interest!"

In the great attic was more furniture, discarded sets put there when her extravagant young mother had ordered new ones. And chairs—uncounted chairs. Senator Welcome used to invite numbers to meet his political friends—and they had delivered glowing orations in the wide, double parlors, the impassioned speakers standing on a temporary dais, now in the cellar; and the enthusiastic listeners disposed more or less comfortably on these serried rows of "folding chairs," which folded sometimes, and let down the visitor in scarlet confusion to the floor.

She sighed as she remembered those vivid days and glittering nights. She used to steal downstairs in her little pink wrapper and listen to the eloquence. It delighted her young soul to see her father rising on his toes, coming down sharply on his heels, hammering one hand upon the other; and then to hear the fusillade of applause.

Here were the chairs, often borrowed for weddings, funerals, and church affairs, somewhat worn and depleted, but still numerous. She mused upon them. Chairs—hundreds of chairs. They would sell for very little.

She went through her linen room. A splendid stock in the old days; always carefully washed by Sally; surviving even the boarders. Plenty of bedding, plenty of towels, plenty of napkins and tablecloths. "It would make a good hotel—but I *can't* have it so—I *can't*! Besides, there's no need of another hotel here. The poor little Haskins House is never full."

The stock in the china closet was more damaged than some other things, naturally; but she inventoried it with care. The countless cups of crowded church receptions were especially prominent. Later additions these, not very costly cups, but numerous, appallingly.

When she had her long list of assets all in order, she sat and studied it with a clear and daring mind. Hotel—boarding-house—she could think of nothing else. School! A girls' school! A boarding school! There was money to be made at that, and fine work done. It was a brilliant thought at first, and she gave several hours, and much paper and ink, to its full consideration. But she would need some capital for advertising; she must engage teachers—adding to her definite obligation; and to establish it, well, it would require time.

Mr. Butts, obstinate, pertinacious, oppressively affectionate, would give her no time. He meant to force her to marry him for her own good—and his. She shrugged her fine shoulders with a little shiver. Marry Peter Butts! Never! Mrs. Morrison still loved her husband. Some day she meant to see him again—God willing—and she did not wish to have to tell him that at fifty she had been driven into marrying Peter Butts.

Better live with Andrew. Yet when she thought of living with Andrew, she shivered again. Pushing back her sheets of figures and lists of personal property, she rose to her full graceful height and began to walk the floor. There was plenty of floor to walk. She considered, with a set deep thoughtfulness, the town and the townspeople, the surrounding country, the hundreds upon hundreds of women whom she knew—and liked, and who liked her.

It used to be said of Senator Welcome that he had no enemies; and some people, strangers, maliciously disposed, thought it no credit to his character. His daughter had no enemies, but no one had ever blamed her for her unlimited friendliness. In her father's wholesale entertainments the whole town knew and admired his daughter; in her husband's popular church she had come to know the women of the countryside about them. Her mind strayed off to these women, farmers' wives, comfortably off in a plain way, but starving

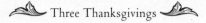

for companionship, for occasional stimulus and pleasure. It was one of her joys in her husband's time to bring together these women—to teach and entertain them.

Suddenly she stopped short in the middle of the great high-ceiled room, and drew her head up proudly like a victorious queen. One wide, triumphant, sweeping glance she cast at the well-loved walls—and went back to her desk, working swiftly, excitedly, well into the hours of the night.

Presently the little town began to buzz, and the murmur ran far out into the surrounding country. Sunbonnets wagged over fences; butcher carts and peddler's wagon carried the news farther; and ladies visiting found one topic in a thousand houses.

Mrs. Morrison was going to entertain. Mrs. Morrison had invited the whole feminine population, it would appear, to meet Mrs. Isabelle Carter Blake, of Chicago. Even Haddleton had heard of Mrs. Isabelle Carter Blake. And even Haddleton had nothing but admiration for her.

She was known the world over for her splendid work for children—for the school children and the working children of the country. Yet she was known also to have lovingly and wisely reared six children of her own—and made her husband happy in his home. On top of that she had lately written a novel, a popular novel, of which everyone was talking; and on top of that she was an intimate friend of a certain conspicuous Countess—an Italian.

It was even rumored, by some who knew Mrs. Morrison better than others—or thought they did—that the Countess was coming, too! No one had known before that Delia Welcome was a schoolmate of Isabel Carter, and a life-long friend; and that was ground for talk in itself.

The day arrived, and the guests arrived. They came in

hundreds upon hundreds, and found ample room in the great white house.

The highest dream of the guests was realized—the Countess had come, too. With excited joy they met her, receiving impressions that would last them for all their lives, for those large widening waves of reminiscence which delight us the more as years pass. It was an incredible glory—Mrs. Isabelle Carter Blake, *and* a Countess!

Some were moved to note that Mrs. Morrison looked the easy peer of these eminent ladies, and treated the foreign nobility precisely as she did her other friends.

She spoke, her clear quiet voice reaching across the murmuring din, and silencing it.

"Shall we go into the east room? If you will all take chairs in the east room, Mrs. Blake is going to be so kind as to address us. Also perhaps her friend—"

They crowded in, sitting somewhat timorously on the unfolded chairs.

Then the great Mrs. Blake made them an address of memorable power and beauty, which received vivid sanction from that imposing presence in Parisian garments on the platform by her side. Mrs. Blake spoke to them of the work she was interested in, and how it was aided everywhere by the women's clubs. She gave them the number of these clubs, and described with contagious enthusiasm the inspiration of their great meetings. She spoke of the women's club houses, going up in city after city, where many associations meet and help one another. She was winning and convincing and most entertaining—an extremely attractive speaker.

Had they a women's club there? They had not.

Not *yet*, she suggested, adding that it took no time at all to make one.

They were delighted and impressed with Mrs. Blake's

speech, but its effect was greatly intensified by the address of the Countess.

"I, too, am American," she told them; "born here, reared in England, married in Italy." And she stirred their hearts with a vivid account of the women's clubs and associations all over Europe, and what they were accomplishing. She was going back soon, she said, the wiser and happier for this visit to her native land, and she should remember particularly this beautiful, quiet town, trusting that if she came to it again it would have joined the great sisterhood of women, "whose hands were touching around the world for the common good."

It was a great occasion.

The Countess left next day, but Mrs. Blake remained, and spoke in some of the church meetings, to an ever-widening circle of admirers. Her suggestions were practical.

"What you need here is a 'Rest and Improvement Club,'" she said. "Here are all you women coming in from the country to do your shopping—and no place to go to. No place to lie down if you're tired, to meet a friend, to eat your lunch in peace, to do your hair. All you have to do is organize, pay some small regular due, and provide yourselves with what you want."

There was a volume of questions and suggestions, a little opposition, much random activity.

Who was to do it? Where was there a suitable place? They would have to hire someone to take charge of it. It would only be used once a week. It would cost too much.

Mrs. Blake, still practical, made another suggestion. Why not combine business with pleasure, and make use of the best place in town, if you can get it? I *think* Mrs. Morrison could be persuaded to let you use part of her house; it's quite too big for one woman."

Then Mrs. Morrison, simple and cordial as ever, greeted with warm enthusiasm by her wide circle of friends.

"I have been thinking this over," she said. "Mrs. Blake has been discussing it with me. My house is certainly big enough for all of you, and there am I, with nothing to do but entertain you. Suppose you formed such a club as you speak of—for Rest and Improvement. My parlors are big enough for all manner of meetings; there are bedrooms in plenty for resting. If you form such a club I shall be glad to help with my great, cumbersome house, shall be delighted to see so many friends there so often; and I think I could furnish accommodations more cheaply than you could manage in any other way.

Then Mrs. Blake gave them facts and figures, showing how much clubhouses cost—and how little this arrangement would cost. "Most women have very little money, I know," she said, "and they hate to spend it on themselves when they have; but even a little money from each goes a long way when it is put together. I fancy there are none of us so poor we could not squeeze out, say ten cents a week. For a hundred women that would be ten dollars. Could you feed a hundred tired women for ten dollars, Mrs. Morrison?"

Mrs. Morrison smiled cordially. "Not on chicken pie," she said, "But I could give them tea and coffee, crackers and cheese for that, I think. And a quiet place to rest, and a reading room, and a place to hold meetings."

Then Mrs. Blake quite swept them off their feet by her wit and eloquence. She gave them to understand that if a share in the palatial accommodation of the Welcome House, and as good tea and coffee as old Sally made, with a place to meet, a place to rest, a place to talk, a place to lie down, could be had for ten cents a week each, she advised them to clinch the arrangement at once before Mrs. Morrison's natural good sense had overcome her enthusiasm.

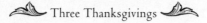

Before Mrs. Isabelle Carter Blake had left, Haddleton had a large and eager women's club, whose entire expenses, outside of stationery and postage, consisted of ten cents a week *per capita*, paid to Mrs. Morrison. Everybody belonged. It was open at once for charter members, and all pressed forward to claim that privileged place.

They joined by hundreds, and from each member came this tiny sum to Mrs. Morrison each week. It was very little money, taken separately. But it added up with silent speed. Tea and coffee, purchased in bulk, crackers by the barrel, and whole cheeses—these are not expensive luxuries. The town was full of Mrs. Morrison's ex-Sunday-school boys, who furnished her with the best they had—at cost. There was a good deal of work, a good deal of care, and room for the whole supply of Mrs. Morrison's diplomatic talent and experience. Saturdays found the Welcome House as full as it could hold, and Sundays found Mrs. Morrison in bed. But she liked it.

A busy, hopeful year flew by, and then she went to Jean's for Thanksgiving.

The room Jean gave her was about the same size as her haven in Andrew's home, but one flight higher up, and with a sloping ceiling. Mrs. Morrison whitened her dark hair upon it, and rubbed her head confusedly.

Then she shook it with renewed determination.

The house was full of babies. There was little Joe, able to get about, and into everything. There were the twins, and there was the new baby. There was one servant, over-worked and cross. There was a small, cheap, totally inadequate nurse-maid. There was Jean, happy but tired, full of joy, anxiety and affection, proud of her children, proud of her husband, and delighted to unfold her heart to her mother.

By the hour she babbled of their cares and hopes, while

Mrs. Morrison, tall and elegant in her well-kept old black silk, sat holding the baby or trying to hold the twins. The old silk was pretty well finished by the week's end. Joseph talked to her also, telling her how well he was getting on, and how much he needed capital, urging her to come and stay with them; it was such a help to Jeannie; asking questions about the house.

There was no going visiting here. Jeannie could not leave the babies. And few visitors; all the little suburb being full of similarly overburdened mothers. Such as called found Mrs. Morrison charming. What she found them, she did not say. She bade her daughter an affectionate goodbye when the week was up, smiling at their mutual contentment.

"Goodbye, my dear children," she said. "I am so glad for all your happiness. I am thankful for both of you."

But she was more thankful to get home.

Mr. Butts did not have to call for his interest this time, but he called none the less.

"How on earth'd you get it, Delia?" he demanded. "Screwed it out o' these club-women?"

"Your interest is so moderate, Mr. Butts, that it is easier to meet than you imagine," was her answer. "Do you know the average interest they charge in Colorado? The women vote there, you know."

He went away with no more personal information than that; and no nearer approach to the twin goals of his desire than the passing of the year.

"One more year, Delia," he said; "then you'll have to give in."

"One more year!" she said to herself, and took up her chosen task with renewed energy.

The financial basis of the undertaking was very simple, but it would never have worked so well under less skillful

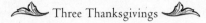

management. Five dollars a year these country women could not have faced, but ten cents a week was possible to the poorest. There was no difficulty in collecting, for they brought it themselves; no unpleasantness in receiving, for old Sally stood at the receipt of custom and presented the covered cash box when they came for their tea.

On the crowded Saturdays the great urns were set going, the mighty array of cups arranged in easy reach, the ladies filed by, each taking her refection and leaving her dime. Where the effort came was in enlarging the membership and keeping up the attendance, and this effort was precisely in the line of Mrs. Morrison's splendid talents.

Serene, cheerful, inconspicuously active, planning like the born statesman she was, executing like a practical politician, Mrs. Morrison gave her mind to the work, and thrived upon it. Circle within circle, and group within group, she set small classes and departments at work, having a boys' club by and by in the big room over the woodshed, girls' clubs, reading clubs, study clubs, little meetings of every sort that were not held in churches, and some that were—previously.

For each and all there was, if wanted, tea and coffee, crackers and cheese; simple fare, of unvarying excellence, and from each and all, into the little cashbox, ten cents for these refreshments. From the club members this came weekly; and the club members, kept up by a constant variety of interests, came every week. As to numbers, before the first six months was over The Haddleton Rest and Improvement Club numbered five hundred women.

Now, five hundred times ten cents a week is twenty-six hundred dollars a year. Twenty-six hundred dollars a year would not be very much to build or rent a large house, to furnish five hundred people with chairs, lounges, books, and magazines, dishes and service; and with food and drink even of the simplest. But if you are miraculously supplied with a club-house, furnished, with a manager and servant on the spot, then that amount of money goes a long way.

On Saturdays Mrs. Morrison hired two helpers for half a day, for half a dollar each. She stocked the library with many magazines for fifty dollars a year. She covered fuel, light, and small miscellanies with another hundred. And she fed her multitude with the plain viands agreed upon, at about four cents apiece.

For her collateral entertainments, her many visits, the various new expenses entailed, she paid as well; and yet at the end of the first year she had not only her interest, but a solid thousand dollars of clear profit. With a calm smile she surveyed it, heaped in neat stacks of bills in the small safe in the wall behind her bed. Even Sally did not know it was there.

The second season was better than the first. There were difficulties, excitements, even some opposition, but she rounded out the year triumphantly. "After that," she said to herself, "they may have the deluge if they like."

She made all expenses, made her interest, made a little extra cash, clearly her own, all over and above the second thousand dollars.

Then did she write to son and daughter, inviting them and their families to come home to Thanksgiving, and closing each letter with joyous pride: "Here is the money to come with."

They all came, with all the children and two nurses. There was plenty of room in the Welcome House, and plenty of food on the long mahogany table. Sally was as brisk as a bee, brilliant in scarlet and purple; Mrs. Morrison carved her big turkey with queenly grace.

"I don't see that you're over-run with club women, mother," said Jeannie.

"It's Thanksgiving, you know; they're all at home. I hope

they are all as happy, as thankful for their homes as I am for mine," said Mrs. Morrison.

Afterward Mr. Butts called. With dignity and calm unruffled, Mrs. Morrison handed him his interest—and principal.

Mr. Butts was almost loath to receive it, though his hand automatically grasped the crisp blue check.

"I didn't know you had a bank account," he protested, somewhat dubiously.

"Oh, yes; you'll find the check will be honored, Mr. Butts."

"I'd like to know how you got this money. You *can't* 'a' skinned it out o' that club of yours."

"I appreciate your friendly interest, Mr. Butts; you have been most kind."

"I believe some of these great friends of yours have lent it to you. You won't be any better off, I can tell you."

"Come, come, Mr. Butts! Don't quarrel with good money. Let us part friends."

And they parted.

The Cottagette

"WHY NOT?" SAID Mr. Mathews. "It is far too small for a house, too pretty for a hut, too—unusual—for a cottage."

"Cottagette, by all means," said Lois, seating herself on a porch chair. "But it is larger than it looks, Mr. Mathews. How do you like it, Malda?"

I was delighted with it. More than delighted. Here this tiny shell of fresh unpainted wood peeped out from under the trees, the only house in sight except the distant white specks on far off farms, and the little wandering village in the river-threaded valley. It sat right on the turf,—no road, no path even, and the dark woods shadowed the back windows.

"How about meals?" asked Lois.

"Not two minutes' walk," he assured her, and showed us a little furtive path between the trees to the place where meals were furnished.

We discussed and examined and exclaimed, Lois holding her pongee skirts close about her—she needn't have been so careful, there wasn't a speck of dust,—and presently decided to take it.

Never did I know the real joy and peace of living, before that blessed summer at "High Court." It was a mountain

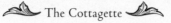

place, easy enough to get to, but strangely big and still and far away when you were there.

The working basis of the establishment was an eccentric woman named Caswell, a sort of musical enthusiast, who had a summer school of music and the "higher thought." Malicious persons, not able to obtain accommodations there, called the place "High C."

I liked the music very well, and kept my thoughts to myself, both high and low, but "The Cottagette" I loved unreservedly. It was so little and new and clean, smelling only of its fresh-planed boards—they hadn't even stained it.

There was one big room and two little ones in the tiny thing, though from the outside you wouldn't have believed it, it looked so small; but small as it was it harbored a miracle—a real bathroom with water piped from mountain springs. Our windows opened into the green shadiness, the soft brownness, the bird-inhabited quiet flower-starred woods. But in front we looked across whole counties—over a far-off river—into another state. Off and down and away—it was like sitting on the roof of something—something very big.

The grass swept up to the door-step, to the walls—only it wasn't just grass of course, but such a procession of flowers as I had never imagined could grow in one place.

You had to go quite a way through the meadow, wearing your own narrow faintly marked streak in the grass, to reach the town-connecting road below. But in the woods was a little path, clear and wide, by which we went to meals.

For we ate with the highly thoughtful musicians, and highly musical thinkers, in their central boarding-house nearby. They didn't call it a boarding-house, which is neither high nor musical; they called it "The Calceolaria." There was plenty of that growing about, and I didn't mind what they called it so long as the food was good—which it was, and the prices reasonable—which they were.

The people were extremely interesting—some of them at least; and all of them were better than the average of summer boarders.

But if there hadn't been any interesting ones it didn't matter while Ford Mathews was there. He was a newspaper man, or rather an ex-newspaper man, then becoming a writer for magazines, with books ahead.

He had friends at High Court—he liked music—he liked the place—and he liked us. Lois liked him too, as was quite natural. I'm sure I did.

He used to come up evenings and sit on the porch and talk.

He came daytimes and went on long walks with us. He established his workshop in a most attractive little cave not far beyond us,—the country there is full of rocky ledges and hollows,—and sometimes asked us over to an afternoon tea, made on a gipsy fire.

Lois was a good deal older than I, but not really old at all, and she didn't look her thirty-five by ten years. I never blamed her for not mentioning it, and I wouldn't have done so, myself, on any account. But I felt that together we made a safe and reasonable household. She played beautifully, and there was a piano in our big room. There were pianos in several other little cottages about—but too far off for any jar of sound. When the wind was right we caught little wafts of music now and then; but mostly it was still—blessedly still, about us. And yet that Calceolaria was only two minutes off—and with raincoats and rubbers we never minded going to it.

We saw a good deal of Ford and I got interested in him, I couldn't help it. He was big. Not extra big in pounds and inches, but a man with big view and a grip—with purpose and real power. He was going to do things. I thought he was

doing them now, but he didn't—this was all like cutting steps in the ice-wall, he said. It had to be done, but the road was long ahead. And he took an interest in my work too, which is unusual for a literary man.

Mine wasn't much. I did embroidery and made designs.

It is such pretty work! I like to draw from flowers and leaves and things about me; conventionalize them sometimes, and sometimes paint them just as they are,—in soft silk stitches.

All about up here were the lovely small things I needed; and not only these, but the lovely big things that make one feel so strong and able to do beautiful work.

Here was the friend I lived so happily with, and all this fairy land of sun and shadow, the free immensity of our view, and the dainty comfort of the Cottagette. We never had to think of ordinary things till the soft musical thrill of the Japanese gong stole through the trees, and we trotted off to the Calceolaria.

I think Lois knew before I did.

We were old friends and trusted each other, and she had had experience too.

"Malda," she said, "let us face this thing and be rational." It was a strange thing that Lois should be so rational and yet so musical—but she was, and that was one reason I liked her so much.

"You are beginning to love Ford Mathews—do you know it?"

I said yes, I thought I was.

"Does he love you?"

That I couldn't say. "It is early yet," I told her. "He is a man, he is about thirty I believe, he has seen more of life and probably loved before—it may be nothing more than friendliness with him."

"Do you think it would be a good marriage?" she asked.

We had often talked of love and marriage, and Lois had helped me to form my views—hers were very clear and strong.

"Why yes—if he loves me," I said. "He has told me quite a bit about his family, good western farming people, real Americans. He is strong and well—you can read clean living in his eyes and mouth." Ford's eyes were as clear as a girl's, the whites of them were clear. Most men's eyes, when you look at them critically, are not like that. They may look at you very expressively, but when you look at them, just as features, they are not very nice.

I liked his looks, but I liked him better.

So I told her that as far as I knew it would be a good marriage—if it was one.

"How much do you love him?" she asked.

That I couldn't quite tell,—it was a good deal,—but I didn't think it would kill me to lose him.

"Do you love him enough to do something to win him—to really put yourself out somewhat for that purpose?"

"Why—yes—I think I do. If it was something I approved of. What do you mean?"

Then Lois unfolded her plan. She had been married,—unhappily married, in her youth; that was all over and done with years ago; she had told me about it long since; and she said she did not regret the pain and loss because it had given her experience. She had her maiden name again—and freedom. She was so fond of me she wanted to give me the benefit of her experience—without the pain.

"Men like music," said Lois; "they like sensible talk; they like beauty of course, and all that,—"

"Then they ought to like you!" I interrupted, and, as a matter of fact they did. I knew several who wanted to marry her, but she said "once was enough." I don't think they were "good marriages" though.

"Don't be foolish, child," said Lois, "this is serious. What they care for most after all is domesticity. Of course they'll fall in love with anything; but what they want to marry is a homemaker. Now we are living here in an idyllic sort of way, quite conducive to falling in love, but no temptation to marriage. If I were you—if I really loved this man and wished to marry him, I would make a home of this place."

"Make a home?—why it *is* a home. I never was so happy anywhere in my life. What on earth do you mean, Lois?"

"A person might be happy in a balloon, I suppose," she replied, "but it wouldn't be a home. He comes here and sits talking with us, and it's quiet and feminine and attractive— and then we hear that big gong at the Calceolaria, and off we go stopping through the wet woods—and the spell is broken. Now you can cook." I could cook. I could cook excellently. My esteemed Mama had rigorously taught me every branch of what is now called "domestic science;" and I had no objection to the work, except that it prevented my doing anything else. And one's hands are not so nice when one cooks and washes dishes,—I need nice hands for my needlework. But if it was a question of pleasing Ford Mathews—

Lois went on calmly. "Miss Caswell would put on a kitchen for us in a minute, she said she would, you know, when we took the cottage. Plenty of people keep house up here,—we, can if we want to."

"But we don't want to," I said, "we never have wanted to. The very beauty of the place is that it never had any house-keeping about it. Still, as you say, it would be cosy on a wet night, we could have delicious little suppers, and have him stay—"

"He told me he had never known a home since he was eighteen," said Lois.

That was how we came to install a kitchen in the Cottagette.

The men put it up in a few days, just a lean-to with a window, a sink and two doors. I did the cooking. We had nice things, there is no denying that; good fresh milk and vegetables particularly, fruit is hard to get in the country, and meat too, still we managed nicely; the less you have the more you have to manage—it takes time and brains, that's all.

Lois likes to do housework, but it spoils her hands for practicing, so she can't; and I was perfectly willing to do it—it was all in the interest of my own heart. Ford certainly enjoyed it. He dropped in often, and ate things with undeniable relish. So I was pleased, though it did interfere with my work a good deal. I always work best in the morning; but of course housework has to be done in the morning too; and it is astonishing how much work there is in the littlest kitchen. You go in for a minute, and you see this thing and that thing and the other thing to be done, and your minute is an hour before you know it.

When I was ready to sit down the freshness of the morning was gone somehow. Before, when I woke up, there was only the clean wood smell of the house, and then the blessed out-of-doors: now I always felt the call of the kitchen as soon as I woke. An oil stove will smell a little, either in or out of the house; and soap, and—well you know if you cook in a bedroom how it makes the room feel differently? Our house had been only bedroom and parlor before.

We baked too—the baker's bread was really pretty poor, and Ford did enjoy my whole wheat, and brown, and especially hot rolls and gems. It was a pleasure to feed him, but it did heat up the house, and me. I never could work much—at my work—baking days. Then, when I did get to work, the people would come with things,—milk or meat or vegetables, or children with berries; and what distressed me most was the wheel-marks on our meadow. They soon made quite a road—

they had to of course, but I hated it—I lost that lovely sense of being on the last edge and looking over—we were just a bead on a string like other houses. But it was quite true that I loved this man, and would do more than this to please him. We couldn't go off so freely on excursions as we used, either; when meals are to be prepared someone has to be there, and to take in things when they come. Sometimes Lois stayed in, she always asked to, but mostly I did. I couldn't let her spoil her summer on my account. And Ford certainly liked it.

He came so often that Lois said she thought it would look better if we had an older person with us; and that her mother could come if I wanted her, and she could help with the work of course. That seemed reasonable, and she came. I wasn't very fond of Lois's mother, Mrs. Fowler, but it did seem a little conspicuous, Mr. Mathews eating with us more than he did at the Calceolaria. There were others of course, plenty of them dropping in, but I didn't encourage it much, it made so much more work. They would come in to supper, and then we would have musical evenings. They offered to help me wash dishes, some of them, but a new hand in the kitchen is not much help, I preferred to do it myself; then I knew where the dishes were.

Ford never seemed to want to wipe dishes; though I often wished he would.

So Mrs. Fowler came. She and Lois had one room, they had to,—and she really did a lot of the work, she was a very practical old lady.

Then the house began to be noisy. You hear another person in a kitchen more than you hear yourself, I think,—and the walls were only boards. She swept more than we did too. I don't think much sweeping is needed in a clean place like that; and she dusted all the time; which I know is unnecessary. I still did most of the cooking, but I could get off more to draw, out-of-doors; and to walk. Ford was in and out continually, and, it seemed to me, was really coming nearer. What was one summer of interrupted work, of noise and dirt and smell and constant meditation on what to eat next, compared to a lifetime of love? Besides—if he married me—I should have to do it always, and might as well get used to it.

Lois kept me contented, too, telling me nice things that Ford said about my cooking. "He does appreciate it so," she said.

One day he came around early and asked me to go up Hugh's Peak with him. It was a lovely climb and took all day. I demurred a little, it was Monday, Mrs. Fowler thought it was cheaper to have a woman come and wash, and we did, but it certainly made more work.

"Never mind," he said, "what's washing day or ironing day or any of that old foolishness to us? This is walking day—that's what it is." It was really, cool and sweet and fresh,—it had rained in the night,—and brilliantly clear.

"Come along!" he said. "We can see as far as Patch Mountain I'm sure. There'll never be a better day."

"Is anyone else going?" I asked.

"Not a soul. It's just us. Come."

I came gladly, only suggesting—"Wait, let me put up a lunch."

"I'll wait just long enough for you to put on knickers and a short skirt," said he. "The lunch is all in the basket on my back. I know how long it takes for you women to 'put up' sandwiches and things."

We were off in ten minutes, light-footed and happy, and the day was all that could be asked. He brought a perfect lunch, too, and had made it all himself. I confess it tasted better to me than my own cooking; but perhaps that was the climb.

When we were nearly down we stopped by a spring on a broad ledge, and supped, making tea as he liked to do out-of-doors. We saw the round sun setting at one end of a world view, and the round moon rising at the other; calmly shining each on each.

And then he asked me to be his wife.—

We were very happy.

"But there's a condition!" said he all at once, sitting up straight and looking very fierce. "You mustn't cook!"

"What!" said I. "Mustn't cook?"

"No," said he, "you must give it up—for my sake."

I stared at him dumbly.

"Yes, I know all about it," he went on, "Lois told me. I've seen a good deal of Lois—since you've taken to cooking. And since I would talk about you, naturally I learned a lot. She told me how you were brought up, and how strong your domestic instincts were—but bless your artist soul dear girl, you have some others!" Then he smiled rather queerly and murmured, "surely in vain the net is spread in the sight of any bird."

"I've watched you, dear, all summer;" he went on, "it doesn't agree with you.

"Of course the things taste good—but so do my things! I'm a good cook myself. My father was a cook, for years—at good wages. I'm used to it you see.

"One summer when I was hard up I cooked for a living—and saved money instead of starving."

"O ho!" said I, "that accounts for the tea—and the lunch!"

"And lots of other things," said he. "But you haven't done half as much of your lovely work since you started this kitchen business, and—you'll forgive me, dear—it hasn't been as good. Your work is quite too good to lose; it is a beautiful and distinctive art, and I don't want you to let it go. What would you think of me if I gave up my hard long years of writing for the easy competence of a well-paid cook!"

I was still too happy to think very clearly. I just sat and looked at him. "But you want to marry me?" I said.

"I want to marry you, Malda,—because I love you—because you are young and strong and beautiful—because you are wild and sweet and—fragrant, and—elusive, like the wild flowers you love. Because you are so truly an artist in your special way, seeing beauty and giving it to others. I love you because of all this, because you are rational and high-minded and capable of friendship,—and in spite of your cooking!"

"But—how do you want to live?"

"As we did here—at first," he said. "There was peace, exquisite silence. There was beauty—nothing but beauty. There were the clean wood odors and flowers and fragrances and sweet wild wind. And there was you—your fair self, always delicately dressed, with white firm fingers sure of touch in delicate true work. I loved you then. When you took to cooking it jarred on me. I have been a cook, I tell you, and I know what it is. I hated it—to see my wood-flower in a kitchen. But Lois told me about how you were brought up to it and loved it—and I said to myself, 'I love this woman; I will wait and see if I love her even as a cook.' And I do, Darling: I withdraw the condition. I will love you always, even if you insist on being my cook for life!"

"O I don't insist!" I cried. "I don't want to cook—I want to draw! But I thought—Lois said—How she has misunderstood you!"

"It is not true, always, my dear," said he, "that the way to a man's heart is through his stomach; at least it's not the only way. Lois doesn't know everything, she is young yet! And perhaps for my sake you can give it up. Can you sweet?"

Could I? Could I? Was there ever a man like this?

When I Was a Witch

IF I HAD understood the terms of that one-sided contract with Satan, the Time of Witching would have lasted longer—you may be sure of that. But how was I to tell? It just happened, and has never happened again, though I've tried the same preliminaries as far as I could control them.

The thing began all of a sudden, one October midnight—the 30th, to be exact. It had been hot, really hot, all day, and was sultry and thunderous in the evening; no air stirring, and the whole house stewing with that ill-advised activity which always seems to move the steam radiator when it isn't wanted.

I was in a state of simmering rage—hot enough, even without the weather and the furnace—and I went up on the roof to cool off. A top-floor apartment has that advantage, among others—you can take a walk without the mediation of an elevator boy!

There are things enough in New York to lose one's temper over at the best of times, and on this particular day they seemed to all happen at once, and some fresh ones. The night before, cats and dogs had broken my rest, of course. My morning paper was more than usually mendacious; and my neighbor's morning paper—more visible than my own as I went down town—was more than usually salacious. My cream wasn't cream—my egg was a relic of the past. My "new" napkins were giving out.

Being a woman, I'm supposed not to swear; but when the motorman disregarded my plain signal, and grinned as he rushed by; when the subway guard waited till I was just about to step on board and then slammed the door in my face— standing behind it calmly for some minutes before the bell rang to warrant his closing—I desired to swear like a mule-driver.

At night it was worse. The way people paw one's back in the crowd! The cowpuncher who packs the people in or jerks them out—the men who smoke and spit, law or no law—the women whose saw-edged cart-wheel hats, swashing feathers and deadly pins, add so to one's comfort inside.

Well, as I said, I was in a particularly bad temper, and went up on the roof to cool off. Heavy black clouds hung low overhead, and lightning flickered threateningly here and there.

A starved, black cat stole from behind a chimney and mewed dolefully.

Poor thing! She had been scalded.

The street was quiet for New York. I leaned over a little and looked up and down the long parallels of twinkling lights. A belated cab drew near, the horse so tired he could hardly hold his head up.

Then the driver, with a skill born of plenteous practice, flung out his long-lashed whip and curled it under the poor beast's belly with a stinging cut that made me shudder. The horse shuddered too, poor wretch, and jingled his harness with an effort at a trot.

I leaned over the parapet and watched that man with a spirit of unmitigated ill-will.

"I wish," said I, slowly—and I did wish it with all my heart—"that every person who strikes or otherwise hurts a horse unnecessarily, shall feel the pain intended—and the horse not feel it!"

It did me good to say it, anyhow, but I never expected any result. I saw the man swing his great whip again, and—lay on heartily. I saw him throw up his hands—heard him scream—but I never thought what the matter was, even then.

The lean, black cat, timid but trustful, rubbed against my skirt and mewed.

"Poor Kitty" I said; "poor Kitty! It is a shame!" And I thought tenderly of all the thousands of hungry, hunted cats who stink and suffer in a great city.

Later, when I tried to sleep, and up across the stillness rose the raucous shrieks of some of these same sufferers, my pity turned cold. "Any fool that will try to keep a cat in a city!" I muttered, angrily.

Another yell—a pause—an ear-torturing, continuous cry. "I wish," I burst forth, "that every cat in the city was comfortably dead!"

A sudden silence fell, and in course of time I got to sleep.

Things went fairly well next morning, till I tried another egg. They were expensive eggs, too.

"I can't help it!" said my sister, who keeps house.

"I know you can't," I admitted. "But somebody could help it. I wish the people who are responsible had to eat their old eggs, and never get a good one till they sold good ones!"

"They'd stop eating eggs, that's all," said my sister, "and eat meat."

"Let 'em eat meat!" I said, recklessly. "The meat is as bad as the eggs! It's so long since we've had a clean, fresh chicken that I've forgotten how they taste!"

"It's cold storage," said my sister. She is a peaceable sort; I'm not.

"Yes, cold storage!" I snapped. "It ought to be a blessing—

to tide over shortages, equalize supplies, and lower prices. What does it do? Corner the market, raise prices the year round, and make all the food bad!"

My anger rose. "If there was any way of getting at them!" I cried. "The law don't touch 'em. They need to be cursed somehow! I'd like to do it! I wish the whole crowd that profit by this vicious business might taste their bad meat, their old fish, their stale milk—whatever they ate. Yes, and feel the prices as we do!"

"They couldn't you know; they're rich," said my sister.

"I know that," I admitted, sulkily. "There's no way of getting at 'em. But I wish they could. And I wish they knew how people hated 'em, and felt that, too—till they mended their ways!"

When I left for my office I saw a funny thing. A man who drove a garbage cart took his horse by the bits and jerked and wrenched brutally. I was amazed to see him clap his hands to his own jaws with a moan, while the horse philosophically licked his chops and looked at him.

The man seemed to resent his expression, and struck him on the head, only to rub his own poll and swear amazedly, looking around to see who had hit him. The horse advanced a step, stretching a hungry nose toward a garbage pail crowned with cabbage leaves, and the man, recovering his sense of proprietorship, swore at him and kicked him in the ribs. That time he had to sit down, turning pale and weak. I watched with growing wonder and delight.

A market wagon came clattering down the street; the hard-faced young ruffian fresh for his morning task. He gathered the ends of the reins and brought them down on the horse's back with a resounding thwack. The horse did not notice this at all, but the boy did. He yelled!

I came to a place where many teamsters were at work

hauling dirt and crushed stone. A strange silence and peace hung over the scene where usually the sound of the lash and sight of brutal blows made me hurry by. The men were talking together a little, and seemed to be exchanging notes. It was too good to be true. I gazed and marveled, waiting for my car.

It came, merrily running along. It was not full. There was one not far ahead, which I had missed in watching the horses; there was no other near it in the rear.

Yet the coarse-faced person in authority who ran it, went gaily by without stopping, though I stood on the track almost, and waved my umbrella.

A hot flush of rage surged to my face. "I wish you felt the blow you deserve," said I, viciously, looking after the car. "I wish you'd have to stop, and back to here, and open the door and apologize. I wish that would happen to all of you, every time you play that trick."

To my infinite amazement, that car stopped and backed till the front door was before me. The motorman opened it, holding his hand to his cheek. "Beg your pardon, madam!" he said.

I passed in, dazed, overwhelmed. Could it be? Could it possibly be that—that what I wished came true. The idea sobered me, but I dismissed it with a scornful smile. "No such luck!" said I.

Opposite me sat a person in petticoats. She was of a sort I particularly detest. No real body of bones and muscles, but the contours of grouped sausages. Complacent, gaudily dressed, heavily wigged and ratted, with powder and perfume and flowers and jewels—and a dog.

A poor, wretched, little, artificial dog—alive, but only so by virtue of man's insolence; not a real creature that God made. And the dog had clothes on—and a bracelet! His fitted jacket had a pocket—and a pocket-handkerchief! He looked sick and unhappy.

I meditated on his pitiful position, and that of all the other poor chained prisoners, leading unnatural lives of enforced celibacy, cut off from sunlight, fresh air, the use of their limbs; led forth at stated intervals by unwilling servants, to defile our streets; overfed, under-exercised, nervous and unhealthy.

"And we say we love them!" said I, bitterly to myself. "No wonder they bark and howl and go mad. No wonder they have almost as many diseases as we do! I wish—" Here the thought I had dismissed struck me again. "I wish that all the unhappy dogs in cities would die at once!"

I watched the sad-eyed little invalid across the car. He dropped his head and died. She never noticed it till she got off; then she made fuss enough.

The evening papers were full of it. Some sudden pestilence had struck both dogs and cats, it would appear. Red headlines struck the eye, big letters, and columns were filled out of the complaints of those who had lost their "pets," of the sudden labors of the board of health, and interviews with doctors.

All day, as I went through the office routine, the strange sense of this new power struggled with reason and common knowledge. I even tried a few furtive test "wishes"—wished that the waste basket would fall over, that the inkstand would fill itself; but they didn't.

I dismissed the idea as pure foolishness, till I saw those newspapers, and heard people telling worse stories.

One thing I decided at once—not to tell a soul. "Nobody'd believe me if I did," said I to myself. "And I won't give 'em the chance. I've scored on cats and dogs, anyhow—and horses."

As I watched the horses at work that afternoon, and thought of all their unknown sufferings from crowded city stables,

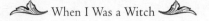

bad air and insufficient food, and from the wearing strain of asphalt pavements in wet and icy weather, I decided to have another try on horses.

"I wish," said I, slowly and carefully, but with a fixed intensity of purposes, "that every horse owner, keeper, hirer and driver or rider, might feel what the horse feels, when he suffers at our hands. Feel it keenly and constantly till the case is mended."

I wasn't able to verify this attempt for some time; but the effect was so general that it got widely talked about soon; and this "new wave of humane feeling" soon raised the status of horses in our city. Also it diminished their numbers. People began to prefer motor drays—which was a mighty good thing.

Now I felt pretty well assured in my own mind, and kept my assurance to my self. Also I began to make a list of my cherished grudges, with a fine sense of power and pleasure.

"I must be careful," I said to myself; "very careful; and, above all things, make the punishment fit the crime."

The subway crowding came to my mind next; both the people who crowd because they have to, and the people who make them. "I mustn't punish anybody, for what they can't help," I mused. "But when it's pure meanness!" Then I bethought me of the remote stockholders, of the more immediate directors, of the painfully prominent officials and insolent employees—and got to work.

"I might as well make a good job of it while this lasts," said I to myself. "It's quite a responsibility, but lots of fun." And I wished that every person responsible for the condition of our subways might be mysteriously compelled to ride up and down in them continuously during rush hours.

This experiment I watched with keen interest, but for the life of me I could see little difference. There were a few more well-dressed persons in the crowds, that was all. So

I came to the conclusion that the general public was mostly to blame, and carried their daily punishment without knowing it.

For the insolent guards and cheating ticket-sellers who give you short change, very slowly, when you are dancing on one foot and your train is there, I merely wished that they might feel the pain their victims would like to give them, short of real injury. They did, I guess.

Then I wished similar things for all manner of corporations and officials. It worked. It worked amazingly. There was a sudden conscientious revival all over the country. The dry bones rattled and sat up. Boards of directors, having troubles enough of their own, were aggravated by innumerable communications from suddenly sensitive stockholders.

In mills and mints and railroads, things began to mend. The country buzzed. The papers fattened. The churches sat up and took credit to themselves. I was incensed at this; and, after brief consideration, wished that every minister would preach to his congregation exactly what he believed and what he thought of them.

I went to six services the next Sunday—about ten minutes each, for two sessions. It was most amusing. A thousand pulpits were emptied forthwith, refilled, re-emptied, and so on, from week to week. People began to go to church; men largely—women didn't like it as well. They had always supposed the ministers thought more highly of them than now appeared to be the case.

One of my oldest grudges was against the sleeping-car people; and now I began to consider them. How often I had grinned and borne it—with other thousands—submitting helplessly.

Here is a railroad—a common carrier—and you have to use it. You pay for your transportation, a good round sum.

Then if you wish to stay in the sleeping car during the day, they charge you another two dollars and a half for the privilege of sitting there, whereas you have paid for a seat when you bought your ticket. That seat is now sold to another person—twice sold! Five dollars for twenty-four hours in a space six feet by three by three at night, and one seat by day; twenty-four of these privileges to a car—$120 a day for the rent of the car—and the passengers to pay the porter besides. That makes $44,800 a year.

Sleeping cars are expensive to build, they say. So are hotels; but they do not charge at such a rate. Now, what could I do to get even? Nothing could ever put back the dollars into the millions of pockets; but it might be stopped now, this beautiful process.

So I wished that all persons who profited by this performance might feel a shame so keen that they would make public avowal and apology, and, as partial restitution, offer their wealth to promote the cause of free railroads!

Then I remembered parrots. This was lucky, for my wrath flamed again. It was really cooling, as I tried to work out responsibility and adjust penalties. But parrots! Any person who wants to keep a parrot should go and live on an island alone with their preferred conversationalist!

There was a huge, squawky parrot right across the street from me, adding its senseless, rasping cries to the more necessary evils of other noises.

I had also an aunt with a parrot. She was a wealthy, ostentatious person, who had been an only child and inherited her money.

Uncle Joseph hated the yelling bird, but that didn't make any difference to Aunt Mathilda.

I didn't like this aunt, and wouldn't visit her, lest she think I was truckling for the sake of her money; but after I had wished this time, I called at the time set for my curse to work; and it did work with a vengeance. There sat poor Uncle Joe, looking thinner and meeker than ever; and my aunt, like an overripe plum, complacent enough.

"Let me out!" said Polly, suddenly. "Let me out to take a walk!"

"The clever thing!" said Aunt Mathilda. "He never said that before."

She let him out. Then he flapped up on the chandelier and sat among the prisms, quite safe.

"What an old pig you are, Mathilda!" said the parrot.

She started to her feet—naturally.

"Born a Pig—trained a Pig—a Pig by nature and education!" said the parrot. "Nobody'd put up with you, except for your money; unless it's this longsuffering husband of yours. He wouldn't, if he hadn't the patience of Job!"

"Hold your tongue!" screamed Aunt Mathilda. "Come down from there! Come here!"

Polly cocked his head and jingled the prisms. "Sit down, Mathilda!" he said, cheerfully. "You've got to listen. You are fat and homely and selfish. You are a nuisance to everybody about you. You have got to feed me and take care of me better than ever—and you've got to listen to me when I talk. Pig!"

I visited another person with a parrot the next day. She put a cloth over his cage when I came in.

"Take it off!" said Polly. She took it off.

"Won't you come into the other room?" she asked me, nervously.

"Better stay here!" said her pet. "Sit still—sit still!"

She sat still.

"Your hair is mostly false," said pretty Poll. "And your teeth—and your outlines. You eat too much. You are lazy. You ought to exercise, and don't know enough. Better apologize to this lady for backbiting! You've got to listen."

The trade in parrots fell off from that day; they say there is no call for them. But the people who kept parrots, keep them yet—parrots live a long time.

Bores were a class of offenders against whom I had long borne undying enmity. Now I rubbed my hands and began on them, with this simple wish: That every person whom they bored should tell them the plain truth.

There is one man whom I have specially in mind. He was blackballed at a pleasant club, but continues to go there. He isn't a member—he just goes; and no one does anything to him.

It was very funny after this. He appeared that very night at a meeting, and almost every person present asked him how he came there. "You're not a member, you know," they said. "Why do you butt in? Nobody likes you."

Some were more lenient with him. "Why don't you learn to be more considerate of others, and make some real friends?" they said. "To have a few friends who do enjoy your visits ought to be pleasanter than being a public nuisance."

He disappeared from that club, anyway.

I began to feel very cocky indeed.

In the food business there was already a marked improvement; and in transportation. The hubbub of reformation waxed louder daily, urged on by the unknown sufferings of all the profiters by iniquity.

The papers thrived on all this; and as I watched the loud-voiced protestations of my pet abomination in journalism, I had a brilliant idea, literally.

Next morning I was down town early, watching the men open their papers. My abomination was shamefully popular, and never more so than this morning. Across the top was printing in gold letters:

All intentional lies, in adv., editorial, news, or any other column … Scarlet

All malicious matter … Crimson

All careless or ignorant mistakes … Pink

All for direct self-interest of owner … Dark green

All mere bait—to sell the paper … Bright green

All advertising, primary or secondary … Brown

All sensational and salacious matter … Yellow

All hired hypocrisy … Purple

Good fun, instruction and entertainment … Blue

True and necessary news and honest editorials … Ordinary print

You never saw such a crazy quilt of a paper. They were bought like hot cakes for some days; but the real business fell off very soon. They'd have stopped it all if they could; but the papers looked all right when they came off the press. The color scheme flamed out only to the bona-fide reader.

I let this work for about a week, to the immense joy of all the other papers; and then turned it on to them, all at once. Newspaper reading became very exciting for a little, but the trade fell off. Even newspaper editors could not keep on feeding a market like that. The blue printed and ordinary printed matter grew from column to column and page to page. Some papers—small, to be sure, but refreshing—began to appear in blue and black alone.

This kept me interested and happy for quite a while; so much so that I quite forgot to be angry at other things. There was *such* a change in all kinds of business, following the mere printing of truth in the newspapers. It began to appear as if we had lived in a sort of delirium—not really knowing the facts about anything. As soon as we really knew the facts, we began to behave very differently, of course.

What really brought all my enjoyment to an end was

women. Being a woman, I was naturally interested in them, and could see some things more clearly than men could. I saw their real power, their real dignity, their real responsibility in the world; and then the way they dress and behave used to make me fairly frantic. 'Twas like seeing archangels playing jackstraws—or real horses only used as rocking-horses. So I determined to get after them.

How to manage it! What to hit first! Their hats, their ugly, inane, outrageous hats—that is what one thinks of first. Their silly, expensive clothes—their diddling beads and jewelry— their greedy childishness—mostly of the women provided for by rich men.

Then I thought of all the other women, the real ones, the vast majority, patiently doing the work of servants without even a servant's pay—and neglecting the noblest duties of motherhood in favor of house-service; the greatest power on earth, blind, chained, untaught, in a treadmill. I thought of what they might do, compared to what they did do, and my heart swelled with something that was far from anger.

Then I wished—with all my strength—that women, all women, might realize Womanhood at last; its power and pride and place in life; that they might see their duty as mothers of the world—to love and care for everyone alive; that they might see their duty to men—to choose only the best, and then to bear and rear better ones; that they might see their duty as human beings, and come right out into full life and work and happiness!

I stopped, breathless, with shining eyes. I waited, trembling, for things to happen.

Nothing happened.

You see, this magic which had fallen on me was black magic—and I had wished white.

It didn't work at all, and, what was worse, it stopped all the other things that were working so nicely.

Oh, if I had only thought to wish permanence for those lovely punishments! If only I had done more while I could do it, had half appreciated my privileges when I was a Witch!

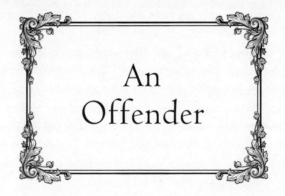

An Offender

"WHERE'S HARRY?" WAS Mr. Cortlandt's first question.

"He's gone to the country, to mother. It was so hot this last day or two, I've sent him out, with Miss Colton. I'm going Saturday. Sit down."

"I miss him," said her visitor, "more than I thought I could. I've learned more in these seven years than I thought there was to know. Or in the last two perhaps, since I've found you again."

She looked at him with a little still smile, but there was a puzzled expression behind it, as of one whose mind was not made up.

They sat in the wide window of a top floor apartment, awning-shaded. A fresh breeze blew in upon them, and the city dust blew in upon them also, lying sandy on the broad sill.

She made little wavy lines in it with one finger—

"These windows ought to be shut tight, I suppose, and the blinds, and the curtains. Then we should be cleaner."

"As to furniture," he agreed, "but not as to our lungs."

"I don't know about that," she said; "we get plenty of air—but see what's in it."

"A city is a dirty place at the best; but Mary—I didn't come to consider the ethics of the dust—how much longer must I wait?" he asked, after a little pause. "Isn't two years courting, re-courting—enough? Haven't I learned my lesson yet?"

"Some of it, I think," she admitted, "but not all."

"What more do you ask?" he pursued earnestly. "Can't we come to a definite understanding? You'll be chasing off again in a few days; it's blessed luck that brought you to town just now, and that I happened to be here too."

"I don't how about the luck," said she. "It was business that brought me. I never was in town before when it was so hot."

"Why don't you go to a hotel? This apartment is right under the roof, gets the sun all day."

"It gets the breeze too, and sunlight is good. No, I'm better off in the apartment, with Harry. It was very convenient of the Grants to be away, and let me have it."

"How does Hal stand the weather?"

"Pretty well. But he was getting rather fretful, so I sent him off two hours ago. I do hope he won't run away from Miss Colton again. She's as nervous as I am about him."

"Don't you think he is fond of me?" asked the man. "I've got to catch up, you see. He can't help being mine—half mine," he hastily added, seeing a hint of denial in her look.

"Why yes, he seems fond of you, he is fond of you," she conceded. "I hope he always will be, and I believe you are beginning to love him."

"A pretty strong beginning, Mary," said the man. "Of course I don't pretend to have cared much at first, but now!—why he's so handsome, and quick, and such a good little duffer; and so affectionate! When he gives a jump and gets his arms around my neck and his legs around my waist and 'hugs me all over' as he calls it, I almost feel as if I was a mother! I can't say more than that, can I?"

"No, you certainly can't say more than that. I believe you, I'm not questioning," for he looked up sharply at her tone.

"I've never had much to do with children, you see," he went on slowly, "no little brothers or sisters, and then only— What astonishes me is how good they feel in your arms! The little fellow's body is so firm and sinewy—he wriggles like a fish—a big fish that you're trying to hold with both hands."

The mother smiled tenderly. She knew the feel of the little body so well! From the soft pink helplessness, the little head falling so naturally into the hollow of the arm or neck, the fumbling little hands; then the gradual gain in size and strength, till now she held that eager bounding little body, almost strong enough to get away from her—but not wanting to. He still loved to nestle up to "Muzz," and was but newly and partially won by this unaccustomed father.

"It's seven years Mary! That makes a man all over, they say. I'm sure it has made me over. I'm an older man—and I think, wiser. I've repented, I've outgrown my folly and seen the justice of my punishment. I don't blame you an atom for divorcing me—I think you did right, and I respect you for it. The biggest lesson I've learned is to love you! I can see— now—that I didn't before."

Her face hardened as she looked at him. "No, you didn't, Harry, you certainly didn't, nor the child—When I think of what I was when you married me! Of my proud health!—"

"*You* are not hurt!" he cried. "I don't mean that you haven't been hurt, I could kill myself when I think of how I made you suffer! But you are a finer woman now than you were then; sweeter, stronger, wiser, and more beautiful. When I found you again in Liverpool two years ago it was a revelation. Now see—I don't even ask you to forgive me! I ask you to try me again and let me prove I can make it up to you and the boy!"

"It's not easy for me to forgive," she answered slowly—"I'm not of the forgiving nature. But there is a good deal of reason in your position. You were my husband, you are Hal's father, there's no escaping that."

"Perhaps, if you will let the rest of my life make up for that time of my God-forsaken meanness, you won't want to escape it, Mary! See—I have followed you about for two years. I accepted your terms, you did not promise me anything, but for the child's sake I might try once more, try only as one of many, to see if I could win you—again. And I love you now a hundred times better than I did when I married you!"

She fanned herself slowly with a large soft fan, and looked out across the flickering roofs. Below them lay the highly respectable street on which the house technically fronted, and the broad, crowded, roaring avenue which it really overlooked.

The rattle of many drays and more delivery wagons rose up to them. An unusual jangle drowned his words just then and she smilingly interpreted "that's railroad iron—or girders, I can tell lots of them now. About four A. M. there is a string of huge milk wagons. But the worst is the cars. Hear that now—that's a flat wheel. How do you like it?"

"Mary—why do you bring up these cars again when I'm trying my best to show you my whole heart? Don't put things like that between us!"

"But they are between us, Henry, all the time. I hear you tell me you love me, and I don't doubt you do in a way; yes, as well as you can, very much indeed!—I know. But when it comes to this car question; when I talk to you of these juggernauts of yours; you are no more willing to do the right thing than you were when I first knew you."

Mr. Cortlandt's face hardened. He drew himself up from

the eager position in which he had leaned forward, and evidently hesitated for a moment as to his words.

In spite of his love for this woman, who, as he justly said, was far more beautiful and winsome than the strong, angular, over-conscientious girl he had married, neglected and shamed, his feelings as a business man were strong within him.

"My dear—I am not personally responsible for the condition of these cars."

"You are President of the Company. You hold controlling shares of the stock. It was your vote that turned down the last improvement proposition."

He looked at her sharply.

"I'm afraid someone has been prejudicing you against me Mary. You have more technical information than seems likely to have reached you by accident."

"It's not prejudice, but it is information; and Mr. Graham did tell me, if that's what you mean. But he cares. You know how hard the Settlement has worked to get the Company to make the streets safer for children—and you wouldn't do a thing."

Mr. Cortlandt hesitated. It would never do to pile business details on his suit for a love once lost and not yet regained.

"You make it hard for me Mary," he said. "Hard because it is difficult to explain large business questions to a—to anyone not accustomed to them. I cannot swing the affairs of a great corporation for personal ends, even to please you."

"That is not the point," she said quickly.

He flushed, and hastily substituted "Even to suit the noblest humanitarian feelings."

"Why not?" said she.

"Because that is not what street cars are run for," he pursued patiently. "But why must we talk of this? It seems to put you so far away. And you have given me no answer."

"I am sorry, but I am not ready yet."

"Is it Hugh Graham?" he demanded.

The hot color leaped to her face, but she met his eyes steadily. "I am much interested in Mr. Graham," she said, "and in the noble work he is doing. I think I should really be happier with him than with you. We care for the same things, he calls out the best in me. But I have made no decision in his favor yet, nor in yours. Both of you have a certain appeal to my heart, both to my duty. With you the personal need, with him the hope of greater service. But—you are the father of the child, and that gives you a great claim. I have not decided."

The man looked relieved, and again drew his chair a little closer. The sharp clangor of the cars rose between them.

"You think I dragged in this car question," she said. "Really, I did it because it is that sort of thing which does most to keep us apart, and—I would like to remove it."

He leaned forward, playing with her big fan. "Let's remove it by all means!" he said.

She looked at his bent head, the dark hair growing somewhat thin on top, almost tenderly.

"If I could feel that you were truly on the right side, that you considered your work as social service, that you tried to run your cars to carry people—not to kill them! If you could change your ground here I think—almost—" she stopped, smiling up at him, her fan in her lap, her firm delicate white hands eagerly clasped; then went on,

"Don't you care at all for the lives lost every day in this great city—under your cars?"

"It cannot be helped, my dear. Our men are as careful as men can be. But these swarming children will play in the streets—"

"Where else can they play!" she interjected.

"And they get right in front of the cars. We are very sorry; we pay out thousands of dollars in damages: but it cannot be helped!"

She leaned back in her chair and her face grew cold.

"You speak as if you never heard of such things as fenders," she said.

"We have fenders!—almost every car—"

"Fenders! Do you call that piece of rat-trap a fender! Henry Cortlandt! We were in Liverpool when this subject first came up between us! They have fenders there that *fend* and no murder list!"

"Conditions are different there," said he with an enforced quiet. "Our pavement is different."

"Our children are not so different, are they?" she demanded. "Our mothers are made of the same stuff I suppose?"

"You speak as if I wanted to kill them! As if I liked to!"

"I thought at first it would hurt you as it did me," she said warmly. "I turned to you with real hope when we met in Liverpool. I was glad to think I knew you, and I had not been glad of that for long! I thought you would care, would do things."

Do what he would his mouth set hard in its accustomed lines. "Those English fenders are not practicable in this country, Mary. They have been tried."

"When? Where? By whom?" she threw at him. "I have read about it, and heard about it. I know there was an effort to get them adopted, and that they were refused. They cost more than this kind!" and she pointed disdainfully at the rattling bit of stub-toed slat-work in front of a passing car.

"Do you expect me to make a revolution in the street car system of America—to please you? Do you make it a condition? Perhaps I can accomplish it. Is it a bargain? Come—"

"No," she said slowly. "I'm not making bargains. I'm only

wishing, as I have wished so often in years past—that you were a different kind of man—"

"What kind do you want me to be?"

"I want you to be—I wish you were—a man who cared to give perfect service to his country, in his business."

"Perhaps I can be yet. I can try. If I had you to help me, with your pure ideals, and the boy to keep my heart open for the children. I don't know much about these things, but I can learn. I can read, you can tell me what to read. We could study together. And in my position perhaps, I could really be of some service after all."

"Perhaps?" She watched him, the strong rather heavy face, the attractive smile, the eyes that interested and compelled. He was an able, masterful man. He surely loved her now. She could feel a power over him that her short miserable marriage had never given her; and her girlhood's attraction toward him reasserted itself.

A new noise rose about them, a dissonant mingled merry outcry, made into a level roaring sound by their height above the street.

"That's when the school up here lets out," she said. "We hear it every day. Just see the crowds of them!"

They leaned on the broad sill and watched the many-colored torrent of juveniles pouring past.

"One day it was different," she said. "A strange jarring shrillness in it, a peculiar sound. I looked out, and there was a fight going on; two boys tumbling about from one side of the street to the other, with a moving ring around them, a big crowd, all roaring in one key."

"You get a birds-eye view of life in these streets, don't you. Can you make out that little chap with the red hair down there?"

"No—we are both nearsighted, you know. I can't distinguish faces at this distance. Can you?"

"Not very clearly," he said. "But what a swarm they are!"

"Come away," said she, "I can't bear to look at them. So many children in that stony street, and those cars going up and down like roaring lions!"

They drew back into the big sunny room, and she seated herself at the piano and turned over loose sheets of music.

He watched her with a look of intensest admiration, she was so tall, so nobly formed, her soft rich gown flowed and followed as she walked, her white throat rose round and royal from broad smooth shoulders.

He was beside her; he took away the music, laid it out of reach, possessed himself of her hands.

"Give them back to me, Mary," he pleaded. "Come to me and help me to be a better man! Help me to be a good father. I need you!"

She looked at him almost pleadingly. His eyes, his voice, his hands, they had their old-time charm for her. Yet he had only said "Perhaps"—and he *might* study, *might* learn.

He asked her to help him, but he did not say "I will do this"—only "I may."

In the steady bright June sunshine, in the sifting dust of a city corner, in the dissonant, confused noise of the traffic below, they stood and looked at one another.

His eyes brightened and deepened as he watched her changing color. Softly he drew her towards him. "Even if you do not love me now, you shall in time, you shall, my darling!"

But she drew back from him with a frightened start, a look of terror.

"What has happened!" she cried. "It's so still!"

They both rushed to the window.

The avenue immediately below them was as empty as midnight, and as silent. A great stillness widened and spread for the moment around one vacant motionless open car.

Without passenger, driver, or conductor, it stood alone in the glaring space; and then, with a gasp of horror, they both saw.

Right under their eyes, headed towards them, under the middle of the long car—a little child.

He was quite still, lying face downward, dirty and tumbled, with helpless arms thrown wide, the great car holding him down like a mouse in a trap.

Then people came rushing.

She turned away, choking, her hands to her eyes.

"Oh!" she cried, "Oh! It's a child, a little child!"

"Steady, Mary, steady!" said he, "the child's dead. It's all over. He's quite dead. He never knew what hit him." But his own voice trembled.

She made a mighty effort to control herself, and he tried to take her in his arms, to comfort her, but she sprang away from him with fierce energy.

"Very well!" she said. "You are right! The child is dead. We cannot save him. No one can save him. Now come back—come here to the window—and see what follows. I want to see with my own eyes—and have you see—what is done when your cars commit murder! Child murder!"

She held up her watch. "It's 12:10 now," she said.

She dragged him back to the window, and so evident was the struggle with which she controlled herself, so intense her agonized excitement, that he dared not leave her.

"Look!" she cried. "Look! See then the crowd now!"

The first horrified rush away from the instrument of death was followed by the usual surging multitude.

From every direction people gathered thickly in astonishing numbers, hustling and pushing about the quiet form upon the ground; held so flat between iron rails and iron wheels, so great a weight on so small a body! The car, still empty, rose like an island from the pushing sea of heads. Men and

women cried excited directions. They tried with swarming impotent hands to lift the huge mass of wood and iron off the small broken thing beneath it, so small that it did not raise the crushing weight from the ground.

A whole line of excited men seized the side rail and strove to lift the car by it, lifting only the rail.

The crowd grew momently, women weeping, children struggling to see, men pushing each other, policemen's helmets rising among them. And still the great car stood there, on the body of the child.

"Is there no means of lifting these monsters?" she demanded. "After they have done it, can't they even get it off?"

He moistened his lips to answer.

"There is a jacking crew," he said. "They will be here presently."

"Presently!" she cried. "Presently! Couldn't these monsters use their own power to lift themselves somehow? not even that?"

He said nothing.

More policemen came, and made a scant space around the little body, covering it with a dark cloth. The motorman was rescued from many would-be avengers, and carried off under guard.

"Ten minutes," said she looking at her watch. "Ten minutes and it isn't even off him yet!" and she caught her breath in a great sob.

Then she turned on the man at her side: "Suppose his mother is in that crowd! She may be! Their children go to this school, they live all about below here, she can't even get in to see! And if she could, if she knew it was her child, she can't *get him out!*"

Her voice rose to a cry.

"Don't, Mary," said he, hoarsely. "It's—it's horrible! Don't make it worse!"

She kept her eyes on her watch-face, counting the minutes. She looked down at the crowd shudderingly, and said over and over, under breath, "A little child! A little soft child!"

It was twelve minutes and a half before the jacking crew drove up, with their tools. It was a long time yet before they did their work, and that crushed and soiled little body was borne to a nearby area grating and laid there, wrapped in its dingy shroud, and guarded by a policeman.

It was a full half hour before the ambulance arrived to take it away.

She drew back then and crouched sobbing by the sofa. "O the poor mother! God help his mother!"

He sat tense and white for a while; and when she grew quieter he spoke.

"You were right, Mary. I—naturally, I never—visualized it! It is horrible! I am going to have those fenders on every car of the four systems!"

She said nothing. He spoke again.

"I hate to leave you feeling so, Dear. Must I go?"

She raised a face that was years older, but did not look at him.

"You must go. And you must never come back. I cannot bear to see your face again!"

And she turned from him, shuddering.

The Boys and the Butter

YOUNG HOLDFAST AND J. Edwards Fernald sat grimly at their father's table, being seen and not heard, and eating what was set before them, asking no questions for conscience' sake, as they had been duly reared. But in their hearts were most unchristian feelings toward a venerable guest, their mother's aunt, by name Miss Jane McCoy.

They knew, with the keen observation of childhood, that it was only a sense of hospitality, and duty to a relative, which made their father and mother polite to her—polite, but not cordial.

Mr. Fernald, as a professed Christian, did his best to love his wife's aunt, who came as near being an "enemy" as anyone he knew. But Mahala, his wife, was of a less saintly nature, and made no pretense of more than decent courtesy.

"I don't like her and I won't pretend to; it's not honest!" she protested to her husband, when he remonstrated with her upon her want of natural affection. "I can't help her being my aunt—we are not commanded to honor our aunts and uncles, Jonathan E."

Mrs. Fernald's honesty was of an iron hardness and heroic mold. She would have died rather than have told a lie, and classed as lies any form of evasion, deceit, concealment or even artistic exaggeration.

Her two sons, thus starkly reared, found their only imaginative license in secret converse between themselves, sacredly guarded by a pact of mutual faith, which was stronger than any outward compulsion. They kicked each other under the table, while enduring this visitation, exchanged dark glances concerning the object of their common dislike, and discussed her personal peculiarities with caustic comment later, when they should have been asleep.

Miss McCoy was not an endearing old lady. She was heavily built, and gobbled her food, carefully selecting the best. Her clothing was elaborate, but not beautiful, and on close approach aroused a suspicion of deferred laundry bills.

Among many causes for dislike for her aunt, Mrs. Fernald cherished this point especially. On one of these unwelcome visits she had been at some pains to carry up hot water for the Saturday evening bath, which was all the New England conscience of those days exacted, and the old lady had neglected it not only once but twice.

"Goodness sake, Aunt Jane! aren't you ever going to take a bath?"

"Nonsense!" replied her visitor. "I don't believe in all this wetting and slopping. The Scripture says, 'Whoso washeth his feet, his whole body shall be made clean.'"

Miss McCoy had numberless theories for other people's conduct, usually backed by well-chosen texts, and urged them with no regard for anybody's feelings. Even the authority of parents had no terrors for her.

Sipping her tea from the saucer with deep swattering inhalations, she fixed her prominent eyes upon the two boys as they ploughed their way through their bread and butter. Nothing must be left on the plate, in the table ethics of that time. The meal was simple in the extreme. A New Hampshire farm furnished few luxuries, and the dish of quince preserves had already been depleted by her.

"Mahala," she said with solemn determination, "those boys eat too much butter."

Mrs. Fernald flushed up to the edging of her cap. "I think I must be the judge of what my children eat at my table, Aunt Jane," she answered, not too gently.

Here Mr. Fernald interposed with a "soft answer." (He had never lost faith in the efficacy of these wrath turners, even on long repeated failure. As a matter of fact, to his wife's temper, a soft answer, especially an intentionally soft answer, was a fresh aggravation.) "The missionary, now, he praised our butter; said he never got any butter in China, or wherever 'tis he lives."

"He is a man of God," announced Miss McCoy. "If there is anybody on this poor earth deserving reverence, it is a missionary. What they endure for the Gospel is a lesson for us all. When I am taken I intend to leave all I have to the Missionary Society. You know that."

They knew it and said nothing. Their patience with her was in no way mercenary.

"But what I am speaking of is children," she continued, not to be diverted from her fell purpose. "Children ought not to eat butter."

"They seem to thrive on it," Mrs. Fernald replied tartly. And in truth both the boys were sturdy little specimens of humanity, in spite of their luxurious food.

"It's bad for them. Makes them break out. Bad for the blood. And self-denial is good for children. 'It is better to bear the yoke in thy youth.'"

The youth in question spread its butter more thickly, and ate it with satisfaction, saying nothing.

"Here, boys!" she suddenly assailed them. "If you will go without butter for a year—a whole year, till I come round again—I'll give each of you fifty dollars!"

This was an overwhelming proposition.

Butter was butter—almost the only alleviation of a dry and monotonous bill of fare, consisting largely of bread. Bread without butter! Brown bread without butter! No butter on potatoes! No butter on anything! The young imagination recoiled. And this measureless deprivation was to cover a whole year. A ninth or an eleventh of a lifetime to them respectively. About a fifth of all they could really remember. Countless days, each having three meals; weeks, months, the long dry butterless vista stretched before them like Siberian exile to a Russian prisoner.

But, on the other hand, there was the fifty dollars. Fifty dollars would buy a horse, a gun, tools, knives—a farm, maybe. It could be put in the bank, and drawn on for life, doubtless. Fifty dollars at that time was like five hundred today, and to a child it was a fortune.

Even their mother wavered in her resentment as she considered the fifty dollars, and the father did not waver at all, but thought it a Godsend.

"Let 'em choose," said Miss McCoy.

Stern is the stock of the Granite State. Self-denial is the essence of their religion; and economy, to give it a favorable name, is for them Nature's first law.

The struggle was brief. Holdfast laid down his thickspread slice. J. Edwards laid down his. "Yes, ma'am," said one after the other. "Thank you, ma'am. We'll do it."

It was a long year. Milk did not take the place of it. Gravy and drippings, freely given by their mother, did not take the place of it, nor did the infrequent portions of preserves.

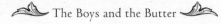

Nothing met the same want. And if their health was improved by the abstinence it was in no way visible to the naked eye. They were well, but they were well before.

As to the moral effect—it was complex. An extorted sacrifice has not the same odor of sanctity as a voluntary one. Even when made willingly, if the willingness is purchased, the effect seems somewhat confused. Butter was not renounced, only postponed, and as the year wore on the young ascetics, in their secret conferences, indulged in wild visions of oleaginous excess so soon as the period of dearth should be over. But most they refreshed their souls with plans for the spending and the saving of the hard-earned wealth that was coming to them. Holdfast was for saving his, and being a rich man—richer than Captain Briggs or Deacon Holbrook. But at times he wavered, spurred by the imagination of J. Edwards, and invested that magic sum in joys unnumbered.

The habit of self-denial was perhaps being established, but so was the habit of discounting the future, of indulging in wild plans of self-gratification when the ship came in.

Even for butterless boys, time passes, and the endless year at last drew to a close. They counted the months, they counted the weeks, they counted the days. Thanksgiving itself shone pale by contrast with this coming festival of joy and triumph. As it drew nearer and nearer their excitement increased, and they could not forget it even in the passing visit of a real missionary, a live one, who had been to those dark lands where the heathen go naked, worship idols and throw their children to the crocodiles.

They were taken to hear him, of course, and not only so, but he came to supper at their house and won their young hearts by the stories he told them. Gray of hair and beard was the preacher and sternly devout; but he had a twinkling eye none the less, and told tales of wonder and amazement that were sometimes almost funny and always interesting.

"Do not imagine, my young friends," he said, after filling them with delicious horror at the unspeakable wickedness of those "godless lands,""that the heathen are wholly without morality. The Chinese, among whom I have labored for many years, are more honest than some Christians. Their business honor is a lesson to us all. But works alone cannot save." And he questioned them as to their religious state, receiving satisfactory answers.

The town turned out to hear him; and, when he went on circuit, preaching, exhorting, describing the hardships and dangers of missionary life, the joys of soulsaving, and urging his hearers to contribute to this great duty of preaching the Gospel to all creatures, they had a sort of revival season; and arranged for a great missionary church meeting with a special collection when he should return.

The town talked missionary and thought missionary; dreamed missionary, it might well be; and garrets were ransacked to make up missionary boxes to send to the heathen. But Holdfast and J. Edwards mingled their interest in those unfortunate savages with a passionate desire for butter, and a longing for money such as they had never known before.

Then Miss McCoy returned.

They knew the day, the hour. They watched their father drive down to meet the stage, and tormented their mother with questions as to whether she would give it to them before supper or after.

"I'm sure I don't know!" she snapped at last. "I'll be thankful when it's over and done with, I'm sure. A mighty foolish business, I think!"

Then they saw the old chaise turn the corner. What? Only one in it! The boys rushed to the gate—the mother, too.

"What is it, Jonathan? Didn't she come?"

"Oh, father!"

"Where is she, father?"

"She's not coming," said Mr. Fernald. "Says she's going to stay with Cousin Sarah, so's to be in town and go to all the missionary doin's. But she's sent it."

Then he was besieged, and as soon as the horse was put up, by three pairs of busy hands, they came to the supper table, whereon was a full two pounds of delicious butter, and sat down with tingling impatience.

The blessing was asked in all due form—a blessing ten miles long, it seemed to the youngsters, and then the long, fat envelope came out of Mr. Fernald's pocket.

"She must have written a lot," he said, taking out two folded papers, and then a letter.

"My dear great-nephews," ran the epistle, "as your parents have assured me that you have kept your promise, and denied yourselves butter for the space of a year, here is the fifty dollars I promised to each of you—wisely invested."

Mr. Fernald opened the papers. To Holdfast Fernald and to J. Edwards Fernald, duly made out, receipted, signed and sealed, were two $50 life memberships in the Missionary society!

Poor children! The younger one burst into wild weeping. The older seized the butter dish and cast it on the floor, for which he had to be punished, of course, but the punishment added nothing to his grief and rage.

When they were alone at last, and able to speak for sobbing, those gentle youths exchanged their sentiments; and these were of the nature of blasphemy and rebellion against God. They had learned at one fell blow the hideous lesson of human depravity. People lied—grown people—religious people—they lied! You couldn't trust them! They had been deceived, betrayed, robbed! They had lost the actual joy renounced, and the potential joy promised and withheld. The money they might some day earn, but not heaven itself could give back that year of butter. And all this in the name of religion—and of missionaries! Wild, seething outrage filled their hearts at first; slower results would follow.

The pious enthusiasm of the little town was at its height. The religious imagination, rather starved on the bald alternatives of Calvinism, found rich food in these glowing tales of danger, devotion, sometimes martyrdom; while the spirit of rigid economy, used to daylong saving from the cradle to the grave, took passionate delight in the success of these noble evangelists who went so far afield to save lost souls.

Out of their narrow means they had scraped still further; denied themselves necessaries where no pleasures remained; and when the crowning meeting was announced, the big collection meeting, with the wonderful brother from the Church in Asia to address them again, the meeting house was packed in floor and gallery.

Hearts were warm and open, souls were full of enthusiasm for the great work, wave on wave of intense feeling streamed through the crowded house.

Only in the Fernalds' pew was a spirit out of tune.

Fernald, good man though he was, had not yet forgiven. His wife had not tried.

"Don't talk to me!" she had cried passionately, when he had urged a reconciliation. "Forgive your enemies! Yes, but she hasn't done any harm to *me*! It's my boys she's hurt! It don't say one word about forgiving other people's enemies!"

Yet Mrs. Fernald, for all her anger, seemed to have some inner source of consolation, denied her husband, over which she nodded to herself from time to time, drawing in her thin lips, and wagging her head decisively.

Vengeful bitterness and impotent rage possessed the hearts of Holdfast and J. Edwards.

This state of mind in young and old was not improved when, on arriving at the meeting a little late, they had found the head of the pew was occupied by Miss McCoy.

It was neither the time nor the place for a demonstration. No other seats were vacant, and Mrs. Fernald marched in and sat next to her, looking straight at the pulpit. Next came the boys, and murder was in their hearts. Last, Mr. Fernald, inwardly praying for a more Christian spirit, but not getting it.

Holdfast and young J. Edwards dared not speak in church or make any protest; but they smelled the cardamom seeds in the champing jaws beyond their mother, and they cast black looks at each other and very secretly showed clenched fists, held low.

In fierce inward rebellion they sat through the earlier speeches, and when the time came for the address of the occasion, even the deep voice of the brother from Asia failed to stir them. Was he not a missionary, and were not missionaries and all their works proved false?

But what was this?

The address was over; the collection, in cash, was in the piled plates at the foot of the pulpit. The collection in goods was enumerated and described with full names given.

Then the hero of the hour was seen to confer with the other reverend brothers, and to rise and come forward, raising his hand for silence.

"Dearly beloved brethren and sisters," he said, "in this time of thanksgiving for gifts spiritual and temporal I wish to ask your patience for a moment more, that we may do justice.

There has come to my ears a tale concerning one of our recent gifts which I wish you to hear, that judgment may be done in Israel.

"One among us has brought to the House of the Lord a tainted offering—an offering stained with cruelty and falsehood. Two young children of our flock were bribed a year ago to renounce one of the scant pleasures of their lives for a year's time—a whole long year of a child's life. They were bribed with a promise—a promise of untold wealth to a child, of fifty dollars each."

The congregation drew a long breath.

Those who knew of the Fernald boys' endeavor (and who in that friendly radius did not?) looked at them eagerly. Those who recognized Miss McCoy looked at her, too, and they were many. She sat, fanning herself, with a small, straight-handled palm-leaf fan, striving to appear unconscious.

"When the time was up," the clear voice went on remorselessly, "the year of struggle and privation, and the eager hearts of childhood expected the reward; instead of keeping the given word, instead of the money promised, each child was given a paid life membership in our society!"

Again the house drew in its breath. Did not the end justify the means?

He went on:

"I have conferred with my fellow members, and we are united in our repudiation of this gift. The money is not ours. It was obtained by a trick which the heathen themselves would scorn."

There was a shocked pause. Miss McCoy was purple in the face, and only kept her place for fear of drawing more attention if she strove to escape.

"I name no names," the speaker continued, "and I regret the burden laid upon me to thus expose this possibly well-

meant transaction, but what we have at stake tonight is not this handful of silver, nor the feelings of one sinner, but two children's souls. Are we to have their sense of justice outraged in impressionable youth? Are they to believe with the Psalmist that all men are liars? Are they to feel anger and blame for the great work to which our lives are given because in its name they were deceived and robbed? No, my brothers, we clear our skirts of this ignominy. In the name of the society, I shall return this money to its rightful owners. 'Whoso offendeth one of these little ones, it were better that a millstone be hanged about his neck and he cast into the depths of the sea.'"

A Coincidence

O THAT! IT was a fortunate coincidence, wasn't it? All things work together for good with those who love the Lord, you know, and Emma Ordway is the most outrageously Christian woman I ever knew. It did look that Autumn as if there was no way out of it, but things do happen, sometimes.

I dropped in rather late one afternoon to have a cup of tea with Emma, hoping against hope that Mirabella Vlack wouldn't be on hand; but she was, of course, and gobbling. There never was such a woman for candy and all manner of sweet stuff. I can remember her at school, with those large innocent eyes, and that wide mouth, eating Emma's nicest tidbits even then.

Emma loves sweets but she loves her friends better, and never gets anything for herself unless there is more than enough for everybody. She is very fond of a particular kind of fudge I make, has been fond of it for thirty years, and I love to make it for her once in a while, but after Mirabella came—I might as well have made it for her to begin with.

I devised the idea of bringing it in separate boxes, one for each, but bless you! Mirabella kept hers in her room, and ate Emma's!

"O I've left mine upstairs!" she'd say; "Let me go up and

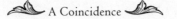

get it;"—and of course Emma wouldn't hear of such a thing. Trust Emma!

I've loved that girl ever since she was a girl, in spite of her preternatural unselfishness. And I've always hated those Vlack girls, both of them, Mirabella the most. At least I think so when I'm with her. When I'm with Arabella I'm not so sure. She married a man named Sibthorpe, just rich.

They were both there that afternoon, the Vlack girls I mean, and disagreeing as usual. Arabella was lean and hard and rigorously well dressed, she meant to have her way in this world and generally got it. Mirabella was thick and soft. Her face was draped puffily upon its unseen bones, and of an unwholesome color because of indigestion. She was the type that suggests cushioned upholstery, whereas Arabella's construction was evident.

"You don't look well, Mirabella," said she.

"I am well," replied her sister, "Quite well I assure you."

Mirabella was at that time some kind of a holy thoughtist. She had tried every variety of doctor, keeping them only as long as they did not charge too much, and let her eat what she pleased; which necessitated frequent change.

Mrs. Montrose smiled diplomatically, remarking "What a comfort these wonderful new faiths are!" She was one of Emma's old friends, and was urging her to go out to California with them and spend the winter. She dilated on the heavenly beauty and sweetness of the place till it almost made my mouth water, and Emma!—she loved travel better than anything, and California was one of the few places she had not seen.

Then that Vlack girl began to perform. "Why don't you go, Emma?" she said. "I'm not able to travel myself," (she wouldn't admit she was pointedly left out), "but that's no reason you should miss such a delightful opportunity. I can be housekeeper for you in your absence." This proposition had been tried once. All Emma's old servants left, and she had to come back in the middle of her trip, and re-organize the household.

Thus Mirabella, looking saintly and cheerful. And Emma—I could have shaken her soundly where she sat—Emma smiled bravely at Mrs. Montrose and thanked her warmly; she'd love it above all things, but there were many reasons why she couldn't leave home that winter. And we both knew there was only one, a huge thing in petticoats sitting gobbling there.

One or two other old friends dropped in, but they didn't stay long; they never did any more, and hardly any men came now. As I sat there drinking my pale tea I heard these people asking Emma why she didn't do this any more, and why she didn't come to that any more, and Emma just as dignified and nice as you please, telling all sorts of perforated paper fibs to explain and decline. One can't be perfect, and nobody could be as absolutely kind and gracious and universally beloved as Emma if she always told the plain truth.

I'd brought in my last protégé that day, Dr. Lucy Barnes, a small quaint person, with more knowledge of her profession than her looks would indicate. She was a very wise little creature altogether. I had been studying chemistry with her, just for fun. You never know when you may want to know a thing.

It was fine to see Dr. Lucy put her finger on Mirabella's weakness.

There that great cuckoo sat and discoursed on the symptoms she used to have, and would have now if it wasn't for "science"; and there I sat and watched Emma, and I declare she seemed to age visibly before my eyes.

Was I to keep quiet and let one of the nicest women that ever breathed be worn into her grave by that—Incubus? Even

if she hadn't been a friend of mine, even if she hadn't been too good for this world, it would have been a shame. As it was the outrage cried to heaven,—and nobody could do anything.

Here was Emma, a widow, and in her own house; you couldn't coerce her. And she could afford it, as far as money went, you couldn't interfere that way. She had been so happy! She'd got over being a widow—I mean got used to it, and was finding her own feet. Her children were all married and reasonably happy, except the youngest, who was unreasonably happy; but time would make that all right. Then Emma really began to enjoy life. Her health was good; she'd kept her looks wonderfully; and all the vivid interests of her girlhood cropped up again. She began to study things; to go to lectures and courses of lectures; to travel every year to a new place; to see her old friends and make new ones. She never liked to keep house, but Emma was so idiotically unselfish that she never would enjoy herself as long as there was anybody at home to give up to.

And then came Mirabella Vlack.

She came for a visit, at least she called one day with her air of saintly patience, and a miserable story of her loneliness and unhappiness, and how she couldn't bear to be dependent on Arabella—Arabella was so unsympathetic!—and that misguided Emma invited her to visit her for awhile.

That was five years ago. Five years! And here she sat, gobbling, forty pounds fatter and the soul of amiability, while Emma grew old.

Of course we all remonstrated—after it was too late.

Emma had a right to her own visitors—nobody ever dreamed that the thing was permanent, and nobody could break down that adamantine wall of Christian virtue she suffered behind, not owning that she suffered.

It was a problem.

But I love problems, human problems, better even than problems in chemistry, and they are fascinating enough.

First I tried Arabella. She said she regretted that poor Mirabella would not come to her loving arms. You see Mirabella had tried them, for about a year after her husband died, and preferred Emma's.

"It really doesn't look well," said Arabella. "Here am I alone in these great halls, and there is my only sister preferring to live with a comparative stranger! Her duty is to live with me, where I can take care of her."

Not much progress here. Mirabella did not want to be taken care of by a fault-finding older sister—not while Emma was in reach. It paid, too. Her insurance money kept her in clothes, and she could save a good deal, having no living expenses. As long as she preferred living with Emma Ordway, and Emma let her—what could anybody do?

It was getting well along in November, miserable weather.

Emma had a cough that hung on for weeks and weeks, she couldn't seem to gather herself together and throw it off, and Mirabella all the time assuring her that she had no cough at all!

Certain things began to seem very clear to me.

One was the duty of a sister, of two sisters. One was the need of a change of climate for my Emma.

One was that ever opening field of human possibilities which it has been the increasing joy of my lifetime to study.

I carried two boxes of my delectable fudge to those ladies quite regularly, a plain white one for Emma, a pretty colored one for the Incubus.

"Are you sure it is good for you?" I asked Mirabella; "I love to make it and have it appreciated, but does your Doctor think it is good for you?"

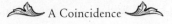

Strong in her latest faith she proudly declared she could eat anything. She could—visibly. So she took me up short on this point, and ate several to demonstrate immunity—out of Emma's box.

Nevertheless, in spite of all demonstration she seemed to grow somewhat—queasy—shall we say? and drove poor Emma almost to tears trying to please her in the matter of meals.

Then I began to take them both out to ride in my motor, and to call quite frequently on Arabella; they couldn't well help it, you see, when I stopped the car and hopped out. "Mrs. Sibthorpe's sister" I'd always say to the butler or maid, and she'd always act as if she owned the house—that is if Arabella was out.

Then I had a good talk with Emma's old doctor, and he quite frightened her.

"You ought to close up the house," he said, "and spend the winter in a warm climate. You need complete rest and change, for a long time, a year at least," he told her. I urged her to go.

"Do make a change," I begged. "Here's Mrs. Sibthorpe perfectly willing to keep Mirabella—she'd be just as well off there; and you do really need a rest."

Emma smiled that saintly smile of hers, and said, "Of course, if Mirabella would go to her sister's awhile I could leave? But I can't ask her to go."

I could. I did. I put it to her fair and square,—the state of Emma's health, her real need to break up housekeeping, and how Arabella was just waiting for her to come there. But what's the use of talking to that kind? Emma wasn't sick, couldn't be sick, nobody could. At that very moment she paused suddenly, laid a fat hand on a fat side with an expression that certainly looked like pain; but she changed it for one of lofty and determined faith, and seemed to feel better. It made her cross though, as near it as she ever gets. She'd have been rude I think, but she likes my motor, to say nothing of my fudge.

I took them both out to ride that very afternoon, and Dr. Lucy with us.

Emma, foolish thing, insisted on sitting with the driver, and Mirabella made for her pet corner at once. I put Dr. Lucy in the middle, and encouraged Mirabella in her favorite backsliding, the discussion of her symptoms—the symptoms she used to have—or would have now if she gave way to "error."

Dr. Lucy was ingeniously sympathetic. She made no pretense of taking up the new view, but was perfectly polite about it.

"Judging from what you tell me", she said, "and from my own point of view, I should say that you had a quite serious digestive trouble; that you had a good deal of pain now and then; and were quite likely to have a sudden and perhaps serious attack. But that is all nonsense to you I suppose."

"Of course it is!" said Mirabella, turning a shade paler.

We were running smoothly down the long avenue where Arabella lived.

"Here's something to cheer you up," I said, producing my two boxes of fudge. One I passed around in front to Emma; she couldn't share it with us. The other I gave Mirabella.

She fell upon it at once; perfunctorily offering some to Dr. Lucy, who declined; and to me. I took one for politeness's sake, and casually put it in my pocket.

We had just about reached Mrs. Sibthorpe's gate when Mirabella gave in.

"Oh I have such a terrible pain!" said she. "Oh Dr. Lucy! What shall I do?"

"Shall I take you down to your healer?" I suggested; but Mirabella was feeling very badly indeed.

"I think I'd better go in here a moment," she said; and in five minutes we had her in bed in what used to be her room.

Dr. Lucy seemed averse to prescribe.

"I have no right to interfere with your faith, Mrs. Vlack," she said. "I have medicines which I think would relieve you, but you do not believe in them. I think you should summon your—practitioner, at once."

"Oh Dr. Lucy!" gasped poor Mirabella, whose aspect was that of a small boy in an August orchard. "Don't leave me! Oh do something for me quick!"

"Will you do just what I say?"

"I will! I will; I'll do *anything*!" said Mirabella, curling up in as small a heap as was possible to her proportions, and Dr. Lucy took the case.

We waited in the big bald parlors till she came down to tell us what was wrong. Emma seemed very anxious, but then Emma is a preternatural saint.

Arabella came home and made a great to-do. "So fortunate that she was near my door!" she said. "Oh my poor sister! I am so glad she has a real doctor!"

The real doctor came down after a while. "She is practically out of pain," she said, "and resting quietly. But she is extremely weak, and ought not to be moved for a long time."

"She shall not be!" said Arabella fervently. "My own sister! I am so thankful she came to me in her hour of need!"

I took Emma away. "Let's pick up Mrs. Montrose," I said. "She's tired out with packing—the air will do her good."

She was glad to come. We all sat back comfortably in the big seat and had a fine ride; and then Mrs. Montrose had us both come in and take dinner with her. Emma ate better than

I'd seen her in months, and before she went home it was settled that she leave with Mrs. Montrose on Tuesday.

Dear Emma! She was as pleased as a child. I ran about with her, doing a little shopping.

"Don't bother with anything," I said, "You can get things out there. Maybe you'll go on to Japan next spring with the James's."

"If we could sell the house I would!" said Emma. She brisked and sparkled—the years fell off from her—she started off looking fairly girlish in her hope and enthusiasm.

I drew a long sigh of relief.

Mr. MacAvelly has some real estate interests.

The house was sold before Mirabella was out of bed.

Making
a Living

"THERE WON'T BE any litigation and chicanery to help you out, young man. I've fixed that. Here are the title deeds of your precious country-place; you can sit in that handmade hut of yours and make poetry and crazy inventions the rest of your life! The water's good—and I guess you can live on the chestnuts!"

"Yes, sir," said Arnold Blake, rubbing his long chin dubiously. "I guess I can."

His father surveyed him with entire disgust. "If you had wit enough you might rebuild that old saw-mill and make a living off it!"

"Yes, sir," said Arnold again. "I had thought of that."

"You had, had you?" sneered his father. "Thought of it because it rhymed, I bet you! Hill and mill, eh? Hut and nut, trees and breeze, waterfall—beat-'em-all? I'm something of a poet myself, you see! Well, there's your property. And with what your Mother left you will buy books and writing paper! As for my property—that's going to Jack. I've got the papers for that too. Not being an idiot I've saved out enough for myself—no Lear business for mine! Well, boy—I'm sorry you're a fool. But you've got what you seem to like best."

"Yes, sir," said Arnold once more. "I have, and I'm really

much obliged to you, Father, for not trying to make me take the business."

Then young John Blake, pattern and image of his father, came into possession of large assets and began to use them in the only correct way; to increase and multiply without end.

Then old John Blake, gazing with pride on his younger son, whose acumen almost compensated him for the bitter disappointment of being father to a poet; set forth for a season of rest and change.

"I'm going to see the world! I never had time before!" quoth he; and started off for Europe, Asia, and Africa.

Then Arnold Blake, whose eyes were the eyes of a poet, but whose mouth had a touch of resemblance to his father's, betook himself to his Hill.

But the night before they separated, he and his brother both proposed to Ella Sutherland. John because he had made up his mind that it was the proper time for him to marry, and this was the proper woman; and Arnold because he couldn't help it.

John got to work first. He was really very fond of Ella, and made hot love to her. It was a painful surprise to him to be refused. He argued with her. He told her how much he loved her.

"There are others!" said Miss Ella.

He told her how rich he was.

"That isn't the point," said Ella.

He told her how rich he was going to be.

"I'm not for sale!" said Ella, "even on futures!"

Then he got angry and criticized her judgment.

"It's a pity, isn't it," she said, "for me to have such poor judgment—and for you to have to abide by it!"

"I won't take your decision," said John. "You're only a child yet. In two years' time you'll be wiser. I'll ask you again then."

"All right," said Ella. "I'll answer you again then."

John went away, angry, but determined.

Arnold was less categorical.

"I've no right to say a word," he began, and then said it. Mostly he dilated on her beauty and goodness—and his overmastering affection for her.

"Are you offering marriage?" she inquired, rather quizzically.

"Why yes—of course!" said he, "only—only I've nothing to offer."

"There's you!" said Ella.

"But that's so little!" said Arnold. "O! if you will wait for me!—I will work!"

"What will you work at?" said Ella.

Arnold laughed. Ella laughed. "I love to camp out!" said she.

"Will you wait for me a year?" said Arnold.

"Ye-es," said Ella. "I'll even wait two—if I have to. But no longer!"

"What will you do then?" asked Arnold miserably.

"Marry you," said Ella.

So Arnold went off to his Hill.

What was one hill among so many? There they arose about him, far green, farther blue, farthest purple, rolling away to the real peaks of the Catskills. This one had been part of his mother's father's land; a big stretch, coming down to them from an old Dutch grant. It ran out like a promontory into the winding valley below; the valley that had been a real river when the Catskills were real mountains. There was some river there yet, a little sulky stream, fretting most of the year in its sunken stony bed, and losing its temper altogether when the spring floods came.

Arnold did not care much for the river—he had a brook

of his own; an ideal brook, beginning with an overflowing spring; and giving him three waterfalls and a lake on his own land. It was a very little lake and handmade. In one place his brook ran through a narrow valley or valleyette—so small it was; and a few weeks of sturdy work had damned the exit and made a lovely pool. Arnold did that years ago, when he was a great hulking brooding boy, and used to come up there with his mother in summer; while his father stuck to the office and John went to Bar Harbor with his chums. Arnold could work hard even if he was a poet.

He quarried stone from his hill—as everyone did in those regions; and built a small solid house, adding to it from year to year; that was a growing joy as long as the dear mother lived.

This was high up, near the dark, clear pool of the spring; he had piped the water into the house—for his mother's comfort. It stood on a level terrace, fronting south-westward; and every season he did more to make it lovely. There was a fine smooth lawn there now and flowering vines and bushes; every pretty wild thing that would grow and bloom of itself in that region, he collected about him.

That dear mother had delighted in all the plants and trees; she studied about them and made observations, while he enjoyed them—and made poems. The chestnuts were their common pride. This hill stood out among all the others in the flowering time, like a great pompon, and the odor of it was by no means attractive—unless you happened to like it, as they did.

The chestnut crop was tremendous; and when Arnold found that not only neighboring boys, but business expeditions from the city made a practice of rifling his mountain garden, he raged for one season and acted the next. When the first frost dropped the great burrs, he was on hand, with

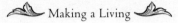

a posse of strong young fellows from the farms about. They beat and shook and harvested, and sack upon sack of glossy brown nuts were piled on wagons and sent to market by the owner instead of the depredator.

Then he and his mother made great plans, the eager boy full of ambition. He studied forestry and arboriculture; and grafted the big fat foreign chestnut on his sturdy native stocks, while his father sneered and scolded because he would not go into the office.

Now he was left to himself with his plans and hopes. The dear mother was gone, but the hill was there—and Ella might come some day; there was a chance.

"What do you think of it?" he said to Patsy. Patsy was not Irish. He was an Italian from Tuscany; a farmer and forester by birth and breeding, a soldier by compulsion, an American citizen by choice.

"Fine!" said Patsy. "Fine. Ver' good. You do well."

They went over the ground together. "Could you build a little house here?" said Arnold. "Could you bring your wife? Could she attend to my house up there? and could you keep hens and a cow and raise vegetables on this patch here— enough for all of us? you to own the house and land—only you cannot sell it except to me?"

Then Patsy thanked his long neglected saints, imported his wife and little ones, took his eldest daughter out of the box factory, and his eldest son out of the printing office; and by the end of the summer they were comfortably established and ready to attend to the chestnut crop.

Arnold worked as hard as his man. Temporarily he hired other sturdy Italians, mechanics of experience; and spent his little store of capital in a way that would have made his father swear and his brother jeer at him.

When the year was over he had not much money left, but

he had by his second waterfall a small electrical plant, with a printing office attached; and by the third a solid little mill, its turbine wheel running merrily in the ceaseless pour. Millstones cost more money than he thought, but there they were—brought up by night from the Hudson River—that his neighbors might not laugh too soon. Over the mill were large light rooms, pleasant to work in; with the shade of mighty trees upon the roof; and the sound of falling water in the sun.

By next summer this work was done, and the extra workmen gone. Whereat our poet refreshed himself with a visit to his Ella, putting in some lazy weeks with her at Gloucester, happy and hopeful, but silent.

"How's the chestnut crop?" she asked him.

"Fine. Ver' good," he answered. "That's what Patsy says—and Patsy knows."

She pursued her inquiries. "Who cooks for you? Who keeps your camp in order? Who washes your clothes?"

"Mrs. Patsy," said he. "She's as good a cook as anybody need want."

"And how is the prospect?" asked Ella.

Arnold turned lazily over, where he lay on the sand at her feet, and looked at her long and hungrily. "The prospect," said he, "is divine."

Ella blushed and laughed and said he was a goose; but he kept on looking.

He wouldn't tell her much, though. "Don't, dear," he said when she urged for information. "It's too serious. If I should fail—"

"You won't fail!" she protested. "You can't fail! And if you do—why—as I told you before, I like to camp out!"

But when he tried to take some natural advantage of her friendliness she teased him—said he was growing to look just like his father! Which made them both laugh.

Then Arnold returned and settled down to business. He purchased stores of pasteboard, of paper, of printers ink, and a little machine to fold cartons. Thus equipped he retired to his fastness, and set dark-eyed Caterlina to work in a little box factory of his own; while clever Guiseppe ran the printing press, and Mafalda pasted. Cartons, piled flat, do not take up much room, even in thousands.

Then Arnold loafed deliberately.

"Why not your Mr. Blake work no more?" inquired Mrs. Patsy of her spouse.

"O he work—he work hard," replied Patsy. "You women—you not understand work!"

Mrs. Patsy tossed her head and answered in fluent Italian, so that her husband presently preferred out of doors occupation; but in truth Arnold Blake did not seem to do much that summer. He loafed under his great trees, regarding them lovingly; he loafed by his lonely upper waterfall, with happy dreaming eyes; he loafed in his little blue lake—floating face to the sky, care free and happy as a child. And if he scribbled a great deal—at any sudden moment when the fit seized him, why that was only his weakness as a poet.

Toward the end of September, he invited an old college friend up to see him; now a newspaper man—in the advertising department. These two seemed to have merry times together. They fished and walked and climbed, they talked much; and at night were heard roaring with laughter by their hickory fire.

"Have you got any money left?" demanded his friend.

"About a thou—" said Arnold. "And that's got to last me till next spring, you know."

"Blow it in—blow in every cent—it'll pay you. You can live through the winter somehow. How about transportation?"

"Got a nice electric dray—light and strong. Runs down hill

with the load to tidewater, you see, and there's the old motor-boat to take it down. Brings back supplies."

"Great! It's simply great! Now, you save enough to eat till spring and give me the rest. Send me your stuff, all of it! and as soon as you get in a cent above expenses—send me that—I'll 'tend to the advertising!"

He did. He had only $800.00 to begin with. When the first profits began to come in he used them better; and as they rolled up he still spent them. Arnold began to feel anxious, to want to save money; but his friend replied: "You furnish the meal—I'll furnish the market!" And he did.

He began it in the subway in New York; that place of misery where eyes, ears, nose, and common self-respect are all offended, and even an advertisement is some relief.

"Hill" said the first hundred dollars, on a big blank space for a week. "Mill" said the second. "Hill Mill Meal," said the third.

The fourth was more explicit.

"When tired of every cereal
Try our new material—
Hill Mill Meal."

The fifth—
"Ask your grocer if you feel
An interest in Hill Mill Meal.
Samples free."

The sixth—
"A paradox! Surprising! True!
Made of chestnuts but brand new!
Hill Mill Meal."

And the seventh—
"Solomon said it couldn't be done,
There wasn't a new thing under the sun—
He never ate Hill Mill Meal!"

Seven hundred dollars went in this one method only; and meanwhile diligent young men in automobiles were making arrangements and leaving circulars and samples with the grocer.

Anybody will take free samples and everybody likes chestnuts. Are they not the crown of luxury in turkey stuffing? The gem of the confection as *marrons glacés*? The sure profit of the corner-merchant with his little charcoal stove, even when they are half scorched and half cold? Do we not all love them, roast, or boiled—only they are so messy to peel.

Arnold's only secret was his process; but his permanent advantage was in the fine quality of his nuts, and his exquisite care in manufacture. In dainty, neat, easily opened cartons (easily shut too, so they were not left gaping to gather dust), he put upon the market a sort of stamp, chestnuts perfectly shelled and husked, roasted and ground, both coarse and fine. Good? You stood and ate half a package out of your hand, just tasting of it. Then you sat down and ate the other half.

He made pocket-size cartons, filled with whole ones, crafty man! And they became "The Business Man's Lunch" forthwith. A pocketful of roast chestnuts—and no mess nor trouble! And when they were boiled—well, we all know how good boiled chestnuts are. As to the meal, a new variety of mush appeared, and gems, muffins, and pancakes that made old epicures feel young again in the joys of a fresh taste, and gave America new standing in the eyes of France.

The orders rolled in and the poetry rolled out. The market for a new food is as wide as the world; and Jim Chamberlain was mad to conquer it, but Arnold explained to him that his total output was only so many bushels a year.

"Nonsense!" said Jim. "You're a—a—well, a *poet*! Come! Use your imagination! Look at these hills about you—they could grow chestnuts to the horizon! Look at this valley, that rattling river, a bunch of mills could run here! You can support a fine population—a whole village of people—there's no end to it, I tell you!"

"And where would my privacy be then and the beauty of the place?" asked Arnold, "I love this green island of chestnut trees, and the winding empty valley, just freckled with a few farms. I'd hate to support a village!"

"But you can be a Millionaire!" said Jim.

"I don't want to be a Millionaire," Arnold cheerfully replied.

Jim gazed at him, opening and shutting his mouth in silence. "You—confounded old—*poet*!" he burst forth at last.

"I can't help that," said Arnold.

"You'd better ask Miss Sutherland about it, I think," his friend drily suggested.

"To be sure! I had forgotten that—I will," the poet replied.

Then he invited her to come up and visit his Hill, met her at the train with the smooth, swift, noiseless, smell-less electric car, and held her hand in blissful silence as they rolled up the valley road. They wound more slowly up his graded avenue, green-arched by chestnut boughs.

He showed her the bit of meadowy inlet where the mill stood, by the heavy lower fall; the broad bright packing rooms above, where the busy Italian boys and girls chattered gaily as they worked. He showed her the second fall, with his little low-humming electric plant; a bluestone building, vine-covered, lovely, a tiny temple to the flower-god.

"It does our printing," said Arnold, "gives us light, heat and telephones. And runs the cars."

Then he showed her the shaded reaches of his lake, still, starred with lilies, lying dark under the curving boughs of water maples, doubling the sheer height of flower-crowned cliffs.

She held his hand tighter as they wound upward, circling the crown of the hill that she might see the splendid range of outlook; and swinging smoothly down a little and out on the green stretch before the house.

Ella gasped with delight. Gray, rough and harmonious, hung with woodbine and wild grape, broad-porched and wide-windowed, it faced the setting sun. She stood looking, looking, over the green miles of tumbling hills, to the blue billowy far-off peaks swimming in soft light.

"There's the house," said Arnold, "furnished—there's a view room built on—for you, dear; I did it myself. There's the hill—and the little lake and one waterfall all for us! And the spring, and the garden, and some very nice Italians. And it will earn—my Hill and Mill, about three or four thousand dollars a year—above *all* expenses!"

"How perfectly splendid!" said Ella. "But there's one thing you've left out!"

"What's that?" he asked, a little dashed.

"*You!*" she answered. "Arnold Blake! My Poet!"

"Oh, I forgot," he added, after some long still moments. "I ought to ask you about this first. Jim Chamberlain says I can cover all these hills with chestnuts, fill this valley with people, string that little river with a row of mills, make breakfast for all the world—and be a Millionaire. Shall I?"

"For goodness sake—*No!*" said Ella. "Millionaire, indeed! And spoil the most perfect piece of living I ever saw or heard of!"

Then there was a period of bliss, indeed there was enough to last indefinitely.

But one pleasure they missed. They never saw even the astonished face, much less the highly irritated mind, of old John Blake, when he first returned from his two years of travel. The worst of it was he had eaten the stuff all the way home and liked it! They told him it was Chestnut Meal—but that meant nothing to him. Then he began to find the jingling advertisements in every magazine; things that ran in his head and annoyed him.

"When corn or rice no more are nice,
When oatmeal seems to pall,
When cream of wheat's no longer sweet
And you abhor them all—"

"I do abhor them all!" the old man would vow, and take up a newspaper, only to read:

"Better than any food that grows
Upon or in the ground,
Strong, pure and sweet
And good to eat
Our tree-born nuts are found."

"Bah!" said Mr. Blake, and tried another, which only showed him:

"Good for mother, good for brother,
Good for child;
As for father—well, rather!
He's just wild."

He was.
But the truth never dawned upon him till he came to this one:

"About my hut
There grew a nut
Nutritious;
I could but feel
'Twould make a meal
Delicious.

I had a Hill,
I built a Mill
Upon it.
And hour by hour
I sought for power
To run it.

To burn my trees
Or try the breeze
Seemed crazy;
To use my arm
Had little charm—
I'm lazy!

The nuts are here,
But coal!—Quite dear
We find it!
We have the stuff.
Where's power enough
To grind it?

What force to find
My nuts to grind?—
I've found it!
The Water-fall
Could beat 'em all—

And ground it!
PETER POETICUS."

"Confound your impudence!" he wrote to his son. "And confound your poetic stupidity in not making a Big Business now you've got a start? But I understand you do make a living, and I'm thankful for that."

Arnold and Ella, watching the sunset from their hammock, laughed softly together, and lived.

Martha's Mother

IT WAS NINE feet long.

It was eight feet high.

It was six feet wide.

There was a closet, actually!—a closet one foot deep—that was why she took this room. There was the bed, and the trunk, and just room to open the closet door part way—that accounted for the length. There was the bed and the bureau and the chair—that accounted for the width. Between the bedside and the bureau and chair side was a strip extending the whole nine feet. There was room to turn around by the window. There was room to turn round by the door. Martha was thin.

One, two, three, four—turn.

One, two, three, four—turn.

She managed it nicely.

"It is a stateroom," she always said to herself. "It is a luxurious, large, well-furnished stateroom with a real window. It is *not* a cell."

Martha had a vigorous constructive imagination. Sometimes it was the joy of her life, her magic carpet, her Aladdin's lamp. Sometimes it frightened her—frightened her horribly, it was so strong.

The cell idea had come to her one gloomy day, and she had foolishly allowed it to enter—played with it a little while. Since then she had to keep a special bar on that particular intruder, so she had arranged a stateroom "set," and forcibly kept it on hand.

Martha was a stenographer and typewriter in a real estate office. She got $12 a week, and was thankful for it. It was steady pay, and enough to live on. Seven dollars she paid for board and lodging, ninety cents for her six lunches, ten a day for carfare, including Sundays; seventy-five for laundry; one for her mother—that left one dollar and sixty-five cents for clothes, shoes, gloves, everything. She had tried cheaper board, but made up the cost in doctor's bills; and lost a good place by being ill.

"Stone walls do not a prison make, nor hall bedrooms a cage," said she determinedly. "Now then—here is another evening—what shall I do? Library? No. My eyes are tired. Besides, three times a week is enough. 'Tisn't club night. Will *not* sit in the parlor. Too wet to walk. Can't sew, worse'n reading—O good *land!* I'm almost ready to go with Basset!"

She shook herself and paced up and down again.

Prisoners form the habit of talking to themselves—this was the suggestion that floated through her mind—that cell idea again.

"I've got to get out of this!" said Martha, stopping short. "It's enough to drive a girl crazy!"

The driving process was stayed by a knock at the door. "Excuse me for coming up," said a voice. "It's Mrs. MacAvelly."

Martha knew this lady well. She was a friend of Miss Podder at the Girls' Trade Union Association. "Come in. I'm glad to see you!" she said hospitably. "Have the chair—or the bed's really more comfortable!"

"I was with Miss Podder this evening and she was anxious to know whether your union has gained any since the last meeting—I told her I'd find out—I had nothing else to do. Am I intruding?"

"Intruding!" Martha, gave a short laugh. "Why, it's a godsend, Mrs. MacAvelly! If you knew how dull the evenings are to us girls!"

"Don't you—go out much? To—to theaters—or parks?" The lady's tone was sympathetic and not inquisitive.

"Not very much," said Martha, rather sardonically. "Theaters—two girls, two dollars, and twenty cents carfare. Parks, twenty cents—walk your feet off, or sit on the benches and be stared at. Museums—not open evenings."

"But don't you have visitors—in the parlor here?"

"Did you see it?" asked Martha.

Mrs. MacAvelly had seen it. It was cold and also stuffy. It was ugly and shabby and stiff. Three tired girls sat there, two trying to read by a strangled gaslight overhead; one trying to entertain a caller in a social fiction of privacy at the other end of the room.

"Yes, we have visitors—but mostly they ask us out. And some of us don't go," said Martha darkly.

"I see, I see!" said Mrs. MacAvelly, with a pleasant smile; and Martha wondered whether she did see, or was just being civil.

"For instance, there's Mr. Basset," the girl pursued, somewhat recklessly; meaning that her visitor should understand her.

"Mr. Basset?"

"Yes, 'Pond & Basset'—one of my employers."

Mrs. MacAvelly looked pained. "Couldn't you—er—avoid it?" she suggested.

"You mean shake him?" asked Martha. "Why, yes—I could.

Might lose my job. Get another place—another Basset, probably."

"I see!" said Mrs. MacAvelly again. "Like the Fox and the Swarm of Flies! There ought to be a more comfortable way of living for all you girls! And how about the union—I have to be going back to Miss Podder."

Martha gave her the information she wanted, and started to accompany her downstairs. They heard the thin jangle of the doorbell, down through the echoing halls, and the dragging feet of the servant coming up. A kinky black head was thrust in at the door.

"Mr. Basset, callin' on Miss Joyce," was announced formally.

Martha stiffened. "Please tell Mr. Basset I am not feeling well to-night—and beg to be excused."

She looked rather defiantly at her guest, as Lucy clattered down the long stairs; then stole to the railing and peered down the narrow well. She heard the message given with pompous accuracy, and then heard the clear, firm tones of Mr. Basset:

"Tell Miss Joyce that I will wait."

Martha returned to her room in three long steps, slipped off her shoes and calmly got into bed. "Goodnight, Mrs. MacAvelly," she said. "I'm so sorry, but my head aches and I've gone to bed! Would you be so very good as to tell Lucy so as you're going down."

Mrs. MacAvelly said she would, and departed, and Martha lay conscientiously quiet till she heard the door shut far below.

She was quiet, but she was not contented.

Yet the discontent of Martha was as nothing to the discontent of Mrs. Joyce, her mother, in her rural home. Here was a woman of fifty-three, alert, vigorous, nervously active; but an automobile-agitated horse had danced upon her, and her usefulness, as she understood it, was over. She could not get about without crutches, nor use her hands for needlework,

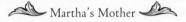

though still able to write after a fashion. Writing was not her *forte,* however, at the best of times.

She lived with a widowed sister in a little, lean dusty farmhouse by the side of the road; a hill road that went nowhere in particular, and was too steep for those who were going there.

Brisk on her crutches, Mrs. Joyce hopped about the little house, there was nowhere else to hop to. She had talked her sister out long since—Mary never had much to say. Occasionally they quarreled and then Mrs. Joyce hopped only in her room, a limited process.

She sat at the window one day, staring greedily out at the lumpy rock-ribbed road; silent, perforce, and tapping the arms of her chair with nervous intensity. Suddenly she called out, "Mary! Mary Ames! Come here quick! There's somebody coming up the road!"

Mary came in, as fast as she could with eggs in her apron. "It's Mrs. Holmes!" she said. "And a boarder, I guess."

"No, it ain't," said Mrs. Joyce, eagerly. "It's that woman that's visiting the Holmes—she was in church last week, Myra Slater told me about her. Her name's MacDowell, or something."

"It ain't MacDowell," said her sister. "I remember; it's MacAvelly."

This theory was borne out by Mrs. Holmes' entrance and introduction of her friend.

"Have you any eggs for us, Mrs. Ames?" she said.

"Set down—set down," said Mrs. Ames cordially. "I was just getting in my eggs—but here's only about eight yet. How many was you wantin'?"

"I want all you can find," said Mrs. Holmes. "Two dozen, three dozen—all I can carry."

"There's two hens layin' out—I'll go and look them up.

And I ain't been in the woodshed chamber yet. I'll go'n hunt. You set right here with my sister." And Mrs. Ames bustled off.

"Pleasant view you have here," said Mrs. MacAvelly politely, while Mrs. Holmes rocked and fanned herself.

"Pleasant! Glad you think so, ma'am. Maybe you city folks wouldn't think so much of views if you had nothing else to look at!"

"What would you like to look at?"

"Folks!" said Mrs. Joyce briefly. "Lots of folks! Somethin' doin'."

"You'd like to live in the city?"

"Yes, ma'am—I would so! I worked in the city once when I was a girl. Waitress. In a big restaurant. I got to be cashier— in two years! I like the business!"

"And then you married a farmer?" suggested Mrs. Holmes.

"Yes, I did. And I never was sorry, Mrs. Holmes. David Joyce was a mighty good man. We was engaged before I left home—I was workin' to help earn, so 't we could marry."

"There's plenty of work on a farm, isn't there?" Mrs. MacAvelly inquired.

Mrs. Joyce's eager eyes kindled.

"There is *so!*" she agreed. "Lots to do. And lots to manage! We kept help then, and the farm hands, and the children growin' up. And some seasons we took boarders."

"Did you like that?"

"I did. I liked it first rate. I like lots of people, and to do for 'em. The best time I ever had was one summer I ran a hotel."

"Ran a hotel! How interesting!"

"Yes'm—it was interesting! I had a cousin who kept a summer hotel up here in the mountains a piece—and he was shorthanded that summer and got me to go up and help him

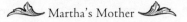

out. Then he was taken sick, and I had the whole thing on my shoulders! I just enjoyed it! And the place cleared more that summer'n it ever did! He said 'twas owin' to his advantageous buyin'. Maybe 'twas! But I could 'a bought more advantageous than he did—I could a' told him that. Point o' fact, I did tell him that—and he wouldn't have me again."

"That was a pity!" said Mrs. Holmes. "And I suppose if it wasn't for your foot you would do that now—and enjoy it!"

"Of course I could!" protested Mrs. Joyce. "Do it better 'n ever, city or country! But here I am, tied by the leg! And dependent on my sister and children! It galls me terribly!"

Mrs. Holmes nodded sympathetically. "You are very brave, Mrs. Joyce," she said. "I admire your courage, and—" she couldn't say patience, so she said, "cheerfulness."

Mrs. Ames came in with more eggs. "Not enough, but some," she said, and the visitors departed therewith.

Toward the end of the summer, Miss Podder at the Girls' Trade Union Association, sweltering in the little office, was pleased to receive a call from her friend, Mrs. MacAvelly.

"I'd no idea you were in town," she said.

"I'm not, officially," answered her visitor, "just stopping over between visits. It's hotter than I thought it would be, even on the upper west side."

"Think what it is on the lower east side!" answered Miss Podder, eagerly. "Hot all day—and hot at night! My girls do suffer so! They are so crowded!"

"How do the clubs get on?" asked Mrs. MacAvelly. "Have your girls any residence clubs yet?"

"No—nothing worth while. It takes somebody to run it right, you know. The girls can't; the people who work for money can't meet our wants—and the people who work for love, don't work well as a rule."

Mrs. MacAvelly smiled sympathetically. "You're quite right

about that," she said. "But really—some of those 'Homes' are better than others, aren't they?"

"The girls hate them," answered Miss Podder. "They'd rather board—even two or three in a room. They like their independence. You remember Martha Joyce?"

Mrs. MacAvelly remembered. "Yes," she said, "I do—I met her mother this summer."

"She's a cripple, isn't she?" asked Miss Podder. "Martha's told me about her."

"Why, not exactly. She's what a Westerner might call 'crippled up some,' but she's livelier than most well persons." And she amused her friend with a vivid rehearsal of Mrs. Joyce's love of the city and her former triumphs in restaurant and hotel.

"She'd be a fine one to run such a house for the girls, wouldn't she?" suddenly cried Miss Podder.

"Why—if she could," Mrs. MacAvelly admitted slowly.

"*Could!* Why not? You say she gets about easily enough. All she'd have to do is *manage*, you see. She could order by 'phone and keep the servants running!"

"I'm sure she'd like it," said Mrs. MacAvelly. "But don't such things require capital?"

Miss Podder was somewhat daunted. "Yes—some; but I guess we could raise it. If we could find the right house!"

"Let's look in the paper," suggested her visitor. "I've got a *Herald*."

"There's one that reads all right," Miss Podder presently proclaimed. "The location's good, and it's got a lot of rooms—furnished. I suppose it would cost too much."

Mrs. MacAvelly agreed, rather ruefully.

"Come," she said, "it's time to close here, surely. Let's go and look at that house, anyway. It's not far."

They got their permit and were in the house very shortly.

"I remember this place," said Miss Podder. "It was for sale earlier in the summer."

It was one of those once spacious houses, not of "old," but at least of "middle-aged" New York; with large rooms arbitrarily divided into smaller ones.

"It's been a boarding-house, that's clear," said Mrs. MacAvelly.

"Why, of course," Miss Podder answered, eagerly plunging about and examining everything. "Anybody could see that! But it's been done over—most thoroughly. The cellar's all whitewashed, and there's a new furnace, and new range, and look at this icebox!" It was an ice-closet, as a matter of fact, of large capacity, and a most sanitary aspect.

"Isn't it too big?" Mrs. MacAvelly inquired.

"Not for a boarding-house, my dear," Miss Podder enthusiastically replied. "Why, they could buy a side of beef with that icebox! And look at the extra ovens! Did you ever see a place better furnished—for what we want? It looks as if it had been done on purpose!"

"It does, doesn't it?" said Mrs. MacAvelly.

Miss Podder, eager and determined, let no grass grow under her feet. The rent of the place was within reason.

"If they had twenty boarders—and some 'mealers,' I believe it could be done!" she said. "It's a miracle—this house. Seems as if somebody had done it just for us!"

Armed with a list of girls who would agree to come, for six and seven dollars a week, Miss Podder made a trip to Willettville and laid the matter before Martha's mother.

"What an outrageous rent!" said that lady.

"Yes—New York rents *are* rather inconsiderate," Miss Podder admitted. "But see, here's a guaranteed income if the girls stay—and I'm sure they will; and if the cooking's good you could easily get table boarders besides."

Mrs. Joyce hopped to the bureau and brought out a hard, sharp-pointed pencil, and a lined writing tablet.

"Let's figure it out," said she. "You say that house rents furnished at $3,200. It would take a cook and a chambermaid!"

"And a furnace man," said Miss Podder. "They come to about fifty a year. The cook would be thirty a month, the maid twenty-five, if you got first-class help, and you'd need it."

"That amounts to $710 altogether," stated Mrs. Joyce.

"Fuel and light and such things would be $200," Miss Podder estimated, "and I think you ought to allow $200 more for breakage and extras generally."

"That's $4,310 already," said Mrs. Joyce.

"Then there's the food," Miss Podder went on. "How much do you think it would cost to feed twenty girls, two meals a day, and three Sundays?"

"And three more," Mrs. Joyce added, "with me, and the help, twenty-three. I could do it for $2.00 a week apiece."

"Oh!" said Miss Podder. "*Could* you? At New York prices?"

"See me do it!" said Mrs. Joyce.

"That makes a total expense of $6,710 a year. Now, what's the income, ma'am?"

The income was clear—if they could get it. Ten girls at $6.00 and ten at $7.00 made $130.00 a week—$6,760.00 a year.

"There you are!" said Mrs. Joyce triumphantly. "And the 'mealers'—if my griddlecakes don't fetch 'em I'm mistaken! If I have ten—at $5.00 a week and clear $3.00 off 'em—that'll be another bit $1,560.00 more. Total income $8,320.00. More'n one thousand clear! Maybe I can feed 'em a little higher—or charge less!"

The two women worked together for an hour or so; Mrs.

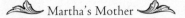

Ames drawn in later with demands as to butter, eggs, and "eatin' chickens."

"There's an ice-box as big as a closet," said Miss Podder.

Mrs. Joyce smiled triumphantly. "Good!" she said. "I can buy my critters of Judson here and have him freight 'em down. I can get apples here and potatoes, and lots of stuff."

"You'll need, probably, a little capital to start with," suggested Miss Podder. "I think the Association could—"

"It don't have to, thank you just the same," said Mrs. Joyce. "I've got enough in my stocking to take me to New York and get some fuel. Besides, all my boarders is goin' to pay in advance—that's the one sure way. The mealers can buy tickets!"

Her eyes danced. She fairly coursed about the room on her nimble crutches. "My!" she said, "it will seem good to have my girl to feed again."

The house opened in September, full of eager girls with large appetites long unsatisfied. The place was new-smelling, fresh-painted, beautifully clean. The furnishing was cheap, but fresh, tasteful, with minor conveniences dear to the hearts of women.

The smallest rooms were larger than hall bedrooms, the big ones were shared by friends. Martha and her mother had a chamber with two beds and space to spare!

The dining-room was very large, and at night the tables were turned into "settles" by the wall and the girls could dance to the sound of a hired pianola. So could the "mealers," when invited; and there was soon a waiting list of both sexes.

"I guess I can make a livin'," said Mrs. Joyce, "allowin' for bad years."

"I don't understand how you feed us so well—for so little," said Miss Podder, who was one of the boarders.

"'Sh!" said Mrs. Joyce, privately. "Your breakfast don't

really cost more'n ten cents—nor your dinner fifteen—not the way I order! Things taste good 'cause they're *cooked* good—that's all!"

"And you have no troubles with your help?"

"'Sh!" said Mrs. Joyce again, more privately. "I work 'em hard—and pay 'em a bonus—a dollar a week extra, as long as they give satisfaction. It reduces my profits some—but it's worth it!"

"It's worth it to us, I'm sure!" said Miss Podder.

Mrs. MacAvelly called one evening in the first week, with warm interest and approval. The tired girls were sitting about in comfortable rockers and lounges, under comfortable lights, reading and sewing. The untired ones were dancing in the dining-room, to the industrious pianola, or having games of cards in the parlor.

"Do you think it'll be a success?" she asked her friend.

"It *is* a success!" Miss Podder triumphantly replied. "I'm immensely proud of it!"

"I should think you would be," said Mrs. MacAvelly.

The doorbell rang sharply.

Mrs. Joyce was hopping through the hall at the moment, and promptly opened it.

"Does Miss Martha Joyce board here?" inquired a gentleman.

"She does."

"I should like to see her," said he, handing in his card.

Mrs. Joyce read the card and looked at the man, her face setting in hard lines. She had heard that name before.

"Miss Joyce is engaged," she replied curtly, still holding the door.

He could see past her into the bright, pleasant rooms. He heard the music below, the swing of dancing feet, Martha's gay laugh from the parlor.

The little lady on crutches blocked his path.

"Are you the housekeeper of this place?" he asked sharply.
"I'm more'n that!" she answered. "I'm Martha's mother."
Mr. Basset concluded he would not wait.

A Middle-
Sized Artist

WHEN ROSAMOND'S BROWN eyes seemed almost too big for her brilliant little face, and her brown curls danced on her shoulders, she had a passionate enthusiasm for picture books. She loved "the reading," but when the picture made what her young mind was trying to grasp suddenly real before her, the stimulus reaching the brain from two directions at once, she used to laugh with delight and hug the book.

The vague new words describing things she never saw suggested "castle," a thing of gloom and beauty; and then upon the page came The Castle itself, looming dim and huge before her, with drooping heavy banners against the sunset calm.

How she had regretted it, scarce knowing why, when the pictures were less real than the description; when the princess, whose beauty made her the Rose of the World (her name was Rosamond, too!), appeared in visible form no prettier, no, not as pretty, as The Fair One with The Golden Locks in the other book! And what an outcry she made to her indifferent family when first confronted by the unbelievable blasphemy of an illustration that differed from the text!

"But, Mother—see!" she cried. "It says, 'Her beauty was crowned by rich braids of golden hair, wound thrice around her shapely head,' and this girl has black hair—in curls! Did the man forget what he just said?"

Her mother didn't seem to care at all. "They often get them wrong," she said. "Perhaps it was an old plate. Run away, dear, Mama is very busy."

But Rosamond cared.

She asked her father more particularly about this mysterious "old plate," and he, being a publisher, was able to give her much information thereanent. She learned that these wonderful reinforcements of her adored stories did not emanate direct from the brain of the beneficent author, but were a supplementary product by some draughtsman, who cared far less for what was in the author's mind than for what was in his own; who was sometimes lazy, sometimes arrogant, sometimes incompetent; sometimes all three. That to find a real artist, who could make pictures and was willing to make them like the picture the author saw, was very unusual.

"You see, little girl," said Papa, "the big artists are too big to do it—they'd rather make their own pictures; and the little artists are too little—they can't make real ones of their own ideas, nor yet of another's."

"Aren't there any middle-sized artists?" asked the child.

"Sometimes," said her father; and then he showed her some of the perfect illustrations which leave nothing to be desired, as the familiar ones by Teniel and Henry Holiday, which make Alice's Adventures and the Hunting of the Snark so doubly dear, Dore and Retsch and Tony Johannot and others.

"When I grow up," said Rosamond decidedly, "I'm going to be a middle-sized artist!"

Fortunately for her aspirations the line of study required was in no way different at first from that of general education. Her parents explained that a good illustrator ought to know pretty much everything. So she obediently went through school and college, and when the time came for real work at her drawing there was no objection to that.

"It is pretty work," said her mother, "a beautiful accomplishment. It will always be a resource for her."

"A girl is better off to have an interest," said her father, "and not marry the first fool that asks her. When she does fall in love this won't stand in the way; it never does; with a woman. Besides—she may need it sometime."

So her father helped and her mother did not hinder, and when the brown eyes were less disproportionate and the brown curls wreathed high upon her small fine head, she found herself at twenty-one more determined to be a middle-sized artist than she was at ten.

Then love came; in the person of one of her father's readers; a strenuous new-fledged college graduate; big, handsome, domineering, opinionated; who was accepting a salary of four dollars a week for the privilege of working in a publishing house, because he loved books and meant to write them some day.

They saw a good deal of each other, and were pleasantly congenial. She sympathized with his criticisms of modern fiction; he sympathized with her criticisms of modern illustration; and her young imagination began to stir with sweet memories of poetry and romance; and sweet hopes of beautiful reality.

There are cases where the longest way round is the shortest way home; but Mr. Allen G. Goddard chose differently. He had read much about women and about love, beginning with a full foundation from the ancients; but lacked an understanding of the modern woman, such as he had to deal with.

Therefore, finding her evidently favorable, his theories and inclinations suiting, he made hot love to her, breathing, "My Wife!" into her ear before she had scarce dared to think "my darling!" and suddenly wrapping her in his arms with hot kisses, while she was still musing on "The Hugenot Lovers" and the kisses she dared dream of came in slow gradation as in the *Sonnets from the Portuguese.*

He was in desperate earnest. "O you are so beautiful!" he cried. "So unbelievably beautiful! Come to me, my Sweet!" for she had sprung away and stood panting and looking at him, half reproachful, half angry.

"You love me, Dearest! You cannot deny it!" he cried. "And I love you—Ah! You shall know!"

He was single-hearted, sincere; stirred by a very genuine overwhelming emotion. She on the contrary was moved by many emotions at once;—a pleasure she was half ashamed of; a disappointment she could not clearly define; as if some one had told her the whole plot of a promising new novel; a sense of fear of the new hopes she had been holding, and of startled loyalty to her long-held purposes.

"Stop!" she said—for he evidently mistook her agitation, and thought her silence was consent. "I suppose I do—love you—a little; but you've no right to kiss me like that!"

His eyes shone. "You Darling! *My* Darling!" he said. "You will give me the right, won't you? Now, Dearest—see! I am waiting!" And he held out his arms to her.

But Rosamond was more and more displeased. "You will have to wait. I'm sorry; but I'm not ready to be engaged, yet! You know my plans. Why I'm going to Paris this year! I'm going to work! It will be ever so long before I'm ready to—to settle down."

"As to that," he said more calmly, "I cannot of course offer immediate marriage, but we can wait for that—together! You surely will not leave me—if you love me!"

"I think I love you," she said conscientiously, "at least I did think so. You've upset it all, somehow—you hurry me so!—no—I can't bind myself yet."

"Do you tell me to wait for you?" he asked; his deep voice still strong to touch her heart. "How long, Dearest?"

"I'm not asking you to wait for me—I don't want to promise anything—nor to have you. But when I have made a place—am really doing something—perhaps then—"

He laughed harshly. "Do not deceive yourself, child, nor me! If you loved me there would be none of this poor wish for freedom—for a career. You don't love me—that's all!"

He waited for her to deny this. She said nothing. He did not know how hard it was for her to keep from crying—and from running to his arms.

"Very well," said he. "Goodbye!"—And he was gone.

All that happened three years ago.

Allen Goddard took it very hard; and added to his earlier ideas about women another, that "the new woman" was a selfish heartless creature, indifferent to her own true nature.

He had to stay where he was and work, owing to the pressure of circumstances, which made it harder; so he became something of a mysogynist; which is not a bad thing when a young man has to live on very little and build a place for himself.

In spite of this cynicism he could not remove from his mind those softly brilliant dark eyes; the earnest thoughtful lines of the pure young face; and the changing lights and shadows in that silky hair. Also, in the course of his work, he was continually reminded of her; for her characteristic drawings appeared more and frequently in the magazines, and grew better, stronger, more convincing from year to year.

Stories of adventure she illustrated admirably; children's stories to perfection; fairy stories—she was the delight of thousands of children, who never once thought that the tiny quaint rose in a circle that was to be found in all those charming pictures meant a name. But he noticed that she never illustrated love stories; and smiled bitterly, to himself.

And Rosamond?

There were moments when she was inclined to forfeit her passage money and throw herself unreservedly into those strong arms which had held her so tightly for a little while. But a bud picked open does not bloom naturally; and her tumultuous feelings were thoroughly dissipated by a long strong attack of *mal de mer*. She derived two advantages from her experience: one a period of safe indifference to all advances from eager fellow students and more cautious older admirers; the other a facility she had not before aspired to in the making of pictures of love and lovers.

She made pictures of him from memory—so good, so moving, that she put them religiously away in a portfolio by themselves; and only took them out—sometimes. She illustrated, solely for her own enjoyment some of her girlhood's best loved poems and stories. "The Rhyme of the Duchess May," "The Letter L," "In a Balcony," "In a Gondola." And hid them from herself even—they rather frightened her.

After three years of work abroad she came home with an established reputation, plenty of orders, and an interest that would not be stifled in the present state of mind of Mr. Allen Goddard.

She found him still at work, promoted to fifteen dollars a week by this time, and adding to his income by writing political and statistical articles for the magazines. He talked, when they met, of this work, with little enthusiasm, and asked her politely about hers.

"Anybody can see mine!" she told him lightly. "And judge it easily."

"Mine too," he answered. "It to-day is—and to-morrow is cast into the wastebasket. He who runs may read—if he runs fast enough."

He told himself he was glad he was not bound to this hard,

bright creature, so unnaturally self-sufficient, and successful.

She told herself that he had never cared for her, really, that was evident.

Then an English publisher who liked her work sent her a new novel by a new writer, "A. Gage." "I know this is out of your usual line," he said, "but I want a woman to do it, and I want you to be the woman, if possible. Read it and see what you think. Any terms you like."

The novel was called "Two and One;" and she began it with languid interest, because she liked that publisher and wished to give full reasons for refusing. It opened with two young people who were much in love with one another; the girl a talented young sculptor with a vivid desire for fame; and another girl, a cousin of the man, ordinary enough, but pretty and sweet, and with no desires save those of romance and domesticity. The first couple broke off a happy engagement because she insisted on studying in Paris, and her lover, who could neither go with her, nor immediately marry her, naturally objected.

Rosamond sat up in bed; pulled a shawl round her, swung the electric light nearer, and went on.

The man was broken-hearted; he suffered tortures of loneliness, disappointment, doubt, self-depreciation. He waited, held at his work by a dependent widowed mother; hoping against hope that his lost one would come back. The girl meanwhile made good in her art work; she was not a great sculptor but a popular portraitist and maker of little genre groups. She had other offers, but refused them, being hardened in her ambitions, and, possibly, still withheld by her early love.

The man after two or three years of empty misery and hard grinding work, falls desperately ill; the pretty cousin helps the mother nurse him, and shows her own affection. He offers the broken remnants of his heart, which she eagerly under-takes to patch up; and they become tolerably happy, at least she is.

But the young sculptor in Paris! Rosamond hurried through the pages to the last chapter. There was the haughty and triumphant heroine in her studio. She had been given a medal—she had plenty of orders—she had just refused a Count. Everyone had gone, and she sat alone in her fine studio, self-satisfied and triumphant.

Then she picks up an old American paper which was lying about; reads it idly as she smokes her cigarette—and then both paper and cigarette drop to the floor, and she sits staring.

Then she starts up—her arms out—vainly. "Wait! O Wait!" she cries—"I was coming back,"—and drops into her chair again. The fire is out. She is alone.

Rosamond shut the book and leaned back upon her pillow. Her eyes were shut tight; but a little gleaming line showed on either cheek under the near light. She put the light out and lay quite still.

Allen G. Goddard, in his capacity as "reader" was looking over some popular English novels which his firm wished to arrange about publishing in America. He left "Two and One" to the last. It was the second edition, the illustrated one which he had not seen yet; the first he had read before. He regarded it from time to time with a peculiar expression.

"Well," he said to himself, "I suppose I can stand it if the others do." And he opened the book.

The drawing was strong work certainly, in a style he did not know. They were striking pictures, vivid, real, carrying out in last detail the descriptions given, and the very spirit of the book, showing it more perfectly than the words. There was the tender happiness of the lovers, the courage, the firmness, the fixed purpose in the young sculptor insisting on her freedom, and the gay pride of the successful artist in her work.

There was beauty and charm in this character, yet the face was always turned away, and there was a haunting suggestion of familiarity in the figure. The other girl was beautiful, and docile in expression; well-dressed and graceful; yet somehow unattractive, even at her best, as nurse; and the man was extremely well drawn, both in his happy ardor as a lover, and his grinding misery when rejected. He was very good-looking; and here too was this strong sense of resemblance.

"Why he looks like *me*!" suddenly cried the reader—springing to his feet. "Confound his impudence!" he cried. "How in thunder!" Then he looked at the picture again, more carefully, a growing suspicion in his face; and turned hurriedly to the title page,—seeing a name unknown to him.

This subtle, powerful convincing work; this man who undeniably suggested him; this girl whose eyes he could not see; he turned from one to another and hurried to the back of the book.

"The fire was out—she was alone." And there, in the remorseless light of a big lamp before her fireless hearth, the crumpled newspaper beside her, and all hope gone from a limp, crouching little figure, sat—why, he would know her among a thousand—even if her face was buried in her hands, and sunk on the arm of the chair—it was Rosamond!

She was in her little downtown room and hard at work when he entered; but she had time to conceal a new book quickly.

He came straight to her; he had a book in his hand, open—he held it out.

"Did you do this?" he demanded. "Tell me—tell me!" His voice was very unreliable.

She lifted her eyes slowly to his; large, soft, full of dancing lights, and the rich color swept to the gold-lighted borders of her hair.

"Did you?" she asked.

He was taken aback. "I!" said he. "Why it's by—" he showed her the title page. "By A. Gage," he read.

"Yes," said she, "Go on," and he went on, "'Illustrated by A. N. Other.'"

"It's a splendid novel," she said seriously. "Real work—great work. I always knew you'd do it, Allen. I'm so proud of you!" And she held out her hand in the sincere intelligent appreciation of a fellow craftsman.

He took it, still bewildered.

"Thank you," he said. "I value your opinion—honestly I do!" And—with a sudden sweep of recognition. "And yours is great work! Superb! Why you've put more into that story than I knew was there! You make the thing live and breathe! You've put a shadow of remorse in that lonely ruffian there that I was too proud to admit! And you've shown the—unconvincingness of that Other Girl; marvelously. But see here—no more fooling!"

He took her face between his hands, hands that quivered strongly, and forced her to look at him. "Tell me about that last picture! Is it—true?"

Her eyes met his, with the look he longed for. "It is true," she said.

After some time, really it was a long time, but they had not noticed it, he suddenly burst forth. "But how did you *know*?"

She lifted a flushed and smiling face; and pointed to the title page again.

"'A. Gage.'—You threw it down."

"And you—" He threw back his head and laughed delight-edly. "You threw down A-N-Other! O you witch! You immeasurably clever darling! How well our work fits. By Jove! What good times we'll have!"

And they did.

A Word in Season

"Children pick up words like pigeons peas,
And utter them again as God shall please."

WHEN GRANDMA CAME to the breakfast table with her sour little smile and her peremptory "Good morning," every one said "good morning" as politely and pleasantly as they could, but they didn't say very much else. They attempted bravely.

"A fine morning, Mother," Papa observed, but she only answered "Too cold."

"Did you sleep well, Mother?" ventured Mama; and the reply to that was, "No, I never do!"

Then Uncle John tried—he always tried once.

"Have you heard of our new machine, Mrs. Grey? We've got one now that'll catch anything in a room—don't have to talk right into it."

Mrs. Grey looked at him coldly.

"I do not take the least interest in your talking machines, Henry, as I have told you before."

She had, many times before, but Uncle Henry never could learn the astonishing fact. He was more interested in his machines than he was in his business, by far; and spent all his spare time in tinkering with them.

"I think they are wonderful," said little Josie.

"You're my only friend, Kid! I believe you understand 'em almost as well is I do," her Uncle answered gaily; and finished his breakfast as quickly as possible.

So did everybody. It was not appetizing to have Grandma say "How you do dawdle over your meals, Louise!"

Little Josephine slipped down from her chair, with a whispered "'Scuse me Mama!" and whisked into her play room.

"How you do spoil that child!" said Grandma, and Mama closed her lips tight and looked at her husband.

"Now Mother, don't you fret about Josie," said he. "She's a good little girl and quiet as a mouse."

"Anything I can do for you downtown, Mother?"

"No thank you Joseph. I'll go to my room and be out of Louise's way."

"You're not in my way at all, Mother—won't you sit down stairs?"

Young Mrs. Grey made a brave effort to speak cordially, but old Mrs. Grey only looked injured, and said "No thank you, Louise," as she went upstairs.

Dr. Grey looked at his wife. She met his eyes steadily, cheerfully.

"I think Mother's looking better, don't you dear?" she said.

"There's nothing at all the matter with my mother—except—" he shut his mouth hard. "There are things I cannot say, Louise," he continued, "but others I can. Namely; that for sweetness and patience and gentleness you—you beat the Dutch! And I do appreciate it. One can't turn one's Mother out of the house, but I do resent her having another doctor!"

"I'd love your Mother, Joseph, if—if she was a thousand

times worse!" his wife answered; and he kissed her with grateful love.

Sarah came in to clear the table presently, and Ellen stood in the pantry door to chat with her.

"Never in my life did I see any woman wid the patience of her!" said Ellen, wiping her mouth on her apron.

"She has need of it," said Sarah. "Any Mother-in-law is a trial I've heard, but this wan is the worst. Why she must needs live with 'em I don't see—she has daughters of her own."

"'Tis the daughter's husbands won't put up wid her," answered Ellen, "they havin' the say of course. This man's her son—and he has to keep her if she will stay."

"And she as rich as a Jew!" Sarah went on. "And never spendin' a cent! And the Doctor workin' night and day!"—

Then Mama came in and this bit of conversation naturally came to an end.

A busy, quiet, sweet little woman was Mama; and small Josie flew into her arms and cuddled there most happily.

"Mama Dearest," she said, "How long is it to Christmas? Can I get my mat done for Grandma? And *do* you think she'll like it?"

"Well, well dear—that's three *questions!* It's two weeks yet to Christmas; and I think you can if you work steadily; and I hope she'll like it."

"And Mama—can I have my party?"

"I'm afraid not, dearest. You see Grandma is old, and she hates a noise and confusion—and parties are expensive. I'm sorry, childie. Can't you think of something else you want, that Mother can give you?"

"No," said the child, "I've wanted a party for three years, Mama! Grandma just spoils everything!"

"No, no, dear—you must always love Grandma because

she is dear Papa's mother; and because she is lonely and needs our love.

"We'll have a party some day, Dearest—don't feel badly. And *we* always have a good time together, don't we?"

They did; but just now the child's heart was set on more social pleasures, and she went sadly back to her playroom to work on that mat for Grandma.

It was a busy day. Mama's married sister came to see her, and the child was sent out of the room. Two neighbors called, and waited, chatting, some time before Mama came down.

Grandma's doctor—who was not Papa—called; and her lawyer too; and they had to wait some time for the old lady to dress as she thought fitting.

But Grandma's doctor and lawyer were very old friends, and seemed to enjoy themselves.

The minister came also, not Grandma's minister, who was old and thin and severe and wore a long white beard; but Mama's minister, who was so vigorous and cheerful, and would lift Josephine way up over his head—as if she was ten years old. But Mama sent her out of the room this time, which was a pity.

To be sure Josephine had a little secret trail from her playroom door—behind several pieces of furniture—right up to the back of the sofa where people usually sat, but she was not often interested in their conversation. She was a quiet child, busy with her own plans and ideas; playing softly by herself, with much imaginary conversation. She set up her largest doll, a majestic personage known as "The Lady Isobel," and talked to her.

"Why is my Grandma so horrid? And why do I have to love her? How can you love people—if you don't, Lady Isobel?

"Other girls' Grandmas are nice. Nelly Elder's got a lovely

Grandma! She lets Nelly have parties and everything. Maybe if Grandma likes my mat she'll—be pleasanter.

"Maybe she'll go somewhere else to live—sometime. Don't you think so, Lady Isobel?"

The Lady Isobel's reply, however, was not recorded.

Grandma pursued her pious way as usual, till an early bedtime relieved the family of her presence. Then Uncle Harry stopped puttering with his machines and came out to be sociable with his sister. If Papa was at home they would have a game of solo—if not, they played cribbage, or quiet.

Uncle Harry was the life of the household—when Grandma wasn't around.

"Well, Lulu," he said cheerfully, "What's the prospect? Can Joe make it?"

"No," said Mama. "It's out of the question. He could arrange about his practice easily enough but it's the money for the trip. He'll have to send his paper to be read."

"It's a shame!" said the young man, "He ought to be there. He'd do those other doctors good. Why in the name of reason don't the old lady give him the money—she could, easy enough."

"Joe never'll ask her for a cent," answered Mrs. Grey, "and it would never occur to her to give him one! Yet I think she loves him best of all her children."

"Huh! *Love!*" said Uncle Harry.

Grandma didn't sleep well at night. She complained of this circumstantially and at length.

"Hour after hour I hear the clock strike," she said. "Hour after hour!"

Little Josephine had heard the clock strike hour after hour one terrible night when she had an earache. She was really sorry for Grandma.

"And nothing to take up my mind," said Grandma, as if her mind was a burden to her.

But the night after this she had something to take up her mind. As a matter of fact it woke her up, as she had napped between the clock's strikings. At first she thought the servants were in her room—and realized with a start that they were speaking of her.

"Why she must live with 'em I don't see—she has daughters of her own—"

With the interest of an eavesdropper she lay still, listening, and heard no good of herself.

"How long is it to Christmas?" she presently heard her grandchild ask, and beg her mother for the "party"—still denied her.

"Grandma spoils everything!" said the clear childish voice, and the mother's gentle one urged love and patience.

It was some time before the suddenly awakened old lady, in the dark, realized the source of these voices—and then she could not locate it.

"It's some joke of that young man's" she said grimly—but the joke went on.

It was Mrs. Grey's sister now, condoling with her about this mother-in-law.

"Why do you have to put up with it Louise? Won't any of her daughters have her?"

"I'm afraid they don't want her," said Louise's gentle voice. "But Joe is her son, and of course he feels that his home is his mother's. I think he is quite right. She is old, and alone— she doesn't *mean* to be disagreeable."

"Well, she achieves it without effort, then! A more disagreeable old lady I never saw, Louise, and I'd like nothing better than to tell her so!"

The old lady was angry, but impressed. There is a fascina-

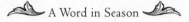

tion in learning how others see us, even if the lesson is unpleasant. She heard the two neighbors who talked together before Mama came down, and their talk was of her—and of how they pitied young Mrs. Grey.

"If I was in her shoes," said the older of the two, "I'd pick up and travel! She's only sixty-five—and sound as a nut."

"Has she money enough?" asked the other.

"My, yes! Money to burn! She has her annuity that her father left her, and a big insurance—and house rents. She must have all of three thousand a year."

"And doesn't she pay board here?"

"Pay board! Not she. She wouldn't pay anything so long as she has a relative to live on. She's saved all her life. But nobody'll get any good of it till she's dead."

This talk stopped when their hostess entered, changing to more general themes; but the interest revived when men's voices took up the tale.

"Yes—wants her will made again. Always making and unmaking and remaking. Harmless amusement, I suppose."

"She wastes good money on both of us—and I tell her so. But one can't be expected to absolutely refuse a patient."

"Or a client!"

"No. I suppose not."

"She's not really ill then?"

"Bless you, Ruthven, I don't know a sounder old woman anywhere. All she needs is a change—and to think of something besides herself! I tell her that, too—and she says I'm so eccentric."

"Why in all decency don't her son do her doctoring?"

"I suppose he's too frank—and not quite able to speak his mind. He's a fine fellow. That paper of his will be a great feature of our convention. Shame he can't go."

"Why can't he? Can't afford it?"

"That's just it. You see the old lady don't put up—not a cent—and he has all he can do to keep the boys in college."

And their conversation stopped, and Grandma heard her own voice—inviting the doctor up to her room—and making another appointment for the lawyer.

Then it was the young minister, a cheerful, brawny youth, whom she had once described as a "Godless upstart!"

He appeared to be comforting young Mrs. Grey, and commending her. "You are doing wonders," he said, as their voices came into hearing, "and not letting your right hand know it, either."

"You make far too much of it, Mr. Eagerson," the soft voice answered, "I am so happy in my children—my home—my husband. This is the *only* trouble—I do not complain."

"I know you don't complain, Mrs. Grey, but I want you to know that you're appreciated! 'It is better to dwell in a corner of the housetop, than with a woman in a wide house'—especially if she's your mother-in-law."

"I won't allow you to speak so—if you are my minister!" said young Mrs. Grey with spirit; and the talk changed to church matters, where the little lady offered to help with time and service, and regretted that she had no money to give.

There was a silence, save for small confused noises of a daytime household; distant sounds of doors and dishes; and then in a sad, confidential voice—"Why is Grandma so horrid? And why do I have to love her? How can you love people you don't, Lady Isobel?"

Grandma was really fond of quiet little Josephine, even if she did sometimes snub her as a matter of principle. She lay and listened to these strictly private remarks, and meditated upon them after they had ceased. It was a large dose, an omnibus dose, and took some time to assimilate; but the old lady had really a mind of her own, though much of it was uninhabited, and this generous burst of light set it to working.

She said nothing to anyone, but seemed to use her eyes and ears with more attention than previously, and allowed her granddaughter's small efforts toward affection with new receptiveness. She had one talk with her daughter-in-law which left that little woman wet-eyed and smiling with pleasure, though she could not tell about it—that was requisite.

But the family in general heard nothing of any change of heart till breakfast time on Christmas morning. They sat enjoying that pleasant meal, in the usual respite before the old lady appeared, when Sarah came in with a bunch of notes and laid one at each plate, with an air of great importance.

"She said I was to leave 'em till you was all here—and here they are!" said Sarah, smiling mysteriously, "and that I was to say nothing—and I haven't!" And the red-cheeked girl folded her arms and waited—as interested as anybody.

Uncle Harry opened his first. "I bet it's a tract!" said he. But he blushed to the roots of his thick brown hair as he took out, not a tract, but a check.

"A Christmas present to my son-in-law-by-marriage; to be spent on the improvement of talking machines—if that is necessary!"

"Why bless her heart!" said he, "I call that pretty handsome, and I'll tell her so!"

Papa opened his.

"For your Convention trip, dear son," said this one, "and for a new dress suit—and a new suit case, and a new overcoat—a nice one. With Mother's love."

It was a large check, this one. Papa sat quite silent and looked at his wife. She went around the table and hugged him—she had to.

"You've got one, too, Louise," said he—and she opened it.

"For my dear daughter Louise; this—to be spent on other people; and *this*" (*this* was much bigger) "to be inexorably spent on herself—every cent of it! On her own special needs and pleasures—if she can think of any!"

Louise was simply crying—and little Josephine ran to comfort her.

"Hold on Kiddie—you haven't opened yours," said Uncle Harry; and they all eagerly waited while the child carefully opened her envelope with a clean knife, and read out solemnly and slowly, "For my darling Grand-child Josephine, to be spent by herself, for herself, with Mama's advice and assistance; and in particular to provide for her party!"

She turned over the stiff little piece of paper—hardly understanding.

"It's a check, dear," said Papa. "It's the same as money. Parties cost money, and Grandma has made you a Christmas present of your party."

The little girl's eyes grew big with joy.

"Can I?—Is there really—a party?"

"There is really a party—for my little daughter, this afternoon at four!"

"O where is Grandma!" cried the child—"I want to hug her!"

They all rose up hurriedly, but Sarah came forward from her scant pretense of retirement, with another note for Dr. Grey.

"I was to give you this last of all," she said, with an air of one fulfilling grave diplomatic responsibility.

"My dear ones," ran the note, "I have gathered from my family and friends, and from professional and spiritual advisers the idea that change is often beneficial. With this in mind I have given myself a Christmas present of a Cook's

Tour around the world—and am gone. A Merry Christmas and a Happy New Year to you all!"

She was gone.

Sarah admitted complicity.

"Sure she would have no one know a thing—not a word!" said Sarah. "And she gave us something handsome to help her! And she's got that young widder Johnson for a companion—and they went off last night on the sleeper for New York!"

The gratitude of the family had to be spent in loving letters, and in great plans of what they would do to make Grandma happy when she came back.

No one felt more grateful than little loving Josephine, whose dearest wishes were all fulfilled. When she remembered it she went very quietly, when all were busy somewhere else, climbed up on the step ladder, and took down the forgotten phonograph from the top of the wardrobe.

"Dear Grandma!" she said. "I do hope she liked it!"

In Two Houses

THE BLANK, BOARDED windows, with which the two old Marshall houses faced, or rather sided, each other, told no tales of midnight danger; but shrill infant screams were more successful.

"Fire! Fire! O Lawdy, Lawdy, de house is afire!" yelled little black Polly, her red-tied pigtails seeming to bristle and prance with horror.

"Be still, child!" said Miss Diana sternly. "Hold your tongue—we can put this out. Be still, I tell you!" With a clear head and a strong hand she proceeded to assail the leaping flames in the back kitchen, but could not at the same time capture and quiet the vociferous Polly, who ran out into the moonlit silence of the back yard, shrieking to heaven that they would all be burned alive. The dark house next door stirred inwardly, it would seem reluctantly.

Distant knocks and cries were heard: "Mas'r Marshall! Mas'r Marshall! De house afire nex' door! Dat lady'll be bun in her baid! O Mas'r Marshall!"

Steps were heard; a moving light glimmered through the cracks of the close-shuttered windows and presently a tall man, somewhat incomplete in costume, leaped over the high brick wall and rushed in, followed by an old negro in a state of uncontrolled excitement.

Miss Diana Marshall paused in her task, smoky and disheveled, but a commanding figure none the less.

"I thank you for your kind intentions, Dr. Blair," she said. "There is not the least necessity for assistance." Neither of the men paid any attention to her; Dr. Marshall Blair taking hold with swift intelligence, while the old negro rushed about so madly that he seemed rather to spread the flames than to quench them, adding his cries to Polly's.

"Get out, Polyphemus!" said his master at length. Go out there and choke that child! I can put this out if you'll let it alone."

Polyphemus took himself off at the word, and a sudden silence fell upon him and Polly as they withdrew behind the smoke house.

"Just pass me the water—let me throw it," the visitor commanded, and Miss Marshall, grim and silent, did as she was told. In a few moments the flames were entirely extinguished.

"There is no great damage done," he remarked on examination.

"I did not think there would be," replied Miss Marshall. "I could have put the fire out easily without any man's assistance; but I couldn't stop that foolish child."

"No," he politely agreed, "it is impossible to stop a woman's tongue—even when very young."

She regarded him coldly. Her thick, coppery hair was in a condition only to be described as tousled; a towel-girt wrapper and shapeless bedroom slippers formed her costume; but the free grace of her athletic body, and the rich color of health and sudden exertion made her a lovely picture for all that.

Perhaps the glint of anger in her clear eyes heightened it; at any rate, he looked at her with admiration, though it seemed strangely reluctant.

"I apologize for my intrusion," he said. "Kindly excuse me. I supposed the house was in danger."

"I thank you for your interest in the house, Dr. Blair. As you see, it is still standing."

He bowed with as much dignity as a black-smooched shirt and suspender-belted trousers allowed, and withdrew; taking the high wall with energy, if not grace. His servant must have rejoined him by some easier means, for the sound of severe reproof was presently heard. "The next time you get me out of bed on any such fool's errand will be your last day in this house!" stormed his master, with that disregard for likelihood which is often to be observed in those who scold. Pacificatory "Yassirs" trailed off into silence as doors slammed shut, and darkness reigned again.

Diana Marshall felt an equal rage against her domestic imp of mischief, to whose carelessness the fire was evidently due; but the small, cowed figure that slunk back into the disman-tled kitchen at her call was so pathetic in its remorseful terror, that she sent the child to bed with few words.

"If I was fool enough to take in that ridiculous infant, I must at least be wise enough to put up with her," she said to herself, trying with much cold water to remove the soot from her hands, and the angry flush from her cheeks.

"The *idea* of his coming in like that! The *idea*!"

It was a long time before she could sleep again; and all that her sad-eyed mother had told her of these old houses and the old quarrels within them, rose and revolved in her mind as she lay staring into the dark. She seemed to see them appear before her, the proud old Englishman, Blair Marshall, with his grant of land, his big stone house, and his twin sons, the pride of his heart and apple of his eye. For one of them he built the second house, identical with the first—close to it, connected with a bridge—that bridge which now gaped broken between them.

Marshall's Folly it was called even then—as folk are apt to consider foolish anything unusual. "You can't make any two families live together, not even by a bridge!" the neighbors said. Identical houses, equally beautiful in furniture and decoration, standing in the great estate with wooded hills and rolling fields; monuments of parental love and pride, they were left to young Vance and Gregory on their father's death.

Within a year they had quarreled, quarreled over a cousin— Diana Blair. Vance married her. Vance lived on the estate and Diana Marshall was his granddaughter and sole heir. Gregory became a traveler, bringing home in course of years a brilliant wife from France. Gregory's one child, a daughter, married a Blair; and Gregory's grandson was Dr. Marshall Blair, Diana's second cousin and next neighbor. Between them rose a higher wall than six feet of brick, a wider gulf than that between the sawed-off planks of the once connecting bridge; a wall of hatred, a chasm of total strangeness.

Diana's mother was a Massachusetts girl, won by the handsome Virginian in what she afterwards called a moment of delirium. She bore a bitter widowhood during her husband's frequent absences; suffered a more bitter wifehood when he was at home; and reared her daughter to hate men in general and Marshalls in particular.

"You can't escape the name unless you marry, and I hope you never will!" her mother said to her, "and you can't wholly escape the nature—though you have enough Wentworth to match it, I believe. But I pray Heaven you may steer clear of all Marshalls and their Follies!"

The girl grew up, a wild, free thing, on the old place; wild enough even to scale the wall and secretly study the shut-up house next door. It made her shiver—it was so like their own—and yet so different.

"It's like a Siamese twin," she used to say to herself. "A dead one! Ugh!"

After her husband's unregretted death Mrs. Marshall took Diana back to Massachusetts and gave her the college education she herself had relinquished for love, and always regretted. Then they had gone to England, traveled, studied, living always in the company of women; efficient, contented, successful women; where the girl heard more and more of the delinquencies and offenses of mankind.

When she was twenty-eight her mother died; and Diana, now well established professionally as a writer, felt a strong desire to return to her childhood's home; but first made careful inquiries by letter as to the house next door, learning that it was still blank and vacant. She lived there quite alone, a handsome hermit, hunting, fishing, swimming in the deep cold lake that formed part of the boundary between the places, living on the garden products, on canned goods and biscuit, with what she added with line and gun; and working happily on her Book—a book she had been planning for ten years.

She grew to love the once gloomy house, standing now wide-windowed to the sun and air; most of its handsome furniture still covered and packed away as her mother had left it. She loved the wide, far view—trees, trees, trees; blue curve on blue curve of distant mountain; not another building in sight save the dark house next door. The space, the quiet delighted her; the freedom from all interruption.

"But why no servants?" wrote her friend and classmate, Miss Jane Cass, of Boston. "Surely you cannot keep that great place clean!—and what sort of food to live on! My dear, you'll break down! It must be unsanitary, and aren't you afraid?"

"My dear old Jane," Diana answered, "I don't suppose you ever were alone—really alone—in your life. It is glorious, simply glorious! My morning bath is a dive into the cleanest lake you ever saw, my meals are largely from the garden. I do employ an old darky to take care of that, his name is Polyphemus, he used to belong to us, or his parents did. My bread is pure wheat biscuit—better than any other kind; meat I get by shooting or fishing—better living you never saw. Also I have plenty of excellent canned goods for emergencies.

"And the comfort—the utter luxury of having a house of one's own! You have never known it, my poor old Jane! fear you never will. You see, I don't care at all for what my ancestors thought or what my present relatives or other persons think; this house is now arranged exactly to suit *me*; and I mean to live here, mostly, for the rest of my days. Unless my cousin, Marshall Blair, should come back and prove a disagreeable neighbor.

"Of course I wish I had children. You know how I love them; but not at the price most women pay. I can always adopt, you know. For pure pleasure, I have my music, an excellent resource. Sometimes I wish I had chosen singing instead of writing. But now I have both!

"As to fear—I never knew it. And as to health—you should see me! It was always good, and grows daily better. Come when you can, and we'll be bachelor maids together."

So feeling, proud and happy in her green solitude, with hasty sandals on bare feet and a blue bathrobe about her, she had raced down to the lake one glittering morning, only to see, poised on her favorite diving place, the straight, white body of a man. He leaped, rose, curved, and swept into the water, swimming with easy pride. She returned to the house, furious, and called Polyphemus.

"There is a man in the lake," she said; "you go and tell him this is private property." Polyphemus seemed at a loss.

"Ya'as, Miss Dina," he said, shifting from one foot to the other. "Ya'asm! But, Miss Dina—dat man am Mars' Marshall Blair!"

Slow rage rose and gathered in her heart. Her lovely lake was no longer hers alone, her solitude was spoiled, and by a man; above all by a Marshall.

Polyphemus eyed her apologetically. "And if you please, Miss Dina," he went on, backing a little away from her, "I goin' to bring another nigger to run this yer garden. I'm 'bleeged to work for Mars' Marshall now."

She paid him on the spot and returned to her room, the day's work spoiled. That very afternoon, ranging with her gun, well on her side of the estate, she had found a small scared colored child, howling dismally.

Being interrogated, she told a dismal tale of having no parents and no home; of being beaten and sent oft' by those who had cared for her. "They done tun me loose, Miss Dina, an' I got nowhar to go! an' I dun bring your milk, Miss Dina!" Diana had taken her in, finding the diminutive imp quite as useful in most ways as old Polyphemus.

She avoided the lake thereafter, choosing a small pool in another quarter for her beloved sunrise bath, and plunged into her work with fresh determination.

Should she, Diana Marshall, be disturbed by the mere adjacent presence of a man? Indeed, no!

Polyphemus, who wholly disapproved of his young mistress swimming in that cold and lonely lake, never told his master of the discovery, and Dr. Blair continued to monopolize the quiet water.

He had been educated in England and France, had made his reputation there, and then gradually turned from the prac-

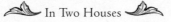

tice of medicine to research work. He, too, had remembered the old place in Virginia, with the big comfortable home belonging to him, and the dark empty shell next door, visited once in his youth, when the estate was settled.

"Just the thing," he said to himself. "I can experiment all I please; no one will be about to bother me. And when I've got this thing worked out!——"

But first he made careful inquiry about the house across the wall. "If that female cousin of mine is at home, I won't live there!" he determined. But he heard that no one had lived there for ten years, and came home rejoicing. Old Polyphemus presented himself humbly as the natural retainer of the place, and was promptly employed.

"Can you cook?—and clean—really clean, you understand? I'll have no woman slopping about in my house!"

"O, ya'as, sir—Lawdy, ya'as, sir! I kin cook better 'n any woman you eber saw, sir!" the old nigger assured him. And because of the proven excellence of his cooking many deficiencies were overlooked in other lines.

Dr. Blair settled down enthusiastically in the old house, conscious of pleasant little thrills of race memory and a comfortable feeling of home. Many rooms he kept shut up; those he used, he furnished in a manner suggesting a laboratory or hospital more than a home, and the great garrets he consecrated to his research work—to slow, careful, continuous experiment and observation, requiring the arbitrary match-making of many mice, much time and no interruption.

He lived well, under the ministrations of the old negro. For exercise he rode far and wide, and found his relaxation and deepest pleasure in his violin. He had scarcely been settled three days, and had not unpacked that beloved instrument, when he heard one evening, rising through the magnolia-scented air, the soft, rich tones of a deep contralto voice.

He called Polyphemus. "Look here—there's someone in the other house!"

"Ya'as, sir; jes' so, sir. It are Miss Dina, sir."

"Name of a pig!" said Marshall Blair, which was certainly unfair, as pigs are seldom called Diana.

He meditated upon it. "Confound all women," said he to himself. "Feeble, sickly, sentimental, selfish, shallow, idle, luxurious, empty-headed, useless trash! And confound This One in particular—spoiling my quiet!" Then he laughed grimly. "If she comes over here we'll let out the mice, Polyphemus," he said. "Don't ever let me hear a word about her."

But Polyphemus was sorely exercised in his mind.

"Dere dey bof are—juxtacomposed to-gedder—and dere dey stick! An' bein' cousins, and bof Blairs *an'* Marshalls, and dis yer property needin' to be looked after and wukked de wust way! Lawdy! Lawdy!"

But just as young Polly's guileless praises of "Mars Marshall nex' door" were met with prompt reproof and tabooed utterly, so were old Polyphemus' more artful suggestions sharply rebuffed.

"I tell you, I want to hear nothing about that woman!" said Dr. Blair. "Not a word. I hope never to set eyes upon her!"

Polyphemus, taking needed rest at hours when his master was engrossed with mice, revolved matters solemnly in the dark recesses of his mind.

"He ain't even willin' to see her," he said to himself; "an' she as hansome as a picter. De Lawd must provide some way to bring dem young people togedder!"

Dr. Blair succeeded in not seeing his cousin until the night of the conflagration, an event which he strove utterly to dismiss from his mind.

"Two fool women together," he summarized them. "Might

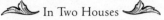

have burned down both houses by their confounded carelessness. I hope I shall never see her again!"

None the less, he was glad when he did see her again—one
hot, still, summer night, when the broad moonlight and the
oppressive heat had tempted him to the lake. He lay too long,
perhaps, with arms outstretched, enjoying the spring-fed coldness of the water, for a fierce pain shot through suddenly
crippled limbs as he struck out for the bank.

He sank, rose, shouted for help with a hopeless thought
of Polyphemus' deafness; sank again, rose struggling weakly,
and saw through half-blinded eyes a great white figure shoot
down through the moonlight and dive after him.

She reached him, rose with him, struck out strongly and
brought him safe to land, worked over him there, till at last
his eyes opened again to a humiliating spectacle. She was
holding his tongue out; Polyphemus, summoned by Polly's
frantic cries, was there, pumping his master's arms up and
down. He experienced great distress of body—and more of
mind. She disappeared on the instant, her tall white figure
shining in the moonlight, sternly Greek in outline under the
wet swathing of her nightdress, vanishing through the trees
like a veritable nymph.

"I certainly am ashamed of you, Mars' Marshall," said the
old negro, when once his charge was safe. "Here you might
'a died without ever wakin' me up, if it hadn't been for that
lady! And she havin' to jump out'n her baid and run down
yer, barfooted, to pull you outen de water. Mighty lucky she's
such a good swimmer!"

In place of that lively gratitude toward one's preserver
which is supposed to move the heart of the rescued, Dr. Blair
felt only an intense mortification and anger. To be caught like
a drowning rat—he, who could swim for miles—and to be
dragged to land, pulled out, and laboriously resuscitated—by

a woman! He thought of how he must have looked, helpless, sodden, with his tongue forcibly pulled out. It was hideously humiliating.

Go to her he would not, but he wrote a courteous note, expressing his obligation in decent terms, though not in warm ones, begging her "to accept the thanks due for saving a worthless life."

She replied with equal courtesy and coldness, also with equal ambiguity. "Pray do not speak of it. It will equal, I trust, your attempt to rescue my house. My efforts are wholly unworthy of mention."

"Women must have the last word," he said grimly, and let it go at that, putting the note in the fire. But he remembered every word of it.

After that the work went on steadily in the two houses. The click of the typewriter resounded faintly on one side of the wall, and the smell of many mice rose like an undesirable incense on the other.

Polyphemus shook his white head, meditating in the old garden. "It did seem like the han' o' Providence—dat yer fire, and den dis yer drownin' upset it all. Hit certainly am a shame! In course, a man don' like to be beholden to a woman dat away; it aint natural. Lawdy! Lawdy! What we guine to do? I must go see dat Voodoo woman after all!"

The hand of Providence soon became strangely active, however, for before many days he approached his master with much timidity, announcing, "If you please, sir, dat good-fer-nuffin Polly chile next door say 'at Miss Dina sick."

"I dare say," replied Dr. Blair, coldly, going on with his supper; "women are always sick."

"Yass, sir; but Miss Dina ain't never been sick in her life before, and she's takin' on turrble; she's clean outn' her haid—just hear to dat, sir!"

The deep contralto voice he had heard so often with irresistible pleasure rose now in sudden, reckless melody; stopped short; broke into laughter; began to sing again, a queer, low chant.

Dr. Blair dropped knife and napkin and rushed into his laboratory, bringing out a long-untouched medicine case; then scaled the wall once more.

He found her standing at the head of the great stairway, brilliantly arrayed in some rich ball dress of a previous generation, with cheeks flaming pink and glittering eyes. She took him for a dangerous assailant, and he was obliged to use all his strength to subdue without hurting her.

He had her quiet at last, and she lay staring at him with fierce eyes, till the sedative he forcibly administered made the white lids close.

Polly, under close questioning, showed as much terror as if she were being blamed for her mistress's condition, and it was only by the exercise of unusual gentleness and the gift of a shining half-dollar that he was able to get any facts in the case.

It appeared that her mistress had been well as usual up to dinner time; had grown more and more flushed and excited ever since, and had been in considerable pain. "She been powerful sick, sir; she sut'nly have!"

"What did she eat for dinner?"

"Some can' soup, and some fish—fraish dis mornin', sir; and some green peas—I picked 'em myself."

"Show me the can."

"Lawdy, sah, I frowed it away."

"Go and get it."

"I can't, sir. I frowed it down de dry well whar I always frow 'em."

His opinion was clear.

"That deadly canned stuff, I don't doubt. Serves anybody right who uses it. I think she's in no danger now." But he had sat by her all night, noting the pulse, the temperature, the action of the lungs; trying to make his knowledge of poisons agree with his theories of the malign composition of canned soup.

She slept heavily most of the following day, and when she opened her eyes he was sitting calmly by her window, reading. She made no sound, no movement, but watched him for a few moments, uncertain whether he was not part of the wild dream which had been drifting through her mind. Then she realized, with a sense of unmeasured amazement, that Marshall Blair was making himself perfectly at home in her house—in her room.

Lying quite still, she spoke calmly. "To what do I owe the honor of this visit, Dr. Blair?"

He rose, looked at his watch, and came to her bedside. "To the fact that you have been suddenly and dangerously ill, and I was the only physician within reach. I make no apologies. If you will allow me, I will take your pulse and temperature once more."

He popped the little thermometer into her mouth before she could say anything further, and held her wrist with an abstracted air, counting.

"I guess you'll do," he said. "It was a case of poison; from eating canned goods I think. You really had a rather close call. I advise your lying still another day, and taking nothing but milk for the rest of the week. Good morning."

He was gone.

She lay still for some time, trying to think, but finding both head and body strangely weak, and presently slept again.

Small Polly waited upon her with spaniel-like devotion.

"Don't look so like a scared mouse, Polly," Miss Diana told her. "Anybody'd think you were to blame for my being sick."

"O, Lawdy, no, ma'am—I aint! I didn't! Please 'scuse me, ma'am," said Polly, still wearing an air of dark remorse.

Diana Marshall remained quiet the next day, as advised, and also lived on milk for a week, her principal entertainment during this time being the melodious sound of her cousin's violin and his pleasant baritone voice, which rose to her window in the still evenings.

At the end of that week Dr. Blair's solo was interrupted by the appearance of his recent patient before his door.

"Good evening," said she calmly; "I've come over to thank you for taking care of me when I needed it, and to say that I think we are making melodramatic fools of ourselves."

He rose and bowed.

"Thank you for your good opinion. Won't you be seated?"

"Not till I know if you share the opinion," she said. "You and I are not children, and we are, I believe, second cousins. I abominate men; but you seem to be a decent sort, and not intrusive."

"And I abominate women," he replied, "but I will say you are the least objectionable of the kind I ever knew."

"You don't disturb my writing, and I don't disturb your mice—I hope."

"Not in the least."

"But it does seem a pity to miss the music we might have. I want so much to try accompanying your violin."

"I have been secretly wishing you would, for a month," said Dr. Blair.

Evenings of mutual music are a pleasant close to days of diverse toil. They played together, they sang together, they talked together, and each learned a real respect for the other's character, together with a deep sympathy for their kindred prejudices.

"If you weren't a woman, Cousin Diana, I really believe I'd ask you to marry me," he said one night.

"If you weren't a man, I might consider it," she replied.

"I have taken seven oaths that no woman should ever live in my house," said he.

"And I, that no man should ever live in mine," she answered.

"I am a scientist, and no family cares must ever interfere with my work," he continued.

"I am a writer, and will never be any man's housekeeper," said she.

"Yet these are happy evenings when the day's work is over," he urged.

"They certainly are," she agreed.

"It can't go on this way," he said.

"Why can't it?" she demanded.

For answer, he suddenly leaned over and kissed her.

There was a silence.

"I see that you are not above Shakespearian argument, Dr. Blair."

"I am glad you admit we are lovers, Cousin Diana."

"But I will not marry you, Cousin Marshall."

"It is only a formality, Cousin Diana. What you really don't want to do is to keep house for me, and I assure you I don't want you to. But suppose—just for the sake of argument—that we went through that little formality and then continued to live as we do now?"

"In two houses?"

"Why not? There is the bridge—we can mend it."

"Well," said Diana, "on those conditions—and merely as a formality——"

So they mended the bridge.

After the wedding old Polyphemus withdrew young Polly to the depths of the woods, a dim place, utterly removed, and addressed her with solemnity:

"Now dis yere thing am accomplished, I'se obliged to chastise you for all you' foolishness."

"I never done nothin' but what you told me to," she pleaded.

"You are a mizzerble, good for nuffin' female child," he declared. "Couldn't you do nuffin' without over-doin' it? Did I tell you to let de house get all a burnin' before you hollered fire? Did I tell you to pison Miss Dina till she near went out of her haid forever, with your double doses? Heah am I, a-wearin' myself to a shadder and a-riskin' my immortal soul to bring dese yere houses togedder, what natchally belong togedder, and you pretty neah to ruin everything with yo' foolishness! You come heah to me!"

And Polly wailed loud and long beneath the severity of an ungrateful grandfather.

Making a Change

"WA-A-A-A! WAA-A-A-AAA!"

Frank Gordins set down his coffee cup so hard that it spilled over into the saucer.

"Is there no way to stop that child crying?" he demanded.

"I do not know of any," said his wife, so definitely and politely that the words seemed cut off by machinery.

"*I do*," said his mother with even more definiteness, but less politeness.

Young Mrs. Gordins looked at her mother-in-law from under her delicate level brows, and said nothing. But the weary lines about her eyes deepened; she had been kept awake nearly all night, and for many nights.

So had he. So, as a matter of fact, had his mother. She had not the care of the baby—but lay awake wishing she had.

"There's no need at all for that child's crying so, Frank. If Julia would only let me——"

"It's no use talking about it," said Julia. "If Frank is not satisfied with the child's mother he must say so—perhaps we can make a change."

This was ominously gentle. Julia's nerves were at the breaking point. Upon her tired ears, her sensitive mother's heart, the grating wail from the next room fell like a lash—burnt

in like fire. Her ears were hypersensitive, always. She had been an ardent musician before her marriage, and had taught quite successfully on both piano and violin. To any mother a child's cry is painful; to a musical mother it is torment.

But if her ears were sensitive, so was her conscience. If her nerves were weak her pride was strong. The child was her child, it was her duty to take care of it, and take care of it she would. She spent her days in unremitting devotion to its needs, and to the care of her neat flat; and her nights had long since ceased to refresh her.

Again the weary cry rose to a wail.

"It does seem to be time for a change of treatment," suggested the older woman acidly.

"Or a change of residence," offered the younger, in a deadly quiet voice.

"Well, by Jupiter! There'll be a change of some kind, and p. d. q.!" said the son and husband, rising to his feet.

His mother rose also, and left the room, holding her head high and refusing to show any effects of that last thrust.

Frank Gordins glared at his wife. His nerves were raw, too. It does not benefit any one in health or character to be continuously deprived of sleep. Some enlightened persons use that deprivation as a form of torture.

She stirred her coffee with mechanical calm, her eyes sullenly bent on her plate.

"I will not stand having Mother spoken to like that," he stated with decision.

"I will not stand having her interfere with my methods of bringing up children."

"Your methods! Why, Julia, my mother knows more about taking care of babies than you'll ever learn! She has the real love of it—and the practical experience. Why can't you let her take care of the kid—and we'll all have some peace!"

She lifted her eyes and looked at him; deep inscrutable wells of angry light. He had not the faintest appreciation of her state of mind. When people say they are "nearly crazy" from weariness, they state a practical fact. The old phrase which describes reason as "tottering on her throne," is also a clear one.

Julia was more near the verge of complete disaster than the family dreamed. The conditions were so simple, so usual, so inevitable.

Here was Frank Gordins, well brought up, the only son of a very capable and idolatrously affectionate mother. He had fallen deeply and desperately in love with the exalted beauty and fine mind of the young music teacher, and his mother had approved. She too loved music and admired beauty.

Her tiny store in the savings bank did not allow of a separate home, and Julia had cordially welcomed her to share in their household.

Here was affection, propriety and peace. Here was a noble devotion on the part of the young wife, who so worshipped her husband that she used to wish she had been the greatest musician on earth—that she might give it up for him! She had given up her music, perforce, for many months, and missed it more than she knew.

She bent her mind to the decoration and artistic management of their little apartment, finding her standards difficult to maintain by the ever-changing inefficiency of her help. The musical temperament does not always include patience; nor, necessarily, the power of management.

When the baby came her heart overflowed with utter devotion and thankfulness; she was his wife—the mother of his child. Her happiness lifted and pushed within till she longed more than ever for her music for the free pouring current of expression, to give forth her love and pride and happiness. She had not the gift of words.

So now she looked at her husband, dumbly, while wild visions of separation, of secret flight—even of self-destruction—swung dizzily across her mental vision. All she said was "All right, Frank. We'll make a change. And you shall have—some peace."

"Thank goodness for that, Jule! You do look tired, Girlie—let Mother see to His Nibs, and try to get a nap, can't you?"

"Yes," she said. "Yes … I think I will." Her voice had a peculiar note in it. If Frank had been an alienist, or even a general physician, he would have noticed it. But his work lay in electric coils, in dynamos and copper wiring—not in woman's nerves—and he did not notice it.

He kissed her and went out, throwing back his shoulders and drawing a long breath of relief as he left the house behind him and entered his own world.

"This being married—and bringing up children—is not what it's cracked up to be." That was the feeling in the back of his mind. But it did not find full admission, much less expression.

When a friend asked him, "All well at home?" he said, "Yes, thank you—pretty fair. Kid cries a good deal—but that's natural, I suppose."

He dismissed the whole matter from his mind and bent his faculties to a man's task—how he can earn enough to support a wife, a mother, and a son.

At home his mother sat in her small room, looking out of the window at the ground glass one just across the "well," and thinking hard.

By the disorderly little breakfast table his wife remained motionless, her chin in her hands, her big eyes staring at nothing, trying to formulate in her weary mind some reliable reason why she should not do what she was thinking of doing. But her mind was too exhausted to serve her properly.

Sleep—Sleep—Sleep—that was the one thing she wanted. Then his mother could take care of the baby all she wanted to, and Frank could have some peace... . Oh, dear! It was time for the child's bath.

She gave it to him mechanically. On the stroke of the hour she prepared the sterilized milk, and arranged the little one comfortably with his bottle. He snuggled down, enjoying it, while she stood watching him.

She emptied the tub, put the bath apron to dry, picked up all the towels and sponges and varied appurtenances of the elaborate performance of bathing the firstborn, and then sat staring straight before her, more weary than ever, but growing inwardly determined.

Greta had cleared the table, with heavy heels and hands, and was now rattling dishes in the kitchen. At every slam the young mother winced, and when the girl's high voice began a sort of doleful chant over her work, young Mrs. Gordins rose to her feet with a shiver, and made her decision.

She carefully picked up the child and his bottle, and carried him to his grandmother's room.

"Would you mind looking after Albert?" she asked in a flat, quiet voice; "I think I'll try to get some sleep."

"Oh, I shall be delighted," replied her mother-in-law. She said it in a tone of cold politeness, but Julia did not notice.

She laid the child on the bed and stood looking at him in the same dull way for a little while, then went out without another word.

Mrs. Gordins, senior, sat watching the baby for some long

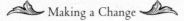

moments. "He's a perfectly lovely child!" she said softly, gloating over his rosy beauty. "There's not a *thing* the matter with him! It's just her absurd ideas. She's so irregular with him! To think of letting that child cry for an hour! He is nervous because she is. And of course she couldn't feed him till after his bath—of course not!"

She continued in these sarcastic meditations for some time, taking the empty bottle away from the small wet mouth, that sucked on for a few moments aimlessly, and then was quiet in sleep.

"I could take care of him so that he'd *never* cry!" she continued to herself, rocking slowly back and forth. "And I could take care of twenty like him—and enjoy it! I believe I'll go off somewhere and do it. Give Julia a rest. Change of residence, indeed!"

She rocked and planned, pleased to have her grandson with her, even while asleep.

Greta had gone out on some errand of her own. The rooms were very quiet. Suddenly the old lady held up her head and sniffed. She rose swiftly to her feet and sprang to the gas jet—no, it was shut off tightly. She went back to the dining-room—all right there.

"That foolish girl has left the range going and it's blown out!" she thought, and went to the kitchen. No, the little room was fresh and clean; every burner turned off.

"Funny! It must come in from the hall." She opened the door. No, the hall gave only its usual odor of diffused basement. Then the parlor—nothing there. The little alcove called by the renting agent "the music room," where Julia's closed piano and violin case stood dumb and dusty—nothing there.

"It's in her room—and she's asleep!" said Mrs. Gordins, senior; and she tried to open the door. It was locked. She knocked—there was no answer; knocked louder—shook it—rattled the knob. No answer.

Then Mrs. Gordins thought quickly. "It may be an accident, and nobody must know. Frank mustn't know. I'm glad Greta's out. I *must* get in somehow!" She looked at the transom, and the stout rod Frank had himself put up for the portieres Julia loved.

"I believe I can do it, at a pinch."

She was a remarkably active woman of her years, but no memory of earlier gymnastic feats could quite cover the exercise. She hastily brought the stepladder. From its top she could see in, and what she saw made her determine recklessly.

Grabbing the pole with small strong hands, she thrust her light frame bravely through the opening, turning clumsily but successfully, and dropping breathlessly and somewhat bruised to the floor, she flew to open the windows and doors.

When Julia opened her eyes she found loving arms around her, and wise, tender words to soothe and reassure.

"Don't say a thing, dearie—I understand. I *understand* I tell you! Oh, my dear girl—my precious daughter! We haven't been half good enough to you, Frank and I! But cheer up now—I've got the *loveliest* plan to tell you about! We are going to make a change! Listen now!"

And while the pale young mother lay quiet, petted and waited on to her heart's content, great plans were discussed and decided on.

Frank Gordins was pleased when the baby "outgrew his crying spells." He spoke of it to his wife.

"Yes," she said sweetly. "He has better care."

"I knew you'd learn," said he, proudly.

"I have!" she agreed. "I've learned—ever so much!"

He was pleased too, vastly pleased, to have her health improve rapidly and steadily, the delicate pink come back to her cheeks,

the soft light to her eyes; and when she made music for him in the evening, soft music, with shut doors—not to waken Albert—he felt as if his days of courtship had come again.

Greta the hammer-footed had gone, and an amazing French matron who came in by the day had taken her place. He asked no questions as to this person's peculiarities, and did not know that she did the purchasing and planned the meals, meals of such new delicacy and careful variance as gave him much delight. Neither did he know that her wages were greater than her predecessors. He turned over the same sum weekly, and did not pursue details.

He was pleased also that his mother seemed to have taken a new lease of life. She was so cheerful and brisk, so full of little jokes and stories—as he had known her in his boyhood; and above all she was so free and affectionate with Julia, that he was more than pleased.

"I tell you what it is!" he said to a bachelor friend. "You fellows don't know what you're missing!" And he brought one of them home to dinner—just to show him.

"Do you do all that on thirty-five a week?" his friend demanded.

"That's about it," he answered proudly.

"Well, your wife's a wonderful manager—that's all I can say. And you've got the best cook I ever saw, or heard of, or ate of—I suppose I might say—for five dollars."

Mr. Gordins was pleased and proud. But he was neither pleased nor proud when someone said to him, with displeasing frankness, "I shouldn't think you'd want your wife to be giving music lessons, Frank!"

He did not show surprise nor anger to his friend, but saved it for his wife. So surprised and so angry was he that he did a most unusual thing—he left his business and went home early in the afternoon. He opened the door of his flat. There was no one in it. He went through every room. No wife; no child; no mother; no servant.

The elevator boy heard him banging about, opening and shutting doors, and grinned happily. When Mr. Gordins came out Charles volunteered some information.

"Young Mrs. Gordins is out, Sir; but old Mrs. Gordins and the baby—they're upstairs. On the roof, I think."

Mr. Gordins went to the roof. There he found his mother, a smiling, cheerful nursemaid, and fifteen happy babies.

Mrs. Gordins, senior, rose to the occasion promptly.

"Welcome to my baby garden, Frank," she said cheerfully. "I'm so glad you could get off in time to see it."

She took his arm and led him about, proudly exhibiting her sunny roof-garden, her sand-pile, and big, shallow, zinc-lined pool; her flowers and vines, her seesaws, swings, and floor mattresses.

"You see how happy they are," she said. "Celia can manage very well for a few moments." And then she exhibited to him the whole upper flat, turned into a convenient place for many little ones to take their naps or to play in if the weather was bad.

"Where's Julia?" he demanded first.

"Julia will be in presently," she told him, "by five o'clock anyway. And the mothers come for the babies by then, too. I have them from nine or ten to five."

He was silent, both angry and hurt.

"We didn't tell you at first, my dear boy, because we knew you wouldn't like it, and we wanted to make sure it would go well. I rent the upper flat, you see—it is forty dollars a month, same as ours—and pay Celia five dollars a week, and pay Dr. Holbrook downstairs the same for looking over my little ones every day. She helped me to get them, too. The mothers pay me three dollars a week each, and don't have to keep a nursemaid. And I pay ten dollars a week board to Julia, and still have about ten of my own."

"And she gives music lessons?"

"Yes, she gives music lessons, just as she used to. She loves it, you know. You must have noticed how happy and well she is now—haven't you? And so am I. And so is Albert. You can't feel very badly about a thing that makes us all happy, can you?"

Just then Julia came in, radiant from a brisk walk, fresh and cheery, a big bunch of violets at her breast.

"Oh, Mother," she cried, "I've got tickets and we'll all go to hear Melba—if we can get Celia to come in for the evening."

She saw her husband, and a guilty flush rose to her brow as she met his reproachful eyes.

"Oh, Frank!" she begged, her arms around his neck. "Please don't mind! Please get used to it! Please be proud of us! Just think, we're all so happy, and we earn about a hundred dollars a week—all of us together. You see I have Mother's ten to add to the house money, and twenty or more of my own!"

They had a long talk together that evening, just the two of them. She told him, at last, what a danger had hung over them—how near it came.

"And Mother showed me the way out, Frank. The way to have my mind again—and not lose you! She is a different woman herself now that she has her heart and hands full of babies. Albert does enjoy it so! And *you've* enjoyed it—till you found it out!

"And dear—my own love—I don't mind it now at all! I love my home, I love my work, I love my mother, I love you. And as to children—I wish I had six!"

He looked at her flushed, eager, lovely face, and drew her close to him.

"If it makes all of you as happy as that," he said, "I guess I can stand it."

And in after years he was heard to remark, "This being married and bringing up children is as easy as can be—when you learn how!"

The Jumping-Off Place

TWO NEW GUESTS were expected at The Jumping-Off Place that night. The establishment was really too full already of Professors, Professorins and—shall we take a lingual liberty and say Professorinii?

The extra ones however had special claims in the mind of Miss Shortridge; claims well weighed by her when she answered their letters.

The Reverend Joseph Whitcomb had been one of her oldest and most honored friends; her minister for some thirty years. She could remember as if of yesterday the hot still Sunday in late May when he was installed in the white wooden church; the warm approval of the entire congregation, with the possible exception of the two oldest deacons and Miss Makepeace—whose name belied her; the instant and continuous adoration of the women, young and old; their artless efforts to attract his attention, win his favor—she herself among the eagerest, worshipping devoutly and afar; and the chill that fell upon them all when after a few years of this idolatry he brought home a wife after his vacation absence.

A higher call, with a higher salary attached, had taken him to the big city afterward, and in later days she had sat under him there, still worshipping, though with a chastened adoration. It was nine years since she had left that city:——

He had heard of the excellence of her accommodation, his letter read; the quiet intellectual atmosphere of the place—could she be his old parishioner, Miss Shortridge, of Brooktown? And could she put him up for a week or so?

Then she had asked one of the young unmarried Professors if he would mind having his bill reduced three dollars, and sleeping in the woodshed chamber, for a week; and by a comfortable coincidence of desires he was very glad to.

The other letter she was slower in answering.

"Can it be possible that you are the Jean Shortridge I used to know in Brooktown?" this ran. "Perhaps you won't remember me—Bessie Moore that was—then Mrs. Paul Olcott—now Mrs. Weatherby. I'm not at all strong, and I've heard of your place as being so refined and quiet, with really excellent food and beds, and very reasonable prices. Could you give me a nice room for two weeks or a month—a large comfortable room, near a bathroom, corner room if possible, and not too many stairs—and what would you charge an old friend?"

There was just one such room unrented, and that was Miss Shortridge's own. With a fortitude rare among those who give board and lodging, she always retained for herself a restful, convenient, quiet room; and enjoyed it.

She read Mrs. Weatherby's letter over more than once, her amused smile growing as she studied it.

"I believe I will," she said to herself at length, "just for the fun of it. I can manage to dress in the garret for a little while. It won't affect my sleeping, anyhow."

So she wrote to both that for a week's time she would gladly accommodate them, and found continuing entertainment in the days before their coming in memories and speculations.

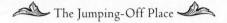

"You're not really going to give up your room at last," protestingly inquired Mrs. Professor Joran, who had tried vainly to secure it for a friend.

"Only for a week," Miss Shortridge explained, "and under rather exceptional circumstances: The lady coming was a—I have known her since early girlhood."

The advent of Dr. Whitcomb excited more discussion, and was hailed with a better grace, as no one begrudged the young unmarried Professor's room, while many had desired Miss Shortridge's. They were all extremely polite to their entertainer, however, she not being, so to speak, a professional; taking only a few during the summer months to accommodate; and accommodating beyond the dreams of local competitors.

No professional comments reached her ears regarding the expected arrivals, but she, in her own mind, dwelt upon them with growing interest. She remembered Bessie Moore with sharp, almost painful clearness, from the day she was "teacher's pet" in school, up through her pink and ringleted girlhood, to the white delicacy of her beauty as a bride.

Miss Shortridge had seen her twice as a bride—and as long as she lived would remember those occasions. She could see her still, at nineteen, standing there in soft veiled whiteness, her small face, pink as a rose beneath the tulle, beside Paul Olcott with his slim young dignity and serious, intellectual face; while she, plain Jean Shortridge, sat, watching, with a pain in her heart that she had honestly believed would kill her.

Not dying, she had gone away to work; and twelve years later found her comfortably established in the office of Horace Weatherby; his trusted, valued and fairly well-paid secretary.

Slowly, and not unnaturally, through long association she had grown to think more and more of this rather burly and florid gentleman, a successful man, cold and peremptory with subordinates, yet always distinctly courteous to a woman of any class.

As a married man her thoughts of him had been but distantly admiring; when she knew him a widower she had allowed herself to sympathize, afar; when he grew more gracious and approachable with the passing of time, why then—

"What an uncommon old fool I must have been!" said Miss Shortridge to herself, as she summoned those days before her.

Yet she was not old then, only thirty-five, and if a fool, by no means an uncommon one. She had lived in a fool's paradise for a while, it is true, building castles in Spain out of the veriest sticks and straws of friendliness. And then one day, in a burst of exceptionable cordiality, he had invited her to his wedding. And she had gone, veiled, shrinking behind a pillar, scarce able to force herself there, yet wholly unable to stay away.

There was the big, impressive church, her church too, though she hardly knew it with these accessories of carpets, canopies, carriages, crowds; its heaped flowers and triumphant bursts of music. And then, up the aisle, pinker and plumper than ever, in tightly gleaming pearl gray satin, with pearls and lace and a profusion of orange blossoms—Bessie Moore again!

And that was more than twenty years ago!

As the slow train struggled on from little town to little town, its crushed commuters scattering like popped corn at every station, Mrs. Horace Weatherby speculated more and more as to the impressive clerical figure a few seats in front of her. The broad square shoulders, the thick gray hair with a wave that was almost a curl—surely she had seen them somewhere.

Sudden need for a glass of water took her down the aisle beyond him, and a returning view brought recognition.

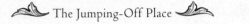

"Dr. Whitcomb!—Oh this *is* a pleasure! Do you remember an old parishioner?"

The reverend gentleman rose to the occasion with that marked deference and suave address which had always distinguished his manner to ladies. Remember her! He did indeed. Had he not twice had the privilege of marrying her—with its invaluable perquisite!

Mrs. Weatherby could still blush at fifty-three, and did so, prettily.

"It's a great pleasure to meet you, I'm sure," she said; and then, in a burst of intuition—"perhaps you're going to Jean Shortridge's too!"

He complimented her on her marvelous perception—"I am indeed! And you also?—What a pleasure!"

"I've heard such nice things of her place," said the lady. "Some friends of mine knew a Professor's family from Lincoln, Nebraska, that went there—they said it was ideal!"

"We are very fortunate, I am sure," agreed Dr. Whitcomb, "though our stay is but a short one."

"If I like it I shall stay," the lady asserted, smiling, "She'd never turn out an old friend."

"You have known her a long time?" he inquired.

"O mercy, yes! Since we were babies. She was such a plain little thing—poor dear!—with her hair combed straight back, and a skimpy little pigtail. Grew up plain, too—as you may remember! She had a Sunday school class, you know, in your church. She was a good girl, and clever in a way; clever at books; but not at all brilliant. I think—I don't know as it's any harm to say it after all these years—but I *think* she was very much in love with my first husband—before he married me, of course."

Dr. Whitcomb looked gravely interested, and made appropriate murmurs as occasion allowed.

"She went to the city to work after that," continued the lady in continuous flow, "and the next I heard of her—years later—she was secretary to Mr. Weatherby—or had been. That was before I married him. And then—when did I hear of her next? O, yes. My sister met her somewhere about ten years ago. She must have been all of fifty then!—How time does fly!"

"The lady must be much older than you, I am sure," said Dr. Whitcomb.

"Yes, she is; quite a little; but I'm old enough!" She smiled archly.

"Exactly old enough—and not a bit more," he promptly agreed.

"Lulu said she was a perfect wreck!" Mrs. Weatherby continued. "Looked sixty instead of fifty, and *so* shabby! I don't know what she's done with herself since, I'm sure, but she's somehow got the place at Crosswater (where they have that scientific summer school—fish and things—) and takes boarders in summer—that's all I know."

"It will be very interesting for you to see her again," he suggested. "So many old memories."

"Some very sad ones, Dr. Whitcomb," murmured the lady, and was easily led or rather was not to be withheld from confiding to his practiced ear the sorrows of her life.

As a recipient of women's griefs Dr. Whitcomb was past master; and this assortment was not a novel one. The first husband had proved a consumptive. There were four little children, three little graves, one grown son, always delicate, now haunting the southwest in search of health; with even more of a shadow on his mother's face in speaking of him than his invalidism alone seemed to justify.

Then the husband's early death—her utter loss—her loneliness—did he blame her for marrying again?

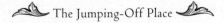

Indeed he did not. Marriage was an honorable estate; women especially needed a protecting arm. He trusted that her later happiness had overcome the memory of pain.

But here the appeal to his sympathies was stronger than before.

"O, Dr. Whitcomb! You don't know! I can never tell anyone all I've been through! I lived with Mr. Weatherby for twenty years—it was a martyrdom, Dr. Whitcomb!"

The worthy doctor had a fairly accurate knowledge of his former wealthy parishioner's life and character, and he nodded his head in grave sympathy; the long clean-shaven upper lip pursed solemnly.

"It was not only drink, Dr. Whitcomb—that I could have forgiven!—It is such a relief to speak to you!—Of course I never say a word against him—but you know!"

"I do indeed, Mrs. Weatherby. You have my sincerest sympathy. You have suffered much—but suffering often leads us Heavenward!"

Meanwhile the lady did not forget a truth long known to her—that men like sympathy as well as women—and presently drew from him the admission that his health was far from good, asthma admitted, other troubles merely hinted at; and that widower-hood was also lonely.

He did not, however, confide to her the uncertain condition of his financial outlook; his lifelong inability to save; his increasing difficulty in finding a pulpit to satisfy his pride—or even his necessity.

Nor did she, for all her fluent recital, hint at the sad deficiencies revealed when the estate of the late Horace Weatherby came to settlement; which was indeed unnecessary, for he had heard these facts.

The Crosswater stage took them, swaying and joggling in its lean-cushioned seats, through the shadowy afternoon woods and along a sluggish brook that curved through encroaching bushes and spread lazily out in successive ponds, starred with white lilies.

When the road seemed to stop short off and end nowhere, with only blue water and blue sky as alternatives, a short turn round a bunch of cedars brought them to Miss Shortridge's door.

"Why, Jean Shortridge! I'd never have known you in the world!" cried Mrs. Weatherby, trying to kiss her affectionately, and somehow missing it as her hostess turned to greet Dr. Whitcomb.

"I am delighted to meet you again, Miss Shortridge," he said, holding her hand impulsively in both his. "How well you look! How young—if you will pardon me—how young you look!"

Even; Mrs. Weatherby, jealously scrutinizing her old friend, could not deny that there was something in what he said. Her own bright color and plump outlines had long since given way to the dragging softness of a face well nursed, but little used; expressing only the soft negation of an old child; and her figure now took shape more from the stays without than from the frame within.

Jean Shortridge stood erect and lightly upon her feet. She moved with swift alertness, and carried herself with agility. Her face was healthily weatherbeaten; high colored from sun and wind; her eyes bright and steady.

She was cordial, but not diffuse; installed them presently in their respective rooms, and sat smiling and well-gowned at the head of her table when they came to supper.

In the days that followed the new guests learned from the old ones much of their hostess's present and recent achievements. This was her third season here, it appeared, and she was regarded as a wonder; she had bought this old place—mortgaged—and was understood to be paying the mortgage,

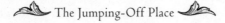

or to have paid it; she was liked and respected in the little community, and considered a solid citizen in spite of her wild eccentricity—she slept out of doors!

All this was commonly known, but what Mrs. Weatherby wanted to know, and, if the truth must be told, Dr. Whitcomb also, was the tale of those years unaccounted for since Jean Shortridge had last been "sighted"—and set down as an absolute wreck.

It was extremely difficult to get Miss Shortridge's ear. Her bedchamber on the roof of a porch was inaccessible to others, and she sought that skyey chamber immediately after supper. She was a-foot at dawn and at work, really at work, in her garden. Not a rose garden this, but several acres of highly cultivated land, which the active lady "worked with her hands," enough to satisfy the most ardent Tolstoyan.

Small time had she for casual conversation save at meals, and then competition was heavy.

So Mrs. Weatherby must needs content herself, during a too short week of good air, good sleep, good food, and good company, with a very pretty campaign of "friendliness" directed against that smoothly defended fortress of Dr. Whitcomb's elderly affections.

Well used was the plump widow to these lines of attack; but even better used was he to all the arts of courteous evasion. Not for nothing had he been a popular minister for nearly fifty years.

It was Friday evening (they had arrived on a Saturday) before, at Dr. Whitcomb's direct solicitation, Miss Shortridge agreed to give him an hour, Mrs. Weatherby promptly chipping in to urge "her room" as an excellent place for a talk.

It was; and Miss Shortridge in her own favorite chair looked more than ever the hostess; cordial, friendly, quite at ease.

"Now, Jean Shortridge!" Mrs. Weatherby began, "we are

old friends, and you needn't make any mystery with us. We want to know what you *did*—what on earth you did—to—well to *arrive* like this!"

"Is this what you call 'arriving'?" asked Miss Shortridge. "I'm simply a hard-working woman with her living to earn—and earning it!"

"And a benefactor to society in that process!" blandly interposed the clergyman.

"So is every honest worker, surely!" she suggested, "but I know what you mean, Mrs. Weatherby—I met your sister some seven or eight years ago and I fancy she gave a pretty bad account of me."

"A sad account, Jean—not bad. She said you were not looking at all well."

"No, I was not looking well—nor feeling well—nor doing well," Miss Shortridge admitted.

"And now you are all three," said Dr. Whitcomb, with an inclination of the head and his admiring smile.

She laughed happily. "Thank you—I am," she frankly agreed. "Well, this is what happened. I was fifty, practically—forty-eight, that is—no money—no health—no happiness." Here her eyes rested a moment on Mrs. Weatherby's soft sagging face. "You see I never married and all I had earned was spent as it came; for mother for a long time—and doctors. I had no talent in particular, and it was increasingly hard to get work as a stenographer. They want them young and quick and pretty. So—it seemed to me then that I had come to the jumping-off place."

Her hearers exchanged glances.

"Yes, that's why I named the place—but it's a good name anyhow—and then I got hold of a book—found it by chance in the public library——" Miss Shortridge paused and heaved a large sigh. "That *was* a book!" she said.

"What was it?" eagerly inquired Mrs. Weatherby.

"It was called 'The Woman of Fifty'; author, one 'A. J. Smith.' But that book was written for *me*! It told me what to do and I did it—and it was all true."

"What was it? Oh, do tell us! What did you do?" Mrs. Weatherby urged.

"I began to live," said Miss Shortridge. "You see I thought my life was ended—such as it was—and pitied myself abominably. I got a new notion out of the book—that there was just as much life as ever there was, and it was mine; health—power—success—happiness."

"And so you 'demonstrated'—is that the phrase?" Dr. Whitcomb asked benignly.

"And so I went to work," she replied.

"Work isn't always easy to get, is it?" inquired Mrs. Weatherby.

"Oh, yes—the kind I did. I selected a healthy suburban town—with a good library—and took a kitchen job for five months. Made my own terms—a good reading lamp and a place to sleep out of doors. I worked hard, slept well, ate good food, and saved money. Every evening I read an hour."

"May we ask what you read?"' asked Dr. Whitcomb.

"About nature; about health; about market gardening; and the lives of people who dared to be different. That was a good winter! By June I had over a hundred dollars. All that summer I lived on it. I tramped, rode on trolley cars, lived out of doors—rested. How I rested! Never before in my life had I learned what this world was really like."

"In wet spells I'd board at some farm house. And I gradually settled on the place where I wanted to live the next year—the man was a market gardener—I wanted to learn the business. I worked out doors and in that year; no time to read, slept like a log, grew strong—saved money.

"I got acquainted, too, and learned a lot about horses and pigs and hens, as well as garden stuff. By the end of the second year I had 450 dollars and some experience. Then I went in with a woman who took summer boarders. She rented me her garden, I furnished enough for the house to pay for it; and I could sell what I had left. I made a lot that year.

"Then I heard of this place, got it on good terms (it was heavily mortgaged you see), and—well, I've paid the mortgage. I own it clear."

"A magnificent record!" said Dr. Whitcomb.

"But how hard you have worked—how hard you work now!" Mrs. Weatherby exclaimed. "I don't see how you stand it."

"I like it, you see," said their hostess. "I like it while I'm doing it, I make a good living by it, and I've got something to look forward to. When I've saved enough I'm going to take a year off, and travel."

"But—it's not like having a family," Mrs. Weatherby ventured.

"No, it's not. I wish I had a family.... But since I haven't— why, I might as well have a life of my own. By the time I'm sixty I mean to take that year abroad I speak of. After that I'll keep on earning. Buy me an annuity, perhaps. There is a home for old people in Los Angeles, I've heard, that's pretty near perfect. I might go there to finish up."

She looked so cheerful, so alert, so capable and assured, and full of hope, so perplexingly young in spite of her gray hair, that Mrs. Weatherby was puzzled in her estimate of age.

"Aren't you older than I am, Jean," she said. "You used to be."

Jean laughed. "Certainly I am. I'm fifty-seven; you're fifty-three. We've both got many years to look forward to."

"I don't see how you work such financial miracles, Miss

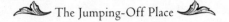

Shortridge," the clergyman protested. "Surely it is not open to every woman of middle age to achieve independence as easily."

"Perhaps they wouldn't all find it easy," she answered. "It did take some courage, and a definite, sustaining purpose. But the way is wide open. You see I have three lines of work: I raise vegetables and fruits and sell them during the summer. I preserve and can all I do not sell or use, and the boarders during the summer are a great help. By the way, Mrs. Weatherby, are you to take the morning stage, or the afternoon?"

"Why, I was hoping you'd let me stay longer," said that lady lamely; "I'm very comfortable here: it has done me ever so much good."

"I am sorry, but I cannot spare the room," Miss Shortridge replied.

Dr. Whitcomb did not wait for her to ask his hour of leaving—"The morning stage, if you please; and I am extremely grateful for this pleasant visit. It has been a great pleasure, too, to renew our old acquaintance."

He was up betimes next morning, early enough to find Miss Shortridge in her well kept garden hard at work. He begged a few moments' talk with her, and used his best powers to attract and hold her attention. He spoke of the changes of life; of her long, patient struggle to support herself and care for her mother; of her phenomenal enterprise and success.

She listened gravely, picking her beans with a deft, practiced hand, and stepping slowly along between the dew-wet rows, while he followed.

Then in deeper, softer tones he referred to his own life; to the pain of loss and loneliness; the injury to his work. He longed for true companionship to the end of the journey. Would she, for the time of rich autumnal peace, be his companion?

It is said that all women have at least one offer of marriage; but Jean Shortridge never expected to receive her first at fifty-seven. She thanked him sincerely for the compliment he paid her, but was not inclined to accept it.

He urged her to take time; to think it over. This was no boyish appeal, but a calm proposal for the joining of their declining years; no mad young passion, but real friendship; understanding; a warm, appreciative affection; she must think it over.

He went away on the morning stage, Mrs. Weatherby accompanying him, at some inconvenience in the matter of packing.

Miss Shortridge considered her first offer of marriage for a full week, and then declined it.

"Why should I?" she said to herself. "I always hated nursing. Let Bessie have him, too!"

But Bessie failed this time.

The Widow's Might

JAMES HAD COME on to the funeral but his wife had not; she could not leave the children—that is what he said. She said, privately, to him, that she would not go. She never was willing to leave New York except for Europe or for Summer vacations; and a trip to Denver in November—to attend a funeral—was not a possibility to her mind.

Ellen and Adelaide were both there: they felt it a duty—but neither of their husbands had come. Mr. Jennings could not leave his classes in Cambridge, and Mr. Oswald could not leave his business in Pittsburg—that is what they said.

The last services were over. They had had a cold, melancholy lunch and were all to take the night train home again. Meanwhile the lawyer was coming at four to read the will.

"It is only a formality. There can't be much left," said James.

"No," agreed Adelaide, "I suppose not."

"A long illness eats up everything," said Ellen, and sighed. Her husband had come to Colorado for his lungs years before and was still delicate.

"Well," said James rather abruptly, "What are we going to do with Mother?"

"Why, of course—" Ellen began, "We *could* take her. It

would depend a good deal on how much property there is—I mean, on where she'd want to go. Edward's salary is more than needed now," Ellen's mental processes seemed a little mixed.

"She can come to me if she prefers, of course," said Adelaide. "But I don't think it would be very pleasant for her. Mother never did like Pittsburg." James looked from one to the other.

"Let me see—how old is Mother?"

"Oh she's all of fifty," answered Ellen, "and much broken, I think. It's been a long strain, you know." She turned plaintively to her brother. "I should think you could make her more comfortable than either of us, James—with your big house."

"I think a woman is always happier living with a son than with a daughter's husband," said Adelaide. "I've always thought so."

"That is often true," her brother admitted. "But it depends." He stopped, and the sisters exchanged glances. They knew upon what it depended.

"Perhaps if she stayed with me, you could—help some," suggested Ellen.

"Of course, of course, I could do that," he agreed with evident relief. "She might visit between you—take turns—and I could pay her board. About how much ought it to amount to? We might as well arrange everything now."

"Things cost awfully in these days," Ellen said with a crisscross of fine wrinkles on her pale forehead. "But of course it would be only just *what* it costs. I shouldn't want to make anything."

"It's work and care, Ellen, and you may as well admit it. You need all your strength—with those sickly children and Edward on your hands. When she comes to me, there need be no expense, James, except for clothes. I have room enough and Mr. Oswald will never notice the difference in the house bills—but he does hate to pay out money for clothes."

"Mother must be provided for properly," her son declared. "How much ought it to cost—a year—for clothes."

"You know what your wife's cost," suggested Adelaide, with a flicker of a smile about her lips.

"Oh, *no*," said Ellen. "That's no criterion! Maude is in society, you see. Mother wouldn't *dream* of having so much."

James looked at her gratefully. "Board and clothes—all told; what should you say, Ellen?"

Ellen scrabbled in her small black hand bag for a piece of paper, and found none. James handed her an envelope and a fountain pen.

"Food—just plain food materials—costs all of four dollars a week now for one person," said she. "And heat—and light—and extra service. I should think six a week would be the *least*, James. And for clothes and carfare and small expenses—I should say—well, three hundred dollars!

"That would make over six hundred a year," said James slowly. "How about Oswald sharing that, Adelaide?"

Adelaide flushed. "I do not think he would be willing, James. Of course if it were absolutely necessary—"

"He has money enough," said her brother.

"Yes, but he never seems to have any outside of his business—and he has his own parents to carry now. No—I can give her a home, but that's all."

"You see, you'd have none of the care and trouble, James," said Ellen. "We—the girls—are each willing to have her with us, while perhaps Maude wouldn't care to, but if you could just pay the money—"

"Maybe there's some left, after all," suggested Adelaide. "And this place ought to sell for something."

"This place" was a piece of rolling land within ten miles of Denver. It had a bit of river bottom, and ran up towards the foothills. From the house the view ran north and south along the precipitous ranks of the "Big Rockies" to westward. To the east lay the vast stretches of sloping plain.

"There ought to be at least six or eight thousand dollars from it, I should say," he concluded.

"Speaking of clothes," Adelaide rather irrelevantly suggested, "I see Mother didn't get any new black. She's always worn it as long as I can remember."

"Mother's a long time," said Ellen.

"I wonder if she wants anything, I'll go up and see."

"No," said Adelaide, "She said she wanted to be let alone—and rest. She said she'd be down by the time Mr. Frankland got here."

"She's bearing it pretty well," Ellen suggested, after a little silence.

"It's not like a broken heart," Adelaide explained. "Of course Father meant well—"

"He was a man who always did his duty," admitted Ellen, "But we—none of us—loved him—very much."

"He is dead and buried," said James. "We can at least respect his memory."

"We've hardly seen Mother—under that black veil," Ellen went on. "It must have aged her. This long nursing."

"She had help toward the last—a man nurse," said Adelaide.

"Yes, but a long illness is an awful strain—and Mother never was good at nursing. She has surely done her duty," pursued Ellen.

"And now she's entitled to a rest, said James, rising and walking about the room. "I wonder how soon we can close up affairs here—and get rid of this place. There might be enough in it to give her almost a living—properly invested."

Ellen looked out across the dusty stretches of land.

"How I did hate to live here!" she said.

"So did I," said Adelaide.

"So did I," said James.

And they all smiled rather grimly.

"We don't any of us seem to be very affectionate, about Mother," Adelaide presently admitted, "I don't know why it is—we never were an affectionate family, I guess."

"Nobody could be affectionate with Father," Ellen suggested timidly.

"And Mother—poor Mother! She's had an awful life."

"Mother has always done her duty," said James in a determined voice, "and so did Father, as he saw it. Now we'll do ours."

"Ah," exclaimed Ellen, jumping to her feet, "Here comes the lawyer, I'll call Mother."

She ran quickly upstairs and tapped at her mother's door.

"Mother, oh Mother, Mr. Frankland's come."

"I know it," came back a voice from within. "Tell him to go ahead and read the will. I know what's in it. I'll be down in a few minutes."

Ellen went slowly back downstairs with the fine crisscross of wrinkles showing on her pale forehead again, and delivered her mother's message.

The other two glanced at each other hesitatingly, but Mr. Frankland spoke up briskly.

"Quite natural, of course, under the circumstances. Sorry I couldn't get to the funeral. A case on this morning." The will was short. The estate was left to be divided among the children in four equal parts, two to the son and one each to the daughters after the mother's legal share had been deducted, if she were still living. In such case they were furthermore directed to provide for their mother while she lived. The estate, as described, consisted of the ranch, the large, rambling house on it, with all the furniture, stock and implements, and some $5,000 in mining stocks.

"That is less than I had supposed, said James.

"This will was made ten years ago," Mr. Frankland explained. "I have done business for your father since that time. He kept his faculties to the end, and I think that you will find that the property has appreciated. Mrs. McPherson has taken excellent care of the ranch, I understand—and has had some boarders."

Both the sisters exchanged pained glances.

"There's an end to all that now," said James.

At this moment, the door opened and a tall black figure, cloaked and veiled, came into the room.

"I'm glad to hear you say that Mr. McPherson kept his faculties to the last, Mr. Frankland," said the widow. "It's true. I didn't come down to hear that old will. It's no good now."

They all turned in their chairs.

"Is there a later will, madam?" inquired the lawyer.

"Not that I know of. Mr. McPherson had no property when he died."

"No property! My dear lady—four years ago he certainly had some."

"Yes, but three years and a half ago he gave it all to me. Here are the deeds."

There they were, in very truth—formal and correct, and quite simple and clear—for deeds, James R. McPherson, Sr., had assuredly given to his wife the whole estate.

"You remember that was the panic year," she continued. "There was pressure from some of Mr. McPherson's creditors; he thought it would be safer so."

"Why—yes," remarked Mr. Frankland, "I do remember

now his advising with me about it. But I thought the step unnecessary."

James cleared his throat.

"Well, Mother, this does complicate matters a little. We were hoping that we could settle up all the business this afternoon—with Mr. Frankland's help—and take you back with us."

"We can't be spared any longer, you see, Mother," said Ellen.

"Can't you deed it back again, Mother," Adelaide suggested, "to James, or to—all of us, so we can get away?"

"Why should I?" she cried.

"Now, Mother," Ellen put in persuasively, "we know how badly you feel, and you are nervous and tired, but I told you this morning when we came, that we expected to take you back with us. You know you've been packing—"

"Yes, I've been packing," replied the voice behind the veil.

"I dare say it was safer—to have the property in your name—technically," James admitted, "but now I think it would be the simplest way for you to make it over to me in a lump, and I will see that Father's wishes are carried out to the letter."

"Your father is dead," remarked the voice.

"Yes, Mother, we know—we know how you feel," Ellen ventured.

"I am alive," said Mrs. McPherson.

"Dear Mother, it's very trying to talk business to you at such a time. We all realize it," Adelaide explained with a touch of asperity, "But we told you we couldn't stay as soon as we got here."

"And the business has to be settled," James added conclusively.

"It is settled."

"Perhaps Mr. Frankland can make it clear to you," went on James with forced patience.

"I do not doubt that your mother understands perfectly," murmured the lawyer. "I have always found her a woman of remarkable intelligence."

"Thank you, Mr. Frankland. Possibly you may be able to make my children understand that this property—such as it is—is mine now."

"Why assuredly, assuredly, Mrs. McPherson. We all see that. But we assume, as a matter of course, that you will consider Mr. McPherson's wishes in regard to the disposition of the estate."

"I have considered Mr. McPherson's wishes for thirty years," she replied.

"Now, I'll consider mine. I have done my duty since the day I married him. It is eleven hundred days—today." The last with sudden intensity.

"But madam, your children—"

"I have no children, Mr. Frankland. I have two daughters and a son. These two grown persons here, grown up, married, having children of their own or ought to have—were my children. I did my duty by them, and they did their duty by me—and would yet, no doubt." The tone changed suddenly.

"But they don't have to. I'm tired of duty."

The little group of listeners looked up, startled.

"You don't know how things have been going on here," the voice went on. "I didn't trouble you with my affairs. But I'll tell you now. When your father saw fit to make over the property to me—to save it—and when he knew that he hadn't many years to live, I took hold of things. I had to have a nurse for your father—and a doctor coming; the house was a sort of hospital, so I made it a little more so. I had a half a dozen patients and nurses here—and made money by it. I ran the

garden—kept cows—raised my own chickens—worked out doors—slept out of doors.

I'm a stronger woman today than I ever was in my life!"

She stood up, tall, strong and straight, and drew a deep breath.

"Your father's property amounted to about $8,000 when he died," she continued. "That would be $4,000 to James and $2,000 to each of the girls. That I'm willing to give you now— each of you—in your own name. But if my daughters will take my advice, they'd better let me send them the yearly income—in cash—to spend as they like. It is good for a woman to have some money of her own."

"I think you are right, Mother," said Adelaide.

"Yes indeed," murmured Ellen.

"Don't you need it yourself, Mother?" asked James, with a sudden feeling of tenderness for the stiff figure in black.

"No, James, I shall keep the ranch, you see. I have good reliable help. I've made $2,000 a year—clear—off it so far, and now I've rented it for that to a doctor friend of mine—woman doctor."

"I think you have done remarkably well, Mrs. McPherson— wonderfully well," said Mr. Frankland.

"And you'll have an income of $2,000 a year," said Adelaide incredulously.

"You'll come and live with me, won't you," ventured Ellen.

"Thank you, my dear, I will not."

"You're more than welcome in my big house," said Adelaide.

"No thank you, my dear."

"I don't doubt Maude will be glad to have you," James rather hesitatingly offered.

"I do. I doubt it very much, thank you, my dear."

"But what *are* you going to do?"

Ellen seemed genuinely concerned.

"I'm going to do what I never did before. I'm going to live!"

With a firm swift step, the tall figure moved to the windows and pulled up the lowered shades. The brilliant Colorado sunshine poured into the room. She threw off the long black veil.

"That's borrowed," she said. "I didn't want to hurt your feelings at the funeral."

She unbuttoned the long black cloak and dropped it at her feet, standing there in the full sunlight, a little flushed and smiling, dressed in a wellmade traveling suit of dull mixed colors.

"If you want to know my plans, I'll tell you. I've got $6,000 of my own. I earned it in three years—off my little ranch-sanitarium. One thousand I have put in the savings bank—to bring me back from anywhere on earth, and to put me in an old lady's home if it is necessary. Here is an agreement with a cremation company. They'll import me, if necessary, and have me duly—expurgated—or they don't get the money. But I've got $5,000 to play with, and I'm going to play."

Her daughters looked shocked.

"Why Mother—"

"At your age—"

James drew down his upper lip and looked like his father.

"I knew you wouldn't any of you understand," she continued more quietly.

"But it doesn't matter any more. Thirty years I've given you—and your father. Now I'll have thirty years of my own."

"Are you—are you sure you're—well, Mother," Ellen urged with real anxiety.

Her mother laughed outright.

"Well, really well, never was better, have been doing business up to today—good medical testimony that. No question of my sanity, my dears! I want you to grasp the fact that your mother is a Real Person with some interests of her own and half a lifetime yet. The first twenty didn't count for much—I was growing up and couldn't help myself. The last thirty have been—hard. James perhaps realizes that more than you girls, but you all know it. Now, I'm free."

"Where *do* you mean to go, Mother?" James asked.

She looked around the little circle with a serene air of decision and replied.

"To New Zealand. I've always wanted to go there," she pursued. "Now I'm going. And to Australia—and Tasmania—and Madagascar—and Terra del Fuego. I shall be gone some time."

They separated that night—three going East, one West.

Turned

IN HER SOFT-CARPETED, thick-curtained, richly furnished chamber, Mrs. Marroner lay sobbing on the wide, soft bed.

She sobbed bitterly, chokingly, despairingly; her shoulders heaved and shook convulsively; her hands were tight-clenched; she had forgotten her elaborate dress, the more elaborate bed-cover; forgotten her dignity, her self-control, her pride. In her mind was an overwhelming, unbelievable horror, an immeasurable loss, a turbulent, struggling mass of emotion.

In her reserved, superior, Boston-bred life she had never dreamed that it would be possible for her to feel so many things at once, and with such trampling intensity.

She tried to cool her feelings into thoughts; to stiffen them into words; to control herself—and could not. It brought vaguely to her mind an awful moment in the breakers at York Beach, one summer in girlhood, when she had been swimming under water and could not find the top.

In her uncarpeted, thin-curtained, poorly furnished chamber on the top floor, Gerta Petersen lay sobbing on the narrow, hard bed.

She was of larger frame than her mistress, grandly built and strong; but all her proud young womanhood was prostrate now, convulsed with agony, dissolved in tears. She did not try to control herself. She wept for two.

If Mrs. Marroner suffered more from the wreck and ruin of a longer love—perhaps a deeper one; if her tastes were finer, her ideals loftier; if she bore the pangs of bitter jealousy and outraged pride, Gerta had personal shame to meet, a hopeless future, and a looming present which filled her with unreasoning terror.

She had come like a meek young goddess into that perfectly ordered house, strong, beautiful, full of good will and eager obedience, but ignorant and childish—a girl of eighteen.

Mr. Marroner had frankly admired her, and so had his wife. They discussed her visible perfections and as visible limitations with that perfect confidence which they had so long enjoyed. Mrs. Marroner was not a jealous woman. She had never been jealous in her life—till now.

Gerta had stayed and learned their ways. They had both been fond of her. Even the cook was fond of her. She was what is called "willing," was unusually teachable and plastic; and Mrs. Marroner, with her early habits of giving instruction, tried to educate her somewhat.

"I never saw anyone so docile," Mrs. Marroner had often commented. "It is perfection in a servant, but almost a defect in character. She is so helpless and confiding."

She was precisely that; a tall, rosy-cheeked baby; rich womanhood without, helpless infancy within. Her braided wealth of dead-gold hair, her grave blue eyes, her mighty shoulders, and long, firmly moulded limbs seemed those of a primal earth spirit; but she was only an ignorant child, with a child's weakness.

When Mr. Marroner had to go abroad for his firm, unwillingly, hating to leave his wife, he had told her he felt quite safe to leave her in Gerta's hands—she would take care of her.

"Be good to your mistress, Gerta," he told the girl that last morning at breakfast. "I leave her to you to take care of. I shall be back in a month at latest."

Then he turned, smiling, to his wife. "And you must take care of Gerta, too," he said. "I expect you'll have her ready for college when I get back."

This was seven months ago. Business had delayed him from week to week, from month to month. He wrote to his wife, long, loving, frequent letters; deeply regretting the delay, explaining how necessary, how profitable it was; congratulating her on the wide resources she had; her well-filled, well-balanced mind; her many interests.

"If I should be eliminated from your scheme of things, by any of those 'acts of God' mentioned on the tickets, I do not feel that you would be an utter wreck," he said. "That is very comforting to me. Your life is so rich and wide that no one loss, even a great one, would wholly cripple you. But nothing of the sort is likely to happen, and I shall be home again in three weeks—if this thing gets settled. And you will be looking so lovely, with that eager light in your eyes and the changing flush I know so well—and love so well! My dear wife! We shall have to have a new honeymoon—other moons come every month, why shouldn't the mellifluous kind?"

He often asked after "little Gerta," sometimes enclosed a picture postcard to her, joked his wife about her laborious efforts to educate "the child;" was so loving and merry and wise——

All this was racing through Mrs. Marroner's mind as she lay there with the broad, hemstitched border of fine linen

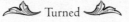

sheeting crushed and twisted in one hand, and the other holding a sodden handkerchief.

She had tried to teach Gerta, and had grown to love the patient, sweet-natured child, in spite of her dullness. At work with her hands, she was clever, if not quick, and could keep small accounts from week to week. But to the woman who held a Ph.D., who had been on the faculty of a college, it was like baby-tending.

Perhaps having no babies of her own made her love the big child the more, though the years between them were but fifteen.

To the girl she seemed quite old, of course; and her young heart was full of grateful affection for the patient care which made her feel so much at home in this new land.

And then she had noticed a shadow on the girl's bright face. She looked nervous, anxious, worried. When the bell rang she seemed startled, and would rush hurriedly to the door. Her peals of frank laughter no longer rose from the area gate as she stood talking with the always admiring tradesmen.

Mrs. Marroner had labored long to teach her more reserve with men, and flattered herself that her words were at last effective. She suspected the girl of homesickness; which was denied. She suspected her of illness, which was denied also. At last she suspected her of something which could not be denied.

For a long time she refused to believe it, waiting. Then she had to believe it, but schooled herself to patience and understanding. "The poor child," she said. "She is here without a mother—she is so foolish and yielding—I must not be too stern with her." And she tried to win the girl's confidence with wise, kind words.

But Gerta had literally thrown herself at her feet and begged her with streaming tears not to turn her away. She would admit nothing, explain nothing; but frantically promised to work for Mrs. Marroner as long as she lived—if only she would keep her.

Revolving the problem carefully in her mind, Mrs. Marroner thought she would keep her, at least for the present. She tried to repress her sense of ingratitude in one she had so sincerely tried to help, and the cold, contemptuous anger she had always felt for such weakness.

"The thing to do now," she said to herself, "is to see her through this safely. The child's life should not be hurt any more than is unavoidable. I will ask Dr. Bleet about it—what a comfort a woman doctor is! I'll stand by the poor, foolish thing till it's over, and then get her back to Sweden somehow with her baby. How they do come where they are not wanted—and don't come where they are wanted!" And Mrs. Marroner, sitting along in the quiet, spacious beauty of the house, almost envied Gerta.

Then came the deluge.

She had sent the girl out for needed air toward dark. The late mail came; she took it in herself. One letter for her—her husband's letter. She knew the postmark, the stamp, the kind of typewriting. She impulsively kissed it in the dim hall. No one would suspect Mrs. Marroner of kissing her husband's letters—but she did, often.

She looked over the others. One was for Gerta, and not from Sweden. It looked precisely like her own. This struck her as a little odd, but Mr. Marroner had several times sent messages and cards to the girl. She laid the letter on the hall table and took hers to her room.

"My poor child," it began. What letter of hers had been sad enough to warrant that?

"I am deeply concerned at the news you send." What news to so concern him had she written? "You must bear it bravely, little girl. I shall be home soon, and will take care of you, of course. I hope there is no immediate anxiety—you do not

say. Here is money, in case you need it. I expect to get home in a month at latest. If you have to go, be sure to leave your address at my office. Cheer up—be brave—I will take care of you."

The letter was typewritten, which was not unusual. It was unsigned, which was unusual. It enclosed an American bill—fifty dollars. It did not seem in the least like any letter she had ever had from her husband, or any letter she could imagine him writing. But a strange, cold feeling was creeping over her, like a flood rising around a house.

She utterly refused to admit the ideas which began to bob and push about outside her mind, and to force themselves in. Yet under the pressure of these repudiated thoughts she went downstairs and brought up the other letter—the letter to Gerta. She laid them side by side on a smooth dark space on the table; marched to the piano and played, with stern precision, refusing to think, till the girl came back. When she came in, Mrs. Marroner rose quietly and came to the table. "Here is a letter for you," she said.

The girl stepped forward eagerly, saw the two lying together there, hesitated, and looked at her mistress.

"Take yours, Gerta. Open it, please."

The girl turned frightened eyes upon her.

"I want you to read it, here," said Mrs. Marroner.

"Oh, ma'am—— No! Please don't make me!"

"Why not?"

There seemed to be no reason at hand, and Gerta flushed more deeply and opened her letter. It was long; it was evidently puzzling to her; it began "My dear wife." She read it slowly.

"Are you sure it is your letter?" asked Mrs. Marroner. "Is not this one yours? Is not that one—mine?"

She held out the other letter to her.

"It is a mistake," Mrs. Marroner went on, with a hard quietness. She had lost her social bearings somehow; lost her usual keen sense of the proper thing to do. This was not life, this was a nightmare.

"Do you not see? Your letter was put in my envelope and my letter was put in your envelope. Now we understand it."

But poor Gerta had no antechamber to her mind; no trained forces to preserve order while agony entered. The thing swept over her, resistless, overwhelming. She cowered before the outraged wrath she expected; and from some hidden cavern that wrath arose and swept over her in pale flame.

"Go and pack your trunk," said Mrs. Marroner. "You will leave my house tonight. Here is your money."

She laid down the fifty-dollar bill. She put with it a month's wages. She had no shadow of pity for those anguished eyes, those tears which she heard drop on the floor.

"Go to your room and pack," said Mrs. Marroner. And Gerta, always obedient, went.

Then Mrs. Marroner went to hers, and spent a time she never counted, lying on her face on the bed.

But the training of the twenty-eight years which had elapsed before her marriage; the life at college, both as student and teacher; the independent growth which she had made, formed a very different background for grief from that in Gerta's mind.

After a while Mrs. Marroner arose. She administered to herself a hot bath, a cold shower, a vigorous rubbing. "Now I can think," she said.

First she regretted the sentence of instant banishment. She went upstairs to see if it had been carried out. Poor Gerta! The tempest of her agony had worked itself out at last as in a child, and left her sleeping, the pillow wet, the lips still grieving, a big sob shuddering itself off now and then.

Mrs. Marroner stood and watched her, and as she watched she considered the helpless sweetness of the face; the defenseless, unformed character; the docility and habit of obedience which made her so attractive—and so easily a victim. Also she thought of the mighty force which had swept over her; of the great process now working itself out through her; of how pitiful and futile seemed any resistance she might have made.

She softly returned to her own room, made up a little fire, and sat by it, ignoring her feelings now, as she had before ignored her thoughts.

Here were two women and a man. One woman was a wife; loving, trusting, affectionate. One was a servant; loving, trusting, affectionate: a young girl, an exile, a dependent; grateful for any kindness; untrained, uneducated, childish. She ought, of course, to have resisted temptation; but Mrs. Marroner was wise enough to know how difficult temptation is to recognize when it comes in the guise of friendship and from a source one does not suspect.

Gerta might have done better in resisting the grocer's clerk; had, indeed, with Mrs. Marroner's advice, resisted several. But where respect was due, how could she criticize? Where obedience was due, how could she refuse—with ignorance to hold her blinded—until too late?

As the older, wiser woman forced herself to understand and extenuate the girl's misdeed and foresee her ruined future, a new feeling rose in her heart, strong, clear, and overmastering; a sense of measureless condemnation for the man who had done this thing. He knew. He understood. He could fully foresee and measure the consequences of his act. He appreciated to the full the innocence, the ignorance, the grateful affection, the habitual docility, of which he deliberately took advantage.

Mrs. Marroner rose to icy peaks of intellectual apprehension, from which her hours of frantic pain seemed far indeed removed. He had done this thing under the same roof with her—his wife. He had not frankly loved the younger woman, broken with his wife, made a new marriage. That would have been heart-break pure and simple. This was something else.

That letter, that wretched, cold, carefully guarded, unsigned letter: that bill far safer than a check—these did not speak of affection. Some men can love two women at one time. This was not love.

Mrs. Marroner's sense of pity and outrage for herself, the wife, now spread suddenly into a perception of pity and outrage for the girl. All that splendid, clean young beauty, the hope of a happy life, with marriage and motherhood; honorable independence, even—these were nothing to that man. For his own pleasure he had chosen to rob her of her life's best joys.

He would "take care of her" said the letter? How? In what capacity?

And then, sweeping over both her feelings for herself, the wife, and Gerta, his victim, came a new flood, which literally lifted her to her feet. She rose and walked, her head held high. "This is the sin of man against woman," she said. "The offense is against womanhood. Against motherhood. Against—the child."

She stopped.

The child. His child. That, too, he sacrificed and injured—doomed to degradation.

Mrs. Marroner came of stern New England stock. She was not a Calvinist, hardly even a Unitarian, but the iron of Calvinism was in her soul: of that grim faith which held that most people had to be damned "for the glory of God."

Generations of ancestors who both preached and practiced

stood behind her; people whose lives had been sternly moulded to their highest moments of religious conviction. In sweeping bursts of feeling they achieved "conviction," and afterward they lived and died according to that conviction.

When Mr. Marroner reached home, a few weeks later, following his letters too soon to expect an answer to either, he saw no wife upon the pier, though he had cabled; and found the house closed darkly. He let himself in with his latchkey, and stole softly upstairs, to surprise his wife.

No wife was there.

He rang the bell. No servant answered it.

He turned up light after light; searched the house from top to bottom; it was utterly empty. The kitchen wore a clean, bald, unsympathetic aspect. He left it and slowly mounted the stair, completely dazed. The whole house was clean, in perfect order, wholly vacant.

One thing he felt perfectly sure of—she knew.

Yet was he sure? He must not assume too much. She might have been ill. She might have died. He started to his feet. No, they would have cabled him. He sat down again.

For any such change, if she had wanted him to know, she would have written. Perhaps she had, and he, returning so suddenly, had missed the letter. The thought was some comfort. It must be so. He turned to the telephone, and again hesitated. If she had found out—if she had gone—utterly gone, without a word—should he announce it himself to friends and family?

He walked the floor; he searched everywhere for some letter, some word of explanation. Again and again he went to the telephone—and always stopped. He could not bear to ask: "Do you know where my wife is?"

The harmonious, beautiful rooms reminded him in a dumb, helpless way of her; like the remote smile on the face of the dead. He put out the lights; could not bear the darkness; turned them all on again.

It was a long night—

In the morning he went early to the office. In the accumulated mail was no letter from her. No one seemed to know of anything unusual. A friend asked after his wife—"Pretty glad to see you, I guess?" He answered evasively.

About eleven a man came to see him; John Hill, her lawyer. Her cousin, too. Mr. Marroner had never liked him. He liked him less now, for Mr. Hill merely handed him a letter, remarked, "I was requested to deliver this to you personally," and departed, looking like a person who is called on to kill something offensive.

"I have gone. I will care for Gerta. Goodbye. Marion."

That was all. There was no date, no address, no postmark; nothing but that.

In his anxiety and distress he had fairly forgotten Gerta and all that. Her name aroused in him a sense of rage. She had come between him and his wife. She had taken his wife from him. That was the way he felt.

At first he said nothing, did nothing; lived on alone in his house, taking meals where he chose. When people asked him about his wife he said she was traveling—for her health. He would not have it in the newspapers. Then, as time passed, as no enlightenment came to him, he resolved not to bear it any longer, and employed detectives. They blamed him for not having put them on the track earlier, but set to work, urged to the utmost secrecy.

What to him had been so blank a wall of mystery seemed not to embarrass them in the least. They made careful inquiries as to her "past," found where she had studied, where taught, and on what lines; that she had some little money of her own, that her doctor was Josephine L. Bleet, M.D., and many other bits of information.

As a result of careful and prolonged work, they finally told him that she had resumed teaching under one of her old professors; lived quietly, and apparently kept boarders; giving him town, street, and number, as if it were a matter of no difficulty whatever.

He had returned in early spring. It was autumn before he found her.

A quiet college town in the hills, a broad, shady street, a pleasant house standing in its own lawn, with trees and flowers about it. He had the address in his hand, and the number showed clear on the white gate. He walked up the straight gravel path and rang the bell. An elderly servant opened the door.

"Does Mrs. Marroner live here?"

"No, sir."

"This is number twenty-eight?"

"Yes, sir."

"Who does live here?"

"Miss Wheeling, sir."

Ah! Her maiden name. They had told him, but he had forgotten.

He stepped inside. "I would like to see her," he said.

He was ushered into a still parlor, cool and sweet with the scent of flowers, the flowers she had always loved best. It almost brought tears to his eyes. All their years of happiness rose in his mind again; the exquisite beginnings; the days of eager longing before she was really his; the deep, still beauty of her love.

Surely she would forgive him—she must forgive him. He would humble himself; he would tell her of his honest remorse—his absolute determination to be a different man.

Through the wide doorway there came in to him two women. One like a tall Madonna, bearing a baby in her arms.

Marion, calm, steady, definitely impersonal; nothing but a clear pallor to hint of inner stress.

Gerta, holding the child as a bulwark, with a new intelligence in her face, and her blue, adoring eyes fixed on her friend—not upon him.

He looked from one to the other dumbly.

And the woman who had been his wife asked quietly:

"What have you to say to us?"

A Council
of War

THERE WAS AN informal meeting of women in a London drawing room, a meeting not over large, between twenty and thirty, perhaps, but of a deadly earnestness. Picked women were these, true and tried, many wearing the broad arrow pin, that badge of shame now turned to honor by sheer heroism. Some would qualify this as "blind" heroism or "senseless" heroism. But then, heroes have never been distinguished by a cautious farsightedness or a canny common sense.

No one, not even a one-ideaed physician, could call these women hysterical or morbid. On the contrary they wore a look of calm, uncompromising determination, and were vigorous and healthy enough, save indeed those who had been in prison, and one rather weazened working woman from the north. Still, no one had ever criticized the appearance of the working women, or called them hysterical, as long as they merely worked.

They had been recounting the measures taken in the last seven years, with their results, and though there was no sign of weakening in any face, neither was there any lively hope.

"It is the only way," said one, a slender pretty woman of over forty, who looked like a girl. "We've just got to keep it up, that's all."

"I'm willing enough," said one who wore the arrow badge, speaking with slow determination. Her courage was proved, and her endurance. "I'm *willing*—but we've got to be dead certain that it's really the best way."

"It's the only way!"—protested Lady Horditch, a tall gentle earnest woman, with a pink face and quiet voice.

"They'll ruin us all—they're after the money now." This from a woman who had none of her own.

"They'll simply kill our leaders—one after another." One of the working women said that with a break in her voice. She could not lead, but she could follow—to the very end.

"One thing we have done, anyhow—we've forced their hand," suggested Mrs. Shortham, a pleasant matronly woman who had been most happily married, the mother of a large and fine family, now all grown and established—"we've made the men say what they really think of us—what they've really thought all the time—only they hid it—owing to chivalry."

"Another thing is that we've brought out the real men—the best ones—we know our friends from our enemies now," said a clear-eyed girl.

"It begins to look like war—in this country, at least," Lady Horwich remarked.

Little Mrs. Wedge suggested:

"It's a sort of strike, I think—begging your Ladyship's pardon. They're willing to have us—and use us—on their own terms. But we're on strike now—that's what we are! We're striking for shorter hours,"—she laughed a grim little laugh, intelligent smiles agreed with her, "and for higher wages, and for" there was a catch in her breath as she looked around at them—"for the Union!"

"Ah!"—and a deep breath all around, a warm handclasp from Lady Horwich who sat next to her, "Hear, Hear!" from several.

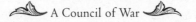

Miss Waltress, a sturdy attractive blonde woman of about thirty, well-known for her highly popular love stories, had been sitting quite silent so far, listening to every word. Now she lifted her head.

"When men began to strike they were in small groups— fiercely earnest, but small and therefore weak. They were frequently violent. They were usually beaten on legal grounds, because of their violence; they were supplemented by others who took their places, or they were starved out—because of their poverty. Why do they so frequently succeed now?"

She looked at Mrs. Wedge from Lancashire, and Mrs. Wedge looked back at her with a kindling eye.

"Because there's so many of 'em now—and they hang together so well, and they keep on the safe side of the law, *and* they've got the brass."

Miss Waltress nodded. "Exactly," said she. "Now friends, I've got something to suggest to you, something very earnest. Mrs. Shortham and I have been talking about it for days,—she has something to say first."

"I think it comes with as good grace from me as from anybody," that lady began quietly. "All of you know how absolutely happy I was with one of the best men God ever made. That shows I'm not prejudiced. And it can't hurt his feelings, now. As to his 'memory'—he put me up to most of this, and urged me to publish it—but I—I just *couldn't* while he was alive."

Most of them had known Hugh Shortham, a tall deep-chested jovial man, always one of the most ardent advocates of the enlargement of women. His big manliness, his efficiency and success, had always made him a tower of strength against those who still talk of "shorthaired women and long-haired men" as the sole supporters of this cause.

What Mrs. Shortham now read was a brief but terrible

indictment of what the title called "The Human Error." It recounted the evil results of male rule, as affecting the health, beauty, intelligence, prosperity, progress and happiness of humanity, in such clear and terrible terms, with such an accumulating pile of injuries, that faces grew white and lips set in hard steely lines as they listened.

"All this does not in the least militate against the beauty and use of true manhood in right relation to women, nor does it contradict the present superior development of men in all lines of social progress. It does, however, in some sort make out the case against man. There follows the natural corollary that we, the women of today, seeing these things, must with all speed possible set ourselves to remove this devastating error in relation, and to establish a free and conscious womanhood for the right service of the world."

There was a hot silence, with little murmurs of horror at some of the charges she had made, and a stir of new determination. Not all of them, keen as they were for the ballot, deeply as they felt the unnecessary sorrows of women, had ever had the historic panorama of injustice and its deadly consequences so vividly set before them.

"I knew it was bad enough," broke forth little Mrs. Wedge, "but I never knew it was as bad as *that*. Look at the consequences."

"That's exactly it, Mrs. Wedge! It's the consequences we are looking at. We are tired of these consequences. We want some new ones!" and Miss Waltress looked around the room, from face to face.

"I'm ready!" said a pale thin woman with an arrow pin.

They were, every one of them. Then Miss Waltress began.

"What I have to suggest, is a wider, deeper, longer, stronger strike."

Mrs. Wedge, her eyes fixed on the calm earnest face, drew in her breath with a big intake.

"Even if we get the ballot in a year—the work is only begun. Men have had that weapon for a good while now, and they have not accomplished everything—even for themselves. And if we do not get it in a year—or five—or ten—are we to do nothing in all that time save repeat what we have done before? I know the ballot is the best weapon, but—there are others. There are enough of us to keep up our previous tactics as long as we hold it necessary. I say nothing whatever against it. But there are also enough of us to be doing other things too.

"Here is my suggestion. We need a government within a government; an organization of women, growing and strengthening against the time when it may come forward in full equality with that of men; a training school for world politics. This may become a world-group, holding international meetings and influencing the largest issues. I speak here only of a definite, practical beginning in this country.

"Let us form a committee, called, perhaps, 'Advisory Committee on Special Measures,' or simpler still, we might call it 'Extension Committee'—that tells nothing, and has no limitations.

"The measures I propose are these:—

"That we begin a series of business undertakings, plain ordinary, every day businesses—farms, market gardens, greenhouses, small fruits, preserves, confections, bakeries, eating-houses, boarding and lodging houses, hotels, milliners and dressmakers' shops, laundries, schools, kindergartens, nurseries—any and every business which women can enter.

"Yes, I know that women are in these things now,—but they are not united, not organized. This is a great spreading league of interconnected businesses, with the economic advantages of such large union."

"Like a trust," said Mrs. Shortham. "A woman's trust."

"Or a Co-operative Society—or a Friendly," breathed little Mrs. Wedge, her cheeks flushing.

"Yes, all this and more. This is no haphazard solitary struggle of isolated women, competing with men, this is a body of women that can grow to an unlimited extent, and be stronger and richer as it grows. But it can begin as small as you please, and without any noise whatever.

"Now see here—you all know how women are sweated and exploited; how they overwork us and underpay us, and how they try to keep us out of trades and professions just as the Americans try to keep out Chinese labor—because they are afraid of being driven out of the market by a lower standard of living.

"Very well. Suppose we take them on their own terms. Because we can live on nothing a week and find ourselves— therefore we can cut the ground out from under their feet!"

The bitter intensity of her tones made a little shiver run around the circle, but they all shared her feeling.

"Don't imagine I mean to take over the business of the world—by no means. But I mean to initiate a movement which means on the surface, in immediate results, only some women going into business—that's no novelty! Underneath it means a great growing association with steady increase of power."

"To what end—as a war measure, I mean?" Lady Horwich inquired.

"To several ends. The most patent, perhaps, is to accumulate the sinews of war. The next is to become owners of halls to speak in, of printing and publishing offices, of paper mills perhaps, of more and more of the necessary machinery needed for our campaign. The third is to train more and more women in economic organization, in the simple daily practice of modern business methods, and to guarantee to more and more of them that foundation stone of all other progress, economic independence. The fourth is to establish in all these businesses as we take them up, *right conditions*—proper hours, proper wages, everything as it should be."

"Employing women, only?"

"As far as possible, Mrs. Wedge. And when men are needed, employing the right kind."

There was a thoughtful silence.

"It's an ENORMOUS undertaking," murmured the Honorable Miss Erwood, a rather grim faced spinster of middle age. "How can you get 'em to do it?"

Miss Waltress met her cheerfully.

"It is enormous, but natural. It does not require a million women to start at once you see; or any unusual undertaking. The advisory central committee will keep books and make plans. Each business, little or big, starts wherever it happens to be needed. The connection is not visible. That connection involves in the first place definite help and patronage in starting, or in increasing the custom of one already started; second, an advantage in buying—which will increase as the allied businesses increase; and then the paying to the central committee of a small annual fee. As the membership increases, all these advantages increase—in arithmetical progression."

"Is the patronage in your plan confined to our society? or to sympathizers?" pursued Miss Erwood.

"By no means. The very essence of the scheme is to meet general demands to prove the advantage of a clean, honest efficiency.

"Now, for instance—" Miss Waltress turned over a few notes she held in a neat package—"here is—let us say—the necktie trade. Now neckties are not laborious to make—as a matter of fact women frequently sell them. Silk itself was first made use of by a woman, and the whole silk industry might be largely in their hands. Designing, spinning, weaving, dyeing, we might do it all. But in the mere matters of making and selling the present day necktie of mankind, there is absolutely nothing to prevent our stretching out a slow soft hand, and gathering in the business. We might begin in the usual spectacular 'feminine' way. A dainty shop in a good street, some fine girls, level-headed ones, who are working for the cause, to sell neckties, or—here is an advertising suggestion— we might call it 'The Widows' Shop' and employ only widows. There are always enough of the poor things needing employment.

"Anyhow we establish a trade in neckties, fine neckties, good taste, excellent materials, reliable workmanship. When it is sufficiently prosperous, it branches—both in town and in the provinces—little by little we could build up such a reputation that 'Widow Shop Neckties' would have a definite market value the world over. Meanwhile we could have our own workrooms, regular show places—patrons could see the neckties made, short hours, good wages, low prices."

She was a little breathless, but very eager. "Now I know you are asking how we are going to make all these things *pay*, for they must, if we are to succeed. You see, in ordinary business each one preys on the others. We propose to have an interconnected group that will help one another—that is where the profit comes. This was only a single instance, just one industry, but now I'll outline a group. Suppose we have a bit of land in some part of the country that is good for small fruit raising, and we study and develop that industry to its best. For the product we open a special shop in town, or at first, perhaps getting patronage by circularizing among our present membership, but winning our market by the goodness of the product and the reasonable price. Then we have a clean, pretty, scientific preserving room, and every bit of the unsold

fruit is promptly turned into jam or jelly or syrup, right in sight of the patrons. They can see it done—and take it home, 'hot' if they wish to, or mark the jars and have them sent. That would be a legitimate beginning of a business that has practically no limits—and if it isn't a woman's business, I don't know what is!

"Now this could get a big backing of steady orders from boarding houses and hotels managed by women, and gradually more and more of these would be run by our members. Then we could begin to effect a combination with Summer lodgings—think what missionary work it would be to establish a perfect chain of Summer boarding houses which should be as near perfect as is humanly possible, and all play into one another's hands and into our small market garden local ventures.

"On such a chain of hotels we could found a growing laundry business. In connection with the service required, we could open an Employment Agency; in connection with that a Training School for Modern Employees—not 'slaveys,' to be 'exploited' by the average household, but swift, accurate, efficient, self-respecting young women, unionized and working for our own patrons. That would lead to club-houses for these girls—and for other working girls; and step by step, as the circles widened, we should command a market for our own produce that would be a tremendous business asset."

She paused, looking about her, eager and flushed. Mrs. Shortham took up the tale in her calm, sweet voice.

"You see how it opens," she said. "Beginning with simple practical local affairs—a little laundry here, a little bakeshop there; a fruit garden—honey, vegetables—what you like; with dressmakers and milliners and the rest. It carries certain definite advantages from the start; good conditions, wages, hours; and its range of possible growth is quite beyond our calculations.

And it requires practically no capital. We have simply to plan, to create, to arrange, and the pledged patronage of say a thousand women of those now interested would mean backing enough to start any modest business."

"There are women among us who have money enough to make several beginnings," Lady Horwich suggested.

"There'll be no trouble about that—we have to be sure of the working plan, that's all," Miss Erwood agreed.

"There's a-plenty of us workers that could put it through— with good will!" Mrs. Wedge confidently asserted. "We're doing most of this work you speak of now, with cruel hours and a dog's wages. This offers a job to a woman with everything better than she had before—you'll have no trouble with the workers."

"But how about the funds?—there might be a great deal of money in time," suggested Mrs. Doughton-Highbridge. "Who would handle it?"

"There would have to be a financial committee of our very best—names we all know and trust; and then the whole thing should be kept open and above board, as far as possible.

"There should be certain small return benefits—that would attract many; a steady increase in the business, and a 'war chest'—the reserve power to meet emergencies."

"I don't quite see how it would help us to get the ballot," one earnest young listener now remarked, and quiet Mrs. Shortham answered out of a full heart.

"Oh, my dear! Don't you see? In the mere matter of funds and membership it will help. In the very practical question of public opinion it will help; success in a work of this sort carries conviction with it. It will help as an immense machine for propaganda—all the growing numbers of our employees and fellow-members, all these shops and their spreading patronage. It will help directly as soon as we can own some

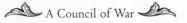

sort of hall to speak in, in all large towns, and our own publishing house and printing shop. And while we are waiting and working and fighting for the ballot, this would be improving life for more and more women all the time."

"And it would carry the proof that the good things we want done are practical and can be done—it would promote all good legislation," Miss Waltress added.

"I see; it's all a practical good thing from the start," said Miss Erwood, rather argumentatively. "To begin with, it's just plain good work. Furnishes employment and improves conditions. And from that up, there is no top to it—it's education and organization, widening good fellowship and increasing power—I'm for it definitely."

"It would be a world within a world—ready to come out full-grown a woman's world, clean and kind and safe and serviceable," Lady Horwich murmured, as if to herself. "Ladies, I move that a committee should be appointed forthwith, consisting of Mrs. Shortham, Mrs. Wedge, and Miss Waltress, with power to consult as widely as they see fit, and to report further as to this proposition at our next meeting."

The motion was promptly seconded, as promptly carried, and the women looked at one another with the light of a new hope in their eyes.

A Partnership

AFTER THE BABY was married—not a real baby, of course, but a girl of twenty-two who could never persuade her parents to call her anything but "Baby"—Mrs. Haven fell to cleaning house.

She set her teeth, put clamps on her heart, and cleaned house from garret to cellar, inclusive. It was so much bigger than it had ever been before, that house.

When they moved in, after quite outgrowing their first one, there had been six of them, and a cook and a second girl and a nursemaid besides. Sometimes there was a trained nurse also, in serious illness. Sometimes there were guests. As the children grew bigger and enjoyed the big house and big yard as children should, they seemed to multiply by some infantile magic into forty children at once—they and their young friends.

Mrs. Haven had so completely given her life to her children after the fashion of conscientious American mothers (who can afford it) that she had never once thought of them as an essentially transient possession.

They had liberally appropriated the life she gave them, had grown up as children will, and were now most undeniably gone—all of them. Both boys in business in other cities; both girls married, in other cities, and Othello's occupation gone—clean gone. Also, as she began to find with a pressing sense of loss—her topics of conversation were gone.

She had always held the pleasant theory that marriage was a partnership.

Of course it is, in parentage; and she had done her part, her royal share of love and care and service, as faithfully as Mr. Haven had paid the bills. But now, as parents, the partnership was closed out. They were has-beens. They could, it is true, read the letters of their absent young people, and discuss their hopes and chances as far as these were confided to them. But talking over occasional letters is not a sufficiently engrossing occupation for really active parents.

After the big house was antiseptically perfect, and four new "spare rooms" left coldly inviting besides the old one, and the nurse's room, and the nursery itself, Mrs. Haven felt a little vacant. She turned to the subject of sewing then, being a busy practical woman. Everything in the line of clothing was put in order, old things cleared out and sent to the proper charities, Mr. Haven's wardrobe wisely scrutinized, her own made perfect—that took some time and was fairly interesting while it lasted.

But a vigorous able energetic woman of forty-nine cannot fill all her time with the clothing of her household, especially when her household is reduced to two.

She had been trying not to face it—the *vacancy*. But it kept gaining on her, rising like a tide, and finally it swept her quite off her feet, and she felt as one swimming in a calm gray horizonless sea.

"Gerald!" she burst out one evening, "how do you *stand* it?"

"Stand what?" he naturally inquired, lowering his newspaper.

"Having them all gone!" she burst out. "All of them—everything!"

"You are not gone, Margie," he said affectionately, coming around to kiss her.

She clung to him. "I don't mean it that way, darling," she urged remorsefully. "But things to *do*—you are just my*self*, Gerry, you are not an occupation."

"Why, there's just as much to do as there ever was, isn't there? I haven't noticed that working hours are any shorter."

She looked at him, lovingly, but realizing as she never had before the difference in their position. Their partnership in parentage was at an end, but his business went right on. His real partner, Mr. Edgers, was a bachelor, yet he had done his half of their common work all these years. They went right on—that partnership—where was hers?

She was sitting by him now, holding his hand as if she was afraid he would go too. He laid the paper down and turned to her definitely, tenderly.

"What is it, Pussy?" he asked. "Is there something you want? You shall have it."

"No." She shook her head slowly. "There's nothing I want—that I know of. Of course I wouldn't have them back—of all things I wouldn't have had the girls not marry—they all have to go, of course. And I've got you—I can't be unhappy, really—while I have you, dearest. But—what am I to *do*?"

"I don't understand, Margie. Here's the house—as big as it always was. Isn't that—an interest?"

"Why, yes, it's something. But that never was the main interest—I can't begin to mother a house at my age. Besides Agnes and Ellen manage it all right now—it runs on wheels. It's not an occupation for me."

"Haven't you your friends, and clothes and things? Don't they fill up?"

"Why, yes—and so have you, Gerry. But that's not your *business*. You have your business—mine's gone!"

Mr. Haven frowned a little. He was very fond of his wife, and of his home. He had been an excellent father, not only holding up the entire household by his efficient labors outside, but really helping her in her more intimate parental problems.

He missed his children, too, but had merely plunged more actively into the affairs of his office, affairs which opened endlessly before him. And he was extremely conservative.

So far he had never thought of his wife as differing from him in his views. He thought "woman's place was the home," and so, apparently, had she. She had always stayed in it, had been continuously busy in it, and apparently happy in it. She still had that home. She still had him. This was only a temporary fit of depression. He must cheer her up.

"I don't see that we can help it, Margie. As you say, you wouldn't have them back. It's the order of nature. I guess all women feel so at first—but they have to get used to it."

He petted her, drew her close to him.

She was silent for a little, but his words called up a dreary vision. She remembered her own mother, what her life had been, of how little she had ever thought about it, being so immersed in her own. She recalled other elderly women, growing grayer and grayer, slowly fading out, as they "got used to it." She thought of the row on the hotel piazzas— middle-aged, elderly, old; rocking, doing fancy work, gossiping,—they were used to it. That gray endless ocean had other women in it, millions of them; some bobbing idly like loose corks, some surrounded by little trays of playthings like the patrons of some German *bad*; some slowly drowning——. She gave a little shiver.

"You must have interests, of course, my dear, and you'll find them—you'll find them."

He thought of it after he went to bed, thought of it at intervals during the next day, and determined to "give her a change." His business was arranged to go on in the hands of Mr. Edgers, and they went off for a long foreign tour, together.

That was a very pleasant experience. It did them both good, and it helped Mrs. Haven to a more settled frame of mind, a sounder health.

When they returned he plunged with renewed vigor and keen zest into his affairs, and she plunged into that gray ocean…

Then she was asked to address the Women's Central Club, to tell them about her travels, and with some enthusiasm she took up "club work." He was pleased to see her returning cheerfulness, to have her chatting gaily across their small bright table of more vital subjects than of old; and, as far as he thought of her problems at all, considered them settled.

They were not settled. The more Mrs. Haven used her mind the more mind she had to use. That trip abroad had given her new angles of vision. The people she had met on the steamer, in hotels and trains; the books she was now reading in connection with club papers; the lectures and discussions she heard; all these furnished a stimulus which resulted in growth, surprising growth.

It surprised her, because, in her thought of the lives of women she had always stopped short as most people do, with the mother period. Never until she came to it had she actively realized that life went right on, after motherhood was accomplished.

There was a paper read at one of the State Federation meetings she attended, on "Ex-Mothers," which she found arresting indeed. The speaker, a woman some considered dangerously "advanced," showed how in the maternal scheme of nature mothers frequently died in the act, as it were—just laid eggs and departed. That in our own early savage period the risks and labors of maternity, with the added toil required of women so shortened their lives that they hardly survived the maternal period. Of them it might be said: "I lived and bore; and though I died, so that I lived to bear, my daughter lived and bore." She showed in later civilization women survived the mother period, but sunk their remaining years in the endless work and care of large families without "modern improvements," and that it was only today, when wealth was larger, families smaller, and education more general, that a new functionary was appearing on the scene—the Ex-Mother.

The paper went on to suggest, what certainly Mrs. Haven had never thought of before, that this opened to women a new vista of life, clear human life, in which they were quite free to take up any human function, having fulfilled the feminine.

In two years' time Margaret Haven came to a vital decision. She valued her husband's love, she would on no account neglect his comfort, but she began to feel sure that he had no right to limit her activities during the hours he was away from her by what she now saw to be mere prejudices.

Discussion was rather difficult. She tried her patient best to persuade him to give his consent to her undertaking some business of her own, but he was immovable.

"It's perfect nonsense, Margie," he insisted. "Business! What do you want of a business? Don't I earn money enough? Don't I give you money enough? It's absurd—utterly absurd!"

She tried to convince him that it was not for the money, but for the sake of the work—a point of view he was utterly unable to grasp. He could not see why she should not be content to "improve her mind" eternally.

"Would you want to go to school all your life?" she asked him. "What is the use of improving my mind if I never *use* it. I tell you, Gerald, I am an able-bodied woman of fifty-one—and I'm going to work."

Finally he dismissed the subject rather snappily.

"You may do what you please, of course. I can't prevent you—it is a little late to begin to interfere with you now, my dear. Do what you like—but don't expect me to enjoy it. Fortunately I'm doing well enough and people know it—they won't think you are helping me, at any rate."

She sighed. It would have been ever so much pleasanter if Gerald had been with her in her new hopes—but she could not give them up; she could not settle down to spend twenty or thirty years in "getting used to it," even to please him.

They lived in a Middle Western city in a famous wheat district; busy, prosperous, progressive, but undeveloped in many lines. Mr. Haven was a dealer in flour, one of many; and so far as his wife knew anything of business, she knew this. Her main interest in the flour had always been lodged in bread in the last step between the producer and consumer, and when they were "changing girls" in her young, less experienced days, she had often heard Gerald complain that such first-class flour should go to make such fourth-class food.

The flour of their city was its pride, but the only city that was proud of its bread—as far as she knew, was Vienna.

Spurred by her husband's criticisms, she had long ago perfected herself in the not too abstruse art of breadmaking, and took great pride in her "homemade" rolls, her white and graham and whole-wheat loaves.

In Europe she had been struck with the excellence of the "baker's bread"—a commodity her mother had taught her to despise; and in discussion with foreign critics had learned to her incredulous mortification that her own country had a very low national standard in breadmaking.

Slowly there had grown in her mind a determination to do something to lift that standard.

"The lady is the loaf-giver, they are always telling us. We ought to give better loaves then. If the man can't we must."

That is why Mrs. Gerald Haven went into the baking business.

She called it "New Home" bread, and began very simply, paying her excellent cook an extra price for extra work, and selling through the woman's exchange. The orders increased, and she hired an earnest young Norwegian woman to learn in her own kitchen, training her herself as she had the cook.

This was quiet and made no trouble. Mr. Haven felt no difference in the domestic regime except heavier fuel bills, which he refused to let her pay—so she put the money in the bank. Her clientele grew and grew, and the boy who came to the back gate with the handcart protested that he needed a horse.

Good bread, like good wine, needs no push and the second year she started a little shop, adding her own especial gingerbread, the "hot water" gingerbread, smooth, sweet, dark, and as porous as a sponge. Also her own sponge cake, real sponge cake that, soaring aloft on unaided eggs.

This grew, too, to the busy manager's delight and pride; grew quite naturally and safely, on the advertisement that follows the pleased customer.

Almost any woman is glad to avoid the baking if she is sure of getting as good and as reliable products outside; and the New Home Bakery furnished better goods than most of its patrons were able to make.

To Mrs. Haven it was a growing joy. Her wide circle of friends approved of the product if they did not approve of the principle and after all, their patronage was worth more than their approval.

She gave a paper at the club, on "Bread-making, Domestic and Foreign," which was warmly received. As one of the committee on schools, she addressed the cooking classes of eager young people.

Her supply of "yesterday's bread" to the Working Girls' Club House was a substantial help to that struggling institution, and the girls said the New Home "yesterday's" was better than anyone else's tomorrow's.

Meanwhile there was a widening range of study to be kept up. It was perhaps the happiest part of Mrs. Haven's work to feel the wonderful sense of *youth* that came with it. Youth is a beginning; it is full of "first times," and enjoys them. To her great surprise she found that this new enterprise roused a vivid, eager joy she had not thought ever to feel again, the joy of beginning.

A Social Service lecturer spoke in the town on labor conditions, and disclosed the revolting circumstances in which so much of the baker's bread is made. She was stirred to the depths by this revelation and her ambition took new shape.

With the profits of three years' work and the base of a steadily widening patronage she opened a Model Bakery. She remembered a sign she had seen over a little London dairy: "The Inspection of the Public is Invited," and invited it here.

As she must have a delivery wagon in any case she found it cheaper to supply her little shop from a distance than to pay heavy downtown rent for the working place; and placed her bakery farther out, a trim comfortable little building, coolly situated in its own garden, adding to the fresh odors of flower and tree its own tempting bouquet of fragrance. Clean comfortable women worked for reasonable hours, and rested under the trees in their leisure moments.

One girl was detailed to take visitors through the place, and the exquisite shining cleanliness, the glass and marble

and nickel fittings, the big gas ovens, only heated for the actual hours of baking, the white-capped, white-uniformed workers, all had their effect on the purchasers.

One of the pleasantest results was an emulous improvement in other bakeries. That kind of competition is indeed "the life of trade." Everywhere in the town the standard of bread and of breadmaking was raised by this woman's honest work, and her happy pride rose with it.

She did not fade and wither and "get used to it." She grew, grew wiser, abler, more efficient, more interested yearly. She was asked far and wide to give "Bread Talks" to schools and clubs.

Her husband—who most sincerely loved her—grew proud of her in spite of himself. After all if breadmaking was not a woman's business, what was?

In the end there came to him an unexpected misfortune. Mr. Edgers suddenly departed with the entire available funds of their business, at a time when it meant ruin.

"Gerald," said his wife. "Oh, my dear! Don't look like that, dear! What if he has! Let the poor wretch go and forget it. You're young enough yet to go ahead and do better than ever. And in the meantime I wish you'd help me out. My work is getting quite beyond my managing ability—I wish you'd take hold and straighten it out for me."

He consented to look at her papers—and was surprised; pleased in spite of himself. A large and growing trade, a demand from neighboring towns, a branch already started in one, and in the city, three—there was need for careful management.

He gave her the help of his experience, his larger business grip; she joyfully shifted the "money end" as she called it, on to his shoulders, and went on developing the "bread end."

In a few more years they formed a Baking Company of solid importance and assured success.

Then one day, as they sat together in the evening, discussing some little difficulty in one of the shops, rejoicing in their growing prosperity, she suddenly came around the table and ran into his arms.

"Oh, Gerry! Gerry!" she cried. "I'm such a happy woman! We *are* partners now, for keeps!"

Fulfilment

TWO WOMEN ROCKED slowly in the large splint chairs on a breezy corner of the hotel piazza. One sat as if she grew there, as if a rocking-chair were her natural habitat, as if she passed her life occupying rocking-chairs, merely eating and sleeping in the necessary intervals between one sitting and the next; as if, without a rocking-chair, she lacked explanation, missing it as a sailor his ship, or a cowboy his horse.

The other looked comfortable enough, and rocked appreciatively, but her air and her garments suggested other seats: desk-chairs, parlor-car chairs, and no chairs at all—long erect standing, brisk continued walking. There was about her even a subtle suggestion of one running easily, and this in spite of pleasant relaxation, such as one sees in the lines of a sleeping hound.

Mrs. Edgar Maxwell, she of the soul affinity to rocking-chairs, was daintily engaged with some bright fancy work, a graceful wild-rose wreath on a large linen centerpiece. Her white fingers were dexterously busy, but her eyes were placid pools of contentment.

Her sister, Irma Russell, did nothing. Her vigorous supple hands were quiet, though carrying their clear suggestion of active power, but her eyes were vividly alive.

They talked freely, with increasing intimacy, with a clear view of two long empty stretches of verandah, and neither of them thought that the closed slats of the long green-blinded window beside them concealed a conscienceless novelist. They did not know he was in the hotel, as indeed he intended no one should. He was only waiting over a day to meet a friend, and carefully avoiding the crowds of female admirers, toward whom decent courtesy and business principles compelled some politeness when unescapable.

The term "conscienceless" is perhaps too severe to describe him; he had an artistic conscience, deep, broad, accurate, relentless, but refused to be bound by the standards of most people.

Mrs. Maxwell held her work off from her approving eyes, and drew a happy little sigh of admiration. Her glance dwelt briefly on the green slopes and blue heights about them, then long and tenderly on her boy and girl, playing tennis with the other young folks in the near distance.

"Oh, Irma!" she said. "If only you were as happy as I am!"

"How do you know I'm not. You haven't seen me for twenty years, you know. Do I look unhappy?"

"Oh, no! I think you look wonderfully well, and you have certainly done well out there."

"Out there" was California. It seemed the end of the earth to Mrs. Maxwell.

Irma smiled. "You are a dear girl—you always were, Elsie. It's a treat to see you. We haven't had a chance at a good talk for all this while—about half our lives. Pitch in now—tell me about your happiness."

Elsie laid down her work for a moment and looked lovingly at her sister.

"You always were—different," she said. "I remember just

as well how we used to talk—just girls! And now we're both forty and over—and here we are together again! But I've nothing to tell—that you don't know."

"I know the facts, of course," her sister agreed. "You wrote me of your engagement, sent wedding cards and baby-cards, and all—and photographs of everybody. But you never were much of a letter-writer—you always did talk better than you wrote, Elsie. What I want you to talk about is first your happiness—and, second, your superiority."

"My superiority! Why, Irma! What do you mean?"

"Just a little air of 'Poor Irma' I detect about you—that's all. I'm perfectly well; I'm doing nicely with my prunes and apricots; I want to know why you think you're happier than I am." Elsie met the affectionate quizzical gray eyes with the peaceful conviction of her own soft blue ones. "You certainly know that, Irma. You've seen Hugh—and the children."

"Yes, I've seen Hugh and the children—they are dears—I cheerfully agree to that. But what I want is the story of your life. Come—I've been a day at your house and here a week, getting acquainted all over again—and this is the first clear safe quiet time we've had together. You're just as sweet as ever, and I love to see you so contented—you haven't changed a bit, for all your 'Hugh and the children.'"

"There isn't anything to tell, Irma, but what you know. Hugh came the year you left. It helped me not to miss you so cruelly. We couldn't marry for some time—he had to save, and I waited. But I was glad to—I'd have waited till now for Hugh... . Then we had to struggle along for a good while— you knew that, too, and often helped, bless you! The children came pretty soon—and then we lost little Bobby ... and the dear baby that never even lived to be named." The blue eyes filled, but she looked at the gay young tennis players again and turned bravely back to her sister. "There was waiting, and work, and going without—there always has been a lot of planning and some sacrifices, of course. But there has been love, always, and the blessed children … even the grief—we had *together*… . It is life, Irma, it is living—and if I seem to say, 'Poor Irma!'—which I deny, it is only on that account. A woman who hasn't married, who isn't a mother—I don't care how successful she is—she hasn't *lived*."

"I see," said Irma, somewhat drily.

"I thought as much. I wanted you to say it, that's all. And now will you answer me a few questions. How do you spend your time?"

"My time?" Elsie looked at her perplexedly. "Spend my time? Why, as any woman does."

"Yes, but specify, please—what do you *do*? Hour by hour— what does your day mean to you?"

The conscienceless novelist behind the green slats had been half dozing on the little hard sofa in the corner, and carrying on a half-hearted skirmish with the rudiments of ordinary people's principles. Now he trampled on those principles, kicked them out entirely, drew forth a worn little notebook, and devoted himself with wholehearted enthusiasm to the business of listening. "Invaluable material!" he murmured inaudibly.

"I don't know as I ever thought of it that way," Elsie said slowly.

"Well—think of it that way now," her sister urged. "You get up at—shall we say seven? What do you do—with brain and hand and heart, all day?"

"I—why, I keep house. You know!" protested Elsie.

"Do you make the fire? Get breakfast? Wash and iron?"

"No indeed—of course not. That was one reason Hugh waited. He said his wife was not to be his servant," quoted

Mrs. Maxwell proudly.

"I see. Well—what *do* you do?"

"Why—when the children were little there was more to do than there is now—of course, night and day too."

"You had no nurse?"

"No—we couldn't afford that. Besides, I preferred to care for my children myself—it is a mother's sacred duty, I think. And a pleasure," she added carefully.

Irma looked at her sister with tender sympathy. She loved her far too much to suggest that for this sacred duty she had never prepared herself by either study or practice, and that in performance of it she had lost fifty per cent of her children. That would have been cruel—and useless.

"We'll skip the babies, Elsie. Your youngest is fifteen. You haven't had to spend many hours a day on them for ten years or so, now have you? Come what do you do with your time? Twenty-four hours a day; eight out for sleep, one for toilet activities, two for three meals—that leaves thirteen. What do you do for a day's work in thirteen hours?"

"Oh, I'm sure it's not that!" protested Elsie. "It can't be!"

Irma produced pencil and paper. "What time do you get up—seven?"

"Ye—es——" agreed her sister, rather faintly.

"Seven-thirty," wrote Irma. "Breakfast at eight?"

"Yes."

"An hour to eat it?"

"Oh, no—half an hour—the children have to get off—and Hugh. We're always through by eight-thirty."

"What time is lunch?"

"One o'clock—that doesn't take long either—the children have to hurry—say half an hour."

"And dinner?"

"Dinner's at seven—Hugh is so often late. I'd like it at

six-thirty—on account of the cook—but it's seven."

"Well, now, my dear sister. I'll give you your evening to play in; but you have from eight-thirty to one, and one-thirty to seven to account for—ten hours. A good working day—what do you do with it?"

"Ten hours!" Elsie would not admit it.

"Ten hours—your own figures. I'll give you another half-hour after breakfast, and after lunch—just to dawdle, read the paper, and so on, but that leaves nine. Now then, Elsie—speak up!"

Elsie spoke up, a little warmly.

"You can't measure housekeeping that way—by hours. Sometimes it's one thing and sometimes another. There is always something to do—always! And then there's one thing you forget—people coming in—and my going out."

"Exercise—we'll allow an hour for exercise—you don't walk more than an hour a day, do you, sister?"

"I don't mean just walking—one hasn't time to walk much. I mean calling—and shopping."

"And you haven't any idea how many hours a day—or a week—you call—or shop?"

"No, I haven't. I tell you it's impossible to figure it out that way. And then when the children come home I have to *be there.*" She grasped a thought, and lifted her head rather defiantly. "That's what housekeeping *is,*" she said proudly. "It's being there!"

"I see," said Irma, and wrote it down. (So did the novelist.) "I'll stop quizzing you as to hours, child—it's evident you never made a time-schedule in your life—much less kept one. Did you ever make a budget? Do you know, as a matter of fact, if your housekeeping is more or less efficient, more or less expensive, than your neighbors?"

Elsie drew herself up, a little hurt. "I am sure nobody could

be more economical than I am. Hugh always says I am such a good manager. I often make my housedresses myself, and Betty's; and I watch the sales——"

"But you don't know—nor Hugh—anything definite about it? Comparing with other families of the same size—on a similar amount?"

"I'd like to know what you're driving at, Irma. No—we neither of us has made any such calculation. No two families are alike. Each one is a law to itself—has to be. If I am satisfied and Hugh is—whose business is it besides?"

"Not mine," agreed Irma cheerfully. "Excuse me, dear, if I've offended you. I wanted to get at the real working of your life if I could, to compare with mine. Let's take a new tack. Tell me have you kept up your physical culture?"

"I have not," said Elsie, a little sharply. "Motherhood interferes with gymnastics."

"Are you as strong and active as you used to be?"

"I am not," still a little sharply. "You don't seem to understand, Irma—I suppose you can't, not being a mother—that if you have children you can't have everything else."

"Have you kept up your music? Or your languages?"

"No—for the same reason."

"Have you learned anything new? Now, Elsie, don't be angry—what I'm getting at is this: You have spent twenty years in one way, I in another. You have certain visible possessions and joys which I have not. You have also had experiences—griefs—cares—which I have not. I'm just trying to see if besides these you have other gains, or if these are the only gains to offset what I may show."

"I'm not angry with you, Irma—how could I be? You are my only sister, and you've always been good to me. I'll make you all the concessions you wish. Marriage is a mutual compromise, dear. A man gives up his freedom and a woman gives up hers. They have their love—their home—their children. But nobody can have everything."

"That's a fact—I'll grant you that, Elsie. But tell me one more thing—what do you look forward to?"

"I don't look forward," protested Elsie stoutly. "I don't believe in it. 'Sufficient unto the day——'"

"'Is the evil thereof'?" asked Irma. "Please do look forward. You are forty-two. You'll live, I hope, to be twice that. What do you expect to accomplish in the next forty years?" There was a deeper note in her voice.

Elsie dropped her work and looked at her, a little shaken.

"As long as you have lived before—and no preliminary childhood to wade through! From now on, full grown, experienced, with your home, your happiness, your motherhood achieved; with your housekeeping surely no great burden by this time. With no more children coming and these two fairly grown—they'll be off your hands entirely soon — college—business—marriage. Then you won't have to 'be there' so much, will you? What are you going to do—with forty years of life?"

"I may not live——" suggested Elsie, rather as if it were an agreeable alternative.

"And you may. We're a long-lived lot, all of us. And you know motherhood really adds to the chances of longevity—if you don't die at it. I'll excuse you from the last ten though; after seventy you can rock all the time. Call it thirty years, ten hours a day—or nine—or eight—why Elsie—don't you even *want* to do anything?"

Elsie gave a little nervous laugh. "I feel like quoting from *Potash and Perlmutter*," she said, "'Whadda y' mean do anything?' Come, you leave off questioning me and let's hear all the fine things you've been doing—you never would write about yourself."

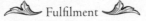

Irma rose and walked softly, smoothly, up and down the piazza, watched with slanting eagerness by the eyes behind the slats. She came back and stood near her sister, leaning against the railing.

"All right—I'll make up for it now. And in the first place, Elsie, I don't want you to think I minimize your happiness—it is a great big splendid slice of life that you've had and I haven't. I'm sorry I've missed it—I'd like to have had that too. Well—here's my record:

"I went to California as you know at twenty-one. Sort of governess-companion. All of our people protested—but I *was* twenty-one—they couldn't stop me. I went because I wanted to grow—and I have grown. I studied the place, the people, the opportunities. I kept at work, saved my salary, added to my capacities. Took that chance to go to Europe with the Cheeseboro kids—saw a lot—learned a lot—got three languages, a world of experience—and a good bit of money. That was at twenty-four.

"Came back to the coast and invested my money in a small private school business."

"You gave me some of it, you dear thing," Elsie interrupted, affectionately.

"Oh, well—that was natural. I had enough left to start. I did well with the school, and set up a sort of boarding-school—a health-and-educational stunt, up in the foothills. Bought land up there—a fine breezy mesa it is, with an artesian well of its own.

"I worked—but it's work I love. Built on, enlarged my staff, cautiously. Added a sort of winter camp for adults—not invalids. By the time I was thirty I had quite a place up there, a lovely home of my own all by itself on a sort of promontory—with such a garden! O Elsie—you're coming out to see me some day—all of you!

"Then I went very cautiously, used my accumulating

experience, invested wisely and slowly. Things move rather quickly out there, but common sense keeps on being useful. As to money I'm very comfortable indeed, and may be rich—rich enough. All sweet, safe, honestly-earned money—my own.

"But that's the least of it. What I'm gladdest of is the *living*. The kind of work I've done has helped people—lots of people—especially children. I've been a sort of foster-mother to hundreds of them, you see, some fifteen years, averaging twenty new ones a year—that's three hundred, besides those in the first five beginning years.

"Also—I adopted some."

Elsie started. "And never said a word about it!"

"No—I wanted to see how it would turn out. But I've got four I call my own—took 'em as babies, you know. They're a splendid lot. Two about the age of Tom and Betty—two younger—I'll show you their pictures presently.

"Personally, physically, I mean, I'm a hundred per cent stronger and more efficient than I used to be. I've trained—years and years of it—in sunlight and mountain air. It's not just strength, but skill. I can climb mountains, ride, shoot, fence, row, swim, play golf, tennis, billiards, dance like a youngster—or a professional. I'm more *alive*, literally, than I was at twenty. I have a good car and can run it as well as the man.

"Then I know more—I've had plenty of time to study. The town is only a half-hour run—the city about an hour.

"I belong to clubs, classes, societies. I'm a citizen, too—I can vote now. I begin to have ambitions of *bigger* service by and by—widening and deepening as I get older I have plans for when I'm fifty—sixty—seventy.

"As to prunes and apricots—they are growing well—pay well, too. I have a little cannery of my own—and a little

settlement of working people near it, and a *crêche* there for the women to tuck the babies in while they work—a jewel of a *crêche*, mind you. And I'm promoting all manner of industries among the women. I've got plans—oh, I couldn't begin to tell you of my plans——!"

"You never did," said Elsie slowly. "I—I never dreamed you had spread out so. How splendid of you, Irma!"

"It isn't what I've done that keeps me so happy," mused her sister. "It's the things I'm going to do! The widening horizon! Every year I feel stronger, braver, see things more clearly. Life is so—glorious!

"You see, Elsie dear, I have had the babies to love and care for, even if not mine born—they were babies—and I do love them. I have a home, too, a lovely one, with comfort and beauty and peace—and space, too. The one thing I haven't got is the husband—there you are ahead. But I'm not wearing the willow, sister. Life is big enough to bring endless happiness, even without that. Don't you ever show me that 'Poor Irma!' look again—now, will you?"

"No——" said Elsie, sitting very quiet, "I never will."

There was a hop at the Hotel that night.

Elsie sat among the matrons, watching her son and daughter frisk with the young people.

Irma, dressed to quiet perfection, danced; danced so well that girls, half her age, were envious of her partners.

"What a woman!" said the unprincipled novelist to himself before he danced with her.

"Which is the quickest route to Southern California?" he inquired, after he had danced with her.

Mr. Peebles's Heart

HE WAS LYING on the sofa in the homely, bare little sitting room; an uncomfortable stiff sofa, too short, too sharply upcurved at the end, but still a sofa, whereon one could, at a pinch, sleep.

Thereon Mr. Peebles slept, this hot still afternoon; slept uneasily, snoring a little, and twitching now and then, as one in some obscure distress.

Mrs. Peebles had creaked down the front stairs and gone off on some superior errands of her own; with a good palm-leaf fan for a weapon, a silk umbrella for a defense.

"Why don't you come too, Joan?" she had urged her sister, as she dressed herself for departure.

"Why should I, Emma? It's much more comfortable at home. I'll keep Arthur company when he wakes up."

"Oh, Arthur! He'll go back to the store as soon as he's had his nap. And I'm sure Mrs. Older's paper'll be real interesting. If you're going to live here you ought to take an interest in the club, seems to me."

"I'm going to live here as a doctor—not as a lady of leisure, Em. You go on—I'm contented."

So Mrs. Emma Peebles sat in the circle of the Ellsworth Ladies' Home Club, and improved her mind, while Dr. J. R.

Bascom softly descended to the sitting room in search of a book she had been reading.

There was Mr. Peebles, still uneasily asleep. She sat down quietly in a cane-seated rocker by the window and watched him awhile; first professionally, then with a deeper human interest.

Baldish, grayish, stoutish, with a face that were a friendly smile for customers, and showed grave, set lines that deepened about the corners of his mouth when there was no one to serve; very ordinary in dress, in carriage, in appearance was Arthur Peebles at fifty. He was not "the slave of love" of the Arab tale, but the slave of duty.

If ever a man had done his duty—as he saw it—he had done his, always.

His duty—as he saw it—was carrying women. First his mother, a comfortable competent person, who had run the farm after her husband's death, and added to their income by Summer boarders until Arthur was old enough to "support her." Then she sold the old place and moved into the village to "make a home for Arthur," who incidentally provided a hired girl to perform the manual labor of that process.

He worked in the store. She sat on the piazza and chatted with her neighbors.

He took care of his mother until he was nearly thirty, when she left him finally; and then he installed another woman to make a home for him—also with the help of the hired girl. A pretty, careless, clinging little person he married, who had long made mute appeal to his strength and carefulness, and she had continued to cling uninterruptedly to this day.

Incidentally a sister had clung until she married, another until she died; and his children—two daughters, had clung also. Both the daughters were married in due time, with sturdy young husbands to cling to in their turn; and now there remained only his wife to carry, a lighter load than he had ever known—at least numerically.

But either he was tired, very tired, or Mrs. Peebles's tendrils had grown tougher, tighter, more tenacious, with age. He did not complain of it. Never had it occurred to him in all these years that there was any other thing for a man to do than to carry whatsoever women came within range of lawful relationship.

Had Dr. Joan been—shall we say—carriageable—he would have cheerfully added her to the list, for he liked her extremely. She was different from any woman he had ever known, different from her sister as day from night, and, in lesser degree, from all the female inhabitants of Ellsworth.

She had left home at an early age, against her mother's will, absolutely ran away; but when the whole countryside rocked with gossip and sought for the guilty man—it appeared that she had merely gone to college. She worked her way through, learning more, far more, than was taught in the curriculum; became a trained nurse, studied medicine, and had long since made good in her profession. There were even rumors that she must be "pretty well fixed" and about to "retire"; but others held that she must have failed, really or she never would have come back home to settle.

Whatever the reason, she was there, a welcome visitor; a source of real pride to her sister, and of indefinable satisfaction to her brother-in-law. In her friendly atmosphere he felt a stirring of long unused powers; he remembered funny stories, and how to tell them; he felt a revival of interests he had thought quite outlived, early interests in the big world's movements.

"Of all unimpressive, unattractive, *good* little men—" she

was thinking, as she watched, when one of his arms dropped off the slippery side of the sofa, the hand thumped on the floor, and he awoke and sat up hastily with an air of one caught off duty.

"Don't sit up as suddenly as that, Arthur, it's bad for your heart."

"Nothing the matter with my heart, is there?" he asked with his ready smile.

"I don't know—haven't examined it. Now—sit still—you know there's nobody in the store this afternoon—and if there is, Jake can attend to 'em."

"Where's Emma?"

"Oh, Emma's gone to her 'club' or something—wanted me to go, but I'd rather talk with you."

He looked pleased but incredulous, having a high opinion of that club, and a low one of himself.

"Look here," she pursued suddenly, after he had made himself comfortable with a drink from the swinging ice-pitcher, and another big cane rocker, "what would you like to do if you could?"

"Travel!" said Mr. Peebles, with equal suddenness. He saw her astonishment. "Yes, travel! I've always wanted to—since I was a kid. No use! We never could, you see. And now—even if we could—Emma hates it." He sighed resignedly.

"Do you like to keep store?" she asked sharply.

"*Like* it?" He smiled at her cheerfully, bravely, but with a queer blank hopeless background underneath. He shook his head gravely. "No, I do not, Joan. Not a little bit. But what of that?"

They were still for a little, and then she put another question. "What would you have chosen—for a profession—if you had been free to choose?"

His answer amazed her threefold; from its character, its

sharp promptness, its deep feeling. It was in one word—"Music!"

"Music!" she repeated. "Music! Why I didn't know you played—or cared about it."

"When I was a youngster," he told her, his eyes looking far off through the vine-shaded window, "father brought home a guitar—and said it was for the one that learned to play it first. He meant the girls of course. As a matter of fact I learned it first—but I didn't get it. That's all the music I ever had," he added. "And there's not much to listen to here, unless you count what's in church. I'd have a Victrola—but—" he laughed a little shamefacedly, "Emma says if I bring one into the house she'll smash it. She says they're worse than cats. Tastes differ you know, Joan."

Again he smiled at her, a droll smile, a little pinched at the corners. "Well—I must be getting back to business."

She let him go, and turned her attention to her own business, with some seriousness.

"Emma," she proposed, a day or two later. "How would you like it if I should board here—live here, I mean, right along."

"I should hope you would," her sister replied. "It would look nice to have you practicing in this town and not live with me—all the sister I've got."

"Do you think Arthur would like it?"

"Of course he would! Besides—even if he didn't—you're *my* sister—and this is my house. He put it in my name, long ago."

"I see," said Joan, "I see."

Then after a little—"Emma—are you contented?"

"Contented? Why, of course I am. It would be a sin not to be. The girls are well married—I'm happy about them both. This is a real comfortable house, and it runs itself—my Matilda is a jewel if ever there was one. And she don't mind company—likes to do for 'em. Yes—I've nothing to worry about."

"Your health's good—that I can see," her sister remarked, regarding with approval her clear complexion and bright eyes.

"Yes—I've nothing to complain about—that I know of," Emma admitted, but among her causes for thankfulness she did not even mention Arthur, nor seem to think of him till Dr. Joan seriously inquired her opinion as to his state of health.

"His health? Arthur's? Why he's always well. Never had a sick day in his life—except now and then he's had a kind of a breakdown," she added as an afterthought.

Dr. Joan Bascom made acquaintances in the little town, both professional and social. She entered upon her practice, taking it over from the failing hands of old Dr. Braithwaite—her first friend, and feeling very much at home in the old place. Her sister's house furnished two comfortable rooms downstairs, and a large bedroom above. "There's plenty of room now the girls are gone," they both assured her.

Then, safely ensconced and established, Dr. Joan began a secret campaign to alienate the affections of her brother-in-law. Not for herself—oh no! If ever in earlier years she had felt the need of someone to cling to, it was long, long ago. What she sought was to free him from the tentacles—without re-entanglement.

She bought a noble gramophone with a set of first-class records, told her sister smilingly that she didn't have to listen, and Emma would sit sulkily in the back room on the other side of the house, while her husband and sister enjoyed the music. She grew used to it in time, she said, and drew nearer, sitting on the porch perhaps; but Arthur had his long denied pleasure in peace.

It seemed to stir him strangely. He would rise and walk, a new fire in his eyes, a new firmness about the patient mouth, and Dr. Joan fed the fire with talk and books and pictures with study of maps and sailing lists and accounts of economical tours.

"I don't see what you two find so interesting in all that stuff about music and those composers," Emma would say. "I never did care for foreign parts—musicians are all foreigners, anyway."

Arthur never quarrelled with her; he only grew quiet and lost that interested sparkle of the eye when she discussed the subject.

Then one day, Mrs. Peebles being once more at her club, content and yet aspiring, Dr. Joan made bold attack upon her brother-in-law's principles.

"Arthur," she said. "Have you confidence in me as a physician?"

"I have," he said briskly. "Rather consult you than any doctor I ever saw."

"Will you let me prescribe for you if I tell you you need it?"

"I sure will."

"Will you take the prescription?"

"Of course I'll take it—no matter how it tastes."

"Very well. I prescribe two years in Europe."

He stared at her, startled.

"I mean it. You're in a more serious condition than you think. I want you to cut clear—and travel. For two years."

He still stared at her. "But Emma—"

"Never mind about Emma. She owns the house. She's got enough money to clothe herself—and I'm paying enough board to keep everything going. Emma don't need you."

"But the store—"

"Sell the store."

"Sell it! That's easy said. Who'll buy it?"

"I will. Yes—I mean it. You give me easy terms and I'll take the store off your hands. It ought to be worth seven or eight thousand dollars, oughtn't it—stock and all?"

He assented, dumbly.

"Well, I'll buy it. You can live abroad for two years, on a couple of thousand, or twenty-five hundred—a man of your tastes. You know those accounts we've read—it can be done easily. Then you'll have five thousand or so to come back to —and can invest it in something better than that shop. Will you do it—?"

He was full of protests, of impossibilities.

She met them firmly. "Nonsense! You can too. She doesn't need you, at all—she may later. No—the girls don't need you—and they may later. Now is your time—*now*. They say the Japanese sow their wild oats after they're fifty—suppose you do! You can't be so *very* wild on that much money, but you can spend a year in Germany—learn the language—go to the opera—take walking trips in the Tyrol—in Switzerland; see England, Scotland, Ireland, France, Belgium, Denmark— you can do a lot in two years."

He stared at her fascinated.

"Why not? Why not be your own man for once in your life—do what *you* want to—not what other people want you to?"

He murmured something as to "duty"—but she took him up sharply.

"If ever a man on earth has done his I prescribe two years in duty, Arthur Peebles, you have. You've taken care of your mother while she was perfectly able to take care of herself; of your sisters, long after they were; and of a wholly able-bodied wife. At present she does not need you the least bit in the world."

"Now that's pretty strong," he protested. "Emma'd miss me—I know she'd miss me—"

Dr. Bascom looked at him affectionately. "There couldn't a better thing happen to Emma—or to you, for that matter—than to have her miss you, real hard."

"I know she'd never consent to my going," he insisted, wistfully.

"That's the advantage of my interference," she replied serenely. "You surely have a right to choose your doctor, and your doctor is seriously concerned about your health and orders foreign travel—rest—change—and music."

"But Emma—"

"Now, Arthur Peebles, forget Emma for awhile—I'll take care of her. And, look here—let me tell you another thing—a change like this will do her good."

He stared at her, puzzled.

"I mean it. Having you away will give her a chance to stand up. Your letters—about those places—will interest her. She may want to go, sometime. Try it."

He wavered at this. Those who too patiently serve as props sometimes underrate the possibilities of the vine.

"Don't discuss it with her—that will make endless trouble. Fix up the papers for my taking over the store—I'll draw you a check, and you get the next boat for England, and make your plans from there. Here's a banking address that will take care of your letters and checks—"

The thing was done! Done before Emma had time to protest. Done, and she left gasping to upbraid her sister.

Joan was kind, patient, firm as adamant.

"But how it *looks*, Joan—what will people think of me! To be left deserted—like this!"

"People will think according to what we tell them and to how you behave, Emma Peebles. If you simply say that Arthur

was far from well and I advised him to take a foreign trip—
and if you forget yourself for once, and show a little natural
feeling for him—you'll find no trouble at all."

For her own sake the selfish woman, made more so by her
husband's unselfishness, accepted the position. Yes—Arthur
had gone abroad for his health—Dr. Bascom was much
worried about him—chance of a complete breakdown, she
said. Wasn't it pretty sudden? Yes—the doctor hurried him
off. He was in England—going to take a walking trip—she
did not know when he'd be back. The store? He'd sold it.

Dr. Bascom engaged a competent manager who ran that
store successfully, more so than had the unenterprising Mr.
Peebles. She made it a good paying business, which he ulti-
mately bought back and found no longer a burden.

But Emma was the principal charge. With talk, with books,
with Arthur's letters followed carefully on maps, with trips
to see the girls, trips in which travelling lost its terrors, with
the care of the house, and the boarder or two they took "for
company," she so ploughed and harrowed that long fallow
field of Emma's mind that at last it began to show signs of
fruitfulness.

Arthur went away leaving a stout, dull woman who clung
to him as if he was a necessary vehicle or beast of burden—
and thought scarcely more of his constant service.

He returned younger, stronger, thinner, an alert vigorous
man, with a mind enlarged, refreshed, and stimulated. He
had found himself.

And he found her, also, most agreeably changed; having
developed not merely tentacles, but feet of her own to stand
on.

When next the thirst for travel seized him she thought
she'd go too, and proved unexpectedly pleasant as a
companion.

But neither of them could ever wring from Dr. Bascom any definite diagnosis of Mr. Peebles's threatening disease. "A dangerous enlargement of the heart" was all she would commit herself to, and when he denied any such trouble now, she gravely wagged her head and said "it had responded to treatment."

If I Were a Man

THAT WAS WHAT pretty little Mollie Mathewson always said when Gerald would not do what she wanted him to—which was seldom.

That was what she said this bright morning, with a stamp of her little high-heeled slipper, just because he had made a fuss about that bill, the long one with the "account rendered," which she had forgotten to give him the first time and been afraid to the second—and now he had taken it from the postman himself.

Mollie was "true to type." She was a beautiful instance of what is reverentially called "a true woman." Little, of course—no true woman may be big. Pretty, of course—no true woman could possibly be plain. Whimsical, capricious, charming, changeable, devoted to pretty clothes and always "wearing them well," as the esoteric phrase has it. (This does not refer to the clothes—they do not wear well in the least; but to some special grace of putting them on and carrying them about, granted to but few, it appears.)

She was also a loving wife and a devoted mother; possessed of "the social gift" and the love of "society" that goes with it, and, with all these was fond and proud of her home and managed it as capably as—well, as most women do.

If ever there was a true woman it was Mollie Mathewson, yet she was wishing heart and soul she was a man.

And all of a sudden she was!

She was Gerald, walking down the path so erect and square-shouldered, in a hurry for his morning train, as usual, and, it must be confessed, in something of a temper.

Her own words were ringing in her ears—not only the "last word," but several that had gone before, and she was holding her lips tight shut, not to say something she would be sorry for. But instead of acquiescence in the position taken by that angry little figure on the veranda, what she felt was a sort of superior pride, a sympathy as with weakness, a feeling that "I must be gentle with her," in spite of the temper.

A man! Really a man; with only enough subconscious memory of herself remaining to make her recognize the differences.

At first there was a funny sense of size and weight and extra thickness, the feet and hands seemed strangely large, and her long, straight, free legs swung forward at a gait that made her feel as if on stilts.

This presently passed, and in its place, growing all day, wherever she went, came a new and delightful feeling of being *the right size*.

Everything fitted now. Her back snugly against the seat-back, her feet comfortably on the floor. Her feet? ... His feet! She studied them carefully. Never before, since her early school days, had she felt such freedom and comfort as to feet—they were firm and solid on the ground when she walked; quick, springy, safe—as when, moved by an unrecognizable impulse, she had run after, caught, and swung aboard the car.

Another impulse fished in a convenient pocket for change—instantly, automatically bringing forth a nickel for the conductor and a penny for the newsboy.

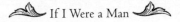

These pockets came as a revelation. Of course she had known they were there, had counted them, made fun of them, mended them, even envied them; but she never dreamed of how it *felt* to have pockets.

Behind her newspaper she let her consciousness, that odd mingled consciousness, rove from pocket to pocket, realizing the armored assurance of having all those things at hand, instantly get-at-able, ready to meet emergencies. The cigar case gave her a warm feeling of comfort—it was full; the firmly held fountain-pen, safe unless she stood on her head; the keys, pencils, letters, documents, notebook, checkbook, bill folder—all at once, with a deep rushing sense of power and pride, she felt all what she had never felt before in all her life—the possession of money, of her own earned money— hers to give or to withhold; not to beg for, tease for, wheedle for—hers.

That bill—why if it had come to her—to him, that is, he would have paid it as a matter of course, and never mentioned it—to her.

Then, being he, sitting there so easily and firmly with his money in his pockets, she wakened to his life-long consciousness about money. Boyhood—its desires and dreams, ambitions. Young manhood—working tremendously for the wherewithal to make a home—for her. The present years with all their net of cares and hopes and dangers; the present moment, when he needed every cent for special plans of great importance, and this bill, long overdue and demanding payment, meant an amount of inconvenience wholly unnecessary if it had been given him when it first came; also, the man's keen dislike of that "account rendered."

"Women have no business sense!" she found herself saying, "and all that money just for hats—idiotic, useless, ugly things!"

With that she began to see the hats of the women in the car as she had never seen hats before. The men's seemed normal, dignified, becoming, with enough variety for personal taste, and with distinction in style and in age, such as she had never noticed before. But the women's——

With the eyes of a man and the brain of a man; with the memory of a whole lifetime of free action wherein the hat, close-fitting on cropped hair, had been no handicap; she now perceived the hats of women.

Their massed fluffed hair was at once attractive and foolish, and on that hair, at every angle, in all colors, tipped, twisted, tortured into every crooked shape, made of any substance chance might offer, perched these formless objects. Then, on their formlessness the trimmings—these squirts of stiff feathers, these violent outstanding bows of glistening ribbon, these swaying, projecting masses of plumage which tormented the faces of bystanders.

Never in all her life had she imagined that this idolized millinery could look, to those who paid for it, like the decorations of an insane monkey.

And yet, when there came into the car a little woman, as foolish as any, but pretty and sweet-looking, up rose Gerald Mathewson and gave her his seat; and, later, when there came in a handsome red-cheeked girl, whose hat was wilder, more violent in color and eccentric in shape than any other; when she stood near by and her soft curling plumes swept his cheek once and again, he felt a sense of sudden pleasure at the intimate tickling touch—and she, deep down within, felt such a wave of shame as might well drown a thousand hats forever.

When he took his train, his seat in the smoking car, she had a new surprise. All about him were the other men, commuters too, and many of them friends of his.

To her, they would have been distinguished as "Mary

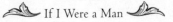

Wade's husband"—"the man Belle Grant is engaged to"—"that rich Mr. Shopworth"—or "that pleasant Mr. Beale." And they would all have lifted their hats to her, bowed, made polite conversation if near enough—especially Mr. Beale.

Now came the feeling of open-eyed acquaintance, of knowing men—as they were. The mere amount of this knowledge was a surprise to her; the whole background of talk from boyhood up, the gossip of barber-shop and club, the conversation of morning and evening hours on trains, the knowledge of political affiliation, of business standing and prospects, of character—in a light she had never known before.

They came and talked to Gerald, one and another. He seemed quite popular. And as they talked, with this new memory and new understanding, an understanding which seemed to include all these men's minds, there poured in on the submerged consciousness beneath a new, a startling knowledge—what men really think of women.

Good average American men were there; married men for the most part, and happy—as happiness goes in general. In the minds of each and all there seemed to be a two-story department, quite apart from the rest of their ideas, a separate place where they kept their thoughts and feelings about women.

In the upper half were the tenderest emotions, the most exquisite ideals, the sweetest memories, all lovely sentiments as to "home" and "mother," all delicate admiring adjectives, a sort of sanctuary, where a veiled statue, blindly adored, shared place with beloved yet commonplace experiences.

In the lower half—here that buried consciousness woke to keen distress—they kept quite another assortment of ideas. Here, even in this clean-minded husband of hers, was the memory of stories told at men's dinners, of worse ones overheard in street or car, of base traditions, coarse epithets, gross experiences—known, though not shared.

And all these in the department "woman," while in the rest of the mind—here was new knowledge indeed.

The world opened before her. Not the world she had been reared in; where Home had covered all the map, almost, and the rest had been "foreign," or "unexplored country;" but the world as it was, man's world, as made, lived in, and seen, by men.

It was dizzying. To see the houses that fled so fast across the car window, in terms of builders' bills, or of some technical insight into materials and methods; to see a passing village with lamentable knowledge of who "owned it"—and of how its Boss was rapidly aspiring to State power, or of how that kind of paving was a failure; to see shops, not as mere exhibitions of desirable objects, but as business ventures, many mere sinking ships, some promising a profitable voyage—this new world bewildered her.

She—as Gerald—had already forgotten about that bill, over which she—as Mollie—was still crying at home. Gerald was "talking business" with this man, "talking politics" with that; and now sympathizing with the carefully withheld troubles of a neighbor.

Mollie had always sympathized with the neighbor's wife before.

She began to struggle violently, with this large dominant masculine consciousness. She remembered with sudden clearness things she had read—lectures she had heard; and resented with increasing intensity this serene masculine preoccupation with the male point of view.

Mr. Miles, the little fussy man who lived on the other side of the street, was talking now. He had a large complacent wife; Mollie had never liked her much, but had always thought him rather nice—he was so punctilious in small courtesies.

And here he was talking to Gerald—such talk!

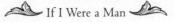

"Had to come in here," he said. "Gave my seat to a dame who was bound to have it. There's nothing they won't get when they make up their minds to it—eh?"

"No fear!" said the big man in the next seat, "they haven't much mind to make up, you know—and if they do, they'll change it."

"The real danger," began the Revd. Alfred Smythe, the new Episcopal clergyman, a thin, nervous, tall man, with a face several centuries behind the times, "is that they will overstep the limits of their God-appointed sphere."

"Their natural limits ought to hold 'em, I think," said cheerful Dr. Jones. "You can't get around physiology, I tell you."

"I've never seen any limits, myself, not to what they want, anyhow," said Mr. Miles, "merely a rich husband and a fine house and no end of bonnets and dresses, and the latest thing in motors, and a few diamonds—and so on. Keeps us pretty busy."

There was a tired gray man across the aisle. He had a very nice wife, always beautifully dressed, and three unmarried daughters, also beautifully dressed—Mollie knew them. She knew he worked hard too, and looked at him now a little anxiously.

But he smiled cheerfully.

"Do you good, Miles," he said. "What else would a man work for? A good woman is about the best thing on earth."

"And a bad one's the worst, that's sure," responded Miles.

"She's a pretty weak sister, viewed professionally," Dr. Jones averred with solemnity, and the Revd. Alfred Smythe added: "She brought evil into the world."

Gerald Mathewson sat up straight. Something was stirring in him which he did not recognize—yet could not resist.

"Seems to me we all talk like Noah," he suggested drily.

"Or the ancient Hindu scriptures. Women have their limitations, but so do we, God knows. Haven't we known girls in school and college just as smart as we were?"

"They cannot play our games," coldly replied the clergyman.

Gerald measured his meagre proportions with a practiced eye.

"I never was particularly good at football myself," he modestly admitted, "but I've known women who could outlast a man in all-round endurance. Besides—life isn't spent in athletics!"

This was sadly true. They all looked down the aisle where a heavy ill-dressed man with a bad complexion sat alone. He had held the top of the columns once, with headlines and photographs. Now he earned less than any of them.

"It's time we woke up," pursued Gerald, still inwardly urged to unfamiliar speech. "Women are pretty much *people*, seems to me. I know they dress like fools—but who's to blame for that? We invent all those idiotic hats of theirs, and design their crazy fashions, and, what's more, if a woman is courageous enough to wear common sense clothes—and shoes—which of us wants to dance with her?

"Yes, we blame them for grafting on us, but are we willing to let our wives work? We are not. It hurts our pride, that's all. We are always criticizing them for making mercenary marriages, but what do we call a girl who marries a chump with no money? Just a poor fool, that's all. And they know it.

"As for those physical limitations, Dr. Jones, I guess our side of the house has some responsibility there, too—eh?

"And for Mother Eve—I wasn't there and can't deny the story, but I will say this, if she brought evil into the world we men have had the lion's share of keeping it going ever since—how about that?"

They drew into the city, and all day long in his business, Gerald was vaguely conscious of new views, strange feelings, and the submerged Mollie learned and learned.

Girls
and Land

IF DACIA BOONE'S father had lived he would have been a rich man, a very rich man, and a power in politics also—for good or ill. He was of the same stamp as Mark Hanna, a born organizer, an accumulator and efficient handler of money. His widow was deeply convinced of this, and expressed her opinion with explicit firmness, more rather than less as the years advanced.

She expressed it to Dacia and her older sisters from infancy up; to all her friends, relatives and associates; and, unfortunately, to Mr. Ordway, her second husband. He was, as she would plaintively explain, a far nicer man to live with than Her First; but he had no gift for making money—which was entirely true. He managed to feed and clothe her three Boone daughters, and the later brood of little Ordways, also to give them a chance at an education, but that appeared to be his limit.

They moved from place to place, in search of better fortune, urged always by the uneasy mother. She seemed to feel that if he could only find his proper place and work he would do well, but as a matter of fact he did fairly well in each attempt, and never any better.

When Dacia was twenty the family had a homestead in the state of Washington, a big fertile place, lacking only a good road to the nearest station to be a profitable fruit ranch. Of this ranch they had hopes, high, but distant. For the rest they lived in a small house on one of Seattle's many hills, and Mr. Ordway worked at what jobs he could get,—as a foreman, manager, small contractor. He had experience enough for a dozen; he could handle men, he was honest and efficient, but blind to the various side issues wherein other men made money.

The two older girls were married, and using what powers they had to spur their husbands on toward high financial achievements; but as for Dacia—she worked in a store. Her mother had opposed it, naturally; but the girl was quietly persistent, and usually got her way.

"Oh, what's the use, mother!" she said. "I shan't marry—I'm too homely, you know that."

"It's not your looks, my dear child," Mrs. Ordway would mournfully reply. "There's plenty of homelier girls than you are—much homelier—that marry. But it is the way you act— you somehow don't try to be—attractive."

Dacia smiled her wide, good-natured smile. "No, I don't, and what's more, I won't. So what between lack of beauty and lack of attractiveness—"

"And lack of money!" her mother broke in. "If your father had only lived!"

"I don't believe I could have loved him any better than I do the father I've got," said the girl loyally. As a matter of fact, for all her frequent references to the departed, the only salient point his widow ever mentioned was that capacity of his for making money.

Dacia went to work, trying several trades, and was in a good position as saleswoman—she flatly refused to say "saleslady"—by the time she was twenty.

She was homely. A strong, square, dark face, determined

and good-natured, but in no way beautiful; rather a heavy figure, but sturdy and active; a quiet girl with a close mouth.

"You certainly are the image of your father!" her mother would say; adding with vain pathos: "If only you had been a man!"

Dacia had no quarrel with being a woman. She had had her woman's experience, too; a deep passionate, wild love for the man who had quite overlooked her and married one of her sisters. They had gone back to Massachusetts to live—for which the lonely girl was deeply thankful. Also she was thankful that no one knew what she had felt, how she had suffered. It was her first great trial in keeping still, and had developed that natural instinct into a settled habit. But though she said little, she thought much; and made plans with a breadth, a length, a daring, that would have made her father proud indeed—had she been a boy.

She saved her money too, steadily laying up a little nest egg for clear purposes of her own. To Mr. Ordway she gave a partial confidence.

"Daddy," said she, "what do you really think would be the best way to develop our ranch—if we had the money."

He had ample views on the subject. There were apples, of course; berries—all kinds of fruit. There was market garden ground, flat and rich where the valley spread out a little; the fruit trees grew best on the slopes. There was timber in plenty—if only they had that road to the station! There was power too—a nice little waterfall—all on their land.

"It'll be worth a lot by and by," he asserted. "And if only I could raise the capital—but what's the use of talkin'!"

"Lots of use, Daddy dear, if you talk to the right person— such as me! Now tell me something else—who *ought* to build that road?"

"Why, there is a kind of a road—it's laid out all right, as

you know—it just needs to be made into a good one. I suppose the town ought to do it, or the county—I don't rightly know."

"If they furnished the labor, could you manage it, Daddy? Could you build a real good road down to Barville? And how much do you think it would cost?"

"Oh, as to labor—it would take—" he scribbled a little, with a flat carpenter's pencil, and showed her the estimate. "'Twould take that many men, at least," his blunt forefinger pointing, "and that long. To pay them—that much; to feed them—that much more to say nothing of shelter. Are you proposing to go into the road-making business next week, my dear?"

She grinned and shook her head. "Not next week, Daddy. But I like to know. And you are so practical! If you had the men—and the County let you—you could build that road and be a public benefactor—couldn't you?"

"I could indeed. There's good road metal there too; a stone crusher could be run by that waterfall—or we'd burn the wood for it. Just advance me a hundred thousand dollars or so out of your wages, and I'll do it! But *what's* the use of talkin'!" he repeated.

"Lots of use," she answered again, "if I talk to the right person—such as you!"

Then she said no more on that subject, though he joked her about it when they were alone, and devoted herself to another branch of tactics. She frequented the YWCA, the Social Settlement, one or two churches, and after some months of quiet inquiry found the woman she wanted, a woman with a high enthusiasm for Working Girls' Clubs.

Dacia was interested, became very friendly, said she could get together quite a number, she thought. She brought to this woman the kind of help she needed, earnest capable girls who saw the value of the work, and inside of two years there were established a whole chain of "R & P Clubs," self-supporting, and very popular.

R & P? Rest and Pleasure, of course.

With a first group of one hundred girls, paying 25 cents a week, they were sure of $100.00 a month for their rent and furnishing. The same number, paying 20 cents a day for lunch, found to their surprise that half of it fed them, and the remaining half, $60.00 a week, paid for the extra fuel and service, with $10.00 left for profit. When two hundred came to the same place for lunch they laid up $50.00 a week for their sinking fund.

Their big rooms were open in the evening for reading and dancing, for club and class work; and their various young gentleman friends who came to see them there and paid a modest five cents for light refreshment, found it the cheapest good time in the city—and the pleasantest.

The idea spread; Tacoma took it up, and Portland, Bellingham, Everett and Spokane; the larger cities had more than one group.

Meanwhile Dacia went to her father with another modest proposition.

"Daddy," she urged. "I've found a nice Swede who is a good carpenter and cabinet maker. He and his wife want a place in the country. Would you be willing to have him cut some of your timber and put up a camp for us—for our clubs, that is—for a Vacation Place?"

"Who's going to pay him?" he asked.

"Oh, I'll pay him, all right; I've got a Fund. But I want you really to sell him a little piece of the property—will you? Just a couple of acres or so, where the garden land is good, and let him pay for it in labor. You can make him agree to sell back to you if he wants to leave."

This being done, and Dacia allowed to dictate the "labor," she set the man to work in good earnest, with some assistants, and soon had camping accommodations for a hundred.

Dacia's Fund, which she had been saving out of her salary for three years, amounted to $500.00, and served to buy the necessary bedding and other supplies. For further gain, she counted as future asset, a Vacation Fund the Clubs had been saving. There were three now in Seattle, comprising well over four hundred working women, and these had been urged to set aside 25 cents a week for a fortnight's vacation. For this $12.50 of a year's easy saving they were to have transportation and board for two weeks in the hills.

Mrs. Olsen, sturdy and industrious, had not been loitering while her husband sawed wood. She had fed him and his assistants; had established a hennery, and a vegetable garden. A few young sheep were kept within safe bounds by a movable wire fence, a device which seemed to Dacia too obvious to avoid, where there were two men to unroll and fasten it to the trees with a quick tap of the hammer, and to reel it up and move it when desired. There were two good cows, also a litter of cheerful young pigs, who basked and grew fat on the little farm.

When it was time for the first detachment of Vacationers, Dacia's fund was all spent, but that hundred times $12.50 was in the savings deposit account of the R & P Clubs, and the girls paid their board with pride and satisfaction. Of the Seattle group of four hundred members, over three hundred had subscribed to this vacation fund; and they came, in self-elected groups, two weeks at a time, all summer long. $3,750.00 they paid in, and when the summer was over Dacia sat down with her father to estimate results of the thirteen weeks.

It had cost $2.40 each to get them there and back, with their baggage. To feed them, using the animals on the place and the garden, was not above $2.00 a week. This left $2,430.00. To Mrs. Olsen and the sturdy flaxen-braided damsel she had to help her, Dacia paid cash,—$10.00 a week, including the girl's board, but this was only $130.00. Then Dacia paid herself back the $500.00 she had invested, allowed $300.00 for refitting, and had a clear $1,500.00 for her further plans.

Dacia smiled and put it in the bank. She was twenty-two now. That winter she rented a pleasant hall; supplied it with refreshments from the lunch room; had dancing classes established under decent and reasonable management; sublet it for part of the time, and added steadily to her little fund.

Another summer's vacation income, with greater patronage and small additional expense, left her, at twenty-three, with quite a little sum. She had all together her first saving of $500.00, additional for a year $200.00 (she earned $15.00 a week, boarded for $7.00, dress and incidentals, $8.00, and saved $4.00), the first year's $1,500.00, the winter's additional earning from her rented hall, amounting to $800.00, and the second year's increased income of $1,800.00—in all $4,800.00.

"Daddy," said she, "let's you and me go into the road business. Can't we rent a stone-crusher? How many horses would it need? Don't you think the county will help?"

Mr. Ordway went up to the ranch with her and looked over the plant. There were the rough but usable sleeping and eating accommodations, and a small saw and planing mill. There were the Olsens, extremely pleased with themselves. The good wife had earned not only her wages but about half of the board money, paid in for milk, meat, eggs and vegetables. This had gone promptly back to Dacia in payment for their stock, and also enabled them to lay in groceries for the winter. Fuel was plenty and Mr. Olsen's two years' work had already covered most of their purchase money.

"But how about labor, Miss Promoter?" asked Mr. Ordway. "Do you realize what it means to feed and pay the force of men we'd need?"

"And how about The Unemployed?" she answered

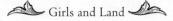

promptly. "Some of them are good workmen—and you know how to pick and manage them. If they are sure of shelter and food and steady work, even at moderate pay—don't you think you could get 'em to come?"

Mr. Ordway consulted with local officials and other owners of homesteads and timber land in the neighborhood. Everyone wanted the road. Here was some capital offered, waterpower, a competent manager and accommodations for the men. And here was "The Problem of The Unemployed" looming ahead for the winter. This would remove a little of that difficulty.

So the County was induced to help.

"It's only a drop in the bucket, "said Dacia, "but if County Canomish can do it, why can't the others? There's Power enough — there's Material enough—there's Brains enough—and there's Labor enough. And a little capital goes a good way, seems to me."

By spring they had a good hard road, opening up much valuable land and adding much to the prosperity of the whole region; and Dacia had just enough money left, from another winter's earnings and saving, to fumigate and refit her camp.

But that year everything was easier on account of the road, and the greater popularity of the place kept it fuller, and longer open. Five hundred girls and women, in different parties, came up; and Dacia invested one dollar from each $12.50 in improving and beautifying the place, still clearing over $2,500.

She was twenty-four now, and very happy. So was Mr. Ordway. He was able to dispose of some of his lumber and start planting the fruit ranch which his heart desired. Mrs. Ordway viewed it all with grudging admiration.

"Yes—it's very nice," she admitted to her daughter. "Very nice, indeed, but I can't help thinking what your father would have done with a chance like this. But then, he was a man of

Financial Genius! If only you had been a boy, Dacia! And if he had only lived to help you!"

"But my second father is helping me," said Dacia. "And I'm perfectly willing to be a girl—rather glad I am one, in fact."

Then she consulted further with Mr. Ordway. "Daddy—can you make furniture out of the kind of wood you've got there?"

"Why, yes—I *could*, I suppose. I never thought of it—plain kitchen sort of furniture. There's not much hard wood."

"But there's some. And you can set out more, can't you?"

"Set out—! Plant hardwood trees! Child, you're crazy. Hardwood timber doesn't grow up like lettuce."

"How long does it take to be—cuttable?"

"Oh—thirty years at least, I should say."

"Well—let's plant some. It will be valuable when I'm fifty-five or so—and your own children will be younger—they may be glad of it. But meantime I want to propose that you start a little Grand Rapids right by our waterfall there. Can't the mill be turned into a furniture factory? Nice cheap plain furniture—painted or stained—and sold to the folks out here that can't pay the freight on Eastern stuff."

"Hm!" Mr. Ordway considered. He got out his pencil. He made some estimates. "There's that young Pedersen," he said, "the Olsen's cousin—he's a good designer—you've seen what he's made for them?"

Dacia had seen it, and had thought about it quite carefully, but she made no admissions.

"Do you think he'd be useful?"

"I'm pretty sure he would," said Mr. Ordway. "Dacia, child, you surely have a business head—why there's no real furniture factory on this coast. We might—we might do pretty well, I think."

Olaf Pedersen thought so too.

"Your wood is much like the wood of our country," he said. "And we make furniture. I have no capital, but I will design and work, gladly."

They began cautiously, with a small workshop, a moderate investment in machinery, and Dacia's big connection of people of small incomes, as advertising ground. She herself had so much faith in the enterprise that she gave up her position and became "the office force" for the undertaking.

Next year they established the firm of Ordway, Boone & Pedersen. The modesty of their methods was such that they encountered practically no opposition until it was too late to crush them.

"A pleased customer is the best advertisement." And there were several hundred pleased customers spreading the good news. Furniture that was solid and strong; that was simple, novel and pretty; that was amazingly cheap; that was made right there in their own state—it really pleased the people, and they supported the business.

Even the railroads, finding that their freight payment was as good as others, and that their trade was steadily growing, ceased to be antagonistic.

Mr. Ordway settled down to steady work that had a future.

"Dacia," said he. "I'm mighty glad that, well, that I inherited you. You see, I can work and I'm honest, but you've got the brains. You can push."

"It's Olaf, too, Daddy—it's mostly Olaf—he puts the novelty and beauty into it."

"Yes, it's Olaf too. You are both good partners. I shall leave the business to you when I go."

And he did,—to two who were partners of a closer sort long before then; and Boone & Pedersen developed a furniture industry which was of immense service to the whole coast.

Dr. Clair's Place

"YOU MUST COUNT your mercies," said her friendly adviser. "There's no cloud so dark but it has a silver lining, you know,—count your mercies."

She looked at her with dull eyes that had known no hope for many years. "Perhaps you will count them for me: Health—utterly broken and gone since I was twenty-four. Youth gone too—I am thirty-eight. Beauty—I never had it. Happiness—buried in shame and bitterness these fourteen years. Motherhood—had and lost. Usefulness—I am too weak even to support myself. I have no money. I have no friends. I have no home. I have no work. I have no hope in life." Then a dim glow of resolution flickered in those dull eyes. "And what is more I don't propose to bear it much longer."

It is astonishing what people will say to strangers on the cars. These two sat on the seat in front of me, and I had heard every syllable of their acquaintance, from the "Going far?" of the friendly adviser to this confidence as to proposed suicide. The offerer of cheerful commonplaces left before long, and I took her place, or rather the back-turned seat facing it, and studied the Despairing One.

Not a bad looking woman, but so sunk in internal misery that her expression was that of one who had been in prison

for a lifetime. Her eyes had that burned out look, as hopeless as a cinder heap; her voice a dreary grating sound. The muscles of her face seemed to sag downward. She looked at the other passengers as if they were gray ghosts and she another. She looked at the rushing stretches we sped past as if the window were ground glass. She looked at me as if I were invisible.

"This," said I to myself, "is a case for Dr. Clair."

It was not difficult to make her acquaintance. There was no more protective tissues about her than about a skeleton. I think she would have showed the utter wreck of her life to any who asked to look, and not have realized their scrutiny. In fact it was not so much that she exhibited her misery, as that she was nothing but misery—whoever saw her, saw it.

I was a "graduate patient" of Dr. Clair, as it happened; and had the usual enthusiasms of the class. Also I had learned some rudiments of the method, as one must who has profited by it. By the merest touch of interest and considerate attention I had the "symptoms"—more than were needed; by a few indicated "cases I had known" I touched that spring of special pride in special misery which seems to be coexistent with life; and then I had an account which would have been more than enough for Dr. Clair to work on.

Then I appealed to that queer mingling of this pride and of the deep instinct of social service common to all humanity, which Dr. Clair had pointed out to me, and asked her—

"If you had an obscure and important physical disease you'd be glad to leave your body to be of service to science, wouldn't you?" She would—anyone would, of course.

"You can't leave your mind for an autopsy very well, but there's one thing you can do—if you will; and that is, give this clear and prolonged self-study you have made, to a doctor I know who is profoundly interested in neurasthenia—melancholia—

all that kind of thing. I really think you'd be a valuable—what shall I say—exhibit."

She gave a little muscular smile, a mere widening of the lips, the heavy gloom of her eyes unaltered.

"I have only money enough to go where I am going," she said. "I have just one thing to do there—that ought to be done before I—leave."

There was no air of tragedy about her. She was merely dead, or practically so.

"Dr. Clair's is not far from there, as it happens, and I know her well enough to be sure she'd be glad to have you come. You won't mind if I give you the fare up there—purely as a scientific experiment? There are others who may profit by it, you see."

She took the money, looking at it as if she hardly knew what it was, saying dully: "All right—I'll go." And, after a pause, as if she had half forgotten it, "Thank you."

And some time later she added: "My name is Octavia Welch."

Dr. Willy Clair—she was Southern, and really named Willy—was first an eager successful young teacher, very young. Then she spent a year or two working with atypical children. Then, profoundly interested, she plunged into the study of medicine and became as eager and successful a doctor as she had been a teacher. She specialized in psychopathic work, developed methods of her own, and with the initial aid of some of her numerous "GPs" established a sanatorium in Southern California. There are plenty of such for "lungers," but this was of quite another sort.

She married, in the course of her full and rich career, one of her patients, a young man who was brought to her by his mother—a despairing ruin. It took five years to make him over, but it was done, and then they were married. He worshipped her; and she said he was the real mainstay of the business—and he was, as far as the business part of it went.

Dr. Clair was about forty when I sent Octavia Welch up there. She had been married some six years, and had, among her other assets, two splendid children. But other women have husbands and children, also splendid—no one else had a psycho-sanatorium. She didn't call it that; the name on the stationery was just "The Hills."

On the southern face of the Sierra Madres she had bought a high-lying bit of mesa-land and steep-sided arroyo, and gradually added to it both above and below, until it was now quite a large extent of land. Also she had her own water; had built a solid little reservoir in her deepest canyon; had sunk an artesian well far up in the hills behind, ran a windmill to keep the water up, and used the overflow for power as well as for irrigation. That had made the whole place such garden land as only Southern California knows. From year to year, the fame of the place increased, and its income also, she built and improved; and now it was the most wonderful combination of peaceful, silent wilderness and blossoming fertility.

The business end of it was very simply managed. On one of the steep flat-topped mesas, the one nearest the town that lay so pleasantly in the valley below, she had built a comfortable, solid little Center surrounded by small tent-houses. Here she took ordinary patients, and provided them not only with good medical advice but with good beds and good food, and further with both work and play.

"The trouble with Sanatoriums," said Dr. Clair to me—we were friends since the teaching period, and when I broke down at my teaching I came to her and was mended—"is that the sick folks have nothing to do but sit about and think of themselves and their 'cases.' Now I let the relatives come too; some well ones are a resource; and I have one or more regularly engaged persons whose business it is to keep them busy—and amused."

She did. She had for the weakest ones just chairs and hammocks; but these were moved from day to day so that the patient had new views. There was an excellent library, and all manner of magazines and papers. There were picture-puzzles too, with little rimmed trays to set them up in—they could be carried here and there, but not easily lost. Then there were all manner of easy things to learn to do; basketwork, spinning, weaving, knitting, embroidery; it cost very little to the patients and kept them occupied. For those who were able there was gardening and building—always some new little place going up, or a walk or something to make. Her people enjoyed life every day. All this was not compulsory, of course, but they mostly liked it.

In the evenings there was music, and dancing too, for those who were up to it; cards and so on, at the Center; while the others went off to their quiet little separate rooms. Everyone of them had a stove in it; they were as dry and warm as need be—which is more than you can say of most California places.

People wanted to come and board—well people, I mean— and from year to year she ran up more cheap comfortable little shacks, each with its plumbing, electric lights and heating—she had water-power, you see—and a sort of cafeteria place where they could eat together or buy food and take to their homes. I tell you it was popular. Mr. Wolsey (that's her husband, but she kept on as Dr. Clair) ran all this part of it, and ran it well. He had been a hotel man.

All this was only a foundation for her real work with the psychopathic cases. But it was a good foundation, and it paid in more ways than one. She not only had the usual string of Grateful Patients, but another group of friends among those boarders. And there's one thing she did which is well worth

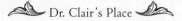

the notice of other people who are trying to help humanity—
or to make money—in the same way.

You know how a hotel will have a string of "rules and
regulations" strung up in every room? She had that—and
more. She had a "Plain Talk With Boarders" leaflet, which
was freely distributed—a most amusing and useful document.
I haven't one here to quote directly, but it ran like this:

> *You come here of your own choice, for your own health and
> pleasure, freely; and are free to go when dissatisfied. The
> comfort and happiness of such a place depends not only on
> the natural resources, on the quality of the accommodations,
> food, service and entertainment, but on the behavior of the
> guests.*
>
> *Each visitor is requested to put in a complaint at the office,
> not only of fault in the management, but of objectionable
> conduct on the part of patrons.*
>
> *Even without such complaint any visitor who is deemed
> detrimental in character or behavior will be requested to
> leave.*

She did it too. She made the place so attractive, so *comfortable,* in every way so desirable, that there was usually a waiting
list; and if one of these fault-finding old women, or noisy,
disagreeable young men, or desperately flirtatious persons
got in, Dr. Clair would have it out with them.

"I am sorry to announce that you have been blackballed
by seven of your fellow guests. I have investigated the
complaints and find them well founded. We herewith return
your board from date (that was always paid in advance) and
shall require your room tomorrow."

People didn't like to own to a thing like that—not and tell
the truth. They did tell all manner of lies about the place, of

course; but she didn't mind—there were far more people to tell the truth. I can tell you a boarding-place that is as beautiful, as healthful, as exquisitely clean and comfortable, and as reasonable as hers in price, is pretty popular. Then, from year to year, she enlarged and developed her plan till she had, I believe, the only place in the world where a sick soul could go and be sure of help.

Here's what Octavia Welch wrote about it. She showed it to me years later:

I was dead—worse than dead—buried decayed—gone to foul dirt. In my body I still walked heavily—but out of accumulated despair I had slowly gathered about enough courage to drop that burden. Then I met the Friend on the train who sent me to Dr. Clair....

I sent the post-card, and was met at the train, by a motor. We went up and up—even I could see how lovely the country was—up into the clear air, close to those shaggy, steep dry mountains.

We passed from ordinary streets with pretty homes through a region of pleasant groups of big and little houses which the driver said was the "boarding section," through a higher place where he said there were "lungers and such," on to "Dr. Clair's Place."

The Place was apparently just out of doors. I did not dream then of all the cunningly contrived walks and seats and shelters, the fruits and flowers just where they were wanted, the marvellous mixture of natural beauty and ingenious loving-kindness, which make this place the wonder it is. All I saw was a big beautiful wide house, flower-hung, clean and quiet, and this nice woman, who received me in her office, just like any doctor, and said:

"I'm glad to see you, Mrs. Welch. I have the card announcing your coming, and you can be of very great service to me, if you are willing. Please understand—I do not undertake to cure you; I do not criticize in the least your purpose to leave an unbearable world. That I think is the last human right—to cut short unbearable and useless pain. But if you are willing to let me study you awhile and experiment on you a little—it won't hurt, I assure you—"

Sitting limp and heavy, I looked at her, the old slow tears rolling down as usual. "You can do anything you want to," I said. "Even hurt—what's a little more pain?—if it's any use."

She made a thorough physical examination, blood-test and all. Then she let me tell her all I wanted to about myself, asking occasional questions, making notes, setting it all down on a sort of chart. "That's enough to show me the way for a start," she said. "Tell me—do you dread anaesthetics?"

"No," said I, "so that you give me enough."

"Enough to begin with," she said cheerfully. "May I show you your room?"

It was the prettiest room I had ever seen, as fair and shining as the inside of a shell.

"You are to have the bath treatment first," she said, "then a sleep—then food—I mean to keep you very busy for a while."

So I was put through an elaborate course of bathing, shampoo, and massage, and finally put to bed, in that quiet fragrant rosy room, so physically comfortable that even my corroding grief and shame were forgotten, and I slept.

It was late next day when I woke. Someone had been watching all the time, and at any sign of waking a gentle anaesthetic was given, quite unknown to me. My special attendant, a sweet faced young giantess from Sweden, brought me a tray of breakfast and flowers, and asked if I liked music.

"It is here by your bed," she said. "Here is the card—you ask for what you like, and just regulate the sound as you please."

There was a light moveable telephone, with a little mega-phone attached to the receiver, and a long list of records. I had only to order what I chose, and listen to it as close or as far off as I desired. Between certain hours there was a sort of "table d'hôte" to which we could listen or not as we liked, and these other hours wherein we called for favorites. I found it very restful. There were books and magazines, if I chose, and a rose-draped balcony with a hammock where I could sit or lie, taking my music there if I preferred. I was bathed and oiled and rubbed and fed; I slept better than I had for years, and more than I knew at the time, for when the restless misery came up they promptly put me to sleep and kept me there.

Dr. Clair came in twice a day, with notebook and pencil, asking me many careful questions; not as a physician to a patient, but as an inquiring scientific searcher for valuable truths. She told me about other cases, somewhat similar to my own, consulted me in a way, as to this or that bit of anal-ysis she had made; and again and again as to certain points in my own case. Insensibly under her handling this grew more and more objective, more as if it were someone else who was suffering, and not myself.

"I want you to keep a record, if you will," she said, "when the worst paroxysms come, the overwhelming waves of despair, or that slow tidal ebb of misery—here's a little chart by your bed. When you feel the worst will you be so good as to try either of these three things, and note the result. The Music, as you have used it, noting the effect of the different airs. The Color—we have not introduced you to the color treatment yet—see here—"

She put in my hand a little card of buttons, as it were, with wire attachments. I pressed one; the room was dark-ened, save for the tiny glow by which I saw the color list. Then, playing on the others, I could fill the room with any lovely hue I chose, and see them driving, mingling, changing as I played.

"There," she said, "I would much like to have you make a study of these effects and note it for me. Then—don't laugh! I want you to try tastes, also. Have you never noticed the close connection between a pleasant flavor and a state of mind?"

For this experiment I had a numbered set of little sweet-meats, each delicious and all beneficial, which I was to deliberately use when my misery was acute or wearing. Still further, she had a list of odors for similar use.

This bedroom and balcony treatment lasted a month, and at the end of that time I was so much stronger physically that Dr. Clair said, if I could stand it, she wanted to use certain physical tests on me. I almost hated to admit how much better I felt, but told her I would do anything she said. Then I was sent out with my attending maiden up the canyon to a certain halfway house. There I spent another month of physical enlargement. Part of it was slowly graduated mountain climbing; part was bathing and swimming in a long narrow pool. I grew gradually to feel the delight of mere ascent, so that every hilltop called me, and the joy of plain physical exhaustion and utter rest. To come down from a day on the mountain, to dip deep in that pure water and be rubbed by my ever careful masseuse; to eat heartily of the plain but delicious food, and sleep—out of doors now, on a pine needle bed—that was new life.

My misery and pain and shame seemed to fade into a remote past, as a wholesome rampart of bodily health grew up between me and it.

Then came the People.

This was her Secret. She had People there who were better than Music and Color and Fragrance and Sweetness,—People who lived up there with work and interests of their own, some teachers, some writers, some makers of various things, but all Associates in her wonderful cures.

It was the People who did it. First she made my body as strong as might be, and rebuilt my worn-out nerves with sleep—sleep—sleep. Then I had the right Contact, Soul to Soul.

And now? Why now I am still under forty; I have a little cottage up here in these heavenly hills; I am a well woman; I earn my living by knitting and teaching it to others. And out of the waste and wreck of my life—which is of small consequence to me, I can myself serve to help new-comers. I am an Associate—even I! And I am Happy!

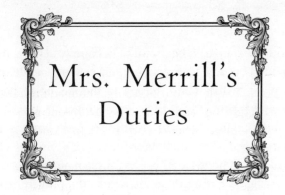

Mrs. Merrill's Duties

GRACE LEROY, IN college, was quite the most important member of the class. She had what her professors proudly pointed out as the rarest thing among women—a scientific mind. The arts had no charms for her; she had no wish to teach, no leaning toward that branch of investigation and alleviation in social pathology we are so apt to call "social service."

Her strength was in genuine research work, and, back of that, greatest gift of all, she showed high promise in "the scientific imagination," the creative synthesizing ability which gives new discoveries to the world.

In addition to these natural advantages a merciful misfortune saved her from the widespread silvery quicksand which so often engulfs the girl graduate. Instead of going home to decorate the drawing-room and help her mother receive, she was obliged to go to work at once, owing to paternal business difficulties.

Her special teacher, old Dr. Welsch, succeeded in getting a laboratory position for her; and for three years she worked side by side with a great chemist and physicist, Dr. Hammerton, his most valued assistant.

She was very happy.

Happy, of course, to be useful to her family at once, instead of an added burden. Happy in her sense of independence and a real place in the world; happy in the feeling of personal power and legitimate pride of achievement. Happiest of all in the brightening dawn of great ideas, big glittering hopes of a discovery that should lighten humanity's burdens. Hardly did she dare to hope for it, yet it did seem almost possible at times. Being of a truly religious nature she prayed earnestly over this; to be good enough to deserve the honor; to keep humble and not overestimate her powers; to be helped to do the Great Work.

Then Life rolled swiftly along and swept her off her feet.

Her father recovered his money and her mother lost her health. For a time there seemed absolute need of her at home.

"I must not neglect plain duty," said the girl, and resigned her position.

There was a year of managing the household, with the care of younger brothers and sisters; a year of travel with the frail mother, drifting slowly from place to place, from physician to physician, always hoping, and always being disappointed.

Then came the grief of losing her, after they had grown so close, so deeply, tenderly intimate.

"Whatever happens," said Grace to herself, "I shall always be glad of these two years. No outside work could justify me in neglecting this primal duty."

What did happen next was her father's turning to her for comfort. She alone could in any degree take her mother's place to him. He could not bear to think of her as leaving the guidance of the family. His dependence was touching.

Grace accepted the new duty bravely.

There was the year of deep mourning, both in symbolic garments and observances and in the real sorrow; and she found herself learning to know her father better than she ever had, and learning how to somewhat make up to him for the companionship he had lost. There was the need of mothering the younger ones, of managing the big house.

Then came the next sister's debut, and the cares and responsibilities involved. Another sister was growing up, and the young brother called for sympathetic guidance. There seemed no end to it.

She bowed her head and faced her duty.

"Nothing can be right," she said, "which would take me away from these intimate claims."

Everyone agreed with her in this.

Her father was understanding and tender in his thoughtfulness.

"I know what a sacrifice you are making, daughter, in giving up your chemistry, but what could I do without you! ... You are so much like your mother ..."

As time passed she did speak once or twice of a housekeeper, that she might have some free hours during the daytime, but he was so hurt at the idea that she gave it up.

Then something happened that proved with absurd ease the fallacy of the fond conclusion that nothing could be right which would take her away. Hugh Merrill took her away, and that was accepted by everyone as perfectly right.

She had known him a long time, but had hardly dared let herself think of marrying him—she was so indispensable at home. But when his patience and his ardor combined finally swept her off her feet; when her father said: "Why, of course, my child! Hugh is a splendid fellow! We shall miss you—but do you think I would stand in the way of your happiness!"— she consented. She raised objections about the housekeeping, but her father promptly met them by installing a widowed sister, Aunt Adelaide, who had always been a favorite with them all.

She managed the home quite as well, and the children really better, than had Grace; and she and her brother played cribbage and backgammon in the evenings with pleasant reversion to their youthful comradeship—he seemed to grow younger for having her there.

Grace was so happy, so relieved by the sudden change from being the mainstay of four other people and a big house to being considered and cared for in every way by a strong resourceful affectionate man, that she did not philosophize at all at the easy dispensibility of the indispensable.

With Hugh she rested; regained her youth, bloomed like a flower. There was a long delightful journey; a pleasant home-coming; the setting up of her very own establishment; the cordial welcome from her many friends.

In all this she never lost sight of her inner hope of the Great Work.

Hugh had profound faith in her. They talked of it on their long honeymoon, in full accord. She should have her labora-tory, she should work away at her leisure, she would do wonderful things—he was sure of it.

But that first year was so full of other things, so crowded with invitations, so crowded with careful consideration of clothes and menus and servants, the duties of a hostess, or a guest—that the big room upstairs was not yet a laboratory.

An unexpected illness with its convalescence took another long period; she needed rest, a change. Another year went by.

Grace was about thirty now.

Then the babies came—little Hugh and Arnold—splendid boys. A happier, prouder mother one would not wish to see. She thanked God with all her heart; she felt the deep and tender oneness with her husband that comes of parentage, with reverent joy.

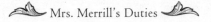

To the task of education she now devoted her warmly loving heart, her clear strong mind. It was noble work. She neglected nothing. This duty was imperative. No low-grade nursemaid should, through ignorance, do some irremediable injury to opening baby minds.

With the help of a fully competent assistant, expensive, but worth all she cost, Mrs. Merrill brought up those boys herself, and the result should have satisfied even the most exacting educator. Hearty, well-grown, unaffected, with clear minds and beautiful manners, they grew up to sturdy boyhood, taking high places when they went to school; loved by their teachers, comrades and friends, and everyone said: "What a lovely mother she is!"

She did not admit to anyone that even in this period of lovely mothering, even with the home happiness, the wife happiness, the pleasant social position, there was still an aching want inside. She wanted her laboratory, her research, her work. All her years of education, from the first chemistry lessons at fourteen to the giving up of her position at twenty-four, had made her a chemist, and nature had made her a discoverer.

She had not read much during these years; it hurt her—made her feel an exile. She had shut the door on all that side of her life, and patiently, gladly fulfilled the duties of the other side, neglecting nothing.

Not till ten more years had passed did she draw a long breath and say: "Now I will have my laboratory!"

She had it. There was the big room, all this time a nursery; now at last fitted up with all the mysterious implements and supplies of her chosen profession.

The boys were at school—her husband at his business—now she could concentrate on the Great Work.

And then Mrs. Merrill began to realize "the defects of her qualities."

There is such a thing as being too good.

We all know that little one-handed tool combination which carries in its inside screwdriver, gouge and chisel, awl and file—a marvellously handy thing to have in the house. Yes—but did you ever see a carpenter use one? The real workman, for real work, must have real tools, of which the value is, not that they will all fit one hollow and feeble handle, but that each will do what it is meant for, well.

We have seen in Grace Leroy Merrill the strength of mind and character, Christian submission, filial duty, wifely love, motherly efficiency. She had other qualities also, all pleasant ones. She was a pre-eminently attractive woman, more than pretty—charming. She was sweet and cordial in manner, quick and witty, a pleasure to talk with for either man or woman. Add to these the possession of special talent for dress, and a gentle friendliness that could not bear to hurt anyone, and we begin to feel "this is too much. No person has a right to be so faultless, so universally efficient and attractive."

Social psychology is a bit complicated. We need qualities, not only valuable for personal, but for social relation. In the growing complexity of a highly specialized organization the law of organic specialization calls for a varying degree of sacrifice in personal fulfillment. It is quite possible, indeed it is usual, to find individuals whose numerous good qualities really stand in the way of their best service to society. The best tools are not those of the greatest "all round" variety of usefulness.

When the boys were grown up enough to be off her mind for many hours a day; when the house fairly ran itself in the hands of well-trained servants; when, at last, the laboratory was installed and the way seemed open; Mrs. Merrill found herself fairly bogged in her own popularity. She had so many friends; they were so unfailingly anxious to have her at their

dinners, their dances, their continuous card parties; they came to her so confidingly, so frequently—and she could never bear to hurt their feelings.

There were, to be sure, mornings. One is not required to play bridge in the morning, or dance, or go to the theatre. But even the daily ordering for a household takes some time, and besides the meals there are the supplies in clothing, linen, china; and the spring and fall extras of putting things away with mothballs, having rugs cleaned and so on—and so on.

Then—clothes; her own clothes. The time to think about them; the time to discuss them; the time to buy them; the time to stand up and be fitted—to plan and struggle with the dressmaker—a great deal of time—and no sooner is the feat accomplished than—presto!—it must be done all over.

Day after day she mounted the stairs to her long looked for workroom, with an hour—or two—or three—before her. Day after day she was called down again; friends at the telephone, friends at the door; friends who were full of cheerful apology and hopes that they did not disturb her; and tradesmen who were void of either.

"If only I could get something *done!*" she said, as she sat staring at her retorts. "If once I could really accomplish a piece of good work, that should command public acknowledgement—then they would understand. Then I could withdraw from all this——"

For she found that her hours were too few, and too broken, to allow of that concentration of mind without which no great work is possible.

But she was a strong woman, a patient woman, and possessed of a rich fund of perseverance. With long waiting, with careful use of summer months when her too devoted friends were out of town, she managed in another five years, to really accomplish something. From her little laboratory, working alone and under all distractions, she finally sent out a new formula; not for an explosive of deadly power, but for a safe and simple sedative, something which induced natural sleep, with no ill results.

It was no patented secret. She gave it to the world with the true scientific spirit, and her joy was like that of motherhood She had at last achieved! She had done something—something of real service to thousands upon thousands. And back of this first little hill, so long in winning, mountain upon mountain, range on range, rose hopefully tempting before her.

She was stronger now. She had gotten back into the lines of study, of persistent work. Her whole mind stirred and freshened with new ideas, high purposes. She planned for further research, along different lines. Two Great Ones tempted her; a cheap combustible fluid; and that biggest prize of all—the mastering of atomic energy.

And now, now that she had really made this useful discovery, which was widely recognized among those who knew of such matters, she could begin to protect herself from these many outside calls!

What did happen?

She found herself quite lionized for a season—name in the papers, pictures, interviews, and a whole series of dinners and receptions where she was wearied beyond measure by the well-meant comments on her work.

Free? Respected? Let alone?

Her hundreds of friends, who had known her so long and so well, as a charming girl, a devoted daughter, an irreproachable wife, a most unusually successful mother, were only the more cordial now.

"Have you heard about Grace Merrill? Isn't it wonderful! She always had ability—I've always said so."

"Such a service to the world! A new anesthetic!"

"Oh, it's not an anesthetic—not really."

"Like the Twilight Sleep, I imagine."

"It's splendid of her anyway. I've asked her to dinner Thursday, to meet Professor Andrews—he's an authority on dietetics, you know, and Dr. North and his wife—they are such interesting people!"

Forty-six! Still beautiful, still charming, still exquisitely gowned. Still a happy wife and mother, with Something Done—at last.

And yet—

Her next younger sister, who had lost her husband and was greatly out of health, now wanted to come and live with her; their father had followed his wife some years back and the old home was broken up.

That meant being tied up at home again. And as to the social engagements, she was more hopelessly popular than ever.

Then one day there came to see her Dr. Hammerton. His brush of hair was quite white, but thick and erect as ever. His keen black eyes sparkled portentously under thick white eyebrows.

"What's this you've been doing, Child? Show me your shop."

She showed him, feeling very girlish again in the presence of her early master. He looked the place over in silence, told her he had read about her new product, sat on the edge of a table and made her take a chair.

"Now tell me about it!" he said.

She told him—all about it. He listened, nodding agreeably as she recounted the steps.

"Mother? Yes. Father? Yes—for awhile at least. Husband?

Yes. Boys? Of course—and you've done well. But what's the matter now?"

She told him that too—urging her hope of forcing some acknowledgment by her proven ability.

He threw back his big head and laughed.

"You've got the best head of any woman I ever saw," he said; "you've done what not one woman in a thousand does—kept a living Self able to survive family relations. You've proven, now, that you are still in the ring. You ought to do—twenty—maybe thirty years of worthwhile work. Forty-six? I was forty-eight when you left me, have done my best work since then, am seventy now, and am still going strong. You've spent twenty-two years in worthwhile woman-work that's *done*—now you have at least as much again to do human work. I daresay you'll do better because of all this daughtering and mothering—women are queer things. Anyhow you've plenty of time. But you must get to work.

"Now, see here—if you let all these childish flub-dubs prevent you from doing what God made you for—you're a Criminal Fool!"

Grace gave a little gasp.

"I mean it. You know it. It's all nonsense, empty nonsense. As for your sister—let her go to a sanitarium—she can afford it, or live with her other sister—or brother. You've earned your freedom.

"As to clothes and parties—Quit!"

She looked at him.

"Yes, I know. You're still pretty and attractive, but *what of it*? Suppose Spencer or Darwin had wasted their time as parlor ornaments—supposing they could have—would they have had a right to?"

She caught at the names. "You think I could do something—Great?" she asked. "You think I am—big enough—to try?"

He stood up. She rose and faced him.

"I think you are great, to have done what you have—a task no man could face. I think you will be greater—perhaps one of the big World Helpers." Then his eyes shot fire—and he thundered: "How Dare you hinder the World's Work by wasting your time with these idle women? It is Treason—High Treason—to Humanity."

"What can I do?" she asked at last.

"That's a foolish question, child. Use your brain—you've got plenty. Learn to assert yourself and stand up to it, that's all. Tell your sister you can't. Disconnect the telephone. Hire some stony-faced menial to answer the door and say: 'Mrs. Merrill is engaged. She left orders not to be disturbed.'

"Decide on how many evenings you can afford to lose sleep, and decline to go out on all others. It's simple enough.

"But you've got to *do it*. You've got to plan it and stand by it. It takes Courage—and it takes Strength."

"But if it is my duty—" said Grace Merrill.

The old man smiled and left her.

"Once that woman sees a Duty!" he said to himself.

The Girl in
the Pink Hat

MY SISTER POLLY and I had a "stateroom," but we did not sit in it all the time. The car was not at all full, and I like to move about and look at the scenery from all sides.

Polly is a dear girl, but her best friends admit she is a trifle odd in appearance. She will wear her red hair pulled down over her ears and forehead and neck—that's a switch, too; with a squishy hat drooping over the whole; and big yellow-glassed shell goggles, and a veil besides. Also one of those long traveling cloaks, sort of black silk duster. I never could see how people can stand veils over their eyes, and mouths, and noses—especially noses; they tickle so.

But I'm very fond of Polly, and she is really a good-looking girl, when properly dressed. She's a romantic soul, and good as gold. I am romantic, too; but not good.

We were coming home from a long trip, away out to the Coast and back, and the home stretch was tiresome. Somewhere about Schenectady it was; Polly was reading another of her interminable magazines, and I was prowling about after variety and amusement.

There was a day-coach just ahead, and I slipped in there for a change, and found an empty seat.

Just in front sat a young couple, with their heads pretty

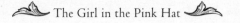

close together, and I watched them idly, for she was a pretty meager looking girl in a soft pink hat, and he quite an impressive fellow,—rather too much so, I thought.

Presently I caught a note of trouble in her voice, and a low insistence in his; low, but quite audible to me. The seat in front of them was empty, and I dare say he thought the one behind was too; at any rate they talked, and I couldn't help hearing them.

The amazing way in which people bare their hearts to one another, in street cars or steam-cars, or in steamer chairs, has always been a wonder to me. You cannot accuse the traveling public of eavesdropping when it hears the immediate fellow sufferers in the New York subway explaining their economic disabilities, or their neighbors in the day-coach exhibiting a painful degree of marital infelicity.

In my own travels I become an unwilling mother confessor to all about me, for my ears are unusually keen, and seem especially so on the cars. Perhaps it is because the speakers, to overcome the noise of the wheels, raise their voices, or sharpen them to a peculiarly penetrating pitch. At any rate I can hear them, right and left, front and rear, which is sometimes interesting, sometimes tedious, sometimes acutely disagreeable.

This time it was interesting, very.

"I tell you it is not my fault," he was saying, in a low restrained voice; but as one whose patience was wearing thin. "I couldn't help it if the car was stalled, could I? And then we *had* to catch this train. I have an engagement in the city I can't afford to miss."

"You can't attend to it tonight, can you?" she asked, evidently trying to keep control of herself, not to be frightened, and not to lose faith in him. Yet a note of suspicion would struggle through in spite of her.

"Why can't we stop off at Albany and——" She spoke low, but I heard it, the little hesitant girlish voice, with a touch of awe at the words "Be married—and then take a later train to New York?"

"What *is* the difference, my dear!" he protested, "whether we're married in Albany, or in New York?"

"What time do we get to New York?" she asked.

"About nine," he said, and then I became really alert, for I knew it would be about eleven.

"And you can arrange for it then—tonight?" she persisted. "Isn't your license for Ohio?"

"What a careful soul you are, my dear," he replied airily. "Yes that license was for Ohio, of course, and I could hardly get one in New York tonight. But there are more ways than one of being married in New York, you will find. People can be married, legally and properly married, before a notary public, and I have a friend who is one. Nothing could be simpler. We call him up, take a taxi to his apartment, make our deposition and have it all properly set down with a big red seal—tonight. Then if you want to go to The Little Church Around the Corner tomorrow and have it 'solemnized,' you may."

He talked too much. Also, though I sat behind, I could "smell his breath." And I saw that the girl was not satisfied. Evidently she was not as green as he had thought her. Either from romances or at "the movies" she had known things of this sort to be done—with sad results.

It must be a terrible thing in the mind of an affectionate young girl to have to distrust her lover. I judged, from what I had gathered, that she had planned a perfectly good marriage, in her home state, before starting on this journey; that some trifle about that incident of the stalled car had upset her, started her to thinking, and that his drinking, on their wedding trip, seemed a suspicious circumstance to her.

She was visibly alarmed, yet striving still to keep her trust, not to accept the horrible alternative which forced itself upon her mind. She sat still for a minute or two, looking out of the window, while he fondled her in vain attempt to substitute caresses she did not want for the reassurance he could not give.

She made up her mind presently.

It was a very firm little chin I now observed, as she turned squarely toward him; a face pale, but quite determined. She smiled too, trying hard to hold her illusions.

"A bride has *some* privileges, surely," she suggested with an effect of buoyancy, "even an eloping bride. I prefer to be married in Albany, if you please, my dear."

It was a pity for this gentleman's purposes that he had taken that drink, or those drinks. It was a little too much, or not quite enough. It made him irritable.

"But I don't please," he said testily. "I did all I could to please you—fixed up to have it all done in Elyria this morning. But we slipped up on that—and now I don't propose to stop over in Albany. It's all nonsense, Jess—only means delay and trouble—I don't know anybody in Albany, and I know plenty in New York. And I tell you I've got to be there in the morning, and I will. And you'll be Mrs. Marsh before midnight, all right, all right——"

"I know somebody in Albany," she answered. "I have an old friend there; she was my Sunday School teacher. I can stay there over-night, or for some days, and you can come up with another license and marry me."

Even then, if he had been quite sober he could have satisfied her. She was fairly trembling at her own daring, and quite ready to break down and cry on his shoulder and own she was a goose—if he said the right thing.

But he did not. He tried to assert a premature authority.

"You'll do nothing of the sort," he told her sharply. "You're my wife, or will be in a few hours, and you're going with me to New York."

She lifted her head at that.

"I am going to get off at Albany," she answered.

"You haven't so much as a nickel, my dear," he said disagreeably, "to 'phone with even, or take a car."

"I'll walk!" she said.

"You haven't your bag either," he told her. It's in the baggage car and I've got the checks."

"I don't care—Miss Pierce will take care of me."

"And suppose Miss Pierce happens not to be there," he suggested. "A nice pickle you'd be in—in Albany—at night—alone—no money and no bag—eh, my dear!"

He put his arm about her and hugged her close. She permitted it, but returned to her plea.

"Julius! You'll stop if I want to, surely! Or if you can't, you'll let me. Just get my bag for me, and give me a dollar or two—you're not going to try to *make* me go to New York—against my will?"

"I'm tired of this," he replied, with sudden irritability. "Of course you are coming to New York. Now just make up your mind to it."

"Julius—I'm sorry to—to—set myself against you so, but I have made up my mind. I mean to get off at Albany. If you won't get my bag, I shall appeal to the conductor——"

He sat up at that, squared his shoulders, and laid an arm across the back of the seat, bending toward her, and speaking low. But I could still hear.

"We've had all we're going to of this—do you hear? You don't know it, but I'm what they call a 'plain clothes man'. Do you see that star?" From his gesture, and the direction of her frightened eyes, her little gasp, I felt as if I saw it too.

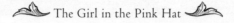

"Now do you sit tight and make no more fuss till we get to the city," he muttered. "If you appeal to the conductor—or anybody else, I'll simply tell 'em that you're a well-known criminal I'm taking back. And if you raise any rough stuff I've got the bracelets—see?"

She saw. I heard them chink in his pocket.

"Shall I put them on, or will you be quiet?" he asked, and she sank down defeated.

"Now a fellow can get a little peace, I guess?" said Mr. Marsh, and leaned his head back on the red plush.

He kept stern watch of her as we drew toward Albany. I knew he would, and I slipped silently out to consult with Polly. She was immensely excited, and full of plans for a dramatic rescue, but I persuaded her it was not safe.

"He's got the star and the handcuffs," I told her. "The girl has nothing but her word—we couldn't do it—not and be sure of it. And besides it would make a terrible scene—she'd never get over the publicity. Wait now—I see how we can work it—would you be willing to get off at Poughkeepsie—take a later train or stop overnight, as you like?"

"What for?" demanded Polly. "Of course I'm willing—but how does it help her?"

"Why, he'll be watching so that she can't get off—but he wouldn't stop you. Here—give me that writing tablet, please. I'll tell you directly—but I want to get this done before we're in—or I'll lose that seat. I'll come back as quick as I can and tell you—I'm sure we can do it."

So I took paper and pencils, and slipped softly back into the seat behind them.

After we left Albany his vigilance relaxed, and presently he was dozing beside her, a sufficient obstacle to her exit.

I swiftly wrote a careful explanation of my overhearing them, of my appreciation of her difficult position, and of her inevitable wish to avoid a noisy scene. Then I proposed my plan—simple enough—and calling only for a little courage and firmness on her part, and slipped it in near the window; he couldn't see it—even if awake.

"Have you a watch?" I wrote. "If you have look at it now, please." And I had the pleasure of seeing her do so.

"We get to Poughkeepsie at nine," I wrote. "At about fifteen minutes before then, say that you must go to the dressing room—he can't refuse that privilege. Go in there first, and shut the door. Take your hat off, and hide it under your dress. I shall be down near there, and when I open the door, you crouch down and slip through into the next car, into the stateroom—this end, close to the door, you know. You'll see my sister there—red hair, veil, yellow glasses. She'll tell you what to do. You can look around and see if you think I'm trusworthy. If you think so, you can nod."

She looked presently, and I'm sure my good natured, strong-lined spinsterish face seemed reliable. So she nodded, with determination.

Then I went back to Polly, and explained all that I had in mind, the two of us engaging in eager preparations. As the time approached I entered the day-coach once more, taking the little shut-in seat just opposite the woman's retiring-room; and was all eyes and ears for my plan's fulfillment.

Sure enough, I saw her coming down the aisle, holding by the seat backs as the car swung forward. He was watching her too, saw her safely inside with the door shut, and seemed satisfied. He knew she could not get off the train going at that rate.

Then I rose, as if to enter the little place myself, and unlatched the door. Finding it occupied, I came forward a little, and stood by the water-cooler, my coat on my arm, filling as much of the aisle as possible. She slipped out like a

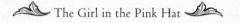

sly child, and I presently followed, stopping to try to enter the dressing-room in vain; opening and closing the rear door with easy indifference.

Before we ran into Poughkeepsie he must have become anxious, for he started to search the train.

Ours was the next car, our stateroom the first place to look, and he looked accordingly. He saw only a lady with low curved red hair, a squishy hat, yellow glasses, a veil, a long duster coat, reading her magazines, and my spinsterish self, knitting for the soldiers.

I watched him go down the aisle, questioning a lady near the door—had she seen a girl in a pink hat go through the car? She had not, and resented being asked.

He rushed into the next one; soon came back, again questioning and searching—and as the train stopped, leaped to the platform. Small chance would any pink-hatted light-coated girl have had of escape on that platform. Only a few got off and he watched every one of them. But naturally he would not know my sister in a neat traveling hat and waterproof coat. How should he?

And as naturally, he would not know my sister, or what certainly appeared to be my sister, wearing that long red switch of which my sister was so proud, her squishy hat, her long duster, her yellow glasses, and her veil. She sat reading as before, and when our friend came through the train again, this time accompanied by the conductor, she barely looked up from her page.

"You need not intrude upon these ladies," said the conductor, glancing at us. "I recognize them both."

"She may have hidden herself in their dressing room," the man insisted. But that was easily shown to be empty, and he backed out, muttering apologies.

"Steady, my dear, steady," I urged, as I saw her trembling

with the excitement of that search. "That's the last of it, I'm sure. He'll go all over the train—and then he'll think he must have missed you at Poughkeepsie."

We had closed our door by this time, and she could breath in peace, and speak even, though she would not raise her voice above a whisper.

"He'll be waiting when we get off—he'll be sure to know me then. I'm so afraid!" she said.

"You haven't a thing to be afraid of, my dear child," I told her. "My car will be there. You shall come home with me for tonight, and tomorrow we'll talk of the future plans. "Or—if you prefer, we'll buy a return ticket to Elyria—and you shall be home again tomorrow."

"I can't think," she said. "I'm so frightened. It has been—just awful! You see, I—I *loved* him! I was going to *marry* him—and to have all that turned into—into this!"

"See here, child, you mustn't talk about it now. You've got to keep a straight face and be Sister Polly till we're out of the woods. Just read one of those foolish stories—it'll take up your mind."

And happening on one of Leroy Scott's doubly involved detective stories, she actually did forget her own distresses for awhile following those of other people.

As we proceeded in a dignified manner up the long plat-form, attended by two red-capped porters, her hand upon my arm, I felt her start slightly.

"There he is," she said. "He's just inside the gate. But how funny! He's got another hat—and another coat—how funny! But I'd know his moustache anywhere."

It was funny, even funnier than she thought. Sister Polly in Poughkeepsie had not been idle, and my young brother, Hugh, had received a telegram as long as a letter and marked "Rush!" He was on hand, standing near the gate, and looking

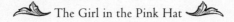

sharply about him, and behind him were two other men who also seemed interested in the crowd.

As we came through, the sharp eyes of Mr. Marsh caught the look of terror in the face beside me, and recognized it in spite of all Polly's wrappings. He started towards her, and she shrank against me with a pitiful little cry, but Mr. Marsh was checked in his career by a strong hand on either arm.

"That's him, and he's wanted all right," said one of his captors, while the other, not too gently, removed his moustache.

Then my young brother, Hugh, with a quizzical smile, took the handcuffs out of that threatening pocket, and they were slipped in place by experienced hands.

"You've certainly had one narrow escape, child," said Hugh to our young guest.

A Surplus Woman

HER FATHER WAS killed in the war. He was a doctor, executed by a well-directed shell that destroyed a hospital; a most efficient shell—some of those wounded might have recovered.

Her brother was killed in the war. He was a non-combatant on principle, a stretcher-bearer, picked off by a well-aimed bullet; a most efficient bullet—why encourage the work of salvage?

Her lover was killed in the war. He was a soldier pure and simple, who expected to be killed and was not disappointed. He had not, however, expected to be burned alive, not having been educated in those methods of warfare.

Moreover most of the young men she knew were killed in the war; and hundreds of thousands of young men she did not know. As there had already been a large majority of surplus women in her country, even before the wholesale destruction of a whole generation of masculine youth, the result was as plain as an example in simple arithmetic; there were now over a million women who could not marry—and she was one of them.

Her younger sister, who was very pretty and as frisky as a healthy kitten, tossed her gay curls and said she wouldn't

give up! She'd wait for some of these nice young boys who were growing so fast and not give them a chance to wait for the still younger girls also growing.

"No single blessedness for me!" said Miss Betty.

Her older sister, who was a widow, but not permanently discouraged, also declined to give up, though she did not say so. She shook her head slowly under its flowing veil of crepe and said that loneliness was cruelly hard for a woman. And there were still many men who had been too old to go to the war—this was vaguely in her mind. "A woman's place is the home," said Mrs. Watson.

We should not overlook one remaining male relative, Uncle Percy. The girls had always called him Uncle, because he was more than old enough to be one, but he was really only a cousin. As he possessed a most exalted sense of duty, both his own duty and those of other persons, he had come to visit them after Dr. Page's death, in order to lend some masculine dignity to the distressed family. This visit continued and repeated itself until Uncle Percy became quite a fixture. At first it had been of some assistance to Mrs. Page, and quite possibly she accepted his presence as another of her "duties"; he certainly interpreted it as his.

Betty did not mind him at all; rather coquetted with the old gentleman indeed, and he made quite a pet of her.

Mrs. Watson declared him invaluable—he used to divide his visits with her, before Mr. Peters assumed headship of that household.

But Susan found him wearing and irritating in the extreme because of his ceaseless emission of advice. Sometimes it was a heavy rain, sometimes a cloudburst, but always a depressing drizzle. She did not enjoy advice.

Susan Page was not pretty, not frisky, not clinging, not "domestic." She had expected to knock about the world with

her soldier-man, and while not herself of a belligerent disposition, she greatly admired the fine organization and high
purpose of the army.

As long as the war lasted she had worked hard enough to
keep down her pain. There was nursing at the front, where
she had learned much not merely in the exacting labors of
her calling, but in the patience and strength of the sufferers
all about her. The sum of that suffering was so great that her
own part of it could not monopolize her.

Being sent home to recover from a serious illness, her
convalescent interest and returning strength were devoted to
the constructive activities of the country; the careful organi-
zations which were handling the civil problems of the
time,—the sick and wounded, the refugees, the cripples, the
blind, the deaf and dumb, the widows and orphans of soldiers.
In all this flood of misery and loss she could not presume to
overestimate her own.

"It's not just my sorrow," she told herself. "It is *our* sorrow.
It is on us all. Why should I pick out mine to fuss over?"

And she did not fuss; she worked.

Having a natural taste for large organized activities, and
the vivid experience of her hospital work, as well as the civil
undertakings which followed, she had been a most useful
helper through all that terrible time of stress and service.

Now it was over. The war was ended; the nation breathed
again. The helpless were cared for and the half-helpless placed
where they could do something for themselves. The men not
killed or wounded came back, and took the places saved for
them, the places which in their absence had been filled by
women. All the wheels began to turn again, slowly and creak-
ingly at first, as the great country turned from its old task of
warfare to the new task of reconstruction.

Susan Page was dispossessed of the place she had held, as

were so many others. She now became one of a larger army than that which had been slain; one of more than a million surplus women.

Susan's grandmother was Irish, a woman of wit and resource, with that streak of genius so frequent among her people. Her mother was Scotch, a stern sense of duty harnessing her unusual statesmanlike abilities to the routine of a mercilessly well-managed household. A strain of Welsh blood was in Susan's veins also; the touch of mystic devotion, the dream of music and beauty. She was an excellent representative of Great Britain; and what she had she held.

Now, twenty-eight, with all her personal life in ruins, the family fortune gone, her mother and grandmother still to be cared for, she faced the years before her.

Betty was provided for; for Mrs. Watson was now Mrs. Peters, and had her home in London, where she said Betty would have more advantages. So Betty went to live with her, thankfully, and waited for her schoolboy.

Susan had no illusions. As a girl she was not misled by baseless hopes, and now—with such grim facts behind her, she was not likely to delude herself.

"Twenty-eight," said Susan. "Mother is fifty-two, strong and eager as ever. Grandmother is seventy-five, and both vigorous and cheerful. I probably have forty or fifty years to live, anyhow. What is the best thing to do?"

In the matter of what was to be done, both by Susan and her countless fellow sufferers, Uncle Percy had much to say.

"It is a lamentable misfortune to the country," quoth he, solemnly to Mrs. Page, who listened with her self-contained patient unsmiling air; and to Susan, who was not so patient nor so easily able to control herself. "It is an unmitigated disaster—this vast mass of helpless women turned loose upon our hands. This is one of the most cruel consequences of war, an economic injury quite outside the pain of bereavement."

He looked at the widowed, son-less mother, the pre-widowed girl, with solemn sympathy, but neither of them seemed grateful.

"Here are a million bread-winners gone, a million producers of wealth, and we are left with many more than that number of dependent females, consumers only; denied their natural place and power; merely adding to the expenses of the nation. You, my dear Margaret," he had a deep respect and some affection for Mrs. Page, "are fortunately provided for, though but narrowly, and your daughters shall not suffer while I live." Uncle Percy was not rich; but he had enough money to keep him living in idleness as a gentleman should. He certainly was not a producer.

He seemed to expect some response from Susan, so she said: "Thank you, Uncle Percy," and soon went to her own room, where she did much clear and careful thinking.

Presently, with a dry smile, she determined to "call a meeting."

"That's the way they begin," she told herself. "I'll get Eleanore to do it."

The meeting was not a large one. There was Lady Eleanore, now the sole survivor of the Wardours of Wardour Hall. She was a neighbor, and a close friend since early girlhood. Gertrude Murray, the tall dark sturdy girl from Manchester, and Joan Whyte from Devon were friends she had made while nursing, and while working in London. Little Mrs. Bates from the village was a plump rosy woman, bubbling over with energy, who had proved her executive force in the crowding activities of local relief work. Lady Eleanore had an immense respect for her, though Mr. Bates had kept a shop—before the war took him; and his wife had kept it since, or tried to.

The five women gathered in the big shadowy drawing-room

of The Hall. All had been brought out by the war, out from their previous limitations, aspirations, and contentments. Every one of them was larger and stronger, abler, more open to idea and to action, because of that cataclysmic experience. They had been democratized by it, not merely in theory, but in the practice of associate labor. Lady Eleanore, eager and devoted, had been in the hospital work for a while, till sent home with her invalided husband; she had learned to know Gertrude and Joan, one at the front, one in the equally necessary civic work; and to honor their courage and ability. As for Susan, she had worked with them all; she loved them all; she knew them all; and felt sure of her ground.

They had their tea, chatting a little of what Mrs. Carson could do, of Maud Westcote's search for employment, and the needs of Molly Masters, and the Simpson girls, till Lady Eleanore said:

"Now, Susan, this is all your doings. You will have to make us a speech to begin with."

Susan looked around her with her guarded earnest little smile, studying each strong kind face in its different grade of power.

"My speech will be mostly questions," she said. "I want a real discussion, a definite long-distance planning as to what 'we-all' are to do."

"'We-all'?" Lady Eleanore looked at her inquiringly.

"It's an expression they have in The States," Susan said. "I read in a story. 'We-all' and 'you-all'—I think it very expressive. What I mean by 'we-all' is all we women of England who are dispossessed, now, at one time—more than a million of us."

"It is a very grave question," agreed Lady Eleanore.

"They can go back to the land—some of them," urged Joan

Whyte. She had been one active in managing the farm-laboring women movement during the war, and believed in it.

"Not by millions, Joan," protested Miss Murray. "The men have something to say, and the land on this island is a bit limited. But there are all the trades—some women have proved their abilities—it's a matter of competition, I suppose.

Mrs. Bates shook her head firmly. "That's all very well for those who have the ability, but how about those who haven't? Just plain working-women, widows and girls, by hundreds of thousands, who have no trade at all—and the men all back now taking up every place there is. Not that I blame 'em," she added hastily. "We've no call to support 'em in idleness."

"There are many of us interested in this problem, Susan, as of course you know," Lady Eleanore gently suggested. "It is proposed that we secure a grant from the government to establish schools, technical schools, I mean, and to devise means of employment for as many as possible."

Susan smiled a little more warmly. "Yes, I know. But—do we need it?"

They looked at her, waiting, and she began to speak, eagerly.

"You know what they say about us—call us 'surplus women,' say we are 'denied our natural functions', and have become 'an economic burden on the state,' call the men 'producers', and us 'consumers'. And then here's this talk about a 'grant' for us, about government aid and so on. It is like—why it is like the way they talked about the suddenly enfranchised negroes in the States."

"Well—" Lady Eleanore narrowed her fine eyes with an air of judicial consideration. "There are points in common, Susan."

"Perhaps—but there are points of difference also. What I have to suggest is this: Everyone of us women, given suitable occupation, is able to produce more than she consumes, even now. Very well; now if we can do three things: A, develop our opportunities; B, increase our efficiency; and, C, decrease our expenses—then we should become not only an independent class of citizens, but a productive class—a positive benefit to the community."

"That's all true enough," agreed Gertrude Murray, "but what miracle is going to do all this?"

"No miracle at all," answered Susan calmly. "Just the laws of nature! What we ought to realize first is that this is not a personal matter; it is a social phenomenon. It is sudden and of course, transient, but the practical fact is that we constitute an enormous body of women who must be celibates."

"Unless——" commented Gertrude grimly.

"Oh, yes, I know the 'unlesses'. But we women of England are not going to accept polygamy, much less prostitution. No—we are a vast mass of enforced celibates. We know perfectly well that the way to bear it is to fill our lives with work that is loved and honored, big satisfying work which not only tires us and feeds us, but fills our hearts."

"We can't all be reformers—even if we earn our living by it," urged Joan.

"Of course not—nor do we wish to be. But here is what I have in mind: a simple form of organization, with some straightforward name like the Women's Economic Alliance, which shall have for its purpose those three things I spoke of: to develop the opportunity, to increase the efficiency, and to decrease the expenses of women."

"Go on," they said, as she looked around for comment.

"Of course I have only a sketch of it in mind," she continued; "but it would be something like this. A headquarters in town, of course; in the very best hands; women known and trusted by everybody. There would be at first a mass of secretarial and research work to do; no less than listing and classifying all the women who wished to join; sending in name, address, capacity, preferred occupation, and one shilling."

"Some mightn't have it," suggested Joan.

"We'd begin with those who had—there would be plenty, and that would carry expenses from the start.

"The first duty of this organization would be to open a national employment agency for women, with branch after branch till every town and village had its 'WEA' office. Then all those who wanted to employ women could have an authoritative place of reference, and the workers too. That would be to take the best advantage of existing conditions.

"Second comes the educational work; to be developed as fast as our funds increased. It could begin with small local classes—you see how this works, locally, don't you? Say that we here, with Lady Eleanore to head it, proceeded to take a little economic census of women, classify it, and send it in to headquarters; then we could open evening classes for such of our girls as had no trade whatever, and not only give them such special instruction as we could, but general education too, lectures, cinema pictures, legitimate helpfulness. In time we'd have a high grade vocational college, with branches everywhere, with a traveling library, with a special corps of lectures and teachers—we would deliberately plan to lift the standard of efficiency among all our women."

"What's to make them come in?" questioned Gertrude.

"Economic advantage of course. Prompt and reliable employment service. The help of solidarity. Every year would build up the value of our 'WEA' recommendation."

"'WE Alliance'," said Gertrude, "'WE All'"—there's your 'we-all!'"

"All right—go on—how are you going to decrease living expenses?"

"By the simplest of economic devices; the same old easy method of organization. The reason we never could do it before was because of the concentric force of the family circle. Now, because we women have lost our chance of having any family circle, we are—by virtue of our misfortune—able to combine."

A steady courage shone on each face. Every one of them had lost that chance—and they knew how many more were with them.

"Don't you see," urged Susan. "It's no fault of ours. We haven't *wanted* to be celibates. The men are—gone, that's all. And it leaves us in the same class as the bees and ants everybody's always quoting. We can't be mothers, but can be—Co-Mothers, Sisters, Co-Workers for the common good."

"I thought all this was for our own advantage," said Gertrude.

"It has to be, primarily. What we have to do first is to take ourselves off the shoulders of our men; to show that we are not mere consumers, but producers also. See, now. Each of us women, to live, has to pay for food, clothing, shelter, service. Now this organization will establish, one after another, residence groups, which will at the same time furnish employment to some of our members and living accommodations to others.

"Take the one field of laundry work; in a given village there is just so much of this work to be done. 'WEA' Laundry is opened, meeting the needs of the town, regularly employing as many laundresses as are needed, and doing the work of all WEA members at cost price. 'WEA Bakery and CookShop', 'WEA Sewing and Mending rooms'—millinery—dressmaking—all *organized*, all furnishing steady employment on the one hand and reduced rates to members on the other. It is good economics—not a new device."

"And living accommodations?"

"Yes—in the big towns we will open Club-houses; not 'Homes,' you know, but agreeable club-houses for working women of different grades and at different rates, but—all WEA.

"Then our producing groups play into the hands of all our living groups——"

Joan Whyte sat up suddenly. "I see!" she said. "We have women on the land—small farmers—market gardeners—fruit-raisers—jam-makers—poultry, eggs, butter——"

"Exactly," said Susan. "Little by little we 'consumers' become producers. We learn to raise our own food—as cheaply as we can, with good conditions and wages for the workers."

"I see, too," said Gertrude. "We work productively, and not competitively; for pure human advantage—not to scrape profits off each other. It's good business."

"Of course I'm looking way ahead—and it is a splendid picture. You see any woman could join. Rich women could, to profit by the employment bureau, and the reliable products—no sweatshops, no starving laborers—no exploitation; and poor women would be enormously advantaged by the wide labor exchange, the reduced living expenses, and the educational features. There need not be any more of these helpless 'unskilled' girls—after a few years.

"But immediately, and locally, we can begin just where we live, starting one WEA branch after another——"

"They are not branches, Susan," suggested Lady Eleanore, "they are roots, separate plants that "run" like strawberries. Also the Central Bureau can begin at once. I'll write to Maud Russell—and Constance Howard—the registration and employment part can start at once. All we need to begin with is a little money for initial advertising—there'll be no trouble about that."

"I can reach every girl in the village, with no expense

whatever," suggested Mrs. Bates, "and so can others in their villages. All it needs is somebody to go around and talk about it. You can do that, Miss Page, I'm sure."

"I can try," said Susan.

In ordinary times a plan like this would have had a hard time in reaching the consciousness of the people; a harder time in rousing action. But this period was one of wide social upheaval, of hearts exalted, of eyes opened to large issues. Moreover these "Surplus Women" were an immediate problem, by some considered an immediate menace.

The Central Bureau was opened at once, under the most reliable management, and its appeal for registration promptly and widely answered. The existing field of employment was soon filled—and then the Alliance set to work on its growing task of education, organization, and industrial development.

As an immediate meeting of a public need its usefulness was undeniable.

As an educational influence it became a power with no visible limits.

And then, from year to year, its income growing from steadily enlarging membership and from its widening industrial enterprise, it became a power in wealth as well as in enlightenment and organization, a band of protection and defense, a basis of safety, a source of hope and a steady inspiration to all those women, no longer a "surplus" but a benefit to the whole nation.

"It is against nature," said Uncle Percy. "Women cannot work together."

"See us do it," replied Susan cheerfully.

Joan's
Defender

JOAN'S MOTHER WAS a poor defense. Her maternal instinct did not present that unbroken front of sterling courage, that measureless reserve of patience, that unfailing wisdom which we are taught to expect of it. Rather a broken reed was Mrs. Marsden, broken in spirit even before her health gave way, and her feeble nerves were unable to stand the strain of adjudicating the constant difficulties between Joan and Gerald.

"Mother! Mo-o-ther!" would rise a protesting wail from the little girl. "Gerald's pulling my hair!"

"Cry baby!" her brother would promptly retort. "Tell tale! Run to mother—do!"

Joan did—there was no one else to run to—but she got small comfort.

"One of you is as much to blame as the other," the invalid would proclaim. And if this did not seem to help much: "If he teases you, go into another room!"

Whether Mrs. Marsden supposed that her daughter was a movable body and her son a fixed star as it were, did not appear, but there was small comfort to be got from her.

"If you can't play nicely together you must be separated. If I hear anything more from you, I'll send you to your room— now be quiet!"

So Joan sulked, helplessly, submitted to much that was painful and more that was contumelious, and made little remonstrance. There was, of course, a last court of appeal, or rather a last threat—that of telling father.

"I'll tell father! I'll tell father! Then you'll be sorry!" her tormentor would chant, jumping nimbly about just out of reach, if she had succeeded in any overt act of vengeance.

"I shall have to tell your father!" was the last resource of the mother on the sofa.

If father was told, no matter by whom, the result was always the same—he whipped them both. Not so violently, to be sure, and Joan secretly believed less violently in Gerald's case than in hers, but it was an ignominious and unsatisfying punishment which both avoided.

"Can't you manage to keep two children in order?" he would demand of his wife. "My mother managed eleven—and did the work of the house too."

"I wish I could, Bert, dear," she would meekly reply. "I do try—but they are so wearying. Gerald is too rough, I'm afraid. Joan is always complaining."

"I should think she was!" Mr. Marsden agreed irritably. "Trust a woman for that!"

And Joan, though but nine years old, felt that life was not worth living, being utterly unjust. She was a rather large-boned, meager child, with a whiney voice, and a habit of crying, "Now stop!" whenever Gerald touched her. Her hair was long, fine and curly, a great trouble to her as well as to her mother. Both were generally on edge for the day, before those curls were all in order, and their principal use appeared to be as handles for Gerald, who was always pulling them. He was a year and a half older than Joan, but not much bigger, and of a somewhat puny build.

Their father, a burly, loud-voiced man, heavy of foot and

of hand, looked at them both with ill-concealed disapproval, and did not hesitate to attribute the general deficiencies of his family wholly to their feeble mother and her "side of the house."

"I'm sure I was strong as a girl, Bert—you remember how I used to play tennis, and I could dance all night."

"Oh I remember," he would answer. "Blaming your poor health on me, I suppose—that seems to be the way nowadays. I don't notice that other women give out just because they're married and have two children—*two!*" he repeated scornfully, as if Mrs. Marsden's product were wholly negligible. "And one of them a girl!"

"Girls are no good!" Gerald quickly seconded. "Girls can't fight or climb or do anything. And they're always hollering. Huh! I wouldn't be a girl—!" Words failed him.

Such was their case, as it says so often in the *Arabian Nights*, and then something pleasant happened. Uncle Arthur came for a little visit, and Joan liked him. He was mother's brother, not father's. He was big, like father, but gentle and pleasant, and he had such a nice voice, jolly but not loud.

Uncle Arthur was a western man, with a ranch, and a large family of his own. He had begun life as a physician, but weak lungs drove him into the open. No one would ever think of him now as ever having been an invalid.

He stayed for a week or so, having some business to settle which dragged on for more days than had been counted on, and gave careful attention to the whole family.

Joan was not old enough, nor Mrs. Marsden acute enough, to note the gradual disappearance of topic after topic from the conversation between Uncle Arthur and his host. But Mr. Marsden's idea of argument was volume of sound, speed in repetition, and a visible scorn for those who disagreed with him, and as Arthur Warren did not excel in these methods he

sought for subjects of agreement. Not finding any, he contented himself with telling stories, or listening—for which there was large opportunity.

He bought sweetmeats for the children, and observed that Gerald got three-quarters, if not more; brought them presents, and found that if Gerald did not enjoy playing with Joan's toys, he did enjoy breaking them.

He sounded Gerald, as man to man, in regard to these habits, but that loyal son, who believed his father to be a type of all that was worthy, and who secretly had assumed the attitude of scorn adopted by that parent toward his visitor, although civil enough, was little moved by anything his uncle might say.

Dr. Warren was not at all severe with him. He believed in giving a child the benefit of every doubt, and especially the benefit of time.

"How can the youngster help being a pig?" he asked himself, sitting quite silent and watching Gerald play ball with a book just given to Joan, who cried "Now sto-op!" and tried to get it away from him.

"Madge Warren Marsden!" he began very seriously, when the children were quarreling mildly in the garden, and the house was quiet: "Do you think you're doing right by Joan— let alone Gerald? Is there no way that boy can be made to treat his sister decently?"

"Of course you take her part—I knew you would," she answered fretfully. "You always were partial to girls—having so many of your own, I suppose. But you've no idea how irritating Joan is, and Gerald is extremely sensitive—she gets on his nerves. As for *my* nerves! I have none left! Of course those children ought to be separated. By and by when we can afford it, we mean to send Gerald to a good school; he's a very bright boy—you must have noticed that?"

"Oh yes, he's bright enough," her brother agreed. "And so is Joan, for that matter. But look here, Madge—this thing is pretty hard on you, isn't it—having these two irreconcilables to manage all the time?"

The ready tears rose and ran over. "Oh Arthur, it's awful! I do my best—but I never was good with children—and with my nerves—*you* know, being a doctor."

He did know, rather more than she gave him credit for. She had responded to his interest with interminable details as to her symptoms and sensations, and while he sat patiently listening he had made a diagnosis which was fairly accurate. Nothing in particular was the matter with his sister except the fretful temper she was born with, idle habits, and the effects of an overbearing husband.

The temper he could not alter, the habits he could not change, nor the husband either, so he gave her up—she was out of his reach.

But Joan was a different proposition. Joan had his mother's eyes, his mother's smile—when she did smile; and though thin and nervous, she had no serious physical disability as yet.

"Joan worries you even more than Gerald, doesn't she?" he ventured. "It's often so with mothers."

"How well you understand, Arthur. Yes, indeed, I feel as if I knew just what to do with my boy, but Joan is a puzzle. She is so—unresponsive."

"Seems to me you would be much stronger if you were less worried over the children."

"Of course—but what can I do? It is my duty and I hope I can hold out."

"For the children's sake you ought to be stronger, Madge. See here, suppose you lend me Joan for a long visit. It would be no trouble at all to us—we have eight, you know, and all

outdoors for them to romp in. I think it would do the child good."

The mother looked uncertain. "It's a long way to let her go——" she said.

"And it would do Gerald good, I verily believe," her brother continued. "I've often heard you say that she irritates him."

He could not bring himself to advance this opinion, but he could quote it.

"She does indeed, Arthur. I think Gerald would give almost no trouble if he was alone."

"And you are of some importance," he continued cheerfully. "How about that? Let me borrow Joan for a year—you'll be another woman when you get rested."

There was a good deal of discussion, and sturdy opposition from Mr. Marsden, who considered the feelings of a father quite outraged by the proposal; but as Dr. Warren did not push it, and as his wife suggested that in one way it would be an advantage—they could save toward Gerald's schooling— adding that her brother meant to pay all expenses, including tickets—he finally consented.

Joan was unaccountably reluctant. She clung to her mother, who said, "There! There!" and kissed her with much emotion. "It's only a visit, dearie—you'll be back to mother bye and bye!"

She kissed her father, who told her to be a good girl and mind her uncle and aunt. She would have kissed Gerald, but he said: "Oh shucks!" and drew away from her.

It was a silently snivelling little girl who sat by the window, with Uncle Arthur reading the paper beside her, a little girl who felt as if nobody loved her in the whole wide world. He put a big arm around her and drew her to him. She snuggled up with a long sigh of relief. He took her in his lap, held her close, and told her interesting things about the flying land-scape. She nestled close to him, and then, starting up suddenly to look at something, her hair caught on his buttons and pulled sharply.

She cried, as was her habit, while he disentangled it.

"How'd you like to have it cut off?" he asked.

"*I'd* like it—but mother won't let me. She says it's my only beauty. And father won't let me either—says I want to be a tom-boy."

"Well, I'm in loco parentis now," said Uncle Arthur, "and I'll let you. Furthermore, I'll do it forthwith, before it gets tangled up tonight."

He produced a pair of sharp little scissors, and a pocket-comb, and in a few minutes the small head looked like one of Sir Joshua Reynold's cherubs.

"You see I know how," he explained, as he snipped cautiously, "because I cut my own youngsters' on the ranch. I think you look prettier short than long," he told her, and she found the little mirror between the windows quite a comfort.

Before the end of that long journey the child was more quietly happy with her uncle than she had ever been with either father or mother, and as for Gerald—the doctor's wise smile deepened.

"Irritated *him*, did she?" he murmured to himself. "The little skate! Why, I can just see her *heal* now she's escaped."

A big, high-lying California ranch, broad, restful sweeps of mesa and plain, purple hills rising behind. Flowers beyond dreams of heaven, fruit of every kind in gorgeous abundance. A cheerful Chinese cook and houseboy, who did their work well and seemed to enjoy it. The uncle she already loved, and an aunt who took her to her motherly heart at once.

Then the cousins—here was terror. And four of them boys— four! But which four? There they all were in a row, giggling happily, standing up to be counted, and to be introduced to

their new cousin. All had short hair. All had bare feet. All had denim knickerbockers. And all had been racing and tumbling and turning somersaults on the cushiony Bermuda grass as Joan and her uncle drove up.

The biggest one was a girl, tall Hilda, and the baby was a girl, a darling dimpled thing, and two of the middle ones. But the four boys were quite as friendly as Hilda, and seeing that their visitor was strangely shy, Jack promptly proposed to show her his Belgian hares, and Harvey to exhibit his Angora goats, and the whole of them trooped off hilariously.

"What a forlorn child!" said Aunt Belle. "I'm glad you brought her, dear. Ours will do her good."

"I knew you'd mother her, Blessing," he said with a grateful kiss. "And if ever a poor kid needed mothering, it's that one. You see, my sister has married a noisy pig of a man—and doesn't seem to mind it much. But she's become an invalid—one of these sofa women; I don't know as she'll ever get over it. And the other child's rather a mean cuss, I'm afraid. They love him the best. So I thought we'd educate Joan a bit."

Joan's education was largely physical. A few weeks of free play, and then a few moments every day of the well-planned exercises Dr. Warren had invented for his children. There were two ponies to ride; there were hills to climb; there was work to do in the well-irrigated garden. There were games, and I am obliged to confess, fights. Every one of those children was taught what we used to grandiloquently call "the noble art of self-defense"; not only the skilled management of their hands, with swift "footwork," but the subtler methods of jiu-jitsu.

"I took the course on purpose," the father explained to his friends, "and the kids take to it like ducks to water."

To her own great surprise, and her uncle's delight, Joan showed marked aptitude in her new studies. In the hours of definite instruction, from books or in nature study and laboratory work, she was happy and successful, but the rapture with which she learned to use her body was fine to see.

The lower reservoir made a good-sized swimming pool, and there she learned to float and dive. The big barn had a little simple apparatus for gymnastics in the rainy season, and the jolly companionship of all those bouncing cousins was an education in itself.

Dr. Warren gave her special care, watched her food, saw to it that she was early put to bed on the wide sleeping porch, and trained her as carefully as if she had some tremendous contest before her. He trained her mind as well as her body. Those children were taught to reason, as well as to remember; taught to think for themselves, and to see through fallacious arguments. In body and mind she grew strong.

At first she whimpered a good deal when things hurt her, but finding that the other children did not, and that, though patient with her, they evidently disliked her doing it, she learned to take her share of the casualties of vigorous childhood without complaint.

At the end of the year Dr. Warren wrote to his brother-in-law that it was not convenient for him to furnish the return ticket, or to take the trip himself, but if they could spare the child a while longer he would bring her back as agreed—that she was doing finely in all ways.

It was nearly two years when Joan Marsden, aged eleven, returned to her own home, a very different looking child from the one who left it so mournfully. She was much taller, larger, with a clear color, a light, firm step, a ready smile.

She greeted her father with no shadow of timidity, and rushed to her mother so eagerly as well-nigh to upset her.

"Why, child!" said the mother. "Where's your beautiful hair? Arthur—how could you?"

"It is much better for her health," he solemnly assured her.

"You see how much stronger she looks. Better keep it short till she's fourteen or fifteen."

Gerald looked at his sister with mixed emotions. He had not grown as much. She was certainly as big as he was now. With her curls gone she was not so easy to hurt. However, there were other places. As an only child his disposition had not improved, and it was not long before that disposition led him to derisive remarks and then to personal annoyance, which increased as days passed.

She met him cheerfully. She met him patiently. She gave him fair warning. She sought to avoid his attacks, and withdrew herself to the far side of the garage, but he followed her.

"It's not fair, Gerald, and you know it," said Joan. "If you hurt me again I shall have to do something to you."

"Oh you will, will you?" he jeered, much encouraged by her withdrawal, much amused by her threat. "Let's see you do it—smarty! 'Fraid cat!" and he struck her again, a blow neatly planted, where the deltoid meets the biceps and the bone is near the surface.

Joan did not say, "Now *stop*!" She did not whine, "*Please* don't!" She did not cry. She simply knocked him down.

And when he got up and rushed at her, furious, meaning to reduce this rebellious sister to her proper place, Joan set her teeth and gave him a clean thrashing.

"Will you give up?"

He did. He was glad to.

"Will you promise to behave? To let me alone?"

He promised.

She let him up, and even brushed off his dusty clothes.

"If you're mean to me any more, I'll do it again," she said calmly. "And if you want to tell mother—or father—or anybody—that I licked you, you may."

But Gerald did not want to.